KEITH WILSON

A Dr. Brett Carson Thriller

PLUNDER

HALLAR PRESS

D1292100

Cover Design by Hallard Press LLC/John W Prince
Cover Image: Mayan Death-Birth Mask, provided by Ancient Sculpture Gallery ©Culture Spot. Used with permission.

Page Design, Typography & Production by Hallard Press LLC/John W Prince

Published by Hallard Press LLC.
www.HallardPress.com   Info@HallardPress.com

Bulk copies of this book can be ordered by contacting Hallard Press LLC, Info@HallardPress.com

Printed in the United States of America   .

ISBN: 978-1-951188-04-7

Dedication

To Cathy

A searing pain ripped the breath from him. His ears were ringing, but he hadn't heard a sound. Why hadn't the gun made a sound? He searched for air, but his breath was gone. An unfamiliar cold seeped into him. His body convulsed, and his hands twitched as he fought against death, but he knew he was losing.

No breath. No light. In that final moment that separated life from death, he was only aware of the girl's skeleton beside him.

They would share the same grave...

Chapter 1

Nine Months earlier....

S. Peter's Cathedral
Chicago
Christmas Eve

Undaunted by a severe winter storm that paralyzed the Windy City with blowing and drifting snow, more than two thousand people crowded into Saint Peter's cathedral on Washington Street at midnight to celebrate Christmas Eve Mass. Soft candlelight illuminated frozen snow veneers on the window panes; branches of pine wrapped with red ribbon wound around marble columns that rose majestically toward the vaulted ceiling.

Pine wreaths decorated the ornate altar, where the old priest struggled to finish the Christmas mass.

Monsignor Joseph Cardone faltered and stumbled over each passage, even though he knew the liturgy by heart. Cold sweat beaded his face and dropped onto the Missal he held with trembling hands, each drop bleeding the print into a dark blotch within the spreading circle of moisture. He squinted, but the blurred words floated aimlessly in front of him. Twice he lost his place.

"And the angel said unto them, Fear not: for behold, I bring you good tidings of great joy...," Cardone repeated as the Missal shook in his hands.

He knew what he'd done was wrong and feared the price he was about to pay for his sins was going to be high.

In spite of his transgression, he believed he was a good man and a faithful servant. Had he not served God well, devoting his life to the people of the parish? What he had done was for God's glory, not personal gain. But he had sinned, and the wrath of God was mighty. He secretly cursed God, and at the same time, prayed for forgiveness.

What he thought the day before was a mild flu had suddenly turned into a malevolent invader that raged through him. The alb under his chasuble was soaked with sweat, and clung to his aching body. His heart pounded against his sternum. The Monsignor struggled to fight back a feeling of impending doom.

For Monsignor Cardone, the past hour had become a distant fog buried somewhere deep within his brain; he now struggled with something much more important than the Christmas liturgy.

Air. He needed air.

He clutched at his collar and pulled it away from his neck. His throat constricted, and his voice grew weaker until it was a barely audible rasp. After mouthing a faint and scratchy, "The mass is ended, go in peace," He made a quick sign of the cross and, desperate to get to the cathedral doors, moved down the aisle past the parishioners who stared at him with concern.

His face contorted in anguish as he gasped for air. The

high, vaulted ceiling with faded frescoes three stories above the sanctuary seemed to close in on him, smothering him.

The combined adult and children's choir began to sing, softly at first, their voices from the choir loft settling on the congregation below like falling snow. *"Silent night, holy night, all is calm, all is bright..."*

But the monsignor did not hear the strains of the carol; the only sound that registered in his brain was a deep, baleful wheeze that rose from his own chest with each labored breath.

Mind and body battled for his attention. His brain screamed for oxygen as a bone-chilling fear rose from his gut: the primal fear as old as life itself—the fear of impending death. The old priest ripped at his collar, trying to loosen it as he strained for air.

Muscles, suddenly devoid of tone, failed him. Just moving his diaphragm to breathe became a monumental effort, each breath agonizing and slow. His eyelids scraped across his dried cornea with each blink, and his legs buckled.

When the priest faltered, one of the altar boys following behind him moved to his side and took his arm to help him the rest of the way to the rear of the church. Cardone's mouth hung open as he gasped for air. His entire body was now drenched in cold sweat.

The young assistant priest, Father O'Higgins, stood by the doors. As the Monsignor grabbed at the assistant's robe for support, he looked up to see horror registered on the young priest's face.

At that moment, Monsignor Cardone knew he was dying.

An EMS van, caked with snow and flashing lights, raced up to the emergency entrance of University of Chicago Hospital, the fifth to arrive in as many minutes. While the rest of Chicago quietly observed Christmas, the emergency department was a madhouse of activity as the staff rushed to evaluate and treat a multitude of medical problems.

The ER staff had been dreading this holiday rotation in the emergency department. Holidays in the ER were chaotic, but Christmas was always the busiest and the craziest. In addition to swallowed toys, sledding accidents, frostbites, and cuts from broken tree ornaments, there were the usual alcoholic binges, drug overdoses, and suicide attempts among those whose expectations went unfulfilled.

An ER staff doctor pulled back the curtain to holding room 14 and turned his attention to the newest admission, an elderly priest with severe respiratory distress. He flipped the chest x-ray onto the viewbox. "Damn, look at that," he said, scrutinizing the details on the film. A dense pneumonic infiltrate flooded both lungs, choking off the tiny alveolar air sacs and depriving the body of oxygen.

"Hell of a pneumonia," one of the residents said over the ER doctor's shoulder.

"Maybe," the ER doctor replied. He leaned closer to the film as if the answer lay hidden somewhere within the dense mess. "Aspiration, Legionnaires', toxic lung... could be anything. Could even be SARS." He turned to the resident. "If that's a pneumonia, it's one of the worst I've seen. Got his blood gases back yet?"

The resident pulled a slip of paper from his pocket. "His PO2 is only thirty percent. And that's with nasal O2 running at six liters."

"What else you got on him?"

"Cardiac enzymes normal. Electrolytes normal, but he was acidotic. I ordered an amp of bicarb."

"Who's his doctor? Any medical history on him?"

"No medical records here," the resident answered, obviously pleased that he had checked that. "They're at the clinic. He's Willard's patient, but Willard's not on call and we can't reach him."

The staff doctor nodded. "Get blood cultures on him, then start him on I.V. Amoxicillin." He put his stethoscope against the priest's chest and bent over him to listen. Through the earpieces came loud, coarse, wheezing sounds from bronchi that were choked with thick secretions.

The priest was barely conscious, his eyes were glazed, and every fiber and muscle were spent trying to get air into his oxygen starved body. A nasal cannula fed oxygen into his nose. Aminophylline, a potent bronchodilator, dripped through an angiocath taped to the back of his withered hand. The priest seemed to shrink as his blood pressure dropped and his life ebbed. His eyes were barely open and unfocused. Then the priest's lips moved.

The resident bent down to listen. "It sounds like he's apologizing for something. What do you think that's all about?"

"He's Catholic—they always think they've done something wrong." The staff doctor leaned close to listen to the priest's breath sounds through his stethoscope. He noticed a strong odor on the priest's breath. It was a familiar smell, but he couldn't place it. Things were deteriorating fast. A small trickle of dark fluid oozed from the corner of the priest's mouth. His cold bluish-gray skin hung loose and gave a dead aura.

"I think we're losing him," he snapped. "I don't know what the hell is going on. Let's intubate him and get him onto a vent. Call

ICU and let them know they're getting a new admit. Put him in isolation until we find out what this is."

But that decision turned out to be meaningless. He noted a faint movement of Cardone's lips again, as if he were saying a prayer, then the priest suddenly grew still. Just as quickly, his body relaxed and sagged into the gurney.

His struggle was over.

The ER doctor stood up and stared down at the lifeless priest. Again, he noticed the odd odor that came from the priest's mouth. It was familiar. Then it hit him.

The smell on his breath was mildew.

Chapter 2

Present Day

Somewhere in the jungles of Guatemala

He stumbled ahead, growing weaker with each step. Blood oozed from his tear ducts and stung his eyes. Everything was a blur. Sweat and grime coated his body. He ignored the insects that ate at him and the tangled vines and thorns that tore at his clothes. He struggled on. He couldn't stop, he didn't dare pause.

A medical clinic and village were just a few hundred yards ahead, but it may as well have been a few hundred miles. He had to make it. He stumbled again but managed to keep his footing as muscles failed him. Breathing and swallowing became more difficult.

He gasped for air and sucked, but weakened chest muscles could not fill his lungs. Blood trickled from his mouth, and he wiped at it with the back of his trembling hand. Dark purple blotches spread on his arms and legs. *Take a few steps, try to breathe, and—most importantly—do not fall!* He knew if he fell, he could never get up.

Ahead, he could just make out the blurred image of a clearing. *Just a few more yards. A few more yards.* But finally, drained of strength and drained of ability to sustain life, he collapsed face down onto the dirt road.

In his last brief moment of remaining consciousness, he knew that his terrifying struggle was over.

4,995 miles North:

Seward Peninsula
Shismaref, Alaska

Frozen snow caked the fur of a husky as she trotted down the dirt road between wooden buildings built on stilts. She held her head low against the bitter wind. Late October days had grown shorter and were already brutally cold. Winter had arrived early along the northern slope of the Seward Peninsula and would not release its frozen grip until spring.

In northern Alaska, winter was more than just a season; it was an over-powering entity. It was the arbiter of life and death. Frozen snow stung the eyes and howling winds froze any exposed skin. Bitter cold brought a swift death to the weak or the careless.

Inuit Eskimos inhabited the villages that hugged the coastline.

Eskimo means "eater of raw meat." And while they no longer ate their meat raw, the Inuit still survived primarily on meat. There was little edible vegetation other than seaweed. They fished during the short summer months and hunted whale, walrus, caribou, and seals during the long winter months. Even the fresh cold wind couldn't blow away the smells of ocean, dead fish, and gasoline that hung in the air.

Shismaref was an insignificant coastal fishing village in the Northwest Arctic Borough, two hundred miles north of Nome. At least it *had* been insignificant; recent events had changed that. It was here that a strange disease had struck with devastating results. Now the rest of the world watched and waited.

For the last five months, Shismaref, along with every tiny village within a hundred-mile radius, had been hit by a deadly epidemic. Most of the victims died; the few who survived were left permanently blind.

All except for one boy.

An Inuit sat in a room in the small clinic with his nine-year-old son. The man had already lost his wife and young daughter to the illness. Now, the disease had infected his son. The motherless boy, with thick gauze taped over his eyes, sat in the chair, obviously terrified, his lower lip quivering. The father kept his arm around the boy's waist, as if to make sure he wouldn't lose him also.

The door opened, and Dr. Brett Carson swept into the room and grabbed a stool. "Good morning, Danny. How are you?" he asked as he gently shuffled his hand through the boy's hair.

"Fine," the boy answered quietly.

"Well, let's get the bandages off and see how the medicine's working." Brett carefully peeled off the tape and slowly removed the gauze from the boy's eyes. His eyes were still swollen, red, and markedly inflamed. But they had also dramatically improved over the past week. When the boy came to him ten days ago, his eyes were crusted, bleeding, swollen, and the sclera had started to split open from the massive inflammation and edema. Brett had recognized the similarities between advanced ocular herpes simplex infection and the newly discovered virus. The usual antiviral eye drops had had no effect in any of the patients.

In a final attempt to save the boy's life and maybe preserve his eyesight, Brett had requested and finally received 5-fluorouracine —commonly called "5-FU"—a strong anti-metabolite usually used to treat cancer. He had combined 5-FU with interferon, steroids, and a new experimental protease inhibitor in the hopes of stopping the growth of the virus and reducing the intense reaction and edema. His hunch seemed to have worked.

Brett still had to wash the topical paste from the boy's eyes, but the boy already had broken into a broad smile.

"I can see you," he said. "And it doesn't hurt anymore." The boy's father wiped tears from his own eyes.

Brett smiled back at him and nodded. Then he took sterile saline from the shelf and gently washed out the boy's eyes. "There. Now you should be able to see a lot better." He handed a small bottle containing a mixture of the drugs to the father and said, "Just make sure to add drops to each eye four times a day for the next two weeks, okay?"

"He's going to be okay, isn't he?"

"I don't know for certain yet. But I think we may have gotten lucky this time." After seeing the father's shoulders sag, Brett added, "Yeah, I think he's going to be okay."

"When do you need to see us again?" the father asked.

"Actually, you won't be seeing me again. I'm being sent back home. In fact, I'm leaving shortly. There will be a public health nurse here in a couple of days to take my place. You'll need to make an appointment in a week to see her."

The father stood and shook Brett's hand. "I will never be able to thank you enough," he said. "I have my son because of you."

Brett smiled. "There was a lot of luck on our side." He patted the boy on the shoulder. "Take good care of yourself, Danny."

"I will, Dr. Carson."

Brett shook the father's hand, turned and hurried out of the room; a plane was waiting for him. Brett was an EIS agent—the Epidemic Intelligence Service—of the Centers for Disease Control in Atlanta. Five months ago, he and a team of five others had been sent by the CDC to identify the cause of the new disease and then try to figure out how to stop it.

The other members of the team had returned to Atlanta more than three weeks ago. His instructions had been to return with the rest of the team, but Brett, not someone who followed orders easily, had stayed behind. He still had work to do. Finally, another plane had been sent just for him. With a winter storm bearing down on them, it might be the last plane until spring, and now he had no choice but to leave.

Brett grabbed his bags and his coat near the door of the small clinic. He was pleasantly surprised to see that many of the villagers and the two public health nurses had gathered to see him off. Five months earlier, he had been a stranger to them, and they had accepted him cautiously. Now, they were saying good-bye to a close friend. As Brett was putting on his parka, there was a chorus of "goodbye, Dr. Carson," "we'll miss you," and "have a safe flight."

After saying his good-byes, he turned and saw that the village men had already picked up his bags, and the two boxes filled with research data. He grabbed his laptop and walked over to the single engine de Havilland Beaver that was waiting on a flat piece of tundra that was used as a landing strip. The pilot loaded the bags and boxes.

"Are you going to be able to fly in this weather?" Brett asked. Wind driven snow stung his face; sudden gusts made the de Havilland shudder, and its aluminum skin groaned and creaked in protest.

"It's blowing pretty hard," the pilot said, "and the temperature's dropping. More weather is on the way. If we don't leave now, we're going to be here for a while."

"So, are you going to be able to fly in this?" he asked again.

"I've flown in worse," the pilot answered.

That wasn't the kind of assurance he'd hoped for. He waved to everyone again, then climbed in, buckled his seatbelt, and let out a sigh. He'd been in Alaska nearly five months, his longest assignment since joining the EIS division of the CDC. The de Havilland turned into the wind, revved its engine, then accelerated down the field, disappearing into clouds of snow that swirled up behind them. The plane lifted, and the Alaskan coast fell away below him.

Brett looked out the window at the steep mountains below him, and his thoughts turned to Atlanta. There had been no cell phone signal for hundreds of miles, and he had called Ashley no more than a dozen times using the clinic phone during his five-month absence. He could have called her more often; he knew he should have. But he hadn't. He wasn't sure why. It didn't matter now. Those five grueling months were over and he was going home.

Strong gusts of wind buffeted the plane, but the violent jarring did little to displace the haunting thoughts of the past five months from his mind. Most would consider his efforts in Alaska a success. He knew it was far from that. Ninety-eight people had died, and the eighteen who survived were left permanently blind—all except for Danny. That was far short of "success." He would have liked to have stayed another few weeks for follow up. But the CDC had decided his job was finished. In fact, they had insisted that he return immediately. He had accomplished what they sent him to do.

He had been with the EIS division of the CDC for the past ten years. This assignment had been the longest and most troubling for him yet. He settled back in his seat, and let out a sigh as the last five months of his life receded behind him.

Twenty-three hours later, Brett was back in his condominium. He was exhausted. A four-hour time difference between Alaska and Atlanta, and four connecting flights had left him drained. He had taken the de Havilland to Nome; then flew from Nome to Fairbanks, Fairbanks to Chicago, and the final leg Chicago to Atlanta. After a hot shower, Brett crawled into his own bed for the first time in more than five months.

The phone rang. He was tempted to let it ring. It couldn't be good news, and there was nobody he wanted to talk to, not as tired as he was. Finally, he fumbled for the phone and picked it up.

"Brett, I see you finally made it back. Welcome home." It was Dr. Mitchell Quinn, the director of the EIS Division of the CDC. "Great job," Quinn continued. "They think you're a hero."

Brett glanced at the clock: 8 p.m. "Who thinks I'm a hero? That's a bunch of bull—"

"Not to them it's not. To them you're a hero."

"Who is 'them'?"

"The press and the general public. This epidemic captured everyone's attention. You've been gone, so you don't know how much press it's gotten. A strange new deadly disease, Eskimos, blindness—it has it all. I've scheduled you to give a short press conference."

"A press conference?" he asked, unable to stifle a yawn.

"Tomorrow at one-thirty. Now get some sleep." And he hung up.

Tomorrow? He plunked the receiver onto the phone, punched his pillow into a soft ball, and fell asleep.

Chapter 3

El Peten Rain Forest,
Guatemala

The first tropical storm of the season struck the rain forest with hurricane-force winds and torrential rains, ripping down thousands of trees, snapping off power lines, and leaving villages isolated. Eight days of unrelenting rain had sent torrents of water roaring through swollen streams, tearing out bridges and roads. Finally, the jungle floor itself yielded to the unrelenting onslaught; tons of rich soil hemorrhaged from the earth and flowed in viscous rivers of mud, turning the dirt streets of villages into quagmires of brown muck.

The village of Lepudro was little more than a clearing in the jungle, filled with dilapidated buildings, mud roads, and chickens roaming around pecking at scraps. Rain pelted the tin roof of the small medical clinic in the center of the village with a deafening staccato and dripped from dozens of leaks. Puddles spread on the tiled floor. The stale air inside was damp and musty.

Doctor Robert Crenshaw yanked off his damp scrub shirt and reached for the last clean one. He hated the incessant dampness that clung like a second skin. He longed to feel dry.

The misery of the jungle was endless: swarms of bloodthirsty insects, the constant rain and humidity, the smothering heat. He developed rashes that lasted for weeks, and mold kept forming inside his shoes. His residency at Mass General in Boston had not prepared him for the poverty and disease he was forced to deal with daily.

Most of his fellow residents had opened offices and gone into practice. Crenshaw, always the idealist, wanted to do something meaningful. His fiancée never fully understood his motives and called him an "idealistic activist." Instead of beginning his medical practice, he had joined the Peace Corps and was assigned to the World Health Organization in Guatemala. She was less than thrilled about that.

After a few months of trying to talk him out of it, she finally told him to go and get it out of his system. Her advice had worked; every last vestige of idealism had vanished.

It was strictly feast or famine at the small medical clinic. Most days were spent suffering through sweltering, boring hours that dragged on interminably, while the rest were filled with terror and panic. He frequently encountered conditions and diseases that he'd only read about in textbooks—malaria, parasites, infected rashes, snake bites, and fungus rot.

Now, he feared something more menacing lurked outside the clinic walls. During the past six weeks, more than eleven patients had died after a short, desperate battle with some disease he had never seen before nor read about. After the third patient died with symptoms similar to the first two, he grew suspicious. When the sixth patient had succumbed, he knew without a doubt that it was from the same disease.

With the tenth death, his curiosity and concern changed to panic. Knowing he needed help, and fearing for his own safety, he had sent messages to the World Health Organization and to the Guatemalan Minister of Health, warning them of his suspicions that something deadly was afoot.

So far there had been no response, and he was growing frustrated and angry. Then, the storm of the century smashed into the center of Guatemala. It devasted remote villages; roads and bridges were washed away. For the last eight days the rain had not let up.

They were now isolated, cut off from the outside world. Crenshaw worried that the WHO and the health minister might not have received his message—or worse, that they had dismissed his concern.

He wanted to pack his bags and leave this hell hole. Just when he felt he'd reached his limit, the tropical storm hit and the deluge began. The storm showed no signs of letting up.

Neither did the flow of the sick and the dying. Three days ago, they had found a man face down in the dirt, dead. There was no doubt he had died from the same disease.

"*Prisa, senor*. Quick! You must come," an old man shouted from the doorway to be heard above the storm. Rain poured from the man's hat onto his mud-splattered clothes. "He's very sick."

Crenshaw followed him out into the storm. Outside, a man on horseback slumped under an oiled poncho. Crenshaw's heart sank. He couldn't be sure without examining him, but he worried the man was dying from the same unknown disease. If so, that made the second one this week.

"Let's get him inside," Crenshaw shouted back. Thick mud sucked at his feet, and rain beat against his face as he helped pull the man from the horse. "How long has he been like this?"

The villager shrugged. "*El es enfermo. Muy enfermo.* He can't breathe. He's very sick," he repeated.

They carried him into the small, cramped isolation room, and Maria Portillo, the only nurse at the clinic, began getting him out of his wet clothes and putting a dry gown on him. Crenshaw snapped on a pair of sterile gloves and did a quick check of the man. He knew immediately it was the same disease. He had seen it before.

Dark fluid oozed from the man's ear, from his nose, and from the corners of his mouth. Purple blotches marked his skin, the result of hemorrhage into tissues. Crenshaw clicked on his penlight and looked at the man's eyes. The conjunctiva were dull and the mucosal tissues dry. From the corner of his eye, a small trickle of dark blood oozed from a tear duct. The man was severely dehydrated, probably had multi-organ failure, and was slowly bleeding to death from every pore.

Crenshaw had no idea what the disease was, had no idea of how to treat it, and certainly was not equipped to handle complex cases such as this. In all likelihood, it was an overwhelming infection that caused some kind of blood dyscrasia.

He knew it was not the plague. Bubonic plague was the opposite of this disease; instead of causing bleeding, bubonic plague caused the victim's entire blood volume to clot into a solid glob. Blood in every artery solidified into gnarly ropes of dark clot, turning the dying victim a dark purplish color known as the *'black plague.'*

In front of him lay the twelfth victim, now an even dozen.

Crenshaw grabbed a stethoscope and listened to his lungs. "He's dehydrated and hemorrhaging. Just like the others. Start an IV," he said.

"Do you want to give him an antibiotic? We're nearly out," Maria reminded him.

They'd been without new supplies for more than a week. Crenshaw might need the antibiotic for someone who had a chance at survival. He knew there was no hope for this man. So far, nobody had survived.

"Then hold off on that for now. It's probably not going to help him anyway," he said. "Someone else might need it. And be very careful. Don't stick yourself."

She stared at him a moment, then nodded and pulled out supplies to start an IV.

He felt as if he'd just signed a death warrant, even though he knew he couldn't have changed anything regardless of what he gave the man. He hadn't been able to save any of them. Because of the shortage of drugs, he was being forced into a difficult medical dilemma of whether to treat or not treat. Thumbs up they live, thumbs down they die. Only in this case it didn't matter what you did with your damned thumbs: they still died.

"Hang a bottle of saline and piggy-back a vial of hydrocortisone," he told the nurse. At least he would try to do something for the poor man. Maybe the steroids would help his breathing, but most likely it would only serve to prolong his agony. Crenshaw already knew what the outcome would be, and he also knew he had neither the supplies nor the stamina to deal with it. This man was going to die. Like all the others.

The problem now was not to try and save them—so far that had proved to be impossible—but to figure out what the disease was and how to stop it. Crenshaw had converted a storage closet into a crude isolation room, a simple but effective solution to separating those with the disease from the other patients. They had managed to squeeze two cots into the cramped space with just enough room to move between them. He and Maria wore masks and gloves and scrubbed thoroughly each time they left the isolation room.

But a fear was always in the back of his mind. A fear that he might become infected. If that happened, he would die alone in the jungle, thousands of miles away from family and friends.

He had already seen two new cases this week. This new patient made the third one in seven days.

And now he had other problems to deal with. He had two other patients in the clinic, and both of them were critical. They needed his full concentration. One was a young girl in labor with a breech pregnancy, and the other was an old man.

The day before, people from a neighboring village brought in the elderly man who had been bitten by a 'bushmaster,' the silent jungle predator feared most by natives. Known to grow up to twelve feet in length, the bushmaster possessed the largest fangs of any snake, and its bite was vicious.

Swift and deadly accurate, the snake dispatched its venom in seconds. The venom caused severe pain, swelling, and a dark discoloration as tissue necrosed. Without amputation or antivenom, gangrene and death would usually follow several agonizing hours later.

Crenshaw had no antivenom to give the man. The leg looked ugly and, in all likelihood would have to be amputated if he were to survive. But there would be no amputation. Crenshaw didn't have surgical saws and instruments needed to cut through bone, didn't have blood for transfusion, didn't have anesthesia, and most importantly, he didn't have the surgical training.

The man was at far greater risk of dying from a botched amputation than from the snake bite. Any concern over the leg would have to wait until the patient survived his more immediate problem of breathing. The man's skin took on a cyanotic bluish tint as his breathing became more labored. The venom had caused an allergic reaction that closed the small bronchioles of the lungs. Crenshaw had been treating him with a combination of high doses of steroids, aminophylline, and epinephrine.

He had little else to offer. Marie put a wet cloth to the old man's forehead.

"What's his temperature?"

"One hundred and four," she said.

"He's developing sepsis from the infected leg. Give him IV Keflex and change the dressing." Crenshaw knew gangrene was probably setting in.

"That's our last bottle."

"Go ahead and use it," he said with a tone of resignation. "It's the only chance he has."

Things had definitely gotten more complicated with the arrival of the latest patient. As if he didn't have enough problems already, with the girl in labor and the man dying from a bushmaster bite. Crenshaw was exhausted, damp, and miserable. And he was worried. He knew that if the worst happened, he would have more deaths on his hands.

And the worst began to happen.

Chapter 4

The Centers for Disease Control
Atlanta, Georgia

B rett Carson sat on the stage beside the podium and looked out over the audience. He had not fully realized how big a story the epidemic in Alaska had generated. Most of the press conferences at the CDC were to discuss flu outbreaks, new vaccines, or the seasonal diseases, and attendances were usually small, with only a dozen or so health or science reporters in the room.

People were more interested in who won on *American Idol* than they were which strain of flu was predicted for the winter. The auditorium could seat three hundred, but was rarely filled except for special events. Today, there were only a few empty seats as dozens of reporters from around the country, news photographers, and live TV cameras from CNN, the major networks, and several local stations filled the auditorium. Thick cables snaked up to the forest of microphones in front of the podium.

Brett was as dressed up as he would ever get: a clean but

unpressed oxford button-down shirt, knit tie, navy blazer, faded jeans, and well-worn leather loafers. His face, bronzed by the Arctic sun, accentuated his pale blue eyes. He ran his hands through his thick black hair as he waited.

The overhead lights dimmed, and Kate Roberson, the communications director for the CDC, walked up to the podium. "On behalf of the Centers for Disease Control, I would like to welcome everyone here today. We will be giving a report on the recent serious epidemic in Alaska that everyone has been anxiously following. There will be time for questions and answers at the end," Roberson said. "I will now turn it over to our EIS agent who was in charge of the investigation, Doctor Brett Carson."

Cameras clicked away as he stepped up to the podium. "Good afternoon. As most of you know, in early May of this year, there was an outbreak of a deadly epidemic in northern Alaska along the coast of the Seward Peninsula."

He described in detail how a newly identified virus, now called the "A9-NC virus," had killed more than ninety people and blinded eighteen others. The mysterious disease had created a sensation in the press for weeks. Meanwhile, scientists at the CDC worried that it would spread into the lower forty-eight. It had taken scientists at the CDC more than five frantic months to find the source of the deadly virus.

"This photo shows the horrific effects of the A9-NC virus," he said. The slide was a close-up of a young Alaskan native woman whose red, swollen eyes looked like over-ripened cherries that might burst open at any moment.

"The inflammatory reaction in the eyes is devastating, often causing blindness in a matter of hours," he said. "After the virus attacks the optic nerve, it spreads quickly along the nerve sheath and invades the brain, resulting in death from encephalitis and massive edema of the brain. If the patient manages to survive, blindness is inevitable." He paused a moment. The silence was palpable as the audience hung onto every word. "Time was of the essence, if we hoped to stop the spread of the virus and prevent more deaths."

Images flashed on the large screen in quick succession, showing victims whose eyes had been ravaged by the virus. "This slide taken by an electron microscope shows a neuron infected with the virus," Brett continued. "Of the few people who survived, all have been left permanently blind—except for one nine-year-old boy."

He concluded his press conference by detailing how he had traced the virus to the tundra lemming. "Fleas carried the A9-CN virus from rodents to humans with devastating results," he said. "Two consecutive mild winters produced lush tundra foliage, which in turn caused an explosion in the tundra lemming population.

"However, this past winter was brutally cold, and it drove the rodents into human dwellings in search of food and shelter, carrying with them the A9-NC virus. In many ways, it was similar to the Hanta virus outbreak in Mesa Verde and the Southwest a few years ago.

"We then instituted an extensive trapping program that drastically reduced the rodents' population and stopped human exposure to the virus. Soon after these measures were introduced, the epidemic seems to have been contained. There have been no new cases reported in the past four weeks. I recently tried a combination of drugs on a nine-year-old patient, and it we are hopeful that he will recover with no significant loss of vision. Our labs here have isolated the virus and are attempting to develop a vaccine for it. Hopefully, this virus will not spread into the lower forty-eight states."

Silence filled the auditorium as the crowd looked at him, processing all they had just heard. Then applause filled the auditorium. The communications director approached the podium.

"Thank you, Dr. Carson, for your presentation. You and your team are to be commended for an outstanding job." Roberson adjusted the microphone. "Are there any questions for Dr. Carson?"

Robyn Deters, a CNN reporter, stood. "Why is this the first time anyone's ever heard of this virus?" she asked. "Where did it come from?"

"That's a very good question," Brett said. "Some of the known viruses, such as the polio virus or the hanta virus, are retroviruses. They are mysterious and disappear for decades, then suddenly appear with new outbreaks of the disease. These retroviruses invade the cells of some obscure host animal, lay dormant for years, then suddenly reappear and begin to spread rapidly. There are dozens of these diseases that seem to appear in cycles, such as monkey pox, bird flu, swine flu, and ebola. The source of the deadly Ebola virus is unknown, but we believe the source is lurking inside a few caves in Africa. Outbreaks of Ebola are probably due to an unsuspecting victim getting exposed to the virus in one of those caves."

He took a sip of water and continued. "Even the ancient bubonic plague is still with us today. This past summer, a ranger in the Rocky Mountain National Park found a dead mountain lion in one of the canyons. There was no sign of injury, so she was curious about what had killed it. She loaded the dead lion into her Jeep and took it back to the garage at the ranger station. She cut it open for a quick autopsy. When she did this, she unknowingly released a cloud of bubonic organisms which she inhaled. She was dead in less than forty-eight hours from the plague—the same dreaded 'black death' of medieval Europe that wiped out more than one third of the human population in Europe during the seventeenth century."

A wave of gasps and murmurs spread through the auditorium.

Brett continued. "There are also rapidly mutating viruses that spread from species to species, a process which creates new viruses, such as this A9-CN virus. They can then suddenly appear in humans with devastating results. Severe Acute Respiratory Syndrome, also known as SARS, killed nearly eight-hundred people before the virus was isolated and identified. Where did that virus come from? Why did the new A9-NC virus in Alaska suddenly appear out of nowhere? We will probably never know the answer to that."

"New, deadly viruses will always surface unannounced and unanticipated," he continued. "There is always the fear of some newly mutated virus that bursts out of the jungle, possibly killing millions before it can be contained or an effective vaccine can be developed."

The audience remained silent as the lights went up. Then reporters and cameramen flooded into the center aisle. Brett was a man of action, but not a man with patience. He had little tolerance for reporters and their questions.

Glancing around the room, a wide smile spread across his face when he spotted a young woman wearing an *Atlanta Journal-Constitution* ID badge moving down the aisle through the crowd of other reporters. Finally, she reached him and stuck out her hand. ""Nice talk," she said. "I'm Ashley Bentley with the *Atlanta*

Journal-Constitution. May I ask a few questions?"

The people pressed around him were visibly shocked when he leaned down, took her in his arms, and kissed the attractive young woman.

"Sure. What did you want to ask me?"

"So, how have you been, Brett?"

El Peten Rain Forest

After more than a difficult hour of struggling with the breech pregnancy, Crenshaw delivered a healthy baby which Maria was now attending to. Crenshaw's scrub shirt was soaked. He needed a break, but he washed his hands and turned his attention again to the old man with the snake bite.

He checked the dressing and adjusted the IV. The aminophylline had improved the man's breathing, and the old man drifted into a deep sleep. Crenshaw slowed the aminophylline drip. He was relieved that the man's breathing had improved, but he'd have to keep a close eye on him; his condition was still critical. But Crenshaw knew there was no way he would attempt an amputation on him. In the next bed the new mother and her baby had both fallen asleep.

For the first time in hours, the clinic was quiet. But Crenshaw's work wasn't finished.

He and Maria put on masks and gloves and entered the dreaded dark isolation room in the corner to check on the newest admission. The man showed no signs of improvement. In fact, he was losing ground fast. His gray face contracted in agony as he struggled for air. His ashen skin hung loose, muscles as soft as bruised bananas sagged from bones, and his sunken eyes were dull and unable to focus.

The disease was both swift and predictable. Within the first two hours of the onset of the illness, its victim developed a scorching fever. After ten to twelve hours, the fever resolved but the victim's skin had turned cold and was already feeling lifeless to the touch.

A thick, musty smell poured from the man's mouth. Crenshaw put his stethoscope against the sunken chest. Noisy, wet lung sounds crackled through the earpieces. He moved the stethoscope and detected a friction rub caused by pleural inflammation.

Crenshaw had seen it before and now, far too often. They all looked the same; a mask of terror and helplessness haunted their faces as life drained away along with blood that oozed from every orifice. Muscles turned gelatinous and useless, making every movement a monumental chore. Breathing, swallowing, even blinking their eyes, became agonizingly slow. The very act of living seemed painful. Their last bit of energy was spent clinging to life.

Death would soon follow for this patient just as it had with the previous twelve patients—or was it thirteen? He'd lost count.

God, he hated this place.

After a desperate clenching of fists and a final gasp at life, the man's struggle ended. Vacant eyes, already clouded, stared at nothing. The man had only been in the clinic for three hours. Crenshaw stopped the IV to save the supply of hydrocortisone.

"We have to move him outside until the family can come for him," Crenshaw said.

"It's raining and the ground is covered with mud," Maria argued. "Where are we going to put him?"

"We can't leave him in here. We'll wrap him in sheets and put him outside until morning. Then we can find a place to put him."

With Maria's help, he wrapped the body in sheets and carried it out into the driving rain; they left it lying in the cold mud to wait for morning light. It seemed cruel, but Crenshaw wanted the body and whatever disease it was carrying out of the clinic as quickly as possible. With luck, wild dogs wouldn't find it before his family came to claim him in the morning.

"What is it? What's killing them?" Maria asked.

"I wish I knew. Whatever it is, it's spreading. Heaven help us," he said as he wiped his forehead with the back of his hand.

"You don't look so good," she said. "Go get some rest. I'll keep an eye on the patients."

Crenshaw stood in the doorway a moment and looked out at the darkness. The jungle seemed to close in around him like an evil presence. Something was out there, something deadly. The rain forest was a breeding ground for many of the world's most exotic and lethal organisms. They might be facing a disease that could kill hundreds—maybe thousands—if someone didn't figure out a way to stop it.

He slumped back against the doorframe and let out a deep sigh. After more than forty hours of chaos, the clinic had again become a place of unsettled worried anticipation. He wondered when the next victims would arrive. He needed help, and soon. More important, he desperately needed sleep. He turned and went back inside.

He scrubbed his hands again and glanced at his reflection in the mirror. His face was gaunt, and he seemed to have aged ten years. Dark circles outlined his bloodshot eyes—eyes that begged to be a million miles away from this damned godforsaken place.

It had been more than eight days since he had contacted both the Guatemalan government and the World Health Organization. He worried that they hadn't received his message because of the storm, or worse—that they didn't believe him.

The one thing he knew for certain—he didn't want to die here.

He walked over to one of the empty cots, pulled a damp sheet around his shoulders, and fell into a deep sleep, unfazed by the pounding rain outside.

Chapter 5

After a round of questions, the reporters and camera crews drifted away to their next assignment, leaving Brett and Ashley alone.

"I just got in yesterday," he said. "I would have called you, but as you can see, it's been pretty hectic around here."

"Let's go get a cup of coffee," she said.

He glanced at his watch a second, then shrugged. "Sure, that'd be great."

They left the conference room and went down the hall to the coffee shop. "How's the reporting business?" he asked, putting his arm around her.

"Great. You look terrific, Brett," she said, looking up and hugging him. "I'm so proud of what you did in Alaska. You were too modest in there."

"I didn't do anything special, and I certainly didn't do it alone."

"That's not what I heard. You can read about it in the Sunday paper."

"Isn't that some kind of conflict of interest?" he asked. "Isn't there some kind of rule that you can't write about your own family or friends?"

She grinned. "Hmm...never heard of it. Besides, I have a great story here."

They quickly caught up on things over coffee. Finally, he glanced at his watch. "I'm really sorry, but I have a mountain of stuff to catch up on." Leaning across the small table, he kissed her. "How about dinner tonight?"

"I've been waiting more than five months to see you. Nothing could keep me away."

He smiled. "Seven-thirty at L'Alouette—meet you there?"

As they stood to leave, Ashley took his arm, pressed her body against him and spoke softly in his ear. "If I were you, I wouldn't plan on getting to work early tomorrow. You might be up late."

Brett watched her, admiring her curves as she walked away. A hint of her perfume hung in the air. He shook his head and smiled again. Then he gathered up his material, refilled his cup, and headed to his office.

He opened the door to the familiar, tiny office. He bumped his elbow while stacking his notes on top of a pile of other papers, sending a wave of coffee splashing across his desk.

"Damn!" he said, as he wiped up the spill. Five months freezing his ass off in Alaska while chasing down a lethal virus, and all he had to come back to was an office that wouldn't have made a good closet. The CDC told him eight years ago it was only temporary and promised him larger office space. But that hadn't happened. After wiping the rest of the spill from his desk, he finally sat down and let out a deep breath.

It was good to be back in Atlanta.

The phone on Brett's desk rang. The EIS director, Dr. Mitchell Quinn—"Mitch" to those who knew him—was on the other end. "How did the news conference go, Brett? Something came up, and I wasn't able to make it."

"It went fine. I could have used a couple of days to prepare for it."

"I need to see you in my office as soon as it's convenient."

The tone of that brief conversation left Brett feeling uneasy. Maybe Quinn was pissed that he hadn't returned with the rest of the Alaskan team. He grabbed the thick folder containing his notes on the A9-CN investigation and headed toward C-Building, which housed the EIS administrative offices.

The large CDC complex was spread out over four acres. With an annual budget of over 1.5 billion dollars, it employed more than six thousand people, including renowned scientists in microbiology, virology, immunology, epidemiology, and biochemistry. The Epidemic Investigative Service was the elite division within the CDC to which Brett was assigned. It had fewer than twenty-five agents—doctors who specialized in tracking down some of the world's deadliest diseases.

On the eighth floor, Brett went to Quinn's office, knocked once, and entered. The large corner office had two walls lined with large windows. The director sat at a large, polished, wooden desk which held multiple computer screens. Quinn's appearance—tie loosened, shirt sleeves rolled up, and reading glasses parked on the bridge of his nose—seemed more appropriate to a city editor than the director of the EIS division.

Quinn stood up and shook his hand. "Nice to see you, Brett. I'm glad you finally decided to come back and join us." He glanced at the folder of papers Brett carried under his arm and jabbed his thumb toward a chair. "Have a seat."

Brett sank into a black leather chair. "It's good to be back. Here are my notes on the A9-NC. I haven't had time to write a report." Brett somehow guessed this wasn't about the virus.

Quinn returned to his desk and dismissed the folder with a wave of his hand as he sat down.

"Brett, everyone here's pleased with your work in Alaska. A senior editor at the *Constitution* called me and said your reporter friend is doing a feature article on the epidemic and the CDC in this Sunday's paper. We're going to get great press coverage. Give us a real PR boost, which doesn't hurt during budget time. But that's not why I called you up here. This isn't about the A9-NC virus. Something else has come up." He paused a moment, then shoved a pile of papers clipped together across the desk to Brett.

"We just received this fax today."

"What's this?"

"It's from the World Health Organization. They're worried about a possible new epidemic in Guatemala. According to them, at least thirty, maybe even as many as forty or more—may have already died from it."

Brett was confused. Why was Quinn telling him this? It

certainly wasn't for advice. That wasn't Quinn's style. "What does the Guatemalan health department have to say about it?"

"Not much actually. The Guatemalan government said they'll cooperate in any way they can. But right now that's going to be limited. They have other concerns—like a civil war that's sapping the country's resources. And they're been hit with a tropical storm that devastated the center of the country."

"What does this have to do with me?" Brett asked, looking at the fax on the desk.

"I want you to go down and check it out." Quinn tapped his pen against a notepad.

"You're not serious. There's no way I can go. I just got back, remember? I've been gone more than five months—"

"Yeah, I know."

"I haven't even unpacked."

Mitch kept tapping his pen but said nothing.

"Who else is on the team?" Brett asked.

"No team. Not yet. It's too risky." Quinn walked over to the coffee pot for a fresh cup, poured a cup, then dumped a packet of NutraSweet into it. "Coffee?" he asked, holding the pot out toward Brett.

"No thanks. I just had some."

Quinn went back to his desk and continued. "Do you know anything about the political situation in Guatemala?" Before Brett could respond, Quinn continued. "Very unstable. And dangerous. Mountain rebels are fighting the government forces in a civil war that's gone on for more than thirty years. Parts of the country are a hell zone right now. Even the Red Cross pulled its people out. Last month, four nuns were murdered, and two other nuns were held captive by government forces. They eventually escaped but not before they were brutalized and raped.

"And three reporters are missing. I can't risk sending a team into that political mess until we know exactly what this report is all about."

To Brett, it suddenly seemed as if he was expendable, and he didn't like the sound of that. Maybe this was Quinn's punishment for staying on in Alaska. "Are you asking me or telling me?"

"Depends on your answer," Quinn said. "If you agree, then I'm asking you. If you say no, then I'm telling you."

Brett shook his head. "I can't go right now. I just got back. I do have a life outside of this place. Not much of one, granted. And I have a lot of paperwork here to catch up on."

Quinn said nothing as he kept tapping his pen against the pad.

Finally he said, "What's with you, Brett? I tell the team to come back from Alaska, and you decide on your own to stay behind. I had to charter a plane to get you back—and that wasn't cheap. Now I tell you I need you to go to Guatemala for a few days, and you say no."

"I need some time here in the office before I take another assignment," Brett continued.

"Sometimes things just don't work out the way they're supposed to," Quinn said. "I need you down there."

"At least let Ross go with me." Dr. Ross Solt was the senior EIS agent, and one of Brett's closest friends. They had been on several assignments together. Brett was younger, more driven and often reckless; Solt was older, more experienced, and savvy. Solt had taught Brett the ropes when he first arrived at the CDC and had got him out of more than one serious situation.

"Can't," Quinn said. "He's headed off to Massachusetts in two days to deal with the equine encephalitis virus outbreak in New England."

Brett suspected the real reason Quinn wouldn't let Solt go with him was because he didn't want to risk losing two EIS agents. Brett reluctantly picked up the fax. "What do you know about the epidemic so far?"

"Not much, except that whatever we're dealing with is hot, if what they're telling us is accurate. It seems most of the victims die within the first twenty-four hours. The symptoms mentioned in the report were vague, but my guess is the cause of death is from pneumonia. What little information we have came from the World Health Organization. The Guatemalan government is not that involved yet, but like I said, they've got other things to worry about."

"What about cultures? Any organisms identified? There must be something to go on."

"Nothing," Quinn answered. "We don't even know if it *is* an infection. It could be toxins, poisons—just don't know. We're starting from the bottom on this one."

Quinn dropped his pen on the desk and leaned forward on his elbows. "I want you to check it out. I know you just got back. This might be nothing, or it could be something very serious and contagious that we need to know about before it gets way out of hand."

"Why me?"

"I need someone who can go down there, find out what's going on, and get the hell out again without me having to worry about them. That's you. You can handle it."

As Brett saw it, there were two ways to interpret this. Either it was a great compliment—or he was expendable. He decided to go for the first option. "I'll take that as a compliment," Brett said.

Quinn said nothing.

This was the kind of assignment that had danger and trouble written all over it. The last five months had been grueling, and he needed a rest. A couple of weeks to regroup and he'd be ready to tackle anything. But he'd only been in Atlanta less than twenty-four hours, and he'd only been in his apartment long enough to get a night's sleep, shower, change clothes, and give a news conference.

He needed some down time.

"We can't wait on this one," Quinn said without apology. "I'll see if I can arrange some time off for you after this matter is finished."

"How soon would I have to leave?"

"Got you booked on an early flight day after tomorrow," Quinn said, looking at him as if he were trying to judge his reaction. "Sorry, Brett, but this is urgent."

Quinn picked up the pen again and used it to stir his coffee. "Be here first thing in the morning. Maybe we'll have more information for you by then."

"Guess I'm getting to be too predictable," Brett said.

"You're a lot of things, Brett, but predictable is not one of them. Here's a folder with the information we have at this time. Tomorrow our travel office will have the usual official documents, money, and papers you'll need for Guatemala."

Quinn stood up, walked over to the door and opened it, indicating that the meeting was over. "See you first thing tomorrow morning."

When Brett returned to his office, there were four phone messages taped to his door, and his message machine was blinking, but he ignored them. He dropped the A9-CN virus notes on top of other papers piled on the file cabinet and turned his attention to the folder. Guatemala? What the hell was he doing?

Still, he knew that this was an opportunity he couldn't pass up, not that he really had any choice in the matter.

He also knew for certain Ashley wasn't going to be pleased.

Chapter 6

Brett had reserved a corner table at L'Alouette. After having been away for five months, he wanted his reunion with Ashley to be special. Because of his job—and occasionally hers when she was away working on an article for the paper—they often went for weeks without seeing each other. Whenever they did manage to have time together, it was like having a first date. It was never the routine or boring familiarity that his married friends occasionally complained about.

He was late and moved quickly through the restaurant. Ashley was already there, and from the empty glass in front of her, he guessed she had already finished her first cosmopolitan. She was dressed in an expensive-looking black dress.

"Sorry I'm late," he said, kissing her on the cheek before sliding into his chair. "Something unexpected came up and I had to deal with it."

The waiter came to the table. "Scotch on the rocks," Brett said. He glanced at the wine list and ordered a bottle of Erath Pinot Noir to have with their dinner. Then he turned to her. "Ashley, you look beautiful," he said.

"Thank you. And you look great, Brett," she said. "That arctic sun gave you a great tan. The women reporters at the conference today were trying to find out more about you—and it had nothing to do with your report."

The waiter delivered Brett's drink. Ashley hesitated a moment, as if she wasn't sure whether or not to ask him something. "You said something unexpected came up. Anything to do with the problem in Alaska?"

"Let's order dinner," he said before answering her. Ashley ordered the evening's special: pheasant with raspberry sauce, yams and wild mushrooms with rice. Brett took a moment to glance over the menu, then ordered chilled carrot soup, spinach salad, broccoli quiche and a side dish of pasta with tomatoes in olive oil.

"Turning into a vegetarian?" she asked.

"I can't remember the last time I had fresh vegetables," Brett said. "Did you know that they can't grow vegetables in northern Alaska? Plenty of sunlight during the summer, but it's still too cold to grow anything because of the permafrost.

"For the past five months I've lived on dried fish, smoked caribou, whale blubber and beef jerky. Whale blubber, for God's sake! The only vegetables available came from cans." He sipped his Scotch and said, "Maybe I will become a vegetarian. The thought of eating meat, just the smell of it—fried, smoked, dried, or baked—makes me sick."

She hesitated, then asked, "So, what's the new problem at work? A new epidemic somewhere in the world?"

"Yeah, actually there is. At least we think so, but we don't know for sure yet."

Their salads arrived. "Fresh ground pepper?" the waiter asked. Ashley said no, and Brett politely waved the waiter away.

"I've got a surprise for you," she said. "I'm having a dinner party this weekend." He shifted uneasily in his chair. She continued. "Saturday evening the whole gang is coming over, and I'm cooking Italian. It's a kind of a welcome home party for you."

Brett stared at the single candle in the center of their table for a moment before answering. "I'm sorry, Ashley, but Saturday's no good. As I said, something's come up." When he looked up at her, her smile was gone.

He continued. "We just received a fax from Guatemala— there's a potentially serious situation down there."

"What's that got to do with you?" she asked.

"They want me to go down there and look into it."

She laughed nervously. "What? That's ridiculous. You *can't* go. You just got back." When he didn't say anything, she grew more serious. "Isn't there supposed to be some kind of break between assignments?"

"Yeah, usually four weeks. Two weeks minimum."

"Four weeks? You've only been back a day. Tell them to send somebody else!" she blurted out. "They can't do that to us, Brett. It seems like we're never together. We go for months without seeing each other. Honestly, I'm tired of being alone, of always waiting for you to get back from some assignment. I need to know where my life is going. I don't always want to be a reporter. Someday, I would like to settle down and have a family. How can we build a life together if you're never here?"

The question went unanswered and the tension grew. The waiter arrived with the wine, showed the label to Brett, opened it and poured. Brett fixed his gaze on the deep-red liquid as it flowed into the glasses.

After the waiter left, Brett took a sip of wine, thought a moment, then quietly said, "Ashley, we're not like other people. We knew that going in. But we wouldn't want to be, would we? Caught in ruts, always doing the same things. You have your job at the paper, and I have my life at the CDC."

"You mean your *job*!" she corrected him. "It's not your *life*."

The waiter arrived with their dinners. After arranging the plates, he poured more wine. "*Bon appétit*," he said and left.

"Look, whenever we're together, it's special," Brett continued. "Most people don't get many special times, some don't get any. All of our times together are special."

She forked mushrooms and rice into her mouth. "Like tonight, you mean?"

"Yes," he said and grinned. "Like tonight."

She didn't' return the smile. Instead, she jabbed her fork into the pheasant, cut off a bite, and ate it in silence.

Brett's mind was already elsewhere. He stared at the candle flame as he pondered what he might be facing deep in the Guatemalan jungle.

Chapter 7

Brett hadn't had time to unpack. His condo was cluttered with luggage, boxes, stacks of journals, and five months of unopened junk mail. Bills were paid automatically by the bank whenever he was gone on assignment, but everything else kept accumulating and had been delivered by the post office that afternoon. So Ashley insisted they go to her place after dinner. After they arrived at her fifth-floor condominium, Ashley poured two glasses of Amaretto on the rocks, and they walked out onto the balcony off her bedroom.

"Beautiful night," he said, looking up at the moon playing hide-and-seek through the maple branches.

"How long will you be gone?" she asked.

"Don't know. A few days, maybe a week. This is going to be a short trip."

"God, I missed you," she said and kissed him. She pressed her body against his.

He put his arms around her and drew her closer. He felt her body against his.

She led him inside and they fell across her bed. Moonlight spilling through the doorway bathed them in a faint glow. He kissed her lips, her hair, and the softness of her neck. His hands slid up her thighs, slowly pushing up her dress. He unzipped her dress and kissed the top of her breast as the dress slipped down. After she was naked, his lips, tongue, and hands moved over her, exploring, tasting. His touch, at first slow and gentle, grew more urgent.

She started to unbutton his shirt, but he quickly tore off his clothes and reached for her again.

"Slow down... take your time," she said in a throaty voice, while trying to catch her breath. But it became obvious that tonight he could do no such thing. His muscles tensed. His breath was hot, and a soft moan rose from her throat as his hands moved between her legs.

She reached down and guided him into her. Her body, pale in the moonlight, rose to meet his. When she finally stopped trembling and caught her breath, she said, "Maybe five months is a little too long to wait, Brett Carson. What do you think?"

He said nothing, but quietly began kissing her breasts again. She rolled over and straddled him, holding his arms against the pillow, and slowly moved her hips against him, tantalizing him. When he pushed up and into her, she gasped as her body responded to his. He drew her face down to his lips as he pressed deeper into her.

A long, relaxing shower the next morning cleared his head, but the previous night's activity and lack of sleep had drained him. Brett still hadn't adjusted to the four-hour time difference between Alaska and Atlanta. He'd used Ashley's shampoo, and now his hair smelled of jasmine.

Ashley handed him a cup of coffee as he walked into the kitchen. "I thought you'd sleep in," she said, and leaned over to kiss him.

He gratefully accepted the coffee. "Got an early meeting with Quinn. And I have a million things to do before I leave tomorrow," he said.

"Tomorrow?" she asked with disbelief in her voice. After a long pause she asked, "You're leaving tomorrow? I thought you'd have at least a couple of days here. They can't send you out again after just one day back, can they?" she asked.

"Ashley, I have to go. Besides, I'll probably only be down there only a few days, a couple of weeks at most." That wasn't exactly the truth, but it was close enough.

"You can't get out of it?"

"No." He took a sip of coffee.

"Well that's just great," she said, throwing the dish towel down on the counter. "Why don't you ask them for an assignment here? They'd do it, wouldn't they?"

"You don't understand. I have to go."

"Why do you do this?" she asked, her eyes filling with tears.

"It's my job. It what makes me feel alive."

"No," she said, "it's what makes you feel *alone*."

The silence between them grew, as if neither knew what to say. He reached out a hand toward her, but she pulled away. He put the cup down on the table. "I have to go. I'll call you later," he said and turned to leave.

"You don't want a relationship," Ashley said, wiping away tears with the back of her hand. "You don't have time for that, do you? You just want somebody to sleep with when you pop into town. That's all." Her voice was starting to crack. "Well, go get someone else to fuck—if you ever show up."

As Brett left, he didn't know if they'd just broken up or merely had a serious fight. Either way, it wasn't good.

Epidemic Intelligence Services Headquarters,
Centers for Disease Control
7:40 a.m.

"More coffee?" Quinn asked as Brett scanned the maps that were spread out on the table in front of him.

Brett held up his cup without taking his eyes from the maps while Quinn filled it. "How many cases reported so far? Brett asked." He was trying to put this morning's ugly scene with Ashley behind him and concentrate on the matter in front of him.

"Don't know exactly. Hard to get an exact count. Looks like just sporadic outbreaks in different areas. The report described a rapid onset of symptoms, followed by a devastating course that has always been fatal. We assume from the sketchy information that we're dealing with some kind of infection, but it could be anything," Quinn said as he added sugar to his cup and stirred his coffee with his pen.

"Have there been any survivors?"

"None that we've been told about. But that's still an unknown."

"Do you think there's any connection to locale, occupation, water supply, that sort of thing?" Brett asked as he flipped through the folder again.

"There's just not enough information yet. Some of the victims were treated with antibiotics, but there's no response. Probably viral rather than bacterial, but could be another Legionaries' scenario where the bacteria are difficult to culture. Medical records of the victims are either sketchy or nonexistent, so at this point we're really in the dark."

"What's your best guess?" Brett asked.

Quinn rubbed his chin as he considered the question. "My guess is it's probably a virus. Possibly one of the deadly hemorrhagic viruses like the Hanta virus or one of its cousins." Quinn paused a moment, then continued. "We have to assume that this is a hot one and that the risk to everyone involved is significant, so we have to be extremely cautious."

A hot one—the term they reserved for the rare, extremely virulent organisms that were highly contagious and could kill victims within a day, sometimes within hours after the onset of symptoms.

"*We* have to be extremely cautious?" Brett said. "You mean *I* have to be cautious."

Quinn's warning reminded Brett of the CDC's recent tragedies. The past year had been the deadliest in the history of the CDC. Last summer, an agent had died of a black mamba snake bite while in Zaire working on the AIDS crisis. Two more EIS agents, both close friends of Brett, had died in the last three months while on assignment—one due to a random shooting in a region torn by civil war, another as a result of fatal meningitis caused by the virus she had been studying in Turkey. As director, Quinn felt responsible and had taken their deaths hard.

It was dangerous work. Poverty and political chaos equaled breeding grounds for disease. Cholera, plague, dysentery, and hepatitis were always a constant threat with social upheaval. Quinn was right; Guatemala was not going to be a friendly place. The information provided by the State Department detailed the brutality of the Guatemalan army, now famous for its daylight kidnappings and roadside executions of those who disagreed with the government. It definitely wasn't Brett's first choice for a destination.

"What are the autopsy results?" Brett asked.

"Unfortunately, there have only been two autopsies," Quinn said. "Lack of funds, the civil war, and of course, jungle heat. Very limited options in Guatemala. But those two autopsies didn't add much."

Brett knew only too well how the jungle heat accelerated decomposition of a body. He had seen the jungle turn a body into a pile of glistening white bones in less than twenty-four hours. What the heat and scavenging animals didn't finish, the insects devoured in short order.

Brett nodded, not wishing to dwell on the image. "These three areas you've circled on the map—"

"Those are the areas where the clusters of deaths have been reported. A small cluster here in the Yucatan Peninsula," Quinn said, pointing his finger at the map, "but most are here in the inner region of Xultun—a rain forest, mountains, and nearly impassable jungles. Land of the ancient Mayans."

"Yeah, along with poisonous snakes, human sacrifices, and a zillion tropical diseases," Brett added.

"Just don't try to be a hero and do anything stupid," Quinn warned him.

"What's that supposed to mean?"

"Truth is, this is a dangerous situation down there and I worry about you, Brett."

"Why's that?"

"First of all, you make up your own rules. And you take too damned many chances. You're not in charge around here. I am. Try not to forget that." He paused a moment to let that sink in, then continued. "And while we're on the subject, why didn't you come back three weeks ago with the rest of the team?"

"I was treating a patient. I wanted to see if there was any way we could save his eyesight. I was using a combination of—"

Quinn cut him off. "If you want to treat patients on an individual basis, then go into private practice. You are an EIS agent. We've got much bigger issues to deal with. We had to charter a plane just for you."

Brett was taken aback at the sudden reprimand from Quinn. He could feel his blood pressure rising and his jaw muscles tighten.

Quinn knew Brett had a short fuse and probably sensed that he'd pushed him too far. "Brett, you're one of my best agents and a damn fine physician, but you're going to get yourself into serious trouble someday. You take unnecessary risks. And as long as you're with the CDC, you play by our rules. Frankly, we can't afford to lose you."

Brett was about to press the issue but decided to drop it. He couldn't tell if it was a pep talk or a scolding.

"Did it work?" Quinn asked.

Brett frowned. "Did what work?"

"Your treatment. Did you save the boy's eyesight?"

"Yes, it looks like a combination of drugs is going to work."

Quinn nodded, then walked over to his desk, pulled the familiar looking large manila travel envelope from his drawer, and handed it to Brett. It contained Brett's assignment papers, travel vouchers, money in Guatemalan Quetzals, airline tickets and the documents he would need while on assignment.

"We've got highly detailed satellite photos of the area," Quinn said, "but unfortunately there's nothing to see but miles of dense jungle. They'd be useless to you." He drained his coffee mug.

"You're to meet with Dr. Manuel Sanchez in Guatemala City tomorrow afternoon. He's the director of the Ministry of Health. He'll bring you up to date on any details I may have left out."

"One more question," Brett said as he took the envelope. "Have there been any similar cases reported anywhere else? Any here in the U.S.?"

"None that we're aware of. We have a computer search underway checking state health reports. But nothing so far. The truth is, we don't even know what we're looking for."

Brett stifled a yawn. "Well, I guess that's it, unless you can think of something else."

"As a matter of fact, there is," Quinn said and handed him a piece of paper. "Stop by the health clinic on your way out of here. According to your records, you'll need three vaccinations before leaving."

Quinn opened the door for him. He looked serious. "Brett, for God's sake, while you're down there, try to remember that you're mortal. Don't take any damned unnecessary risks, okay?"

Brett left C-Building and headed for the health clinic on the first floor of the main building on the other side of the CDC campus. Quinn was obviously concerned. Brett could see it in his face. He didn't want another dead EIS agent.

Brett wondered what the hell he'd gotten himself into.

Again.

Chapter 8

Brett had a dozen loose ends to tie up before he left his office, and it was well after dark when he got back to his apartment. He still had to do laundry and repack for an early morning flight. He was hungry and went into the kitchen to fix something. He hadn't had time to shop for groceries. All he had in the cupboard was a can of chili and some old frozen dinners in the freezer. He shoved them back in frustration and closed the door. He didn't feel like eating anything frozen or from a can.

What he really wanted was a drink. When he went into the living room, he saw that the red light on his answering machine was flashing. There were three messages. The first two were from colleagues at work wanting to know more about his trip to Guatemala, and the last one was from Ashley asking him to call her.

She was sorry about getting so angry that morning. She understood the situation and knew he had to go. She wanted to be with him on his last night. "Please call me when you get in," she'd said before hanging up. "I love you."

He called her back but only got her answering machine. She

hadn't known he'd be getting home late. When he hadn't returned her call earlier, he guessed she had assumed he was mad at her, and now they were just playing phone tag.

He left a short message on her machine, then put a load of clothes in the washer. He would have liked to spend his last evening with Ashley, but he didn't know when she'd be home. He was hungry and thought about ordering a pizza but decided against it. Instead, he called Ross Solt.

"Ross, hi—it's me."

"Brett? I didn't know you were back in town. Congratulations. You scored a really big one in Alaska."

"Thanks. Have you eaten yet?"

"No, I haven't," Solt said. "I just flew in from Boston. What do you have in mind?"

"Meet me at Murray's for dinner."

"I'm on my way. See you there in a few minutes."

Brett left his apartment and headed to Murray's Place, a pub known for its spacious booths, great burgers, and cold beer. It was the favorite hangout for a lot of the gang from the CDC. What he needed now was a friendly face, and he knew seeing Ross, his best friend and mentor, would cheer him up.

Dr. Ross Solt had begun his career as a brilliant internist and the youngest man to become a professor at Columbia medical school. Shortly after his appointment to Columbia at age thirty-one, his young wife whom he adored was killed by a drunk driver running a red light. Devastated, Solt sank into a deep depression and became withdrawn. On the advice of worried friends, he took a leave of absence from Columbia and traveled to Africa. When he visited the Congo, he saw medical problems that would change him forever. His life took a new direction.

After he returned, he resigned his position at Columbia and joined the EIS division of the Centers for Disease Control in Atlanta. Solt had been an EIS agent for twenty years when Brett joined the CDC. He was teamed with Solt on his first assignment with the EIS Division. Over the ensuing years, Solt had shown Brett the ropes and gotten him out of serious trouble more than once on their assignments together. The two men—opposites in many ways—had formed a lasting friendship.

Solt was already sitting at a table outside on the patio, drinking a beer when Brett arrived. Sporting a well-trimmed beard and thinning silver hair, Solt looked distinguished. A wide grin spread across his face when he saw Brett approach. He jumped up and slapped Brett on the back, then shook his hand. "Damn, you're a sight for sore eyes! How've you been, Brett?" They sat down at the table.

"Okay, I guess. How about you?"

"That sounds a little qualified. I thought you'd be basking in the limelight of your success in Alaska. You're all over the news."

"Hell, Ross, you and I both know this was no different than dozens of other assignments we've been on together. It's only big news because the press decided to make it big." The waitress arrived, and Brett ordered an Amstel lager while he glanced at the menu. "But it was one long, tiring assignment," he continued. "I've been away too long."

"They should have sent me up there with you. I missed out on a good one this time." Solt pulled out his pipe, tapped some kind of blend into it, lit a match, and sucked the flame into the bowl. Blowing out a pale cloud he said, "But now you can take it easy for a while."

Brett shook his head. "I guess you haven't heard. Quinn's sending me to Guatemala tomorrow."

"Tomorrow?" Solt blurted out. "You just got back. What's going on in Guatemala? I haven't heard anything."

The waitress arrived with his beer, and Brett ordered lobster bisque and a warm spinach salad. "Actually, we don't know anything for sure yet. I'm going down to check it out. Want to come along?"

"I'd love to. But I'm tied up with Equine encephalitis, I'll be leaving again in two days. It's one big political and social mess in New England right now."

"I'll only be gone a few days. I'll call you when I get back."

Solt nodded and drew deeply from the pipe. "I'll get us tickets to a Falcon's game. With that first-round draft pick from Ohio State, maybe we'll win some games."

Brett shook his head and smiled. "You and that damned pipe. I can't believe that you of all people still smoke that thing."

"Well, Brett, no one lives forever. I enjoy it. Besides, I don't inhale," Solt said, and let out one of his famous laughs. "So, what's the deal in Guatemala?"

"We're not sure," Brett said. "One of the World Health clinics in Guatemala reported several unusual deaths and they're worried that there might be a new epidemic brewing in the jungle. Not much information so far. It may turn out to be nothing. Or—it could be a hot one."

"How does Ashley feel about this? Is she okay about your heading off to Guatemala so soon?"

"Not exactly," Brett said. "We had kind of a misunderstanding this morning about my having to leave again."

"You mean you had a fight. Don't worry about it," Solt said. "She knows it's your job. Besides, it's just for a few days. She'll get over it."

"I'm not so sure this time."

"You know, Brett," Solt said, then paused and rubbed his beard. "I have trouble seeing you in a serious long-term relationship. None of us are ever home for more than a few weeks at a time, and we travel all over the world in some of the worst god-awful conditions."

The waitress brought their meals. Solt grabbed his steak sandwich and took a bite, then washed it down with beer. "My guess is she wants somebody more secure, more reliable. She probably wants what every woman wants. A home, kids, a family. That's not going to happen with you. I'm not sure you and Ashley are actually that compatible."

Brett stared at him with eyebrows furrowed. "Okay, we're different. What's that got to do with it? Opposites attract, right?" He started attacking his spinach salad.

"Honestly," Solt said, "I don't see you settling down anytime in the near future with anybody. You're too... wild. You're restless. I don't think you could ever settle down permanently."

Brett laughed. "Yeah, sure. I'm wild and untamable."

"You know I'm right. I wish I were going with you this time, Brett."

They finished their meals and talked over coffee.

Finally Brett said, "I've got an early flight tomorrow. Hate to rush off, but I have a lot to do." He downed his coffee and peeled bills from his wallet to pay for his meal.

"I'll walk back with you," Solt said.

"Thanks, but I have a lot to do before tomorrow. Stay here and finish your coffee. I'll call you when I get back in a week or so." He slapped him on the back and left.

"Take care of yourself, Brett," Solt called after him.

It was dark and the streetlights were on. As he waded through leaves on his back to his condo, Brett stewed over Solt's remarks about Ashley and him. Deep down he knew Solt was right. His life had been a series of broken relationships, victims of his demanding job. He and Ashley had dated for more than two years, and he thought things might move in a different direction this time.

But once again his job had consumed him and put a severe strain on their relationship. He'd just had a fight with Ashley, something that had become a common pattern for him. Why didn't it ever work out? What was it he really wanted?

Ashley had told him she wanted a commitment, which he couldn't possibly do right now. He began to wonder if he knew how to sustain a relationship—something he'd never had in his life. His parents had both been killed in a car accident when he was twelve.

It was the worst possible age for him; it was a time when parental support and guidance were needed the most. He had been raised by an aunt and uncle on a ranch in the foothills of Colorado. Brett had had lots of space and independence growing up and learned to become self-sufficient. Maybe he'd learned this lesson too well.

Now he was driven by an irrational inner need to succeed at any cost. That drive had served him well in college and medical school, but it also served to shut out others. His total focus and commitment to his job had left a string of relationships that hadn't worked out—doomed by his life-style.

Maybe it was more than his job that was to blame.

Brett was tired. Maybe he should have simply refused to go this time. He wasn't physically or mentally ready to tackle a new assignment. Injuries and infections were part of the job, and he carried the scars to prove it. He'd been infected with more viruses, bacteria and parasites than he could remember.

The malaria he brought back from Mozambique still flared up occasionally. His wrist and jaw—both broken when a small Red Cross Cessna crashed in Zaire—still ached when the temperature plummeted in winter. The accumulated assault on his body over the years had taken its toll.

Still, he knew he wouldn't be happy working full-time in Atlanta, having to rub elbows with Ashley's friends at their frequent gatherings. That wasn't his style. The truth was, he was far too busy to get involved in the kind of serious relationship that Ashley wanted. Maybe Ross was right.

The quiet street swallowed him in dark shadows, and he hurried on alone, deep in thought. He had a plane to catch in less than eight hours.

Chapter 9

Early the next morning Brett caught a 6:40 a.m. flight to Dallas, then another plane to Mexico City. After a three hour wait and another change of planes, he finally arrived in Guatemala City a tiring eighteen hours, three time zones, and four airports later.

At the noisy, smoke-filled and crowded airport, he collected his duffel bag, computer bag and backpack and elbowed his way out to the street. His government pass got him through customs without delay, and he grabbed a taxi. The taxi had no air conditioning, and the windows were down, allowing blistering hot, humid air to blow in. The driver took a route through the outdoor market district. The constant noise of traffic and car horns blended with the occasional mariachi bands that played beside open-air markets, giving the city an aura of both chaos and a never-ending fiesta.

Vendors sold a wide assortment of craft items, baskets, pottery and hand-woven straw hats—as well as fruits and vegetables. Bins were filled with a colorful jumble of red chilies, yellow tropical fruits, green peppers, achiote, wild oregano, golden corn, black beans, and deep purple habanero chilies—the world's hottest. Above the music, he could hear the slap of fresh tortillas hitting a griddle. The aroma of *recados*, the traditional pastas used in the region, saturated the air.

Guatemala City was a city of contradictions, a strange blending of the ancient and the modern, the pagan and the religious. City buses and donkeys crowded the same narrow streets. Mayan Indians, dressed in traditional bright red huipil blouses and straw hats, walked alongside men in business suits.

The city was in decay; streets were rutted and broken; the sidewalks and curbs were crumbling; the buildings were shedding mortar, bricks, and plaster. Rusting tin sheets were stuck on buildings and roofs like band-aids.

Brett had the taxi take him to the Hotel El Dorado. Two armed guards with automatic rifles stood watch by the front entrance as guests unloaded and checked in. In the crowded city bursting with upheaval, a feeling of raw tension filled the air.

After he had checked in and dropped his luggage in his room, Brett took another taxi to the building that housed the government offices. Guatemala City was laid out in zones. Zone 4 was the hub of government offices.

The building Brett sought was a block off Centro Civico, a large plaza bordered by the Cathedral Metropolitana and Portal del Comerico government buildings. Soldiers armed with automatic assault rifles stood at every major building on the plaza, reminding Brett that Guatemala was a country at war with itself. After showing his papers to a guard, he was allowed to enter.

Two physicians from the Ministry of Health greeted him and expressed their gratitude for the CDC's quick response.

The younger of the two, his shiny black hair plastered in place, introduced himself as Doctor Del Vago. "We didn't expect you today, Doctor Carson."

That remark didn't sit well with Brett, whose nerves were already frayed with fatigue. Quinn had assured him everything had been arranged. "I'm scheduled to meet Dr. Sanchez today. Didn't anyone tell you?"

"We were not informed of that. We'll check and let you know if he is available to meet with you. In the meantime, what can we get for you?"

"I would like to review the medical records, x-rays, labs – everything you have on all the cases of the new epidemic." They found a room with an empty desk for him to use and brought him what information they could collect.

He spent the rest of the afternoon reviewing files on the deaths that had been reported at a few remote clinics. Shocked by how unprepared the Ministry of Health was to deal with the problem, Brett knew he faced incredible difficulties. Bacterial cultures from three of the victims were negative, but no blood cultures or serum titers had been obtained, and there had been only two autopsies, which revealed little.

Chest X-rays on three of the victims showed massive overwhelming pneumonia, but Brett had no way of knowing if it was from the disease or a secondary infection. He didn't know if the x-rays were done when the patients first arrived, or just before they died.

Dr. Manuel Sanchez, the Minister of Health, finally arrived at six o'clock, just as Brett was ready to call it a day. Sanchez wore a wrinkled, sweat-stained tan cotton suit. His eyes sagged, and his head and shoulders drooped as he walked. Whether he was bored or exhausted, Brett couldn't discern.

"Dr. Carson, I hope this has been helpful to you," Sanchez said in a deep, slow voice. "Were you able to learn anything from the reports?"

Brett wanted to scream, *What the hell am I supposed to learn from these anemic reports?* Instead, he took a deep breath and said, "Not really. I want to go to the clinic in Lepudro, and I'd like to leave first thing in the morning. I need to talk to the American doctor there who's working for the World Health Organization. It was his report that prompted this investigation. Maybe he'll have more information for us."

"That's more than two hundred miles away. The closest airport to Lepudro is Santa Elena. But the runway was washed out by the storm," Sanchez said.

"I see," Brett said, undaunted. "How far is Santa Elena from Lepudro?"

"More than fifty miles," Sanchez replied, his eyes slowly moving up to meet Brett's. "It's rough terrain through the mountains of the El Peten jungle."

"How can you get me to Lepudro?" Brett asked with a determined voice.

Sanchez thought for a moment. "We can fly you directly to the clinic on a military helicopter," he finally said.

"Great. A helicopter is exactly what I need. Can you have it here for me first thing tomorrow morning?"

"You can't *have* the helicopter," Sanchez corrected him as he slipped a dark cigarette into his mouth and lit it. He took a deep draw. "We can use it for one day at the end of the week to fly you there." Thick, foul smoke poured out slowly with each word.

"Then talk to someone with the authority to do it and get a helicopter assigned to us. I want to leave tomorrow, and I'm going to need a helicopter at my disposal while I'm down here."

"Impossible," Sanchez said. "It can't be done."

Brett was souring quickly on the whole situation. He would need a helicopter to both get there and then fly back. He didn't want to be dropped off in the middle of the jungle and just left there.

"I can't be certain of anything yet," Brett said, "but you may have one nasty epidemic on your hands. I may need to cover a lot of territory. How am I supposed to get around?"

"Sorry, but it won't be by helicopter. Our country has fewer than ninety that can still fly, and they all belong to the military. As you may know, we're quagmired in a nasty civil war with rebel forces. And our country's just been devastated by a hurricane. Dozens of villages were wiped out; others have been isolated and are in need of food and medicine. Our helicopters will be in great demand for some time. Both for civilian and for the military."

Brett let out a sigh and ran his hands through his hair. "Then get me a truck in the meantime."

"You won't need a truck, but I'll get a Jeep for you. And you'll need a driver. You won't make it on your own."

"Why not?"

"The storm has washed away most of the roads, taken out bridges, caused mudslides, and the rivers are overflowing. The jungle would swallow you up. I know of a truck that drove into the El Peten after a storm, streams swollen like they are now. Truck and all the men in it just disappeared. Never seen again. Swallowed in quicksand, buried in a mud slide, swept away in a river—who knows."

That was a sobering thought. "Will I be able to get through?" Brett asked.

"Maybe," Sanchez said, the word falling out of his mouth slowly. "I can't guarantee it. The El Peten jungle has only a few primitive roads, but most will be pure mud, if they haven't disappeared altogether from the storm. Happens every rainy season. And as you know, this was a major storm. There's also the problem of limited fuel."

"That's why I need a helicopter, not a Jeep," Brett shot back. "Consider it an emergency."

"I know, you told me already." Smoke snaked out of his mouth as he spoke. "And I told you we don't have one available. I'll talk to some people and see what we can do. The Jeep is all I can do for now. It will be a rough trip," he said, crushing out the soggy butt, "but you should be able to get through. I'll go see about a Jeep," he said, then left the room.

Brett decided that Sanchez and the rest of them could go straight to hell. If it weren't for the risk that some epidemic might kill dozens—possibly hundreds—of innocent people, Brett would have packed up right then and left. He saw no reason to risk his neck when they didn't seem to give a damn about what was happening.

Sanchez came back with the news, delivered as slowly and dryly as before. "I can get a Jeep and a driver for you, maybe ready by late tomorrow. Two days at the latest"

"Two days? No, I need it tomorrow."

"It'll take a day to get it ready for you. We need to install extra fuel containers. You don't want to get stuck in the jungle out of gas."

"Will there be any trouble finding gasoline once we're there?"

"When the roads are open"—Sanchez paused to light another

cigarette—"a delivery truck goes once a week to Lepudro with supplies, including fuel. But trucks can't get through yet."

His droopy eyes faded behind a blue cloud of smoke. "You might be able to get there, but getting back could prove to be more difficult."

Brett gave Sanchez a list of supplies he would need before he left. After the long trip that morning and a tiring afternoon reviewing medical records, Brett was exhausted. He decided there was nothing more he could do that day and took a taxi back to the hotel.

Chapter 10

He thought about calling Ashley, then calculated the time difference and decided it was too late to call. He'd call her first thing in the morning. He hated the way they'd left things.

Brett's stomach reminded him that the last food he'd had was on the plane that morning. After a hot shower, he put on fresh clothes and went down to the dining room of the El Dorado Hotel, filled with a noisy Friday night crowd. Loud voices and laughter came from the adjacent bar. He found a table and sat down.

A young woman came to his table and handed him a menu. "*Buenos noches, senor.* Welcome to the El Dorado. How are you this evening?"

"Fine, thank you," he said. But his aching muscles said otherwise. The rigors of the past few days had caught up with him. Six days ago he had been more than four thousand miles away in northern Alaska. The day he left Prudhoe Bay, the thermometer at the airport registered minus 10; this afternoon, the mercury in Guatemala City had reached a sweltering 112 degrees.

He glanced at the menu, then ordered a cold Cabro—a pale

lager brewed in Guatemala—and the dinner special that the waitress recommended.

While he nursed the cold beer, he went over his mental list of things to do, trying to make sure he had covered everything. The storm had moved out of Guatemala City and the northern region, but jungle highlands to the south were still being drenched by the tail end of the tropical depression. He would leave early the day after tomorrow, regardless of the weather. He had no choice. A delay of one or two days might mean the difference between containing the disease or allowing it to spread out of control. Brett had seen epidemics wipe out an entire village in less than forty-eight hours.

He couldn't afford to wait for the rain to stop. But a fear kept gnawing at him that he might be taking too big a gamble by not waiting a few days as suggested. He wanted to improve his odds of succeeding.

The soup arrived. Heavily seasoned with spices that defined the regional cooking—epazote, achiote and wild oregano—the first spoonful was full of exotic flavors, but the second spoonful brought tears to his eyes. He'd bitten into a piece of habanero chili that would have made the devil beg for mercy. Tiny beads of sweat formed on his forehead. A gulp of cold beer brought some relief, and he shoved the bowl aside as he held his hand to his mouth.

Just as his dinner came, Brett spotted a stout white-haired man with a beard, a Hemingway look-alike, waiting to be seated. Then Brett saw the young woman accompanying him. She wore a plain black dress. Her dark hair was pulled back, simple and practical. He just caught a brief look at her face, but she was stunning. Brett noticed heads turned and eyes followed her as she and the man crossed the room.

Brett smiled to himself. Solt ought to see this. He'd have something profound to say about it. A rich old man with his young prize. Brett took another drink of cold beer while he watched. Maybe he was just jealous.

Turning his attention back to his dinner, Brett scooped up beans and globs of chilmole—an exotic black recado made from burned chilies, onions, garlic and corn dough—and deposited them onto a pile of tortillas. The chilmole had a deep smoky flavor, but at least it wasn't spicy like the soup. He washed it down with his second bottle of Cabro.

After Brett finished his dinner, he ordered iced pozole, a traditional liqueur of masa, honey and coconut that was as old as the Mayan empire. He felt the effects of the potent cold liquid almost immediately. Glancing again at the two people, he heard bits of conversation above the noise. A few words heightened his interest. He strained to hear more. They spoke English. They were *Americans*. Maybe it was the pozole that caused him to do it, or maybe he just wanted a closer look at the woman. Whatever the reason, he pushed his chair back and walked over to their table.

"Hello," he said, extending his hand. "I'm Brett Carson. Sorry to interrupt your dinner, but I heard you talking and assumed you were Americans."

"Forrest Wheeler," the white-haired man answered and extended his hand to Brett. "Please join us and have some coffee. Always delighted to talk to another American. This is my daughter Kari."

She extended her hand and smiled. "Nice to meet you, Mr. Carson."

He shook her hand and felt his face flush. The first thing

he noticed were her eyes—beautiful, dark, captivating eyes. He realized he was staring and quickly turned to Wheeler.

"What brings you to Guatemala?" he asked. He pulled out a chair and sat down at their table.

"Digging," Wheeler said. He glanced over his shoulder to survey the dining room, as if he were looking for someone, then he continued. "I'm a professor of archeology at the University of Chicago. We've been down here for the past two months excavating pre-Columbian Mayan tombs. And you?"

"I'm with the CDC in Atlanta," Brett said.

"You're a doctor?" Wheeler asked.

"Yes. I'm down here to investigate a possible outbreak of a new epidemic. Have you heard anything about it?"

"Diseases," Wheeler said, shaking his head. "You hear all kinds of rumors down here. You never know if any of them are true. Small outbreaks of diseases in the jungle are not uncommon. Contaminated water, spoiled food, parasites, lack of vaccines for common diseases. Who knows why? But why am I telling *you* that?"

Wheeler said he had been coming to Guatemala for the past eight summers. His rugged, weathered face showed the effects of countless hours of digging in the sun. He was a world expert on ancient Mayan history and artifacts.

"And what about you?" Brett asked, turning to Kari.

"I'm also on the faculty. I'm an associate professor of social anthropology." She pushed a strand of hair back from her face and looked at her father. "I'm just down here during the fall semester to keep an eye on Dad," she said, smiling.

"This is Kari's second trip with me down here in Guatemala," Wheeler said. "I used to come during the summer break, but it's boiling down here then, so this time we came during the fall. Kari hates the jungle, but she worries that I can't take care of myself. So here she is."

Brett once again caught himself staring at her. When she looked at him, he glanced down.

"We're here to get supplies," Wheeler continued, "then we're heading into the jungle."

"You mean the rain forest?" Brett asked.

"Rain forest to you. Jungle to me."

"What's the difference?" Brett pressed him.

"To some liberal politically correct journalist behind his computer in an air-conditioned office in New York, it's a rain forest. But when you're knee-deep in muck, being eaten alive by mosquitoes and fighting your way through poisonous snakes and tangled vines, then it's a goddamned jungle."

The waitress brought them fresh coffee.

"How familiar are you with the rain forest—or jungle?" Brett asked, pulling a map from his jacket and unfolding it.

"Depends," Wheeler said. "I know parts of it really well, some not at all. It covers nearly ten thousand square miles."

"I'm leaving first thing tomorrow morning, and I need to get here," Brett said, and showed Wheeler the map. "What's the best route?"

"Well, now, that's going to be rough going because of the storm. But it can be done. Not for the next few days, though. Some of the roads will be washed out, and most of the streams will be flooded."

Wheeler rubbed his chin a moment while he continued to study the map. "It's going to be damned risky, especially since you're not familiar with El Peten, but if you have to go, follow this route." He pulled a pen from his pocket and marked on the map.

"Avoid the gullies. The jungle will be a mess for at least a week. It'll swallow you up. Try to stay on the upper ridges."

"Where will you be going?" Brett asked.

He noticed that Wheeler balked momentarily at the question.

"Don't know exactly, but somewhere in this region," Wheeler said, pushing his finger roughly across the map. He shot a quick glance over his shoulder, the second time Brett had noticed him doing that.

They had coffee and talked. Wheeler was a likable man and seemed very knowledgeable about the people and their customs. But beneath the friendly exchange, Brett had the feeling there was something else that worried the archaeologist. It made Brett uncomfortable. Was Wheeler afraid of something, or was he trying to hide something from him? Perhaps Wheeler was just worried about the trip they had ahead of them.

Brett finished his coffee, stood, thanked them for their help, and wished them well. "Nice meeting you, Kari." His heart skipped a beat when he shook her hand again.

"It's a dangerous place, Dr. Carson," Wheeler said. "Be careful."

"I will," Brett said. "Thanks for the advice, and good luck." Brett's eyes locked with Kari's for just a moment, then he turned and left. He was convinced something was troubling Wheeler, but what? He shrugged and dismissed it. He had a lot more to worry about than what might be bothering an old archaeologist.

Dismissing Kari from his mind was another matter.

Earlier, a solitary figure had slipped in unnoticed through the side door of El Dorado's restaurant. He sat out of the way in the corner. The location afforded Father Hernandez a complete view of the lounge and dining room. Dressed in peasant clothes, he wasn't worried that he'd be recognized. The noise and commotion of the crowd would be his cover. He ordered a Brandy & Benedictine.

He had to know for certain—once and for all. There could be no mistakes. The consequences for a mistake would be dire. His drink arrived. The dark sweet B & B warmed him with each swallow. He would drink just enough to take the edge off. But never enough to lose control. He scanned the room and almost immediately located his query.

Professor Forrest Wheeler was dining with a young woman. That would be his daughter—an eye-catching beauty. He felt a sharp pang of regret about the course of action he would have to take. He wished she hadn't come to Guatemala. His growing awareness of the consequences was disquieting.

But there were no options. They would have to be dealt with.

Who was the third person who had just joined them? Was he also American? The situation might be far more serious than he had imagined. Maps! Why were they going over maps? What had started out as suspicious concerns had possibly grown into a full-blown crisis. The situation had to be dealt with immediately. He stared at the young woman again with regret. He wished there could be another way to deal with her, but there wasn't.

He was convinced that the old man knew—somehow, despite their extreme precautions and against all odds, the professor had done the unimaginable and somehow stumbled onto it. His discovery threatened everything. There was no reason to delay the inevitable. As he watched Wheeler, he made his decision. With one large final swallow the priest downed the last of his B & B, then slipped out through the side door again.

Back in his room, Brett undressed and climbed into bed for much-needed sleep. Kari Wheeler's face flooded his thoughts. Fatigue, two Mexican beers, and the potent pozole soon propelled him into a deep sleep.

Chapter 11

The next morning Brett showered, put on fresh clothes and went down for breakfast. He hoped to see the Wheelers again. But they weren't there. Before he checked out, he decided to call Sanchez to see if his supplies and Jeep were ready.

"We'll have everything ready first thing tomorrow morning, Dr. Carson. We need to install extra fuel cans. Just relax and enjoy our city before your trip. You have a rough trip ahead of you."

Dammit! Brett was furious. Another day further behind. "Any word on a helicopter?"

"Nothing so far."

"I'm not going to get a chopper, am I?"

"No. I already told you that."

Brett called Quinn next, but he was in a meeting. He left word for him to call back as soon as possible. Then he informed the front desk that he would be staying another night at the El Dorado.

He decided to take a walk through the markets while it was still relatively cool. Near the hotel, a dog hidden in the shade of a large tree let out a soft *woof* as Brett walked past. Dozens of stray dogs roamed the streets and alleys. Stray dogs around the world were of similar size and color, having interbred to a uniformity that made them nearly indistinguishable. But this dog was different, bigger than the street strays, and his fur was thicker and lighter. Brett had noticed the dog the day before in the same spot when he left the hotel, and wondered if the dog was lost or if its owner had abandoned it.

Brett spent the morning walking through several blocks of open markets, sampling fruits and roasted nuts sold by women wearing brightly colored blouses. As the sun burned hotter, the air began to bake, and sweat trickled down his back. He retraced his route back to the hotel. The dog was still lying in the same spot.

In his room, Brett spent an hour studying maps and going over the medical reports again, hoping to pick up something that might have eluded him, but that proved to be useless. There just wasn't enough information to be of any help. Still tired from travel, he took a two-hour nap and woke in the early afternoon feeling refreshed.

He went to the front desk and inquired about any messages. Quinn had called while he was napping but left no message. Brett called him back.

"Brett, how's it going? Sorry I missed your call. Where are you?"

"Still in Guatemala City, and that's the problem. The storm down here washed out airports and roads. I need a helicopter, and they don't have any available. Can you get one for me?"

"That's a tall order. The fact is, Brett, there's probably no way I can do that until we know what's going on down there. Our military sure as hell won't give us one. The State Department let it be known that they don't want to have any involvement in the civil war down there, and a U.S. military helicopter could be interpreted as just that."

"What about the Mexican government? Or the Red Cross?"

"That's not likely to happen. When you get more information for us, maybe the Red Cross could be persuaded to help. I'll start working on it. Be careful, Brett."

He called the *Atlanta Journal-Constitution* and tried to reach Ashley, but she wasn't at her desk. He started to leave a voice message, then changed his mind. He didn't want to get into playing phone tag with Ashley. He didn't need more complications to worry about now.

He inquired at the desk about Wheeler and his daughter, hoping they might join him for dinner later, but was told they had checked out earlier that morning.

After a late lunch he went out for another walk, which seemed preferable to staying inside the hotel, even though the temperature was now well above 110. The dog was still there, and this time Brett knelt down and extended his hand toward the dog. "Hey, fella, don't you have a home somewhere?"

The dog stared at him but didn't move. It was a big dog with a large head, and its eyes never left Brett. It was emaciated, its ribs showing through the dirty, matted fur. Brett opened his hand, and the dog leaned forward, first sniffing then carefully licking his hand. The dog's tongue felt hot. Brett assumed it was because of the heat of the afternoon, but the thought also crossed his mind that the dog might be sick.

Brett went back inside the hotel and returned with a bowl and a bottle of water. As he poured the water, the dog stood, its tail down, and slowly limped over to him, then devoured the water in huge gulps. Brett refilled the bowl, and the dog drank that too. The dog smelled of neglect. Brett looked at the foot that caused the limp, and the dog gave a low growl when he reached for the leg.

"I won't hurt you, fella. Let's have a look at that paw."

He knew that even gentle dogs would often bite when they were injured. The dog watched as Brett's hand moved slowly toward his foot. Finally, Brett took hold of the leg and just held it for a moment. Lips curled back to show teeth, and a low growl rose from its throat, but the dog made no attempt to bite him, and Brett did not let go of the paw.

An ugly rusty wire ran through the paw, which was swollen and infected. The dog would surely die because it couldn't scavenge for food and water or compete with the other wild dogs in the streets. Brett let go of the paw and patted the large head. The dog timidly wagged its tail and licked his hand again. Brett held its muzzle in his hand and looked into its eyes. They were clear, and they were focused squarely on him. "Fella, you're in one hell of a mess."

He made a mental note to bring more water the next day. Then he stood up and took a short walk through the narrow streets as afternoon shadows grew longer. When he returned to the El Dorado, he decided to have dinner and get to bed early. He had a long trip ahead of him, and he wanted to get an early start. Back in his room, he put on a fresh shirt to go to dinner, then hesitated. He was probably going to regret it, but he picked up his canvas first aid kit, which was equipped for minor surgery, then went down to the bar and bought a bottle of tequila. He carried the first aid kit and bottle of tequila outside.

The dog was still there. Brett wasn't yet sure how he was going to get the dog to sit still for him while he worked on the paw.

The dog stood hesitantly, its tail down as Brett approached. He coaxed the dog to sit down. He held the infected paw in his hand to examine it closely. Then he poured tequila and water into a tin cup and held it out. The dog sniffed it, lapped at it tentatively, and—driven by thirst—drank it. Brett offered another small cup, but the dog just looked at him, its tail wagging slowly, its tongue out and panting. Brett slipped a morphine syringe into its shoulder and injected the vial.

After a few minutes, the dog lay down and sighed, putting its head between its paws as the morphine and tequila worked their magic. The dog was feverish. Brett opened a small canvass tool kit and used the pliers to untwist the rusted wire, then carefully pulled the wire out. The wound was swollen and sore, and the dog jerked his leg, but Brett kept a firm grip and didn't let go.

He had debrided dozens of infected wounds; this was old territory for him. He then picked up a scalpel and skillfully opened the wound to drain it, then poured alcohol over it and sutured it. If the infection had spread into the bone, the dog would probably die. Brett applied Neosporin cream over the incision and wrapped it first with gauze, then taped it so the dog wouldn't lick the dressing.

Brett knew the dog might not make it, but at least he had given him a fighting chance. He patted the dog's head. The drowsy dog raised his head slowly, then lay back down, eyes glassy. "Can't hold your liquor, can you?" Brett said softly. He poured water into a can, left it beside the dog, and went back inside.

As Brett ate his dinner, his mind was still on the dog. He tried to put it out of his mind, but it troubled him. Countless abandoned children roamed barefoot on blistering hot cement, selling Chicklet gum for a few quetzals and eating garbage left in the alleys. So why had he chosen to turn his attention to an abandoned dog? He couldn't answer that. He didn't even want to try.

He needed to stay focused on the epidemic. Too many other things had crept into the equation: the destructive tropical storm, a wounded stray dog, and a woman he didn't even know.

After dinner, Brett took part of his meal out to the dog. The dressing was still intact. Brett had buried two Keflex antibiotic capsules in the food. The starving dog gulped down the scraps and sniffed his hand for more. Brett patted the emaciated animal and went back inside.

He went to a phone in the lobby and dialed Ashley's condominium, doubting she would be home. He was surprised when she answered and for a moment was at a loss for words.

"Ashley," he finally said.

A long silent pause followed. "Hi, Brett. How are things going?"

"Fine. Well, actually there a lot more complications down here than I could have ever envisioned. I'm afraid it's going to take more time that I first thought."

More silence. Then she finally said, "Brett, remember you were the one who called me, so what did you want?"

"I was just calling to say hi—"

She cut him off. "Brett, I can't live like this. I've been doing a lot of thinking since you left. It'll always be like this, with you being gone all the time. I can't do it anymore."

"Ashley, it's just going to be for a couple of weeks."

"No, it's not. I love you, Brett, but I have to get on with my life, just as you should with yours. After this trip there'll be another, then another." She paused, but he said nothing, so she continued.

"You've been searching for something your entire life, Brett, and I realize it's neither me nor those viruses you chase. Whatever it is you're looking for, I hope you find it someday. Take care of yourself, Brett."

Click.

The growing silence that followed made his ears ring. He leaned against the wall, ran his hands through his hair and sighed. Once again his job had imperiled a relationship, and he found himself alone again. Even though it hurt, he knew Ashley was right. It could never have been the kind of relationship she was looking for. He returned to his room.

A note pushed under his door relayed a phone message from Sanchez. The Jeep with extra tanks and a driver would be ready in the morning.

Chapter 12

Brett woke up in the middle of the night. He fought his way out of a deep fog, vaguely aware that something had disturbed him. He opened his eyes and remained motionless while he listened in the dark, his senses alert and muscles tensed.

He heard nothing.

Just as he was about to dismiss it as something outside, a faint flash of light on steel caught his eye, and his coiled muscles sprang to life.

A razor-sharp blade sliced into the mattress where Brett had been only a split-second earlier. He kicked his foot out, catching someone in the chest. A grunt was followed by a moan and a thud as the assailant hit the floor, gasping for air.

Brett spun out of bed, rolled to the floor and caught the attacker by the neck in a strangling arm lock. With his other hand, he turned on the light and nearly lost his grip from the shock of what he saw.

A skinny, barefoot boy dressed in dirty clothes stared at him, while struggling against the arm around his neck. Brett guessed him to be maybe twelve. Blood was smeared across the boy's face and ran down Brett's arm. He immediately released the boy.

Before Brett could react, the boy bolted for the door and disappeared down the hall. Shaken, he stared at the knife buried to the handle in the mattress. A chill went through him as he realized his back had been the intended target. Blood ran down his arm, and he felt a stinging in his shoulder.

He hadn't turned quickly enough, and the knife had sliced open a four-inch-long cut in his shoulder. Fortunately, it wasn't a deep cut and hadn't sliced into any muscles. He put a wet cloth against it until the bleeding stopped, then applied Neosporin and tried to bandage it using only his good hand. Why had the boy tried to kill him? What was he after? It certainly didn't seem to be merely a robbery. That wouldn't explain why he had nearly been murdered.

He thought about going down to the front desk and contacting the police. He rubbed his eyes and decided it wouldn't matter. The boy had already melted into the dark streets. Brett was exhausted, and sleep was far more important to him at the moment.

He closed the door, locked it and pulled the dresser in front of it, then slid the bed up against the dresser. He figured only an elephant could get through the door now. He pulled the knife out of the mattress, dropped it on the floor, and crawled back into bed. Sleep seemed out of the question.

He lay in bed thinking and worrying about things: the dog, what he would find in the jungle, and the fact that he might be taking too big a chance this time. Sleep finally brought relief.

When he woke, he threw on his clothes and packed his things. A stinging in his shoulder and the knife lying on the floor brought back the memory of the shocking attack during the night. After a quick breakfast, Brett took his bags and checked out of the hotel. As he climbed into a taxi, he spotted the dog, head up, ears pointed and staring at him expectantly. Brett watched him until the taxi was engulfed in the morning traffic.

Sanchez was waiting for him at the Ministry of Health. The supplies Brett had requested were packed in several canvas bags: bottles of phenol, alcohol, and formaldehyde; sterile syringes, needles, scalpels, culture tubes and slides.

"Good morning, Dr. Carson. You are in luck. The rain in the mountains has stopped. The storm is over. But you are still going to have a rough trip." The words were pushed from his mouth by a cloud of stale smoke. The dark cigarette bounced in Sanchez's lips like a conductor's baton.

"I didn't feel so lucky last night," Brett said. "Somebody tried to kill me." He told Sanchez about the young boy in tattered clothes who had attacked him.

Sanchez looked at him with his sagging, bloodshot eyes. "That wasn't about you, Dr. Carson. It was about poverty. Thousands of children are abandoned and left to survive in the streets and fend for themselves," Sanchez said, taking a long draw from his cigarette. "They are rejects. Their families cannot afford to feed them. They live in alleys that smell of sex and glue. They sell themselves for money and sniff glue for relief from their pain. It's how they survive.

"You take things like unspoiled food and clean water for granted," Sanchez continued. "We take nothing for granted." He crushed out his cigarette, then crumbled the Styrofoam coffee cup in his huge fist. "The driver is outside waiting for you. Have a good trip."

Fuck you, Brett thought. The last thing Brett needed was a social lecture from Sanchez. The boy had tried to kill him! Sanchez had refused to give him a helicopter, and now Brett was risking his life driving through a storm-ravaged jungle. He picked up the canvas bags of supplies and went outside to the rear of the building.

The sergeant who was to be his driver was leaning against a military Jeep that had seen better days. The green paint was faded, the fenders dented, and there were a half-dozen bullet holes in the right side panel. Brett wondered if the occupants had survived the shooting. Sanchez had seen to it that they were provided with maps and supplies. Four extra fuel containers had been strapped to the side of the Jeep.

"Hi, I'm Brett Carson," he said extending his hand.

"Sergeant Alfonso Perez," the man said, then shook his hand and spit in the dirt. "Don't mind how it looks," Perez said. He assured Brett that the four-cylinder engine was in good working condition. "It'll get us there."

Perez, unshaven and disheveled, didn't seem destined for a great military career. That probably explained why he was assigned to the motor pool. Brett hoped Perez could at least get him to Lepudro. He opened a map. "Do you know where we're headed?"

"*Si*. Get in," Perez said, as he slid a semi-automatic rifle onto the floor behind their seats.

Brett loaded his own luggage and equipment into the back, then the pack of supplies Sanchez had provided. The overloaded Jeep with all the fuel strapped to it looked more like an aging pack burro.

"Lepudro," Brett said above the noise of the starter turning over the engine. "We're going to Lepudro," he repeated and climbed in beside Perez.

The engine started after the third attempt, and Perez ground it into gear. The Jeep belched out a blue cloud of exhaust as Perez wove his way around the people, buses, cars, and donkeys clogging the streets with morning traffic.

When they stopped at an intersection, Brett grabbed Perez's arm. "Wait! Turn around. I need to get something back at the hotel. The El Dorado. It'll only take a minute."

Perez looked at him, shrugged, then whipped the Jeep around and headed back into the heart of town. Brett directed him to pull up and stop in front of the large tree near his hotel.

Brett whistled, and the bedraggled dog limped over, its tail dragging. He patted the pile of bags in the back, and the dog, favoring its front paw, climbed carefully into the back and lay down on the canvas packs. Perez shook his head, muttered something in Spanish, then turned around and retraced their route down the street.

It was late morning, and Brett knew they had lost valuable time. But, for reasons he couldn't explain, he couldn't leave the dog. Perez drove recklessly through the crowded streets, punching his fist in the air at everything in his way, nearly hitting a burro, then just missed the front end of an overcrowded bus before they were finally out of town.

Chapter 13

Carlos Mountain Range
New Mexico

A white Federal Express van, small and insignificant against the open expanse of northern New Mexico, snaked its way up a narrow road into the canyon, a cloud of dust trailing behind it. The sage and piñon pine were undisturbed by its presence. At the top of the mesa, the road ended abruptly in front of a large steel gate.

The three-hundred-year-old monastery of Del Cristo de San Sebastian crowned the top of a mesa in the Carlos Mountain Range, eighty-five miles northwest of Santa Fe. Built in 1634 by Franciscan monks, the adobe buildings with red-tiled roofs had withstood more than three centuries of baking summer sun and brutal winter storms.

Inside its tall adobe walls, seventy monks lived and worked in seclusion. Visitors were rare, and the Brothers of San Sebastian only left the monastery to get supplies. Otherwise, they lived and worked in solitude from the outside.

Brother Roberto DiSalle, wearing a brown monk's robe and leather sandals, opened the lock and pulled on the heavy gate. He was a bull of a man with a thick neck and arms of steel, an intimidating presence. DiSalle helped the driver unload two heavy crates, then load several smaller boxes back into the van.

He signed the packing slip and handed it to the driver. The FedEx van headed back down the steep road toward Santa Fe. It made a trip to the monastery each month. After the gates were locked again, the monks carried the crates into one of the adobe buildings and closed the door.

The large building in the center of the monastery was the heart of the monks' daily activities. In contrast to the monks' spartan living quarters, it was connected to the rest of the world by satellite, computers, modems and high-speed fiber optic cables.

A flagstone path twisted up a hill to the Chapel of Saint Francis del Marco, which sat on a small rise overlooking the rest of the monastery. The adobe chapel was the oldest building in the compound, the first structure to be built by the Spanish Franciscans.

The chapel afforded a bird's-eye view of the Chaco River and the deep Canyon de Chelly below the monastery, as well as a panoramic view of the Carlos mountains. The Carlos range was a place of earthly trauma, where the forces of nature had sculpted a rugged, spectacular landscape. Successive waves of sediment had deposited multicolored plateaus and mesas of sandstone and limestone. Weather and erosion had fractured and exposed the rock, peeling away slabs to expose the layers, creating breathtaking natural beauty. The chapel was a place that inspired and was a favorite subject for local artists.

As evening settled in, shadows lengthened, a deep orange

bathed the rocks, and the temperatures dropped. The dry, arid hills, which baked in searing heat during the day, gave up the heat quickly as the sun sank below the horizon. Nights in the Carlos Mountains were cold, and stars filled the dark skies.

A brass bell resonated off the rocky cliffs and summoned the brothers of San Sebastian for their nightly vespers service. They walked up the path in silence to the chapel. Inside, they sang Gregorian chants by candlelight, followed by twenty minutes in silent prayer and meditation before performing vespers.

That night, four of the monks were absent.

In one of the small rooms that housed the monks, Father Jon Menendez, the senior priest and administrator of San Sebastian, was checking on one of the monks who had become seriously ill the day before.

One of the newest arrivals to the monastery, Brother Jonathan Vasquez lay on his narrow cot, wrapped in thick blankets. The only light was a patch of orange on the wall from the late afternoon sunlight that poured through a small open window. Another monk was at his bedside, tending to him.

Brother Daniel, a large monk with a well-trimmed beard, arrived with a bowl of bean soup and a crock of warm tea. "How's he doing?" he asked as he walked over to Jonathan. The room remained silent; nobody answered. Jonathan didn't seem to be aware of Daniel's presence. Turning to Father Menendez, Daniel said, "It's happened again."

Menendez nodded, but said nothing.

"Jonathan is critically ill," Daniel said. "We have to get him to a hospital or send for a doctor." Daniel could never make final decisions on matters pertaining to the monastery. Father Menendez was in charge, and he alone made decisions about San Sebastian. However, the other monks never confided in Menendez; they came to Daniel for spiritual and personal advice.

"No," Menendez said. "Pray for him. We'll see how he's doing in the morning." Menendez, a silver-haired man whose weathered, bronzed face was as craggy and rough as the landscape, mouthed a silent prayer, made the sign of the cross, kissed the silver crucifix hanging from his neck, and left.

The monk taking care of Jonathan grabbed Daniel's sleeve after Menendez left. "Brother Daniel, you must persuade Father Menendez," he said. His voice dropped to a whisper. "Jonathan is very sick and getting worse by the minute."

"Father Menendez will look in on him, and so will I," Daniel said. "You know Father Menendez wouldn't ask someone to drive up to the monastery tonight in the dark unless it's an absolute emergency."

The closest doctor was in Shiprock, and the nearest hospital was in Santa Fe—more than eighty-five miles away, over treacherous canyon roads. Daniel leaned over and looked at Jonathan again.

The young monk's face was drawn and sallow. A wheezing sound rose from deep within his chest with each agonizing breath.

Daniel leaned low over him. "Jonathan, it's me, Daniel. Can you hear me?"

For several seconds Jonathan made no movement. Then, briefly, his eyes focused on Daniel, then quickly glazed over. "I'll be back later," Daniel said to the other monk. "Stay with him."

"He's going to die, isn't he?" the other monk whispered.

Daniel paused as if he were going to say something, but turned and left.

He returned to Jonathan's room just after midnight. A small silver patch of moonlight lighting the wall had replaced the orange sunlight, and the late-night desert chill had settled in. "How is he doing?" he asked in a whisper.

"He's had nothing to eat or drink since yesterday," the monk said. "Look at him. Anyone can see he's dying."

Daniel held a candle close to the young monk's face. Even by the dim flickering light, he could see the gray skin. Dark fluid seeped from the corners of Jonathan's nose and eyes, and an overwhelming sour, musty odor filled the tiny room.

He drew back in horror. "I'll go speak to Father Menendez."

He left the room, went down the long colonnade with stone arches, and headed to the rectory where Father Menendez lived. His leather sandals crunched on gravel as he crossed the courtyard. His breath sent little bursts of vapor into the cold night air.

A full moon created unfamiliar shadows on the terrain. At the rectory, he knocked once, turned the handle and went in without waiting for a response, expecting to find Menendez upstairs asleep in his room.

"You didn't give me time to answer," Menendez said in a stern voice.

"I thought you might be asleep, Father."

"I'm not. Must be the moon. Too bright to sleep. You're here about Jonathan, right?"

"He needs immediate medical attention, Father. We need to call for an ambulance and get him to a hospital."

"He's going to die regardless of what we do," Menendez said.

"We don't know that. We can't just stand by and watch him die," Daniel said, with anger seeping into his voice.

"Most unfortunate, but there's really nothing we can do about it tonight. We must trust God to help us."

Daniel stood silently in the dark, trying to formulate a response.

Menendez continued. "Calling for medical help will do nothing for Jonathan, other than to soothe your conscience. The risk is too great. It could jeopardize everything." Menendez paused a moment, then said, "Pray for him."

"...and for us," Daniel added with bitterness in his voice. He opened the door and went back out into the night.

Chapter 14

For the first two hours, Sergeant Perez followed a wide gravel road that narrowed as it snaked into hills and then canyons that became progressively steeper and more rugged. Brett noticed political graffiti painted on crumbling buildings. The road was pockmarked with ruts, potholes and rocks. The hairpin turns grew more treacherous, and Brett began to wonder if they would reach their destination. Warnings from Wheeler and Sanchez kept haunting him.

By noon the temperature was already well above a hundred, and the searing sun turned the moisture in the air to a suffocating steam that left them bathed in sweat. The dark El Peten jungle was still a hundred miles ahead of them.

They stopped once to refuel from one of the ten-gallon cans they carried with them. They ate a quick lunch, with Brett giving a portion of his food to the mangy dog, and then were on their way again. He tried conversation a few times, but it was hard to talk over the noise of the Jeep's engine as it battled with the road. And Perez seemed in no mood for idle conversation. So Brett endured the jarring, the bouncing, and the sweltering heat in silence.

The dog occasionally sniffed the air but otherwise kept its head down and seemed to be content to be along on the ride. Brett rationalized that it would be easier for the dog to find a home in one of the villages they would be passing through than it would have been for it to survive alone, looking for scraps in the alleys of the city.

In the late afternoon, they pulled into a small village with dirt roads, crumbling shacks of adobe and tin, most with no doors or windows. A few dogs and chickens roamed about. Perez parked in front of a weathered, crumbling stone tavern patched together with mortar under a rusted tin roof.

"What town is this?" Brett wanted to make sure Perez wasn't taking him on a personal side trip. It seemed too early in the day to stop for the night.

"El Chiarco," Perez said, and went into the tavern.

Brett unfolded the map and found the tiny village of El Chiarco. He saw that the jungle was still forty miles away and they were seventy miles from Lepudro. The worst part of the trip still lay ahead and wasn't something to attempt at night. Brett checked his GPS with the map. It turned out that El Chiarco was probably a logical place to stop. Brett gave the dog fresh water, then followed Perez inside. The dog took up a spot in the shade under the Jeep.

Dust-stained windows hung wide open; bugs and hot air blew through the small tavern. A fan overhead did little to relieve the misery from the heat. Sergeant Perez had already started drinking tequila straight, pouring from a bottle with a snake head on the label. Brett guessed the drink probably was as potent as any venom. He sat on a stool beside Perez, ordered a Cabro and was pleasantly surprised that it was cold. "Where're we going to stay for the night?"

"This is it," Perez said and swallowed more tequila. "We eat here, drink here, sleep here. I got us rooms upstairs. We'll leave first thing tomorrow morning."

Perez finally began to talk, and continued effusively for over an hour or so about everything and anything as the tequila loosened his inhibitions. About the rebels in the north, the storm, his several broken marriages, girls, death, and the secret to great sex. Brett tried asking a few questions, hoping to learn something about the area, but Perez wasn't interested in dialogue. He just wanted to talk. When he finally seemed to have exhausted his list, he fell silent. The snake-head bottle was nearly empty.

Brett's four Cabros with slices of lime dulled the pain of a trying day. He hadn't intended to drink four, but he was thirsty and the cold Cabros went down easily as he listened to Perez talk. When Perez ordered another bottle of tequila, Brett moved to a small table, had a hot meal by himself, then took food out for the dog.

When he got to the Jeep, the dog was nowhere in sight. An unexpected sense of loss swept over Brett. He had brought the injured, filthy dog along in the hopes that it would find a home in one of the villages, but now he found himself disappointed when it seemed the dog had done just that. Then, the dog crawled out from under the Jeep, stretched, and barely wagged its tail. Impulsively, Brett put his arm around the dog and held it a second, then put the food down for it. The dog wolfed down the food and looked up for more. It seemed to be limping less.

Brett took the dirty bandage off the paw. He scraped off dried, crusted blood and seepage. It was too early to say how the wound was healing. The dog stretched out while Brett petted him, his tail thumping on the ground. It had been a long day for both of them, and the next day promised to be even more challenging.

Brett sat down beside the dog. "Everybody's gotta have a name, fella. What are we going to call you?" He thought a moment, then smiled. "I think Tequila is fitting, don't you?" The dog barked once and wagged its tail.

The dog was in desperate need of a bath. Dust from the day's trip was layered on top of ground-in filth. Part of its fur was matted into hopeless tangles. Brett cut away the worst of the tangles with scissors, then grabbed a piece of soap from the Jeep and led the dog to a pump outside the tavern. After dousing the dog, he lathered and rinsed it directly under the pump.

Brett's reward for his effort was a sudden and unexpected drenching from the dog as it shook itself. He took the dog back to the Jeep, spread a canvas cover on the ground for him to sleep on, and went back inside.

In his room, Brett washed from a basin of tepid water that had been provided. When he last saw Perez downstairs, the driver was engaging a young local girl and seemed amazingly sober for the amount of snake head he had consumed. Perez was no soldier, Brett decided. But the country's civil war had swallowed him up, and he had become another pathetic victim.

Brett felt pity for Perez, who in some ways seemed as abandoned as the sex-and-glue kids in the alleys.

He realized he had downed too many Cabros, because he was starting to analyze things excessively. Too much alcohol always did that to him. He shook his head and pushed the thoughts away. He had more important things to worry about than the social problems of Guatemala or Sergeant Perez.

Lying in bed in the silence, Brett felt more alone than usual. He got up again, went back down to the Jeep in the dark and quietly brought the dog up to his room. He threw a blanket on the floor, and the dog sniffed it, then lay down.

With memories of the night before at the El Dorado still fresh in his mind, Brett locked the door, jammed a chair against it, pulled hard to test it, then crawled into bed. Alone with a stray dog curled on the floor as his only companion, Brett waited for sleep to come. After fighting with the sheets and struggling to find a comfortable position, he finally fell into an uneasy sleep.

A military Jeep raced into Guatemala City's heavily guarded Government Plaza in the early morning light and braked in front of the Presidential Palace. Colonel Leonardo Zolog, head of Guatemala's Secret Police, stepped out and climbed the wide steps to the palace. At six-four, Zolog was an imposing figure. The soldiers guarding the entrance snapped to attention when they saw one of the most feared men in Guatemala approach them.

Zolog barely acknowledged their salutes and entered the palace. He walked with purpose, his black boots echoing on the polished marble floor of the Great Hall. Both he and General Dimago, head of Guatemala's army, had been summoned to the palace by the president of Guatemala, Jorge del Manguinos.

Zolog wasn't sure why the meeting had been called, but he would be cautious. He had come up the hard way, as the scar along the side of his face showed, the result of a knife attack. Life had taught him always to be wary and to be prepared for the unexpected. Zolog was cunning as well as ambitious, and he didn't intend to ever fall victim to a trap.

He was also savvy and took advantage of every opportunity. When no opportunities presented themselves, he created them. When he was passed over for full colonel, he took it upon himself to speed the process along. He had his predecessor set up on false charges; charges that eventually sent him to the firing squad. Zolog was immediately promoted to colonel and assumed the position as head of the secret police.

Zolog then set his sights on becoming a general. General Dimago had once been a fierce, fearless soldier; but now he was old and tired. He had lost the fire in his belly. Zolog, by contrast, was dangerous, ambitious, and relentless in his quest. However, if he succeeded in becoming a general, he also had to make sure the right side won the war.

If the rebels won—a thought that seemed inconceivable—he would at best spend the rest of his life rotting in prison as a political prisoner. A more likely scenario was that he would also face a firing squad. New governments never liked old army leaders hanging around.

Zolog had no intention of being on the losing side. He planned to crush the rebels, end the civil war, and become a general in the process. He would use every resource available and stop at nothing to achieve that.

Ignoring the elevators, he climbed the three flights of stairs to the president's office. A guard with an AK-47 strapped over his shoulder opened the door. Inside, General Dimago, wearing his uniform with a cluster ribbons and metals, sat in a leather chair while President del Manguinos, dressed in a well-tailored gray suit, stood by the window, smoking a dark cigarette.

Zolog snapped to attention with a salute.

"Colonel Zolog, thank you for coming," President del Manguinos said, and waved his hand toward a chair. "Have a seat. There's coffee if you wish."

"Mr. President, it is nice to see you." Then Zolog nodded to the general and took a seat.

Del Manguinos wasted no time in getting to the point. "It is time for us to end this ridiculous war with the rebels now. We can't keep fighting them indefinitely. It's a drain on our country's resources. It has to stop."

The president was a man under great strain, trying to hold the country and his government together against incredible odds. "I want you to find a way to crush the rebels once and for all," he burst out as he angrily ground out his cigarette in the ashtray.

"Mr. President," General Dimago said, "as you know, our forces have pushed the rebels into the northern mountains—"

"No, General," the President growled, cutting off Dimago. "That's the same combat tactic we've been using year after year! It isn't working. We need a new tactic."

The President took his time lighting another cigarette, then tossed his lighter on the desk. "We need something more than the same military strategy we've been using for nearly thirty years. Thirty years! We must find a way to get rid of the rebels once and for all." Angrily, he pounded his fist into his hand.

Zolog saw his opportunity, but he had to be careful not to offend General Dimago. He would find the appropriate time to deal with the general, but this was not it. He had to move cautiously. Dimago was still in charge of the entire army. Zolog knew he was no match for that kind of power. But Dimago had revealed a soft spot, and Zolog would exploit it to his advantage. The general was busy trying to keep favor with the President.

"Drain their blood and they will die," Zolog said with such ferocity that the President appeared startled. Zolog continued. "I don't mean literally. We don't have to defeat them on the battlefield. When they can no longer fight, the war will end." He stood and walked over to the President's desk. The very act of standing while General Dimago remained seated put Zolog at an advantage—a very calculated move.

"Explain yourself," the president said.

"Money. That's their life blood. The rebels need money for guns, ammunition, and food to continue their war," Zolog said, aware that he had taken temporary control of the meeting. "We need to stop their flow of money," he said, his hand curling into a tight fist for effect. "With no money, they will no longer have guns, ammunition, supplies—their fight will be over."

"And how do you propose to do that?" General Dimago asked dryly.

Zolog picked up a statue from the President's desk and held it. It was a rare Mayan figurine made of gold with inlaid jade. "The obvious question is, where is the money to support the rebels coming from? Other countries? Unlikely. No, the source of their money comes from within our own country."

"Are you suggesting it's from our gold and jade?" the President said, looking at the figurine.

"Preposterous," General Dimago said, staring angrily at Zolog. "How could they possibly steal enough from under our noses to pay for their army? As you know, we already have soldiers guarding our gold and jade mines."

"It is from gold and jade," Zolog said. "But as you've already stated, the mines are heavily guarded. This might be the source of their money." Zolog held the figurine higher.

Suddenly the President's eyes lit up. "Antique Mayan artifacts," he said, almost in a whisper.

Zolog nodded. "Mayan artifacts are among the rarest, most sought after art objects around the world, and they fetch incredible prices. While there's no doubt that smuggled raw gold and jade provide some of the rebels' income, I believe that the majority of their money might come from these rare artifacts."

"Preposterous!" the General bellowed. "There are not enough artifacts to make any difference. The fact that they are extremely rare is what makes them so valuable. And they are more regulated and guarded than raw gold and jade."

"I have to agree with you, General." The President took a deep draw from his dark cigarette and blew out a cloud of smoke while he thought a moment, then said, "So what are you suggesting, Colonel?"

"Please tell us how you plan to stop it, if in fact you are correct," General Dimago said.

The President held up his hand to silence the General, then nodded for Zolog to continue.

"I've already begun to work on the problem, Mr. President," Zolog said, ignoring the general's sarcastic comment. "I am confident the problem can be solved quickly."

The President stood a moment, blowing a stream of smoke through his nose. "I hope you are right about this," he said, flicking the ashes from his cigarette. "I want you to report directly to me. I expect to be kept up to date on everything."

General Dimago's face flushed red with rage at having been taken out of the loop. The President turned toward his aging general. "I want you to give Colonel Zolog all the support he needs to finish this."

"Yes, Mr. President," Dimago said.

"Colonel—" the President said as both men turned to leave. "You had better be right about this." The stern warning hung in the air along with a cloud of smoke as Zolog and the general turned and left.

Chapter 15

Brett woke the next morning feeling refreshed. He went downstairs to the tavern, had breakfast and coffee, then started looking around for Perez. They still had a long trip ahead of them, and he wanted to get started. The woman serving food said the sergeant had gone upstairs with the girl last night and hadn't come down yet.

Brett would have to wake him. He had the owner go upstairs with him and unlock the sergeant's room. When Brett opened the door, he found Perez in bed with the girl, both naked and both in a deep tequila sleep. Brett made a few attempts to rouse him but saw it was useless.

Perez would probably sleep a few more hours, and when he finally woke up, he was going to have one hell of a hangover. He would be in no condition to drive the rough trip that lay ahead. On the other hand, Brett knew nothing of the jungle, which was now even more dangerous because of washed-out roads and bridges.

Brett looked at Perez and the girl lying naked on the bed. They'd both bought companionship for one night, but each had paid a different price. She'd gotten a free meal and all the tequila she could drink for a night of sex. And for a couple of day's military pay, Perez had gotten laid and smashed on cheap booze. A bartering system as old as time itself.

Brett's options were to wait an extra day for Perez or take a considerable risk and leave on his own. While the trip might be difficult, it didn't seem impossible. He'd already lost a full day in Guatemala City waiting for the Jeep to be outfitted with extra tanks.

He decided he would chance it. If he ran into trouble, he could always turn around. He scribbled a quick note to Perez, explaining that he had taken the Jeep; the note also said he would cover for him by telling his superiors that Perez had gotten sick.

Twenty minutes later, with all the gas tanks and water bottles refilled and instructions on the best route to follow, Brett turned the Jeep toward Lepudra. The dog had taken his spot on the packs in the back.

Over the next hour, Brett sipped his coffee and steered the Jeep toward the rain forest. Except for Tequila, Brett found himself alone again. He started thinking about Kari Wheeler. He knew nothing about her but realized he was thinking about her much more than he was Ashley, a woman with whom he'd had a relationship for over two years. Why?

A bump in the road sent the last of his coffee splashing into his face, and he turned his attention from trying to analyze his feelings back to the road. Two hours later, the trees became thicker and the road softer and more treacherous. Before he knew it, he'd entered the El Peten jungle—nearly one-hundred-thousand square miles of rain forest. A thick canopy of immense trees rising two hundred feet above the jungle floor blocked most of the sunlight.

The great cathedral-like space beneath the treetops captured the steamy 100-plus-degree heat and dust. Rare shards of sunlight broke through to the jungle floor. A fuzzy mantle of bright green moss covered everything, and water dripped from every surface. An unsettling silence was occasionally disrupted by the echoing screams of a howler monkey or a scarlet macaw's call. The stagnant, humid air, thick with the smell of earth, mildew, and rotting vegetation grew hotter as he worked his way deeper into the jungle.

Fighting to keep the Jeep on track left him soaked in sweat. The road had washed away in dozens of places, leaving roaring streams or thick mud for him to negotiate. The Jeep moaned, groaned, choked, belched clouds of blue smoke and threatened to stall on several occasions, but never did. Nearly hidden by tangled vines, the moss-covered crumbled ruins of a Mayan tomb loomed out of the mist off to his right, a reminder of a civilization that lived there centuries ago. The large stones had collapsed on themselves and were covered with the ubiquitous green moss; the crumbling structure seemed ominous, a portal to something dark.

He thought about the professor and his daughter. An undefined worry settled over him.

San Sebastian Monastery
New Mexico

With the first hint of dawn, a thin strip of orange grew across the horizon, and a brass bell rang, resonating through New Mexico's crisp morning air. The monks of San Sebastian once again began their day just as they had since 1634.

But the routine would be different on this day. It would be a day of mourning. Brother Jonathan Vasquez, the youngest and newest arrival at San Sebastian, had died during the night. By midmorning, a doctor had arrived, asked questions, filled out a death certificate for the coroner, and taken a few blood samples from Jonathan to send to the state health lab, which was required by New Mexico law, then left.

At twelve o'clock noon, with the sun burning down on the red tiled roofs, Father Menendez said the funeral mass in the Saint Francis del Marco Chapel.

As the brass bell tolled, the monks carried the simple pine coffin from the chapel to an ancient cemetery where monks had been buried for more than three centuries.

Father Menendez read a passage from the Book of Matthew, then recited a prayer written by Father Alfredo de'lLamarco Francisco himself, a prayer that had been used since the founding of the monastery. The monks, standing around the coffin, sang a chant and offered silent prayers as the coffin was lowered into the dry, rocky earth.

"In nomine Patris, et Filius, et Spiritus sanctus," Menendez said as he sprinkled a cross over the coffin with a handful of dirt.

The fresh grave, covered with stones and dark dirt, waited to be absorbed into the mountain like the others before, leaving no other trace except for a simple cross bearing the monk's name. But it wasn't the only recent grave. Nearby were four other mounds already bleached under the intense sun. The deaths of these monks, like that of young brother Jonathan, had also been sudden and inexplicable.

A cloud of fear and uncertainty had settled over San Sebastian. Something evil and mysterious had invaded the walls of the monastery. The recent graves on the mountain were the grim proof.

Things were going to be different at the monastery. That was inevitable. The outside world would be coming to find out what was happening, and the monks would be unable to keep them out.

Burdened with thoughts of death and the events of the past few months, the monks left the cemetery and returned to the seclusion of the monastery. Only a faint wind in the branches of the piñón pine and the squawk of a mountain jay broke the silence.

Guatemala
El Peten jungle

Brett stopped twice to refill the gas tanks, once during the afternoon and the second time just before dark. He and Tequila snacked on dried beef jerky and flour tortillas before pushing on. His arms burned with fatigue from fighting to keep the Jeep on the roads, but he didn't have time to stop and rest.

It had been four days since his arrival in Guatemala. He had lost valuable time; he had to push on.

A big incentive was that he didn't want to spend the night in the jungle, out in the open with no shelter. His global positioning system couldn't receive a signal under the thick canopy of trees, but it wouldn't have helped because the maps Sanchez had provided proved to be worthless in the jungle.

With the onset of darkness, he lost all sense of direction. His world was limited to the small area ahead lit by the headlights. Occasionally, yellow eyes would appear in the headlights, then disappear into darkness. He felt vulnerable sitting in the open Jeep. He could only hope that the bone-jarring ruts that constituted the road would eventually lead him to Lepudro.

Sometime during the night, he stopped and put the last of his fuel into the Jeep, a task that proved to be difficult in the dark, and he spilled a portion of it. He had to find the village. Bone-tired and hungry, he climbed back into the Jeep, turned the key and continued on.

At two o'clock in the morning, Brett finally pulled into a tiny village. He steered the Jeep through the narrow, dark streets of the village until the Jeep's headlights illuminated a modest, stucco building with a rusted tin roof. The building seemed too small to be a clinic, but the sign overhead announced CLINICA DE LA MEDICINA.

The trip had drained him. Exhausted, hungry, and thoroughly miserable from damp clothes caked with mud and sweat, he climbed out of the Jeep. The dog stood up on the packs, stretched, and jumped down to find a place to relieve himself. Brett grabbed the duffel containing a change of clothing and went inside.

The nurse met him at the door. "The doctor's asleep," she

whispered. "I'll wake him if you need him. What brings you here?" she asked Brett, thinking he was a patient.

He held his hand out. "No, I'm not a patient. I'm Doctor Brett Carson. I've been sent here by the CDC in Atlanta. We got your report—"

"Of course!" she interrupted him. "Come in. I'm Maria, the nurse here at the clinic. I'll wake up Doctor Crenshaw." She went behind a curtain to get the doctor.

A freckle-faced, sandy-haired man wiping sleep from his eyes came out and extended his hand. "Hi, I'm Robert Crenshaw."

"I'm Brett Carson with the CDC," Brett said, accepting the eager handshake. "I came down here to investigate your report."

"God, I'm glad to see you," Crenshaw said. "So, they believed me after all. I wasn't even sure they'd gotten my message. I sure as heck didn't expect to see anyone this soon with the roads the way they are. How'd you find your way here in the dark? It's a tough trip, even in daytime. And nearly impossible with the damage from the storm."

"Mostly luck," Brett said. "I wouldn't want to try it again."

"Are you hungry? Would you like some stale coffee?"

"No thanks. I had some beef jerky." He was starved, but it was obvious he had wakened them, and he didn't want to make them cook for him in the middle of the night. Besides, sleep sounded better than food.

Crenshaw rubbed his eyes and nodded. "I've had a long day, and I'm exhausted. It looks like you could use some sleep too. There's a lot to fill you in on. Let's talk in the morning."

"You live here?" Brett asked, looking around the small clinic.

"You mean here in the clinic? Seems like it sometimes. Actually,

I have a small room behind the general store, but I'm rarely there except to get a fresh change of clothes or maybe catch a quick nap when the clinic is quiet. You can use it while you're here. I'll just sack out here. I've got some patients I have to keep an eye on."

Maria brought Brett a towel and soap. "There's a shower out behind the store, right next to Dr. Crenshaw's room," she said.

Brett drove over to the general store and took his packs inside the room attached to the back of the store. He slipped out of his soaked clothes, went outside and took a shower from rain water collected in a tank on the roof of the store. He dried himself and went back inside.

Remembering the knife attack of two nights ago, he decided to let Tequila sleep in his room again. He brought the dog inside, then slid under the sheet on the cot and fell into a much-needed deep sleep with the dog curled on the floor beside him.

Chapter 16

Brett woke with the dog staring at him, wagging his tail. Every muscle ached. He climbed stiffly off the cot and slipped on a clean shirt and jeans. He left Tequila outside by the Jeep and went to the clinic, which was filled with the smell of brewing coffee. He stifled a yawn and glanced at his watch.

"Yeah, it's past nine. We thought you could use the sleep," Crenshaw said. "Maria has breakfast for us."

They sat down at a small table in the corner that doubled as a nurse's station, examining room, reception desk, and apparently cafeteria.

"Thank you. I thought Maria was your nurse."

"She *is* my nurse," Crenshaw said. "But she's a lot more than just a nurse. The government pays her to work at the clinic and help me. That means assisting me with patients and procedures, changing linen, ordering drugs and supplies. And fixing my meals."

Breakfast consisted of cornmeal, black beans, sausage, hot red peppers and coffee that could have passed for motor oil. A taste of the red peppers made Brett's eyes water.

"You'll get used to it," Crenshaw said.

Brett downed some of the bitter coffee. "Don't think so. How long have you been down here?"

"Forever," Crenshaw said disgustedly. "By the calendar, eighteen months. Only six months left on my contract with the WHO."

"I take it you don't like the jungle."

Crenshaw's eyes narrowed. "I hate this damned place. I hate the rain, the mud, the blistering heat, not to mention the *really* bad stuff like a dozen species of poisonous snakes for which we don't have anti-venom, beetles that carry the fatal Chagas disease, quicksand that can swallow you up in less than a minute, poisonous vines that cause festering rashes that never heal, and parasites that grow in your eyeballs leaving you blind. And of course, recently we've had to deal with *the disease*."

"The disease?"

"The epidemic—whatever it is."

"Fill me in on what you know about it," Brett said.

"Over a dozen patients here at my clinic have died so far from what I think is the same illness. There are probably more cases in other clinics throughout Guatemala. We got our thirteenth case today. He arrived early in the morning while you were still sleeping."

Brett looked around the room and saw the six cots, one occupied by an old man, another by a young woman and a baby. "Him?" he asked with some concern in his voice.

"No, in there." Crenshaw nodded toward a closed door.

"What's in there?"

"It's a closet that now serves as our isolation room. I try to keep those with the disease away from the rest of the clinic. We're short on gloves and gowns, just like everything else, but we still change every time we go in there. He's getting the last of my antibiotics now. But I'm sure he'll die anyway. Like all the others."

"When did you first suspect that there might be a new disease?" Brett asked. He could see fatigue and concern etched on the young doctor's face.

"I saw the first case probably three months ago. I became really concerned about a possible epidemic after five more patients showed up with the same symptoms during the following weeks.

This week, I've seen two, in addition to the man they brought in last night."

"Tell me every detail you can remember about them," Brett said.

"The disease comes out of the blue with no hint and hits patients hard with a sudden onset of fatigue, fever, and body aches. After eight to ten hours, muscles begin to fail. Then things rapidly get worse.

"Victims collapse with high fevers, their muscles have no tone, and they lose their ability to move. They can't move their heads, cough, or swallow. They start to choke on their own secretions. Even breathing becomes difficult. Eventually they can't even blink. Their eyes become dull, dried, sunken. There is hemorrhaging around their mouth and eyes, with blood oozing from their nose, mouth, ears.

"The skin hangs loose, as if it were separated from the connective tissue. It's as if they're decomposing while still alive. And their faces are frozen in terror as they struggle to breathe."

Brett was scribbling down notes while Crenshaw talked. He stopped and looked up when Crenshaw paused to fill their cups with coffee.

"Nobody has lived longer than twenty-four hours from the onset of their first symptom," Crenshaw said as he poured. "And nobody has survived more than twelve hours after arriving here. Ever hear of any infection killing that quickly?"

"Yes," Brett said. The hairs on his neck tingled as his mind raced over the possibilities—and none of them good.

"Any ideas?" Crenshaw asked.

"Could be anything. Too early to tell."

"It scares the hell out of me," Crenshaw said.

"It should," Brett said in a somber voice. He worried that Ebola or one of the other deadly hemorrhagic viruses might be raging through the rain forest. If he was right, they were at great risk by just being in the same contaminated building where more than a dozen others had died. He shuddered when he realized he had just eaten there. "Do you know anything about hemorrhagic viruses?"

"I've read about Ebola. You think it could be the Ebola virus?" Crenshaw asked with rising terror in his voice.

"No, probably not," Brett said. "Ebola is mostly found in western Africa in Guinea, except for a few cases that were accidentally brought into the U.S. by infected research lab animals."

"Ebola—in the U.S.? I didn't hear about that," Crenshaw said. "What happened?"

Brett put his coffee down and looked up at Crenshaw. "I'll give you an idea of how dangerous Ebola is. This happened at the army research facility in Maryland. Lab monkeys started to die, in large numbers. When they were found to have somehow gotten infected with Ebola, the entire lot of monkeys was incinerated, the inside of the brick laboratory was torched, then they filled the entire burned-out building with cement. Finally, a one-acre plot around the building was permanently sealed off with double chained link fences."

Crenshaw sat in silence, taking in every word.

"An outbreak in Central America doesn't rule out Ebola," Brett continued, "but it's very unlikely. A more likely guess would be Marburg."

"Marburg?"

"Unless your specialty is tropical infectious diseases, you most likely have never heard of it. Marburg is a hemorrhagic virus in the same family as Ebola—and one of the planet's most lethal diseases. If you're even near infected patients, you're in mortal danger." Crenshaw was staring at him, frozen by the impact of what he was hearing.

Brett continued. "I was in Zaire during an outbreak of Marburg. One of the local health workers slipped off his goggles in the heat of the day for just a second to wipe his eyes. He got infected from a single droplet of saliva on his gloved hand. He was dead the next morning."

Crenshaw put his filled cup down without taking a drink.

"Does that patient live here, in Lepudro?" Brett asked, nodding toward the isolation closet.

"No, he's from a small village at least thirty miles from here."

"They brought him all the way here?"

"He wasn't in his village when he got sick. He was somewhere in the jungle, near here."

"Have you talked to his family, or anyone else from his village?"

"I spoke just briefly with the man who brought him," Crenshaw replied.

"And the other twelve cases..."

"They've come from several different villages. Ten were men, but two of the patients were women."

"Can you get me a list of the patients and names of their villages?" Brett asked.

"Sure, that's not a problem. What I don't understand," Crenshaw continued, "is why everyone in their village doesn't get sick and how it seems to be spread so randomly through the jungle. I guess that's your job to come up with the answers."

"Yeah, I guess it is," Brett said after taking another sip of the bitter coffee. "Let's go see your newest patient." He was curious, but at the same time hesitant and concerned. Behind that door something deadly waited for them. They put on gowns, masks, gloves, and went in. Sunlight and searing humid air poured through the opened window.

Brett cringed when he saw how crude and inefficient the isolation room was. "This room should be sealed. And that means the window has to be kept closed."

"You trying to speed his death?" Crenshaw shot back. "He'll literally boil in this heat if we close the window."

True enough. It was midmorning, and the heat in the small room was already unbearable, even with the window open. He wanted to contain the spread of the organism—if in fact it was an infection—but the jungle seemed to be beating him at every level. He nodded in agreement.

Crenshaw looked down at the patient. "My guess is he's only got a short time now."

Brett felt a chill as he bent down to examine the patient. Shallow breaths with dry wheezing sounds, face staring blankly, sunken eyes dried and dulled from an inability to blink. Brett snapped on his penlight and saw hemorrhages in the conjunctiva, and a trickle of dark fluid at the corner of the mouth.

He put his gloved hand on the man's forehead to check for fever. But the loose skin felt cold, in spite of the jungle heat. That was a bad, ominous sign.

He held a stethoscope to the patient's chest and listened to the faint wheezing as the man tried in vain to suck air into his lungs, but his muscles were already too weakened. The man seemed unaware of their presence. Nearly paralyzed muscles robbed him of vital functions—breathing, eye blinking, swallowing, facial expression—yet he remained semiconscious.

Through the stethoscope Brett heard the gurgling sound of a weakened heart beginning to fail. Crenshaw's assessment was right; for this man, time was very short. Whatever affected the muscles of the extremities had probably also affected the heart muscle. He guessed the involvement of the heart combined with overwhelming pneumonia would be the cause of death.

Brett moved into action and shouted through the door to Maria. "Open my canvas bag, take out the metal box and slide it through the door." When he had it, he opened the lid, took sterile cotton swabs and cultured the man's eyes, nasal cavity, and mouth, then put the swabs into culture tubes and sealed them. After he opened the man's mouth to culture it, it stayed open and he had to push the slack jaw closed again. The muscles felt mushy and flaccid, just useless chunks of tissue attached to bone.

Next, he took out a syringe, pulled a tourniquet tight and slid an 18-gauge needle into a vein. Dark blood filled the vaccu-tube. He was especially cautious so that no blood spilled and that the infected needle was disposed of properly. After taking blood cultures, Brett held up a plastic bag containing the needle, syringe and alcohol swab he had just used. "These have to be incinerated, then the ashes buried. Understood?"

Crenshaw nodded and cautiously gave the bag to Maria. "Burn these," he told her.

Once outside the room again, they snapped off their gloves and scrubbed thoroughly.

"Well, what do you think?" asked Crenshaw.

"I think you're lucky to be alive. And I think we've got a hell of a mess on our hands."

Chapter 17

Hurdoras Pass
El Peten jungle

Ting! Ting! Whack! The ringing sound of the steel blade broke the silence. A peasant in a straw hat, his bare back glistening with sweat, swung his machete to clear the overgrown trail of thick tangled vines. *Ting! Whack! Ting!* The opening in the trail grew wider. Falling branches sent a swarm of insects buzzing into the air.

Professor Forrest Wheeler tugged at his soaked shirt as he watched from his horse. He slapped an insect biting him, then wiped his hand across his sweaty forehead. The clinging heat and hordes of mosquitoes made conditions miserable. They were working their way deeper into the heart of the steamy El Peten rain forest and had to hack their way with greater frequency through thick foliage that choked the trail.

Old roots and vines covered rotting graves and ruins of ancient buildings. At the height of Mayan civilization, more than a hundred thousand people lived in this area. But, now with its poisonous snakes, blood-sucking insects, and quagmires of quicksand waiting to suck the unwary into eternal darkness, the area seemed incapable of providing food and shelter for that many people.

The canopy of trees blocked out the sun except for an occasional thin shaft that broke through, and a thick carpet of green moss covered everything. At times the ground seemed to move; leeches, snakes and beetles as large as rats were everywhere. Wheeler decided that the terrain must have been vastly different when Mayan kings ruled this land.

"Are you sure this is the way?" the man with the machete asked, obviously troubled by what lay ahead.

"I'm not sure of anything, but my instinct tells me this way."

The peasant went back to his horse. Wheeler nudged his own horse through the opening, and they all continued on their way. Exhausted, he stared at the matted mane that hung in wet tendrils from the neck of his bony mare as she threaded her way up the trail. The horses were lean and gaunt, like the peasants who rode them.

They rode in silence, single file through the thick forest of Hurdoras Pass, their mood soured by the wet, miserable conditions. They hadn't seen the sun in three days. A smothering, steamy mist limited their world to a few claustrophobic yards in every direction. The only sounds were those of hoofs on a narrow muddy trail that grew more treacherous along a steep precipice.

The Guatemalan government permitted only certain designated areas to be excavated or explored. Strict laws dictated that all artifacts were the property of the Guatemalan government. The problem was that over the years, most of the approved excavation sites had been studied extensively by dozens of archaeological teams and stripped of any priceless relics. Many of the ruins had been reduced to nothing more than cleaned-up tourist attractions.

There was, though, a consensus that the real art treasures still lay buried in undiscovered tombs hidden deep in the jungle, in remote areas that were now strictly off limits. Ignoring those regulations and restrictions, Wheeler spent his summers in pursuit of new tombs and priceless artifacts. After his wife died ten years ago, he was a lost soul without her. It was then that the search for Mayan art became his obsession.

In spite of the strict regulations, most of the ancient artifacts rarely made it to museums, and almost never to the Guatemalan government. Instead, many of the artifacts were stolen and sold to private collectors through black market dealers. Wheeler had managed to salvage a significant number of artifacts that would have otherwise been sold—or never even found. His contribution to several museums was considerable. He was considered to be the foremost authority on the ancient Mayan civilization. Still, regardless of whatever excuses he made to justify his actions, the truth remained: Forrest Wheeler had become a *sepulcor lardon*—a grave robber.

The seven weathered, olive-skinned men riding with Wheeler were mestizos, a mixed heritage of Spanish and Mayan Indian. In a destitute country where nine out of ten families lived in abject poverty, the mestizos were the poorest. But they were survivors. Out of desperation they plundered ancient ancestral Mayan graves in exchange for a few quetzals.

Wheeler's unholy alliance with the mestizos was not about the money. He was driven by his passion for ancient art treasures untouched by human hands for more than six centuries. Jade, silver, gold, ceramics, stone carvings. To him, they were holy pieces from a civilization centuries ago. They were history. He wanted to save them from greedy art dealers and preserve them in museums and for posterity.

But a week ago, he had stumbled onto something by accident. A secret, something both unthinkable and terrifying because of its implications. He also knew that what he had discovered put both him and Kari in grave danger. After this current trek into the jungle, he would take Kari and return immediately to Chicago. They needed to leave the country as soon as possible.

Kari rode up beside him. "You okay, Dad?"

Wheeler adored his daughter. She had openly expressed her disapproval of his summer trips, but when she couldn't talk him out of it, she had insisted on coming with him the past two years. She despised the jungle, but she loved her father and wanted to keep an eye on him.

A smile spread across his face. At sixty-five, he wasn't as old or as feeble as she imagined. But this time the danger was very real, something she was unaware of. "Yeah, I'm fine," he answered.

Wheeler had previously worked only with villagers he knew. That was a strict rule he had followed until this trip. Looters were desperate and dangerous, and there were horror stories of murderous and machete-armed renegade gangs. He never knew exactly how much was jungle myth or how much was the truth.

But three weeks ago, a stranger had approached him about leading this expedition. The man would provide maps, money to finance the trip, and manpower. Wheeler would be able to keep a few select items for himself, the people sponsoring the trip would get the rest. The man needed his expertise, and Wheeler needed the money, men, and equipment. He had reluctantly agreed to lead the group since they were headed into an area where some of the richest tombs were thought to have been located, but a place also known to be treacherous. The men were heavily armed, but assured him it was only for their own protection.

His brief conversation with the doctor from the CDC had planted a new fear. He wondered which posed the greatest danger: an epidemic, the unforgiving jungle, the unknown mestizos who were with him—or the terrifying secret he had discovered. A growing nagging feeling told him they definitely should have left Guatemala when they were back in Guatemala City.

"Keep your eyes open, Kari," he warned her.

"Open for what, Dad?"

His answer was to nudge his horse on. He was angry at himself for putting Kari in a situation like this. Despite his repeated pleadings for her to remain in the village, she had refused to be left behind. He had tried to coax her, threaten her, bribe her, but she was as stubborn as her mother had been. Now he realized he should have simply refused to let her come. They both should have left Guatemala three days ago while they had the chance.

An eighth man had joined the group as they entered the canyon. After quiet conversation with the others, he fell in line at the back. The stranger was a large man whose face was hidden under a wide-brimmed canvas hat, pulled low. Wheeler stopped and turned toward the man.

"It's okay, Senor Wheeler. He's with us," one of the men assured him.

Wheeler sat a moment, then nodded and nudged his horse on.

He led them farther into a densely tangled ravine that required much hacking at vines and traversing slippery hillsides. An hour later he reined in his mare and scanned the side of the pass. Had he seen a small rise along the crest, maybe a mound at the top of the pass? It was a steep hill; it seemed the right place to look.

A mestizo steered his horse beside Wheeler. "Maybe we should try a different route and go around Hurdoras Pass, senor."

Wheeler shook his head. During the past hour, he had spotted what he thought might have been remnants of a vanished Mayan city. "According to my maps, there may have been a city in this area. This is the area we're looking for."

They looked at him with doubt on their faces but said nothing. The truth was, his maps were useless. There had been a city somewhere in the region, but no one knew exactly where, and the area to search would cover many square miles. Earthquakes, mudslides, and the thick, tangled vines had swallowed up entire cities; ancient tombs were smothered under centuries of tangled jungle growth.

Wheeler turned his horse off the trail and started up the slick, grass-covered slope. The others followed single file. At the top, he searched the area from his horse and felt his pulse quicken when he finally spotted it. At first glance it appeared to be just a moss-covered stone projecting into the air, but to his experienced eye it was too smooth, too flat to be anything but an ancient stela.

He swung his leg over the saddle and dropped to the ground. He knelt down beside the stone, then scraped at the moss with a fingernail. Centuries of wind and rain had eroded most of the hieroglyphic carvings on the limestone stela except for a few indiscernible lines. But the ancient religious stone was a beacon.

The hieroglyphics would have told the story of an important or wealthy Mayan buried nearby.

"What is it, senor?"

Wheeler didn't answer. He stepped back and stared up through the mist, trying to imagine the angle of the sun and where the shadows would fall. The stela was always placed at the top of a mountain or a hill, closest to the sun. To the Mayans, the sun was God. The tomb would be nearby, but never in shadows. He squinted in all directions, looking for the slightest undulation in the undergrowth. Then, with his adrenaline surging, he untied a six-foot steel rod from the saddle.

He knew.

Wheeler wore calf-high boots for protection from poisonous pit vipers and fought his way through tangled brush. He carried the steel rod to a place on the hill where there was an almost imperceptible mound, a pregnant swelling of the earth, like a womb for the dead. He raised the rod at arm's-length, gripped it firmly, then rammed it into the soft flesh of the forest. The rod discovered where the soil had been disrupted more than five-hundred-years ago and sank a full four feet. At the end of the thrust, he felt an unusual crunch.

"Here," he said.

The stela near the telltale mound meant that an elite family or a high priest had been buried there. Probably not royalty, but certainly wealthy. And that meant valuable artifacts.

Sweat poured from the men as they pulled away grass and shrubs. Their picks and shovels clawed at the soil. A pick struck a large stone with a dull thud. Groaning and heaving, they pried away the eighty-pound capstone to reveal the opening, a small black hole leading into a dark cavernous tomb.

One of the men lit a torch and shoved it at Wheeler. "You go first," the man said.

Wheeler felt somewhat uneasy but convinced himself that there was no reason for concern. The new tomb beckoned him, but he had to push away his growing anxiety.

A portion of the roof had collapsed, and large stones were piled on each other. As he moved below the rubble, the chamber of the tomb, a large dark, cavernous space was mostly intact. Thrusting the torch ahead of him, he slid cautiously down into the narrow opening and dropped into the dark, musty tomb, ever aware of the danger of coming face-to-face with poisonous fangs or a cave-in that would bury him. His breath caught in his throat as he surveyed the tomb. A Mayan corpse lay on its back, arms folded across its chest, the moss-covered bones were green. His steel rod had inadvertently punctured the forehead and penetrated through the skull. *The crunch*, he thought, and shuddered.

A gold necklace with inlaid jade around her neck and the shape of her pelvic bone told him it was a young woman. The ribs at the front of her chest gaped open, her sternum split. The Mayans had sacrificed her in a religious ceremony by cutting her heart from her chest while she was still alive. Beside her lay the bones of the wealthy Mayan for whom she had died.

Wheeler dropped to the dirt floor of the tomb and moved with slow, deliberate motions since the slightest vibration could cause a cave-in. He tried to ignore the skull of the girl at his feet. Her jaw was open as if she were screaming at the rod that violated her, even in death.

"Are there any *el tesoro* down there, senor?" a voice asked from the small hole above him.

Treasure—it was all about the money to the mestizos, never about the art, Wheeler thought. He held the torch out at arm's length, moving it in a wide arc around the tomb. The flickering light of his torch revealed rich treasures of pottery, jewelry, and gold. Even after five centuries, the pieces still glittered with magnificent elegance once he rubbed away the cobwebs and slimy moss.

"Yes," Wheeler answered. "This is incredible. We have stumbled on a very ancient, and important tomb. Definitely royalty. You are going to be very pleased." His eyes were drawn to three gold figurines inlaid with polished green jade—the most valuable substance to the Mayans. At Sotheby's they would each go for more than fifty-thousand at auction.

He pushed the torch into a dark corner. Hidden beneath a layer of dust and cobwebs he found more artifacts: a jewel-studded knife, eight pieces of pottery, gold coins, a ring, jade beads, and pyrite carvings. He carefully handed the priceless artifacts up one piece at a time.

The necklace around the girl's neck beckoned, but he left it. It had been her reward for dying, and Wheeler would not take it from her.

He turned and started to climb out, thrusting the torch ahead of him, then froze. Staring him in the face was the big man, the stranger who had just joined the group. Wheeler saw for the first time the grotesque face lit by the flickering torch. The man's right eye was gone, and an ugly deep, scar covered the empty socket. His grin was sinister and revealed gaped, rotting teeth.

A revolver suddenly moved in front of the face, catching the light of the torch—a sight so alarming, Wheeler froze, his breath caught in his throat. The gun was a Spencer, a large, heavy revolver, and its barrel was pointed directly at him. Wheeler's mind raced for answers as he tried to comprehend the situation. *Oh, my God! Kari!* Fear and panic overwhelmed him. He had to get out of this damned hole; he had to get to Kari!

Wheeler put out a hand in front of him, but the Spencer kicked, sending splinters of hell tearing through his chest and knocking him back into the hole. The searing pain ripped the breath from him. His ears were ringing, but he hadn't heard a sound. Why hadn't the gun made a sound?

He searched for air, but his breath was gone. An unfamiliar cold seeped into him. His body convulsed, and his hands twitched as he fought against death, but he knew he was losing. No breath. No light. In that final moment that separated life from death, Wheeler was only aware of the girl's skeleton beside him.

They would share the same grave.

With the crack of the pistol still ringing in her ears, Kari leaped from her horse and ran toward the hole where the mestizos were crouched. A piercing primal scream rose from her chest. "*No-o-o-o-!*"

Kari saw the man holding a gun with smoke curling from its barrel, and she froze. The other men stood and turned toward her. An icy fear surged through her as she realized too late her mistake. She raced back to her horse, grabbed the saddle horn, swung into the saddle, and dug her heels into the side of her horse.

The mare started to bolt forward, then suddenly stopped and reared up as hands grabbed the reins and bridle. A massive hand grabbed Kari's arm and ripped her from the saddle and onto the ground with seemingly little effort.

One man grabbed her around the waist. She elbowed him in the face, shattering his nose, then broke loose from his grip and drove her knee into his groin. He collapsed in a moan, blood pouring down his face. She reached for the saddle horn again, but a fist smashed into her cheek, and she went down. The blow stunned her momentarily, but she got to her feet and looked for an escape.

The men drew close; she kicked out again, but the man she aimed for stepped back, and she caught only air. An elbow in her ribs took her breath and a blow to her stomach took her down again.

The men circled her as she started to get to her feet. Someone clawed at her khaki shirt and tore it open, exposing her breasts. She crouched down, like a cornered animal waiting for the final attack. The men threw her to the ground, ripping at her clothes and grabbing at her legs.

They ripped off her clothes and pinned her naked to the ground. She struggled to move against the probing hands, but it was useless. Her nose was filled with the stench of filth and a musk-like odor of crazed men. Waves of nausea turned her stomach sour.

The giant man holding the pistol suddenly pushed the others aside and leered down at her. He bent down, his face inches from hers, an angular, mean-looking face with only one eye and the empty socket covered by a hideous purple scar.

Kari screamed at the sight and struggled to get away, but it was hopeless. Held spread-eagled by the other men, she couldn't budge. He put his hand between her legs and pushed against her.

She held her breath and tried to brace for the final assault. Just as she started to black out, shots rang out from the trees, and one of the men holding her legs fell to the ground. Another one collapsed and fell across her. The other men scrambled for cover as they returned fire, leaving her lying there tangled under their dead and wounded comrades. Caught in a fierce crossfire, Kari crawled out from under the dead bodies and hid behind a log, trying to catch her breath.

Naked, cold, and shivering—she waited for death.

Chapter 18

Lepudro Medical Clinic

Maria served them a quick lunch, then Brett went back to Crenshaw's room at the rear of the general store, took a cold outdoor shower, shaved, and changed into fresh clothes. He fed Tequila a large portion of food and made a place for the dog to sleep in the room. With the overhead fan on, it would be much cooler than sleeping under the Jeep. He had brought the dog along in the hope that he would find a new home. The truth was that Brett wasn't ready to give him up. Not yet. He enjoyed his company and didn't want him wandering off. Tequila seemed perfectly content to curl up on the floor beside him.

Brett sat at a table and jotted down notes on everything he could remember that Crenshaw had told him. While it was possible they were dealing with something other than an infectious agent, it seemed unlikely. Poor hygiene and unsanitary conditions in the jungle created numerous sources of infection. Heat, stagnant water, and decay made the rain forest a natural incubator for brewing disease, and there were countless insects and rodents to spread it. He left the room and headed back to the clinic.

"He's dead," Crenshaw said, nodding his head toward the isolation room. "I'm going to move his body outside."

"No, leave him in there," Brett said sharply. "I need to get a few more samples and maybe do an autopsy."

"An autopsy? You can't," Crenshaw snapped.

"It won't be any kind of formal autopsy, nothing like you saw in medical school, but we need to get a good look at the major organs and do cultures. If we're lucky we can get a lot more information."

"We can't do that."

"Sure we can," Brett argued. "Like I said, it'll just be a limited autopsy."

"No, I mean you *can't*. Tonight, the weeklong celebration of All Souls' Day begins."

"So?"

"These people are mestizos," Crenshaw said. "Part Spanish, part Mayan. Death is a very important part of their culture. They revere the dead. They don't allow anything to disrespect a body."

"Aren't these the same people who sacrificed thousands, slit their throats and ripped out their hearts, and after a ball game rewarded their athletes by cutting off their heads?" Brett shot back. "Why the hell should anybody care if we do an autopsy?"

"It's true they have had a violent history, but to them, the dead are sacred. A man's soul resides in his body, and in death it's respected."

"Yeah? Well, screw their superstitions. We may to be in the middle of a deadly epidemic, and if we don't figure out what's killing them and do it soon, they are going to become well acquainted with death," Brett said. His patience had evaporated somewhere around the time Sanchez had failed to get him a helicopter. "I intend to find out what we're dealing with, and do it as soon as possible."

Crenshaw reluctantly nodded. They agreed to do the autopsy after dark. That night after a quick dinner, they put on gowns and masks, then pulled on the gloves they had worn once before. Brett knew he had to use extreme caution. He was putting both Crenshaw and himself at great risk, and he knew if he died it might be days or weeks before anyone in Atlanta learned of his death. That delay could be disastrous, possibly putting the CDC so far behind they would never be able to stop a raging epidemic. Besides, he really didn't want to die just yet.

They entered the small room, closed the door behind them, and taped a sheet over the window so nobody could see in. A single bulb hung from the ceiling, illuminating the waxy-blue body. The oven-like air was suffocating.

Outside, the sounds of guitars and trumpets told them that the celebration had begun. Candles and torches flickered past the window as people paraded in the streets carrying skulls and crosses. How appropriate and ironic that they should start All Souls' Day with an autopsy.

"Whatever we do, we have to be very careful with the instruments, blood, and fluids," Brett said.

He had started to question his own judgment for jeopardizing both their lives, but under the circumstances he felt he had no other choice. A limited autopsy would provide them with tissue samples, fluids for culture, and he would be able to examine the lungs and the liver.

He sighed, picked up a scalpel and slit open the abdomen with a single long incision down the middle. "When I'm finished, I'll sew him up tight. It'll look like he had an operation. Tell them you had to do an appendectomy or something."

The abdominal wall gaped open, and a strong odor poured from the peritoneal cavity.

Crenshaw grabbed the light and held it closer. The two men stared into the abdomen, unable to believe what they saw. The abdominal cavity was filled with a purplish-red gelatinous mixture of dissolving organs, old blood and a brownish fluid. Individual organs could no longer be identified. The man appeared to have rotted from the inside while still alive.

Brett stepped back a moment, unprepared for what he saw.

"What is it?" Crenshaw asked, his voice shaky with fear. "Ever see anything like it before?"

Brett didn't answer. Whatever it was wasn't good, and he wanted to finish this quickly. He cultured the fluid and sucked some of the gelatinous material into sterile tubes. He had originally planned to open the chest cavity next and examine the lungs but decided to forego that. His only thought now was to finish and get out of the room as quickly as possible. The heat and a horrible fear were getting to him. He attached a long Chiba needle to a syringe and pushed it through the diaphragm into the chest cavity, then sucked dark fluid from the pleural space into the syringe. That would have to do.

He gripped a curved needle with a hemostat and began to sew up the abdominal incision with quick, decisive sutures. Sweat poured from his forehead and dripped into his eyes and from the end of his nose. The thick air in the tiny room was unbearable.

"You should have been a surgeon," Crenshaw said as he watched. "Where'd you learn to suture like that?"

Brett ignored the question. "This whole building could be contaminated. No more patients are to be admitted to this clinic, understood?" Brett said as he quickly sewed the incision closed. "I want everything in here burned. The gowns, masks, gloves, bed linen, mattress. Everything."

Crenshaw said nothing. The mask covered any expression his face might have shown, but the fear showed in his eyes and his hands were shaking. When Brett finished sewing, they wrapped the body in several sheets. They scrubbed thoroughly, then burned all the contaminated supplies in an incinerator out back.

Neither man slept well that night.

Despite Brett's warning to close the clinic, Crenshaw admitted a new patient during the night, a patient who would change everything.

Chapter 19

Brett woke up in a drenching sweat and threw off the damp sheet. He didn't know whether it was his damned malaria flaring up again or just the stifling heat. He had no idea what time it was, but it was still dark.

Then he remembered the autopsy and couldn't get back to sleep. His body was burning up, and for several minutes he wondered if he were suffering from the early stage of *the disease* but decided it was merely the jungle heat. He lay awake in the dark and didn't doze off until the first shafts of light began to trickle through the jungle canopy.

Tequila finally woke him up with a soft *woof*. Rubbing his eyes and yawning, Brett opened the door and let the dog out. He sat on the edge of the cot in his underwear, rubbing his head while his mind raced over the events of the past day. Quinn would have to send a team down. There was little more he could do here without more help.

He doubted the disease was Marburg, but whatever it was seemed every bit as dangerous. He needed to contact Quinn and get the blood samples shipped back to the CDC lab as soon as possible. He had a lot of ground to cover to get that accomplished. He dressed, stuffed his clothes into his pack, and headed down the narrow alley to the clinic.

"Coffee's almost ready," Crenshaw said. "We've got a new admission. She came in last night," and he nodded toward a cot where a young woman was sleeping.

"Has she got it?" Brett asked. "The disease?"

"No. She and her father were attacked by a renegade gang. They killed her father, and she was beaten up, nearly gang raped. Probably would have been killed, but a group of villagers out hunting in the area heard gunfire and rescued her. They brought her here."

"Nobody was supposed to be admitted. This place is still contaminated."

"What are you suggesting I should have done?" Crenshaw shot back. "Leave her sitting outside in the dark alone, wearing only a blanket?"

Crenshaw was right. Brett moved closer. He could see only her black hair, but something about her looked familiar.

"Oh, my god!" Brett blurted out.

"What?" Crenshaw asked.

Brett stood there stunned, trying to take in what had happened. Finally he answered, "I met her and her father at the hotel in Guatemala City. How is she?"

"She wasn't able to talk much when they brought her in," Crenshaw said. "She was covered in blood, but fortunately most of it wasn't from any of her injuries. We cleaned her up and dressed her cuts. When I examined her I found no fractures. Just minor cuts and lots of bruises from being beaten. I gave her pain meds, a mild sedative and put her to bed."

The woman stirred and sat up. She touched her hand to her swollen lip. A large bruise covered her cheek, and dried blood lined a small cut by her mouth.

"Where am I?" she moaned, groggy from the sedative. She looked around, dazed and confused. Then as the memory of what had happened, panic came flooding back, and she drew in her knees on the bed, sobbing and shaking. Maria went to her side and put her arm around her.

Crenshaw sat down on a cot opposite her. "You're at the Lepudro Medical Clinic. I'm Dr. Crenshaw, and this is my nurse, Maria." Crenshaw sat there a moment, not knowing what else to say. "Is there anything we can get you?"

"Her name is Kari. Kari Wheeler," Brett said.

Kari looked at Brett and wiped her eyes with the back of her hand. Her eyes widened in recognition.

"I'm Brett Carson. I met you and your father at—"

She buried her head in her hands, sobbing.

"I'm so sorry," he said softly. "Is there anything we can do?"

She continued to sob uncontrollably. He was at a loss about what to say or do. He wanted to hold her, comfort her. But he stood frozen as she shook uncontrollably.

Finally, he asked, "Are you able to talk—to tell us what happened?"

She shook her head and picked up a towel, and held it against her face, sobbing.

Brett stood silently beside her. "I'm sorry," he said. "I'm so sorry."

After several moments, she took a deep breath, composed herself, and looked up, her swollen lip quivered, and her voice was a raspy scream. "They killed him! They killed my father!" Tears streamed down her face. "I couldn't stop them! I couldn't save him," she stammered. She wiped her eyes with the towel again. "He'd found a tomb... they were removing artifacts. I heard shouts and gunfire. He was still in the tomb. I was still outside. I couldn't help him. They... they killed him."

She paused and her lips trembled as she fought for control. "Then... they came for me." She started to shake and pressed the towel against her mouth to stifle moans.

Brett gently put his hand on her shoulder. He felt an overwhelming sense of sorrow at what she had gone through, a nightmare of loss and pain. He fought a raging anger at the monsters who had done this to her. His hand clenched into a tight fist. He wanted revenge, he wanted to find them. He wanted to *kill* them.

"According to the men who rescued her, they shot and killed two of the gang, but the others escaped into the jungle," Crenshaw told Brett.

"Are the villagers always armed?" Brett asked.

"When they're hunting in the jungle, they certainly are. Not only to kill their prey, but also to protect themselves from wild boars, cougars, rogue gangs—whatever."

"Honey, can I get you anything to eat?" Maria asked Kari.

She shook her head.

"That's okay. I'm going to fix something anyway, and you can see if you feel like eating." Then she left to fix a breakfast tray.

Brett sat down beside Kari, keeping his hand gently on her shoulder. He was torn with emotions. He never imagined he'd see her again, and now was at a loss to help her. She curled up on the bed and drew the sheet over her.

Brett wanted to stay with her, but there was another matter requiring his immediate attention, something more urgent. He stood and turned to Crenshaw, who was handing him a cup of coffee. "Can you draw me a map to Santa Elena?" he asked quietly.

"Thought you wanted to get back to Guatemala City," Crenshaw said.

"Santa Elena has an airport. I want to get these blood samples back to the CDC immediately so they can do cultures and serologies."

Crenshaw frowned. "That's a gamble. If the runway hasn't been cleared and the airport is still closed, you'll have gone thirty miles out of your way for nothing. Sixty miles round trip. That'll add almost a day to your trip and use up precious gasoline."

Brett unfolded his map and studied it again.

"And you should know the drive back will probably be worse than the trip here," Crenshaw said.

"Why's that?"

"The jungle soil can't hold all the extra water, and there will be tons of flowing mud and runoff after a storm like this. Rivers will be boiling. Extremely dangerous."

Kari sat up slowly and swung her legs over the edge of the bed. "Are you leaving?" she asked.

Both men turned in surprise at the question.

"Will you take me with you?" She put a wet towel against the large bruise on her face and grimaced. "I need to get back."

"Back to where?" Brett asked.

"Back home. To Chicago. I want to get out of here." She reached out and grabbed Brett's arm. "Will you help me?"

"I think it would be better if you wait a day or two before you think about traveling," Crenshaw said.

"I agree," Brett said. "It's a bad idea. It's going to be a rough trip, and I have to cover a lot of distance today. You should rest a few days." He wanted to help her, but this trip was going to be dangerous. He had to try it because he had to get those samples to the CDC lab as quickly as possible. The stress of keeping her safe was just too much, and too risky.

"Are you saying you won't take me with you?" she asked.

Crenshaw turned to Brett. "Maybe you should take her back with you. It could be more risky for her to stay here."

Brett thought about it, then shrugged. "I'm going back to Guatemala City. I guess it will be okay for you to ride along," he said.

"How soon are you leaving?" she asked.

"Immediately—as soon as I can refuel and pack my gear."

"I'll get ready," she said. She got off the cot and tried to stand, wobbled a moment, then caught herself and stood up.

Maria returned with coffee and a tortilla rolled around beans and rice. "What are you doing? Where are you going?" she asked.

"I'm taking her with me," Brett said.

"Well, sit back down and try to eat something before you go," she told Kari. "It's going to be a long trip." Maria turned to Brett and asked, "Are you sure about this? She doesn't look in any condition to travel yet."

"I'll be all right," Kari said. "I have to get back."

Brett was trying to assess the situation and his options. His main goal was to get the samples shipped, then contact Quinn. He wanted to help her, but he also knew that if he was traveling alone, he'd be more willing to take risks and push on. Her presence would slow him down.

"I don't have any clothes to wear," she said almost apologetically.

"Well, this is a clinic, not a clothing store. But we do have something you can wear," Maria said. She returned a moment later and handed her a fresh pair of scrubs. "You can dress behind that curtain."

"Thank you," Kari said and took the clothes.

Kari slipped out of the hospital gown and put on the fresh scrubs.

Crenshaw gave her two vials of pills, one for pain, the other a sedative. "Don't get them mixed up," he said. "The white pills are for pain. The pink for sleep—Tylenol 3 and valium. Are you sure you're up to this?"

"Thank you for everything," she said as she took the pills. Then she turned to Brett. "I'm ready, Dr. Carson."

The determination on her face convinced both of them.

"I'm Brett. Please call me Brett."

"Okay, Brett. I'll be fine."

After shaking hands and thanking Crenshaw and Maria for their help, Brett packed up his supplies and the blood samples and went out.

The dog jumped up on Brett when he appeared. He scratched the dog's head, then loaded the Jeep.

"What's your dog's name?" Kari asked, and stooped to pet him.

"His name is Tequila," Brett said. The dog jumped into the back of the Jeep. "But he's not my dog."

"Well, I don't think Tequila knows that." She noticed the bullet holes in the side of the Jeep and the frayed seats as she climbed in.

Brett packed the Jeep with water and food, then carefully loaded the blood samples and filled the gas tank and the extra containers with the last of the fuel in the village. More than two hours later than he had planned—precious daylight hours he knew he couldn't spare—he drove out of the village into an already sweltering thick morning mist.

He was headed back out into a treacherous jungle in a Jeep of questionable stamina, with an abandoned dog, an emotionally and physically traumatized young woman who had just seen her father murdered, and a dozen vials of blood and tissue samples swarming with something extremely deadly. The complication factors just kept rising.

He took a deep breath and let out an exhausted sigh.

Colonel Zolog was not in a good mood when he entered his office in the Government Secret Police building. His secretary brought him a cup of coffee and slipped out immediately, sensing trouble. Yesterday, he had learned his agents had lost track of Professor Wheeler. He knew they would locate him again—but the lost time could be critical. They'd planned to follow him, learn whom he met with, and uncover whatever method or organization was being used to smuggle artifacts out of the country.

If he had to, he could arrest Wheeler and take him into custody. He knew he could get him to talk. But that method wouldn't be his first choice. In fact, it wasn't even an option at this point. For now, Wheeler, who was his best—and only—link to the money trail, was missing. And that was a huge problem for him. The President was in a impatient, and Zolog had made a promise. He had to find Wheeler, and soon.

He sat at his desk and sipped his coffee. He looked up when someone banged on his door. A frightened-looking captain burst in.

"Colonel," he said, snapping to attention.

"What is it?" Zolog demanded.

"I'm... I'm afraid I have bad news, Colonel," the captain sputtered.

"Well, spit it out!" His patience had evaporated.

"The American—Professor Wheeler—he's dead."

"Dead?" Zolog shot from his chair and slammed his fist on the desk, causing the captain to jump back against the door. "What do you mean? He's dead?" Zolog shouted.

"He was murdered. Our sources learned it from villagers."

"Who killed him? Why?" Zolog's face contorted in rage as the extent of the loss sank in.

"I'm not sure of the exact circumstances," the captain said, with sweat pouring from his face.

"Your orders were for your men to follow him. Not let him out of their sight!" Zolog shouted. "Our men followed from a distance as you instructed. The gang with Wheeler killed him. Shot him point blank."

Zolog paced a moment, then asked, "What happened to the girl? His daughter?"

"No one knows. They think she escaped."

"Dammit!" Zolog banged his fist on the desk again. He walked over to a map of Guatemala that filled half a wall. "Where was he killed?"

The captain approached the map. "It happened somewhere is this region." With a trembling finger, he circled a portion of El

153

Peten rain forest.

Zolog stared at the map. "There are four villages within that general area. We'll start searching there. She has to be somewhere in that area." He walked to his desk and hit the intercom button. "Get my staff!" he roared.

Five nervous officers scrambled down the hall and into his office. An angry Zolog was a dangerous man, and today he was as angry as they'd ever seen him.

He had promised *el Presidente* results, and Wheeler's death was a devastating blow to his plans to quickly end the war.

The officers stood waiting as Zolog went to the map. "The American we were following was killed somewhere in this area. His daughter is missing. Find her!"

He smacked his fist into the palm of his other hand in anger. "Find the girl," he barked. "We can only hope she has the information we need."

"When we find her, what are we to do? Arrest her?" one officer asked hesitantly.

"Bring her to me! Don't let anything happen to her. We have to find out exactly what she knows. This is your top priority." Everyone stared at him, frozen in place.

"Go!" he yelled. "Get moving."

With relief, they saluted and left.

Zolog wasn't sure how much the girl knew, but he was confident she would tell him whatever she did know. He had ways. Eventually they always talked, especially the women.

He picked up the cup and finished the coffee in one furious gulp. Yes, she would definitely talk.

Chapter 20

Brett jammed the Jeep into low gear as they struggled up a steep incline. He wanted to get to the next town, Leguareita, before nightfall, so he pushed the Jeep hard. He'd decided to head for Guatemala City rather than risk a side trip to Santa Elena. If the airport in Santa Elana was still closed, he would lose precious time. And he had to ration his gasoline.

They drove without talking. Brett fought ruts and tangled roots as he tried to keep the Jeep on the road. Landslides, fallen trees, and slick mud had brought the Jeep to a standstill more than once. Kari was alone with her painful memories as she fought to process the trauma and agony of her loss.

The trip was rough but still navigable for the first three hours, but suddenly things changed dramatically. Above the grinding noise of the struggling engine and the thrashing of brush and limbs against the Jeep's sides, another sound grew louder and louder, growing into a deafening roar.

"What is it?" Kari asked.

"Look!" Brett pointed. In the distance they made out a murky turbulence directly in their path. A roaring river, churning with trees and other debris swept across what was to have been their road. There was no visible way of crossing. Brett heart sank. The road he's come in on three days ago was gone.

"Oh, my god." Kari's eyes surveyed the powerful, watery chaos. "Turn around. Let's go back."

"We can't. I have to get the samples back to Guatemala City. I've got to find a way to get across."

Brett stopped, got out and walked to the edge. He stuck a branch in the torrid muddy water racing past to test the bottom. He looked as far as he could in both directions, but there was no other place to cross. He pulled out a map and tried to figure out where he was.

"Is there another way around this?" she asked.

"This map is useless. It doesn't indicate any other way."

"We'll never make it. We'll drown," she argued. "How deep is it?"

"I'm about to find out," Brett said. He took off his boots, stripped down to his boxers, then waded cautiously into the roaring water, pushing a long stick into the bottom. Tequila jumped down and stood at the edge of the bank, barking at him, not knowing whether to follow or stay behind.

"What are you doing?" Kari shouted in alarm, above the roar of the water. "You're going to get washed away!"

"Just checking the bottom," he shouted back. They were in a hell of a situation, but he didn't want to scare her any more than she already was. He waded to the middle, struggling to stand up against the swift current while keeping an eye out for snakes or logs that might be carried down the roaring stream, either of which could prove to be fatal. The water came to his waist—just high enough to cover most of the engine and probably make it stall. If that happened, they would be stranded miles in the middle of nowhere. On the other hand, if the Jeep was going fast enough, the grill would hopefully create a wave and keep just enough water away from the engine to allow them to get across.

He worried about the canvas bag containing tissue and blood samples. He considered carrying it across but decided if he slipped or got knocked down while crossing, the vials would be lost, and the river would be contaminated. He figured that keeping them in the Jeep was his best bet. If the Jeep didn't make it, he and the samples wouldn't be going anywhere.

The slick, muddy bottom made standing treacherous, and the force of the water required all of his energy to remain upright and not be swept away. The ferocity of the water was frightening. He knew he shouldn't have agreed to bring Kari with him. For her safety, he should turn around and go back to Lepudro. But it was imperative to get the samples to the CDC. He'd gotten himself into one hell of a mess; he had no choice but to press on. He turned and carefully made his way back to the Jeep.

She looked at him in his boxers, completely soaked. "What are we going to do?"

He climbed into the Jeep without dressing and started the engine. "We're going to go across." He whistled, and the dog jumped into the back again.

"Then I'm getting out before we get washed away," Kari said emphatically.

He took hold of her arm to keep her from jumping out. "You can't cross on foot. It's too risky. We'll make it."

Before she could react, he ground the gears into reverse, backed up twenty yards, then shifted into first and spun the tires toward the stream. "Hang on!" he yelled, and she grabbed the handle on the dashboard. The dog barked once in protest as they drove into the water at breakneck speed, sending waves of water spraying up around the Jeep, which began to slow. The engine raced, and tires spun wildly as they were caught up in the fury of the water. The Jeep started to slip sideways, and water poured into the vehicle, flooding the floorboards.

"Oh God!" Kari yelled. She grabbed the handle tighter when the Jeep lurched, and she sensed they were being swept downstream.

The dog barked, then jumped into the stream and tried to swim across. But the roaring water swept him downstream and out of sight around a bend in seconds.

"Tequila!" Brett yelled as he watched the dog disappear.

Brett jammed the Jeep into second gear to give the tires less torque. The old Jeep finally found its footing on the muddy bottom and spun its way across, up the other bank, and back onto the road. Muddy water poured from the Jeep.

Brett set the emergency brake, leaped out, and raced barefoot downstream along the bank in the direction of the dog. "Tequila!" he yelled at the top of his lungs.

A bark answered him, and the dog ran out of the brush toward him. Brett stopped and leaned over to catch his breath. The soaked dog jumped on him, knocking him over. Totally winded, Brett lay on his back as the dog licked him.

They walked back to the Jeep. Tequila vigorously shook the water from his coat before he jumped up to his usual spot.

Kari looked at the dog, then at Brett in his soaked underwear covered in dirt and weeds. "That was nearly a disaster," she said, shaking her head in disbelief. "We could've been swept away." She slowly clambered out of the Jeep and started wringing water out of her scrub pants. Her lower lip was trembling from fear.

"We made it. It wasn't that bad." Brett knew she was right. They'd dodged an almost certain disaster. He put on his jeans boots, and shirt, then climbed in.

"You're certifiable," she snapped.

"Yeah, that's what they tell me." He released the brake, shifted into gear and drove on.

They stopped midafternoon to eat. The tropical sun had turned the thick humidity to steam. Their sweat-soaked clothes drew swarms of insects, which they futilely tried to fight off as they unpacked the lunch Maria had made for them. Brett gulped his portion but noticed that Kari ate nothing.

"You should eat something," he said. "It's going to be a long day and you need something in your stomach."

"You can have mine. I'm not hungry." She swallowed two of her Tylenol 3 pills. Tequila had been watching with eager eyes and wolfed down the food Kari tossed back to him.

An hour later, Brett stopped to refill the Jeep's tank from one of the spare gas cans. He had just finished when he heard something coming toward them. Suddenly, he put the can down, and climbed into the Jeep. After slipping it into gear, he quietly eased it into the thick brush, then killed the engine. He pushed Kari, who had been dozing, down onto the seat and put his mouth to her ear.

"Don't move, don't talk, don't even blink," he whispered. She was awake instantly, and her muscles tensed, but she didn't move.

A low, deep growl rose from the back seat. *Tequila*! Brett leaned over Kari and clamped both hands around the dog's mouth, trying to keep him from barking. He whispered in the dog's ear, hoping to calm him and keep him quiet, keeping one hand firmly around the dog's muzzle and rubbed his head with the other, while Kari lay beside him.

They could hear the sound of horses and men approaching. If the men were rebels, they might be friendly. But if they were government forces, or if they were one of the many rogue gangs that roamed about, then he and Kari could be in serious trouble. They could be the same men who killed her father and attacked Kari. That was a possibility he didn't want to entertain.

The Jeep was covered with dried mud and weeds from the crossing and created its own natural camouflage. However, they were only a few feet off the road and still could be spotted. Perez's automatic rifle was buried under their packs and unreachable.

Within moments, the horses were on the road behind them. Brett could smell the horses and heard the sound of hooves, snorting, and the clinking of saddle gear. He guessed there were probably eight to ten horses. A deep, low growl rose from the dog's throat and the hair on his neck bristled. One of the horses snorted loudly. Brett kept his hands firmly around the dog's muzzle. He and Kari remained motionless as the men passed; an agonizing minute later, they were gone.

Finally Kari let out a deep breath. "Who were they?" she whispered.

"Don't know. I didn't get a look at them." He didn't want to suggest that they could be the men who attacked her. He worried she was already thinking that. He kept his hand around the dog's mouth; a bark would alert them, and he couldn't risk it. When Tequila finally wagged his tail, Brett let go of his muzzle and rubbed his head. "Good boy."

He waited a full half hour before starting the engine, then pulled out onto the path and they pressed on. They had lost too much precious daylight. He doubted that they'd get out of the jungle before nightfall, and worried about what they were going to do for shelter. He wondered if the men were just following the road, but his real fear was that the men had been following *them*. He worried about catching up with them around every bend.

In spite of the jarring bumps and the rain-drenched road, Kari dozed during the afternoon, sedated. Brett struggled to keep the battered Jeep moving. He was relieved that she could sleep despite the jolting, bouncing, and grinding of gears.

The thick jungle canopy diminished the late afternoon sun, and night descended around them. Only then did Brett flip on the headlights. Their world became a narrow-lit tunnel created by headlights. Still, he worried that *any* flicker of light might alert their pursuers. He pushed on, wondering who might be watching them from the blackness just beyond their beam of light. An open Jeep wasn't the most reassuring habitat.

Brett's arms were starting to ache from the effort to maintain control as he'd been clenching the steering wheel for hours. Finally, the road straightened and the jungle thinned. A flickering glow bloomed in the distance.

Leguareita!

As they drove closer, Brett found the light becoming increasingly unnatural looking. "Kari," he frowned, "something isn't right. It looks like the place is on fire." He stopped and turned off the engine.

"That's not a fire," she groggily reassured him. "Those are candles and torches. They're celebrating *El Día de los Muertos—*

the Day of the Dead. It lasts for seven days."

"Day of the Dead? I thought that was yesterday."

"Yesterday was All Souls' Day. That's a religious celebration to honor the dead. It's even recognized by the Catholic Church. But the Day of the Dead is pagan, leftover from their Mayan ancestors. It is a wild time of drinking and dancing to mock death, not honor it. The church doesn't sanction it, but also doesn't openly discourage it."

"You know a lot about these people."

"I'm an anthropologist, remember?"

He smiled at her, turned the key and ten minutes later drove into town. He parked on a narrow, dark side street. People milled around the dirt streets carrying brightly painted paper skeletons, skulls, and embellished crosses on poles. They moved through the night sky, lit by flickering candles and torches, and the music of guitars and trumpets played loudly over the noise of the crowd.

"Stay here with Tequila, and I'll try and get us some food and a room for the night," Brett said. He also needed to get a message back to the CDC. He jumped out to join the crowd.

A woman told him his best bet would be the post office, where there was both a phone and a fax machine. He found the post office, but it was dark and locked. Next, he went to the police station where a sergeant behind the desk, drinking a beer, eyed him suspiciously.

"*Buenas noches,*" Brett said. "Do you have a phone? *Teléfono?*" he repeated.

The sergeant belched and nodded toward the wall phone.

Because of downed phone lines, getting through to Atlanta proved to be a daunting and frustrating task. After twenty irritating minutes, Brett finally got through and left a voice mail for Quinn. It was 3 a.m. in Atlanta. Since it was early Saturday, he couldn't be sure Quinn would get the message until Monday morning. Brett would have to call the CDC desk in the morning.

He inquired about getting a room for the night, but nothing was available. He and Kari were exhausted and hungry, and he had to find a place for them. An idea struck him when he walked past a church. He found the priest in the crowd and pulled him aside. A short time later, he was back at the Jeep with two containers of food.

"Any luck?" Kari asked as Brett started the engine.

"Yeah," he said and handed two containers of food to her.

"What is it?"

"Cornbread, tortillas, beans, rice and sausage. And, I found us a place for the night."

"Thank God. I'm beat. All I want now is a shower and a clean bed."

"Not sure about the shower part, or even the clean bed," Brett said and shoved the Jeep into gear and drove off.

"What exactly did you get us besides the food?"

"You'll see." Moments later he pulled the Jeep in front of an adobe church and stopped. "We're here."

"We're going to spend the night in a church?" she asked.

"The padre offered it to us. It's the only space available tonight. It's quiet and it's shelter, so we can get some sleep."

"I lost my sandals when we crossed that stream," she said, as she gingerly got out of the Jeep.

He handed her the containers of food and a flashlight, then pulled their packs from the back of the Jeep and headed into the darkened chapel of San del Champisti.

Kari followed him inside and snapped on the flashlight, moving the beam over the interior. Brightly painted religious icons came to life momentarily, then receded into shadow as the beam passed over them. Christ on the cross with thorns on his head and bright red blood pouring over his face; the Sorrowful Virgin, her sad, pale face looking down; another Jesus looking nine-tenths dead with his bloody, thorn-wrapped heart exposed; a statue of Saint Ignatius.

Other saints and various forms of *la Virgen* appeared briefly, each showing their own sorrow and pain. The pained, tortured faces of the saints reflected the harsh life in the rain forest.

Kari spotted a small balcony along the back of the church. "Let's sleep up there," she said. "At least it's a little more private."

Brett nodded and hauled the packs up the narrow stairs. They sat down, and she handed him both plates of food. "I'm not hungry," she said. "Give mine to Tequila."

"You should eat." He quickly polished off his food, then took off his boots and stripped down to his underwear. "There's a well outside. Give me your clothes and I'll wash them. We're both wearing a lot of mud."

In the dark, Kari stripped out of her damp scrubs and slipped into a sleeping bag. Brett went outside, rinsed their clothes at the well, and hung them over shrubs to dry. Then he washed himself using a bucket. He poured water for Tequila in a bowl, then removed the dressing on his paw, which was healing nicely.

He put on clean jeans, gave the dog the food Kari hadn't eaten, then went back inside and stretched out on his sleeping bag. Apparently deciding that he wasn't expected to sleep alone outside anymore, Tequila had silently followed Brett inside and found a spot on the floor near their sleeping bags.

The darkness of the old chapel engulfed them in an unnerving void. The sounds of the festivities seemed louder. Guitars, drums, trumpets, and voices rolled through in waves.

After several minutes, the door below them opened. An old peasant woman came into the chapel with a candle and walked down the aisle. They both leaned forward and watched the woman from the balcony as she went to the votive stand and lit several candles. Moving as silently as an apparition, she knelt in front of the altar and prayed. Soon she made the sign of the cross, then shuffled back out into the night to join the others. Light from the votives created soft flickering shadows on the ceiling.

Kari sat up and hugged her knees. "Do you believe in life after death?" she asked.

"You mean heaven, ghosts, spirits—things like that? No, I guess not," he answered.

She sat for a while, watching light dance on the ceiling. She hoisted her sleeping bag over her shoulders when she realized it had slipped down, briefly exposing her breasts. "Is everything black and white for you, Brett Carson? No doubts, no what-ifs?"

He didn't answer her. She continued. "Tell me then, what's this all about?"

"What, All Souls' Day? This church? I think it's probably because they can't accept death. Maybe people believe in God and an afterlife to convince themselves that there's more to it than just this life. What if there *is* nothing else?"

She lay down and was silent. Then she said, "You seem so analytical. Is there no allowance for something you can't examine under the microscope? What if you're wrong. Maybe there is more to it than just this." Before he could respond, she said in a voice filled with anguish, "I hate the jungle. I want to go home."

After a long silence, Brett heard her muffled sobbing and saw the blanket shaking. Her father had been murdered and left to rot in the jungle. She had been attacked and nearly raped and was alone in a strange country. A wave of guilt hit him. He suddenly felt inadequate, unable to do anything to help her. He reached out to hold her, his fingers almost touching the trembling sleeping bag, but he hesitated and pulled back.

He wanted to tell her that everything was going to be okay, but he couldn't. He lay on his back and stared up at the shadows flickering on the ceiling. Things were becoming much too complicated.

At some point in the middle of the night, Brett woke up to dead silence. The muffled sounds outside were gone. The revelry and music had come to a halt. Apparently, everyone had gone to bed to get ready for the next day's festivities. The silence and the darkness were overpowering.

Brett was aware of Kari's presence, aware that she was in a sleeping bag next to him. After lying there and not being able to sleep for an agonizing hour, he crawled out of his sleeping bag and went downstairs. He had spotted a guitar leaning against a wall when they entered the church.

Sitting on the floor with his back against a beam, he picked up the guitar and softly began to play a Mendelssohn concerto.

The music filled the dark vastness of the church. After two more pieces, he put the guitar down, went back up to the choir loft, and slipped back into his sleeping bag. Kari hadn't moved, and he thought she was still asleep.

"You are full of surprises, Brett Carson," she whispered, startling him.

"I didn't mean to wake you. I couldn't sleep."

"That was incredible. You should have been a musician."

"I was once."

"What do you mean?"

"Go to sleep. You've had a rough day. Tomorrow isn't going to be any easier."

"What do you mean you were a musician?" she repeated after a few minutes of silence, and rolled over to lean on an elbow and look at him.

"I went through college on a music scholarship," he said. "After college I had to decide between medical school and a career in music."

"So you chose medical school. Do you have any regrets?"

"About what?"

"About not pursuing a career in music."

"You mean 'the road not taken'? I guess with every choice we make in life, you always wonder 'what if,' he said. "But I love medicine, and I still get to play my music, though it's usually for an audience of one." Even in the dark he was aware that she was staring at him.

"You married?" she asked.

"No. You?"

"No. I have a boyfriend, and he's asked me to marry him."

What was her answer to the proposal? He wanted to ask her more about the boyfriend, but he didn't. A long silence followed. He couldn't tell if she was crying or had fallen asleep again. He lay in the dark, thinking about the past few days and how complicated this assignment had become. He was finding it harder and harder to focus on the reason he was there. He finally fell asleep three hours before dawn.

Chapter 21

Borga, Guatemala

Covered with peeling wood siding and a rusted tin roof, the two-story warehouse lay hidden in the crowded slums of Borga, the part of town filled with crumbling houses and the stench of decay.

Armando Galvez pulled back the large bolt lock, slid open the side door of the warehouse and stared out at the three mestizos waiting out in the alley beside their horses. Galvez, less than five feet tall and weighing more than two hundred and sixty pounds, snorted to clear his sinuses, spit phlegm into the street. He looked up and down the alley, then nodded for the men to enter.

"What are you so damned spooked about?" one of the men asked.

"Things are more risky now that the army's stepped up their security," Galvez said, as he pulled the door closed and locked it again. "We have to use extra caution. And I hear they put Zolog in charge of trying to find us. I don't intend to spend my life rotting in prison or ending up in front of a firing squad."

Galvez and eight other men worked in the warehouse. Two

of them guarded the doors as sentries, and the others six cleaned, sorted, and packed artifacts for shipment out of the country. The afternoon sun seared the tin roof and baked the air inside. Armando's swollen belly hung over his belt and he tugged at his baggy trousers. It was too damned hot, even for the man who was part of the decay. Dark blotches of sweat soaked the back and armpits of his shirt.

He had left two wealthy German art dealers waiting in his cramped office, and he went back to tell them there would be a short delay. The new delivery was an unexpected bonus, so he didn't mind making them wait. Galvez knew they considered him to be just necessary scum, a nuisance they tolerated. But Armando Galvez had his own kind of special power within the organization.

The plundered artifacts that made their way to the warehouse were smuggled out of Guatemala by the organization. But Galvez always kept a few isolated prized pieces for himself, which he sold at a nice profit, usually to foreign art dealers. And the Germans were here to do just that. But it was a dangerous game he played; if the organization ever learned of his little side trading, he was a dead man.

Galvez spoke no German, and the Germans knew very little Spanish, so they conversed in English.

He wiped his forehead with a damp handkerchief. "Sorry, but I have business to take care of. It'll only take a few minutes. Brandy." He pointed to the bottle on his desk. The Germans waved him off. The cheap brandy Galvez offered burned the throat, and more than two glasses guaranteed a throbbing headache.

One German pulled out a dark cigarette and lit it. "We'll wait."

Why the hell didn't the damn Germans just do what they came

to do, then leave him alone? Having them here only increased his risk. He wiped his forehead with the back of his hand. He couldn't understand how they managed not to sweat. The overhead fan moved the stale, hot air around in the office, but did little to cool it.

Galvez walked back into the warehouse. The three mestizos in the alley entered the warehouse and carried their canvas bags to a table against the wall. The sweltering building smelled of fresh sawdust and cedar shavings that were used to pack artifacts for shipment out of the country. Four small open crates filled with wood shavings lined the wall beside the table. Against the opposite wall wooden stairs led to a small loft where two men cleaned and packed pieces from an earlier delivery.

The tallest mestizo wore a large hat and had a sunken, purple scar where his right eye should have been. An imposing brute, he towered over Galvez. Galvez had dealt with him before and didn't trust him—the man known only as 'Scar'. Galvez treated the mestizo as one would a mean dog—never showing weakness, always on guard.

"Let's see what you got," Galvez said in a wet, raspy voice. He forced himself not to stare at the grotesque scar.

Galvez carefully pulled pieces from the bags and placed them on the table—religious gold medallions, pottery, turquoise faces, carved stone figures. Galvez picked up a carved pregnant female form with turquoise inlay. It was Mayan, as were all the other artifacts. They'd been exhumed from the earth after being buried for more than thirty-five centuries.

Galvez studied the collection. They were quality pieces that would bring top prices. But the poor mestizos knew nothing about quality, only quantity. What they did was illegal and subject to severe punishment if caught, but poverty drove these men to desperate acts. Fortunately, their efforts also served a larger purpose than they realized.

The mestizos searched for Aztec graves to the north and Mayan tombs to the south, then brought their plunder to Galvez. He paid for their efforts, and they could always borrow a few quetzals from him in an emergency, no small thing in a city as poor as Borga. Some of the mestizos owed him money, but they always repaid him, if not with money, then with stolen pieces of art.

Occasionally they paid with something else.

Armando Galvez craved women. Young women. Girls. The mestizos usually dragged in one of the street girls for him in order to repay a loan. The arrangement fulfilled both their needs.

Galvez put the gold pieces on a scale and wrote down their weight. He noticed dried bloodstains on a piece of pottery but said nothing. The ancient artifacts often followed a violent path to his door. He picked up a Mayan figure of a virgin and ran his finger over the carving, carefully feeling the grooves cut from stone more than five centuries ago. But he wasn't admiring it. He was checking for cracks, for rough edges that might lessen its value. It was a magnificent piece. In auction houses in New York or Paris, a piece like this could bring a half-million dollars.

Galvez sneezed and wiped his nose with the back of his hand, then rubbed his hand on his shirt. He was allergic to the molds and spores carried by the ancient art that he brokered. His eyes were red and swollen, his nostrils crusted and raw. He snorted again and spit on the floor. It was almost as if the ancient dead were getting their revenge.

Galvez finished his inventory, counted the pieces, and wrote in a worn green ledger. Then he went over to an old cast-iron walk-in safe under the stairwell. The name Wells Fargo stood out in gold leaf on the door. He turned the dial on the lock and pulled open the heavy door.

He returned to the table with a metal cash box. "Four thousand quetzals," Galvez said.

"Four thousand? Twenty thousand!" In one swift movement, Scar grabbed Galvez by his shirt and lifted him off the floor as if he were merely an oversized piece of art.

Galvez knew he could never show fear; he could never back down in this business or he was dead. He snorted and spit a mouthful of mucus on the huge hand that held him. "Eight thousand," Armando Galvez said. "And don't ever touch me again." To Galvez, all mestizos stank, but this one had the putrid smell of a rotting dead rat.

The man set Galvez down with a growl. "Ten thousand."

Galvez looked at him, trying to assess his position. "You know, I'm only authorized to pay so much. But I can do ten. If you bring me a girl."

The man smiled, showing yellow stained teeth, then dropped Galvez to the floor. "We might have a special girl for you. Beautiful. American."

Armando's mouth twitched with anticipation. He pulled out two stacks of Quetzals and shoved the money across the table. "Eight thousand, two thousand more when you bring me the girl."

"Three thousand if we get the girl." The giant stared at him with anger on his face, then grabbed the money, unlocked the door, and left with the other two mestizos.

Galvez closed the sliding door behind the men, jammed the

bolt lock into place, spit on the floor again and went back to talk to the Germans. Galvez knew he was burning his candle at both ends, and if he wasn't careful, it might be suddenly snuffed out. He wiped his forehead again.

On the drive back to Guatemala City, Brett began to think about Kari's situation.

"We need to tell the authorities what happened," he said.

"No," Kari shot back. "I don't want the authorities involved. A situation like this can get very messy in Guatemala. I need to get back to Chicago. I can't afford to stay here for days—possibly even weeks—while they do their usual delay tactics."

Brett frowned. She hadn't done anything wrong, so why wouldn't she want the authorities to know about her father's murder?

"Besides," she continued, "what would it accomplish? You think they are going to go into the jungle and look for his killers? That's not going to happen, so why involve them? I don't need more complications. I need to get home."

He didn't know what to say. She was right. It wouldn't accomplish anything except to add to an already difficult situation for her. Still, something didn't sit right with him. He stole a glance at her. A bruised cheek, a swollen lip, and a small cut marred her face.

In spite of that, she was one of the most beautiful women he had ever seen. Her thick dark hair was blowing in the wind. But it was her eyes that had captivated him from the moment she first looked at him. She turned and caught him staring at her.

"What?" she asked.

"Nothing. Just thinking." He gripped the steering wheel tighter and stared at the road as he bit his lip. In a short time, they would be swallowed up in the noisy, crowded city. He had a job to do, which meant both Kari and Tequila would be going their separate ways. He'd had no business getting involved with either of them. But he *had* gotten involved, totally.

Their little trio in the Jeep would soon dissolve, and he would be alone again.

Presidente del Manguinos had left a message asking Colonel Zolog for an update on the situation. The President was growing impatient. He wanted results, results that Zolog had promised to him. Zolog was sitting in his office, pondering the difficult situation that he found himself in, when a knock at the door interrupted his thoughts.

"Come in."

A captain from his staff came in, closed the door and snapped to attention with a smart salute.

"Yes, Captain, what is it?" Zolog asked.

"We think we've found her, Colonel."

"Wheeler's daughter? You have her?" Zolog jumped from his

chair and walked around his desk.

"Not exactly. An American woman was taken to the clinic in Lepudro two days ago, shortly after Wheeler was killed."

"Was it her?" Zolog asked, the muscles in his jaw clenched.

"Probably, but we're not sure. No one at the clinic claimed to know her name, and she'd already left."

"My guess is the doctor and nurse at the clinic know, but they're covering for her. Do we know where she was headed?" Zolog asked.

"No," the captain said, now starting to sweat under his uniform. "We suspect she might be coming here."

"She might be trying to leave the country. We can't let that happen. Check all the hotels. Put men at the airport and the train station. And put men near the American embassy in case she tries to go there. Make sure our men stay out of sight. We'll find her."

The captain started to leave. "Captain," Zolog said, stopping the man in his tracks. "We have to find her. It is absolutely imperative that she does not leave the country. Do I make myself clear?"

"Yes, Colonel," the captain said, as he closed the door.

Zolog went to the window and looked out across the government plaza. He couldn't let her slip through their fingers. There was another scenario he didn't want to think about. What if he found her, but it turned out that she knew nothing? What if her father hadn't told her what he had discovered?

Then what would he do?

Chapter 22

Brett and Kari arrived in Guatemala City in the late afternoon and found themselves facing the overwhelming indigenous traffic—buses, burrows, carts and taxis, all vying for a place on the crowded streets. Brett's first task was to take care of Kari. All her possessions and her money had been left behind in the village where she and her father had stayed. She planned to call her bank in Chicago and have some money wired so she could buy a ticket home.

She was still wearing the scrubs Maria had given her. She was barefoot, had no makeup, and had spent two days in a dusty Jeep, but Brett noted it didn't seem to matter to her.

He stopped in front of a bank, the *Bateria de la Republica,* located beside the government plaza. An armored vehicle parked in the plaza and two soldiers with automatic rifles at the front door of the bank reminded Brett he was in a country at war with itself. A military officer coming out of one of the buildings glanced at them, then got into a Jeep and drove off. Brett went inside and withdrew two thousand dollars on his credit card, had it converted to more than fifteen thousand Quetzals, and hurried back out to the Jeep.

"What's this?" Kari asked when he handed her an envelope filled with money.

"You can pay me back later. It's easier than your having to wire your bank. You can buy your ticket, as well as some clothes. And you're going to need shoes," he persisted. "You can't get on the plane barefoot."

He jammed the Jeep into gear and raced back out into traffic. His own priority was to get the samples to the CDC. He couldn't afford to waste any more time. "I have to go to the airport to ship these blood and tissue samples to Atlanta. You can buy your ticket while we're there."

They parked at the airport lot, and Kari went inside the crowded terminal to get a ticket while Brett carried his pack to the shipping area, which was in a large building at the opposite end of the parking lot. After twenty minutes of trying in broken Spanish to tell them what he needed done, he had only succeeded in confusing everyone.

They were arguing that he needed to take the case through customs for inspection, and he yelled in no uncertain terms that the case was never to be opened. Tempers started to flair. He told them to get Dr. Sanchez at the Ministry of Health on the phone. Kari showed up just before things got completely out of control.

"Looks like you're having a bit of trouble," she said.

"Thank God you're here. Can you explain to them that I need this shipped to Atlanta on the first available flight? Tell them it's a medical emergency and the case can't be tampered with in any way."

She quickly had the attention of the men in shipping as she stepped up to the counter. "*Es absolutamente necesario que estos paquetes llegan a Atlanta por mañana. Gracias,"* she said.

"And tell them they need to mark it 'dangerous—biohazard,'" he added. He had sealed the samples in a locked aluminum case. The chances of anything happening to the case seemed extremely remote, but the consequences would be incredible. The contents could kill hundreds or even thousands if it were somehow opened.

"*Cerciórese de que sean peligrosos marque 'peligroso bioquimico,'"* she said.

"*Si, senorita."* One of the men took the case from her and looked at it suspiciously. Finally he weighed it and put on the necessary shipping labels. He looked at her, then at the case again and applied a tape with *BIO PELIGRO* in bold red letters. He told her it would be sent out on the next available flight and gave her the bill. The clerk was staring at her so hard that Brett didn't think the man had blinked once while they had stood there. He knew the man's attention wasn't on the sealed case.

"Pay them eight hundred and fifty Quetzals," she said. "You're all set."

"Are you sure they understand? It has to be overnight," he persisted.

"Your package is going by air to Mexico City tonight. Tomorrow morning it will be flown to Atlanta and taken by FedEx directly to the CDC. It's all set."

"Nice to have my own personal translator." Brett paid the shipping fee, and they headed back across the blistering asphalt parking lot to the Jeep.

"Ouch, that's hot," she said and stopped to rub her feet.

"We've got to get you some shoes. Here, jump up. The asphalt will burn your feet.

"What?"

"Jump up. I'll carry you."

She jumped onto his back and he carried her piggyback through the parking lot. He could feel her hair against his neck and the warmth of her breath.

"Thank you," she said.

"No big deal. You're not heavy."

"I mean for bringing me back to Guatemala City with you. I know that you have a lot of things to do, and you didn't need to get stuck with me."

"Did you get your ticket?"

"No, I couldn't buy a ticket. I don't have my passport or any kind of ID. Everything is back in the village where we stayed. I won't be able to leave the country or get into the U.S. without proper identification."

Neither of them spoke as he carried her to the Jeep in silence. He stopped at the Jeep and stood there a moment.

"You can put me down now," she said softly.

The Church of San De La Christo
Guatemala City

A huge man wearing a broad-brimmed hat that hid his face in shadow entered the large stone cathedral, closed the heavy wooden door, and waited while he adapted to the darkness. Dusty beams of light streamed through stained-glass windows. The faint orange flicker from a few votive candles reflected from the walls. 'Scar' hated dark confining spaces, and the large church seemed to close in on him. He found it hard to breathe, and small beads of sweat grew on his forehead.

He could make out the tall curved ceiling and heavy beams along narrow aisles that defined the chapel. It seemed as if every icon that hung from the beams stared down at him, passing judgment, condemning him to hell.

Dank alleys had become his home at an early age. With ten other siblings to feed, his parents were unable to care for all of them, and he had been abandoned at the age of four to fend for himself on the streets. His home had consisted of alleys in which stray dogs and other abandoned children competed for the same garbage. He learned early on that violence and brute force were the only means of survival, and the hideous purple scar where his eye had been was testament to that.

His first time in a church many years ago hadn't gone well. At sixteen he had raped a young nun, then savagely beat her when she damned him to hell. He went to church to confess, but when the priest became enraged at the confession, Scar smashed his hand through the lattice wooden panel of the confessional, grabbed the priest and nearly choked him to death with his bare hands.

He paused a moment with the memory still fresh in his mind. That had been a long time ago, and some things had changed since then. Some hadn't. He looked around to make sure he was alone in the church, then moved down the narrow side aisle and slid his bulk into the dark space of a confessional and closed the door.

"It's done," Scar said.

"Are you certain it's taken care of?" a voice on the other side of the confessional asked.

"Yes—well, mostly."

"What do you mean?"

"I found him and made sure he would never talk."

"Wheeler? Are you sure?"

"Yes, I'm sure. He's dead."

"What did you mean by 'mostly' taken care of?" the voice asked.

"The girl got away. His daughter escaped."

"What?" The voice was filled with shock and disbelief. After a considerable silence, it angrily continued. "How did that happen?"

"We were attacked by some villagers. Two of our men were killed and she escaped."

After another long silence, then, "Are you sure he's dead?"

"Between the eyes, dead center."

Another silent pause. Finally, the voice said, "We need take care of the girl also. We have to assume she also knows. Find her and make sure she disappears. We will contact you."

The voice stopped. A door clicked shut. Scar slid his bulk out of the confessional and quickly left the sanctuary, squinting into the sunlight as he opened the door of the church and walked away.

Brett drove them to the El Dorado where he took two rooms for the night. He registered both rooms in his name since Kari had no I.D. He had planned to go to the Ministry of Health to report to Sanchez what he had found and return the Jeep. But at the last minute he changed his mind; he decided he'd keep the Jeep until they could provide him with a helicopter. Besides, it was late in the day and he was tired. The samples were on their way; Sanchez could wait another day.

As he handed a key to Kari, he glanced at the scrubs she was wearing. They did little to hide her figure. "If you try to get on the plane in those clothes," he said, "you're going to start a riot. There are shops right down the street where you can get some clothes," he said. "I need to make a few calls. Meet me here at seven for dinner?"

"Thank you, but I'm kind of tired. I have a long trip tomorrow, assuming I am able to get proper ID so I can buy a ticket and catch a plane. I'm not really hungry. I think I'll just turn in."

"Nothing doing. You haven't eaten in the last two days and you can't wear scrubs. Go buy yourself some clothes, then meet me in the dining room in two hours. We're going to have dinner."

She looked at him for a brief moment, considering her options, then nodded. "Okay," she said, heading toward the front door.

Brett took his packs to his room, then went back downstairs to the lobby to use the phone. He called Quinn's office, but he knew he would only get the answering machine. It was past eight p.m. in Atlanta, and except for those working late in the lab, everyone else at the CDC would be gone. He left a long message, filling Quinn in on everything, and saying he would call again in the morning.

Brett decided to call Sanchez even though he couldn't meet with him in person immediately. He knew he needed to update the minister of health. Unfortunately, he too was gone for the day. Brett left a message detailing what he had found. Now that he'd done everything he reasonably could, he went back up to his room. He took a bath, and put on the last of his fresh clothes.

Scar pulled his large hat low over his face. He walked the busy streets while he surveyed the comings and goings. Then suddenly he thought he spotted who he thought might be her—unbelievably—on the other side of the busy street, weaving through the afternoon crowded sidewalks. She was barefoot and looked shoddily disheveled, and he wasn't sure about the ID. He needed to get closer, but she disappeared into one of the many shops along the street.

He was incredulous that she could be *here* on this sidewalk in Guatemala City. He moved into the shadow of one of the buildings across the street. It provided him with a view of the door to the shop. He couldn't believe his luck. This was going to be easy. They were going to be relieved and pleased with the speed with which he accomplished his assignment.

He ran his tongue over his lips as he thought about having her. There was no reason she should die immediately, and the memory of her lying naked under him back in the jungle made his pulse pound.

He waited with growing impatience when she failed to emerge. Still, he feigned casual interest as he watched people come and go.

As the sun sank lower and the shadows lengthened, he began to have a bad feeling. He knew something had gone terribly wrong. Unable to wait any longer, he crossed the street and looked in the window. No customers. Only the shop keeper remained, and she was closing up for the day.

Had she gone out the back door? Where was she headed? Why would she do that unless she knew she was being followed—but there was no way she could have spotted him.

Damn! His thoughts congealed into a stunned and angry awareness that she'd walked out as a different person, and he'd missed her. It was a clothes shop for god's sake! He stomped away, resolved that she wouldn't get away from him again. She was in the city. He would find her.

Chapter 23

Back at the hotel, Brett took water and food out to Tequila. He was curled up on the backseat of the Jeep now instead of sprawling under the tree where Brett first encountered him. The dog had decided the Jeep was his home now. He thumped his tail on the backseat and stretched his paws as Brett approached.

"Well, we both survived the trip, eh?" Brett said, rubbing Tequila's head. He wondered what would happen to the dog when he and the CDC team headed into the jungle. He should've stuck to his original plan and left the dog in one of the villages where he could find a home.

Brett went back inside to the bar to get a drink and wait for Kari. As usual, it was festive and noisy. A mariachi band was playing, and the drinks were flowing. He slumped down in his chair and sipped his Margarita. The past five days had been hard, and the drink melted some of the tension. Twenty minutes later, he glanced at his watch, starting to worry. She was late. Then he noticed several men turn and look toward the door. He followed their gaze. Kari had arrived.

She had on a black skirt, slit partway up the side, leather sandals, and a traditional red Mayan huipil blouse. A blue sash was tied around her waist. Her freshly washed hair shimmered as she stepped under the lights that hung from the ceiling. He jumped up, hurriedly placed money on the bar's counter, and went into the dining room to meet her.

"You had a successful day shopping, I see," he said looking at her, admiringly.

"Thank you. It felt good to get out of those dirty scrubs. I just bought a few things to hold me until I get home."

They found a table in the corner. He ordered for both of them because he knew she wouldn't order anything substantial on her own.

"Would you like a drink?" he asked.

"I have to get up early. I have a lot to take care of tomorrow if everything goes as planned."

His eyes widened. "You can't leave until you can get replacement documents. That will probably take a several days... or longer, the way things usually work."

"Maybe not. I contacted friends in Chicago. It's possible they can take care of everything from their end. Hopefully they can wire duplicate documents to the American embassy here. Then I can buy a ticket and fly home."

"Great. I'll drive you to the embassy in the morning. Have a glass of wine. It'll help you sleep." He told the waiter to bring a bottle of wine "*pronto*," then filled their glasses as soon as it arrived. He watched her as she sipped the wine.

"I imagine you'll have a lot to do, to take care of... when you get home."

"Yes," she answered and glanced down at her glass. Her eyes started to mist up, then she quickly brushed her eyes with the back of her hand and looked up at him. "Brett... I owe you so much. I'm grateful for all you've gone through to get me here. Her lip quivered as she struggled to continue. "I don't know what I would have done if you hadn't let me come with you. It might have taken weeks... maybe longer to get home."

After they finished their dinner, he walked her back to her room. At her door, they stopped and faced each other.

"Try and get some sleep," he said. "Take a sedative if you need to. I'll wake you in plenty of time in case you have the good fortune to get a plane out of here. Be sure to lock your door."

She looked at him a few seconds. "You're an incredible man, Brett Carson. Take care of yourself." She stood there a moment, then unlocked her door. "Good night," she said as she went inside.

In his room, Brett set the alarm on the clock. He pushed the dresser against the door, then undressed, and climbed into bed. But he didn't fall asleep right away. He knew almost nothing about Kari, but he did know one thing with certainty.

He wasn't ready for her to walk out of his life the following morning.

During the night Brett was startled awake by a knock on his door. He picked up his watch and squinted at it. Three a.m. He went to the door and listened. The door didn't have a peephole, so he couldn't see who was there.

"Who is it?" he asked in a stern voice.

"It's me. Kari."

He shoved his makeshift security system aside and opened the door. She stood in the dimly lit hallway, barefoot and wearing only the large scrub shirt Maria had given her. Her long bare legs below the shirt did not escape his gaze. "Anything wrong?" he asked, glancing up and down the hall.

"I need to go back."

His first thought was she was confused, possibly reacting to one of the medications she was taking. "You *are* going back. First thing this morning, remember?" He tried to sound reassuring.

"No, not to Chicago," she said with certainty, leaving no doubt she wasn't confused. "I just got a call from my friends. Even if I hadn't called so late, they said it wouldn't be possible to clear it for me. I need my passport if I don't want to wait a couple of weeks. And there's something I have to do. I can't leave yet."

What could she possibly have to do? He ran his hand through his hair as he tried to think of a sensitive response. "Even if we could find your father's body..." He didn't want to say that even if they found the location of Wheeler's body, there' would be nothing left but a few bones.

"I'm not going back for my father. I realize we'd never be able to find the place, and I've heard how the jungle devours the dead. I want to go back to the village where my father and I were staying and collect his personal things, including his papers and books. I can't just leave them there. It's important to me to get them. I would feel like I'm abandoning him if I just leave them. And I can also retrieve my passport and visa papers."

"Can't you just contact the American embassy here?"

"The embassy said it would take them a week or more to get duplicate documents. I don't want to wait that long. Also, I need to get some of his things," she said softly.

Brett didn't know what to say.

"Take me with you when you go back," she persisted.

"Kari, I wish I could help, but there's no way I could take you anywhere right now. I've contacted the CDC, and in a day or two a team will be arriving from Atlanta. Once they're here, I'm going to be completely tied up working with them."

She looked down at her feet and frowned as she thought about what he'd said.

"There must be some other way for you to get there," he said.

She looked up at him and shook her head. "No, there isn't. I've been told the railroad tracks and roads were washed out by the storm. No buses, no trains. Besides, a bus wouldn't do me any good. The village where we stayed is too far off the route for me. I'd still have another thirty miles of jungle to travel. I'd need a horse, which of course I don't have."

The last thing he wanted was to have to say no to her, but there was simply nothing he could do.

"Just take me there and bring me back, then I'll be out of your hair for good," she persisted.

"Kari, why don't you just wait a week while the embassy here arranges for a new passport, and then go back to Chicago? After you take care of your affairs there, you could come back down in a couple of weeks. Maybe I'll be able to help you then."

he nodded slowly, as if considering what he said. "Sorry I woke you," she said softly. "Good night."

He watched her walk away and started to say something, but

she turned down a corridor and was gone; he was left staring at an empty hall.

"Damn," he said under his breath. He closed the door. When he crawled back into bed, he felt lonelier than he had ever remembered feeling in his life.

Chapter 24

The next morning the alarm clock went off at five a.m. Brett had set it when he thought he was taking Kari to the airport, and he had forgotten to turn it off. He rolled over and fell asleep again. At 9:30 he finally woke up, shaved, dressed and went down for breakfast.

He felt like hell. The past five days had been harder than the entire five months in Alaska had been. And he hadn't even started the real work in the jungle yet.

The waitress brought him coffee, and he was taking his first sip when three men dressed in military uniforms walked up to his table. He recognized the uniforms of the infamous *Policía del Secreto del Departamento.*

"Doctor Carson? I am Colonel Zolog, head of the Secret Police Section of the Guatemalan government. I need to ask you a few questions." None of the men made a move to sit down but rather remained standing close to Brett.

Zolog was an imposing figure, and his demeanor made it clear that this was not a friendly visit.

"What can I do for you?" Brett asked hesitantly.

"We are looking for Miss Kari Wheeler," Zolog continued, "and we thought you might be able to help us locate her."

Brett's mind scrambled to try and figure out what was going on. What was this all about? Was this concerning Kari and her father's murder, or about the epidemic? Or something else? Of even more concern to him was how they could have known he had been with her. How much had he told Sanchez? Had he been followed? They couldn't have contacted Crenshaw at the clinic because the phone lines were still down.

Or had Zolog visited the clinic? Had he and his men been the group riding on horseback in the jungle? Brett realized he had waited too long before answering the Colonel.

"Can you tell me where we could find her?" Zolog repeated, his voice becoming impatient. "It is extremely important that we talk to her."

"I have no idea where she might be. We met once at a clinic," Brett continued. "Her father was murdered just a few days ago, and she was brutally attacked." The men stared at him in silence. Zolog's composure sent chills down his spine. Brett cleared his throat and asked, "Is this about her father's murder?"

Zolog gave him a stern look before answering. "As I said, we need to talk to her. I urge you to contact us immediately if she gets in touch with you."

Whatever these men wanted, it seemed serious. Brett tried to sound natural as he tiptoed around their questions. "Because of what happened to her father, she wanted to get back to Chicago as soon as possible. She may have already left the country."

Zolog raised his eyebrows. "I do not believe so. I think she is still in Guatemala."

"May I ask how you knew I'd even met her?" Brett asked. His mind was racing. What he really wanted to know was why were they looking for her. Was she in danger, or were they here to help her? Somehow, he didn't think so.

Zolog's face turned red and his eyes narrowed. "That is not important. What is important is that we need to talk to her." Then he dropped a card on the table with the embossed emblem of the *Policia Secreto* and his phone number. "I want to remind you that it is a serious offense to harbor a material witness or withhold information from the police."

"Material witness? Is Kari a suspect? What crime is she suspected of?"

"I didn't say she was. As I said, we just need to talk to her. It would be dangerous for you if you were to withhold any information from us. Call me if you see her," Zolog said. Then they turned and left.

Brett sat there stunned. It seemed apparent that they were not there to investigate Wheeler's murder. Rather, they were on a hunt, and Kari was the prey. Why did they want to find her? What did they need to talk to her about? He breathed a sigh of relief when he realized they didn't know she had been staying at the hotel because he had put both rooms in his name when he signed in.

A quick check at front desk would not have turned up her name. He realized how lucky he and Kari were that they hadn't been more diligent. He stuck Zolog's card in his pocket, pushed his plate aside, and downed his coffee.

What *had* happened to Kari? She had no way of getting back

to the village in the jungle. Had she taken his advice and gone to the embassy? If she was still in the city, he had to find her and warn her.

He sat a few minutes looking around the dining area but spotted nothing out of the ordinary. If anyone was tailing him, he couldn't tell. He went upstairs to Kari's room and knocked, but there was no answer. He pounded loudly. She obviously wasn't in her room. He went back to the lobby and called Quinn.

His secretary answered. "He's been expecting your call, Dr. Carson. I'll put you through."

The response he got from Quinn wasn't what he'd expected.

"Brett, I got your message. What the hell are you doing down there?" Quinn asked. "The government says you threatened them, stole a Jeep, and tried to close down a clinic. I'm assuming none of that is true, is it?"

"Actually, it's all true, Mitch. But it's not as bad as they make it sound," Brett snapped back.

He explained to Quinn what had happened to him over the past few days. Hell yes, the facts on the surface were accurate, but the intent of what actually happened was certainly lost. He hadn't actually stolen a Jeep; he'd just left a drunken Sergeant Perez behind to sleep off a night of tequila. He hadn't threatened the government—he'd just told them their options. Brett couldn't imagine what Quinn would have said if he'd known about his recent visit from Colonel Zolog, head of the Secret Police.

"Brett, for once try to stay under the radar. It makes my job here a hell of a lot easier. Thank god at least you're still alive. So, what have you found out so far?"

"I'm back in Guatemala City. I shipped blood and tissue

samples to you yesterday. They should be there sometime today. Be very careful with the samples. It's worse than we thought."

"Tell me."

"I went to Lepudro and talked to Dr. Crenshaw, the guy who first reported this to the Guatemalan government. According to him, he's seen at least a dozen cases at the clinic where he works. When I was there, we did a limited autopsy on one of the victims. That's where I got the blood, fluid, and tissue samples that I'm sending you."

"You say you did an autopsy?" Quinn asked. "You never do anything halfway, do you? Well—what'd you find?"

Brett described what he had found, then said, "I think this could be one of the hemorrhagic viruses. It looked very similar to what we saw in Zaire, and I suspect it kills as quickly or even quicker than Ebola."

"Marburg!" Quinn said.

"Just what I was thinking," Brett said. "Or one of its nasty close relatives."

"Damn. So that means we really have a hell of a mess on our hands."

"Yep. It's strictly maximum-containment stuff. Get someone from Bio-Four to meet the FedEx and keep the package under tight seal until it's safely inside Bio-Four lab. Then have the lab run serum titers on the blood samples. We might get lucky and get a quick answer."

"At least a dozen cases at one clinic," Quinn said. "Any idea how widespread the disease is? Do you think it's already gotten away from them and it's already out of control?"

"I don't know," Brett said, "but that's the first thing we have to figure out. At least four other clinics have reported cases. And the two hospitals in Guatemala City have several cases. Mostly men, but a half dozen or so women have died. You have to send a team down here. I'm going to need a lot of help."

"Brett, we're stretched to the limit back here. There's been a new salmonella outbreak in California involving a fast food chain. There's a new strain of virulent TB in a New York prison— probably came from Turkey. And the equine encephalitis in New England I mentioned to you before. Now this."

Yeah, now this, Brett thought.

Quinn continued. "I'll try and get a small team down there, possibly as early as tomorrow afternoon. In the meantime, what about having the Guatemalan officials set up quarantines and road blocks so we can contain this?"

"I'll talk to them. And what about getting us a helicopter?" Brett asked.

"Not good. Neither the military nor the State Department wants any kind of a presence in Guatemala right now. The Red Cross is hedging. The Mexican government might be willing to send a chopper. They have a stake in getting the epidemic stopped before it crosses its border."

"How soon can we get it?"

"I said they *might* be willing to help. When we get something more definite on the epidemic, they'll probably be more receptive to actually doing something."

"Well, keep working on them. We're going to need shortwave radios for the team. It'll be almost impossible to communicate with each other in the jungle. The storm has taken out phone lines, and there are large areas are completely isolated."

"Anything else?"

"Yeah. Send the usual field supplies—and lots of latex gloves, masks and disposable gowns. And plenty of bottles of phenol for sterilizing. We going to need full isolation gear."

"No problem. That it?"

"I want Solt down here with me."

"I told you before, he's tied up with the new strain of equine encephalitis virus on the East Coast."

"Screw the equine virus. This is a hot one. It's going to be a hell of a mess down here, and I need him."

"Call me tomorrow," Quinn said. "I'll have more information on the team's arrival time and flight information."

Brett let out a deep breath, ran his fingers through his unruly hair, then called Sanchez.

"Good morning, Dr. Carson. "I received your message." There was a pause, and Sanchez added, "I understand you've been a busy man."

Brett was about to ask him what he meant by that and whether it had anything to do with Zolog, but decided to drop it. "I've got new information since my visit to the clinic in Lepudro," Brett explained. "I was just on the phone with the CDC in Atlanta. I'm afraid this new outbreak is something serious, and we have to move quickly on it. The CDC will be sending an entire team down tomorrow. And we're going to need your full support." Brett went on to tell Sanchez what he would need before the team arrived.

"Of course," Sanchez said. "I'll have a room here at the Ministry of Health set up for you to use as your headquarters while you are here," Sanchez said. "I've arranged for five doctors from my department to be part of your team while you are down here. They will help you any way they can."

"Thank you. Now, what about a helicopter? We'll need

transportation for the team."

"We are still checking. Maybe we will have more information for you this afternoon." The words rolled out slowly and deliberately from the phone. Brett could picture a dark cigarette bouncing to the words.

Brett continued. "In the meantime, I have to keep the Jeep. You've one hell of a medical problem on your hands, and you'd better let other officials know about it. Maybe they can figure a way to get us a helicopter."

"Where's Sergeant Perez?" Sanchez asked, ignoring the comment about a helicopter.

"Sergeant Perez got sick and had a fever," Brett lied to cover for both of them. "I had to leave him in one of the villages." He hoped that would clear Perez of any military discipline and get himself off the hook for abandoning the sergeant and stealing the Jeep.

Then Brett told Sanchez about Professor Wheeler's murder and the attack on his daughter.

"Where did that happen?" Sanchez asked.

"About thirty miles or so from Lepudro. Some villagers who were hunting brought his daughter to the clinic after the attack."

"What were they doing in the jungle?"

"Apparently digging for Mayan artifacts," Brett said. "He was an archeologist."

Sanchez was quiet for a moment, then spoke. "You must be wrong about that," he said, the words rolling out slowly again. "That area is strictly off limits. Everybody knows it is illegal to dig anywhere except at government-approved areas, and then only under strict supervision so that nothing is plundered from our country for personal wealth."

Brett was sure of the location. Sanchez must be wrong.

"I will talk to you tomorrow, Dr. Carson."

"A man named Zolog came to my hotel this morning to ask me some questions."

"Colonel Zolog?" The fear in Sanchez's voice was evident. "What did the *Policia Secreto* want with you? Questions about what?"

"He wanted to know if I knew where they could find Wheeler's daughter."

"I have no idea why Colonel Zolog would have any interest at all in you or the epidemic. I'll talk to you tomorrow."

Chapter 25

Kari showered, dressed in the new clothes she'd bought, and left the El Dorado early that morning. Brett wouldn't be able to help her return to San Angelica to get her father's things, and she wanted to leave this stinking country as soon as possible; she didn't want to wait around until she could get a new passport and papers from the U.S. embassy.

During the night she had come up with another plan. Her father had a friend in Guatemala City, and he might be able to help her. He knew his way around the country and around local government regulations; he might be able to help speed things up.

She decided to walk to his home rather than take a taxi because she would need every bit of the money Brett had given her. She stopped on the street to buy a cup of coffee and fried batter filled with spiced apple, then continued walking toward a residential section near the university.

As much as she tried not to, her thoughts kept turning to Brett Carson. He was different from any other man she had ever met. Most men were attracted to her and did everything they could to show it. She wasn't even sure Brett knew she was a woman. He was brilliant and seemed capable of handling every situation, but he was a driven man.

Still, she couldn't deny it; he was the most intriguing man she had ever met. When she watched him from the church balcony playing the guitar, wearing only jeans and no shirt, she had been completely caught off guard. There was a definite raw male magnetism about him. Most of the smart men she knew tended to be geeks. Nice enough people, but geeks, nonetheless.

Brett Carson was anything but a geek. She let out a deep breath and kept walking.

An hour later she came to a modest white stucco house with a red tiled roof. She knocked on the door and was greeted by an elderly man who looked surprised, then grabbed her in his arms and hugged her.

"Kari. What are you doing here? Come in, come in." Phillip Keiser led her into the living room, which was decorated in Spanish traditional furnishings. An archway from the hall opened into the living room. The couch was a soft, well-worn brown leather; two chairs were made of mesquite wood. A straw woven matt covered the clay-tiled floor. Sunlight from tall, paneled windows spilled across the room. He then noticed her cut lip and bruised face. "What happened? Did you fall or have an accident?"

She shook her head and looked down.

He guided her to the couch. "Sit down. You look tired and hot. Where is Forrest? You didn't leave him all alone in the jungle, did you?" Phillip Keiser was a retired professor of archeology. He worked for the Guatemalan government now as consultant for their national museum of Mayan artifacts and historical documents. He and her father had been friends for many years, and he had known Kari since she was a small child.

Kari was silent for a moment, not knowing how to respond. She hesitated and her eyes teared up. He obviously had not heard about what had happened to them in the jungle.

"Kari, what is it? Did something happen?" Keiser asked, holding her out at arms-length.

Kari nodded, then sat down. She looked at him, and her bottom lip quivered as she spoke. "My father was murdered two"—she put her hand to her head and squinted—"no, three days ago."

"What? Oh my god!" Keiser sat down and put his arm around her shoulder. "What happened?"

"We were ambushed by the men in our group. My dad was murdered and then they... roughed me up." Her eyes had a frightened look and she started to shake uncontrollably.

Keiser sat with his mouth open, trying to comprehend what he'd just heard. He put his hand on his forehead. "My god, I can't believe it. Do the police know? Is there anything I can do for you? Do you need a place to stay?"

"I need your help. All I have now are the clothes I'm wearing and a small amount of cash. I don't have any I.D. or my passport, and I need to get home, back to Chicago. Can you help me?"

"I'll make some calls and see what I can do. And we should call the police." Keiser stood and walked to the phone.

"Wait—I don't really want the police involved," Kari said. "You know how it is down here with the government. Things could get complicated. It wouldn't solve anything. I just want to go home. Is there anybody you can call discreetly?"

Keiser nodded, still shocked and heartbroken by everything

he was she had told him. After a moment of silence while he tried to fathom what he'd just heard, he asked, "Kari, would you like something to drink or eat while I'm making a few calls?"

"Thank you, some water please."

Keiser left the room briefly and returned with a glass and a pitcher of ice water. "I know someone who might be able to pull strings without drawing attention. I'll call him." Keiser put his hand on her shoulder, then left to use the phone.

Kari was hot and thirsty from her long walk. She gulped down a large glass of cold water and wiped her mouth with the back of her hand. She could hear Phillip's voice in the other room but couldn't make out what was being said. Everything was still unreal to her. A week ago, she and father were dining at the hotel. Suddenly, her world had changed forever. She was trapped in a foreign country, had no way of getting home, and for the first time ever, she was alone.

Keiser returned and sat down. "He suggested you call the American embassy here. They would be your best chance, but I'm afraid even that will take some time. He doesn't think there's much he can do, but he will do some checking. He'll call me back this afternoon."

Kari nodded and forced a smile. "Phillip, thank you for your help."

"You looked totally beat. Would you like to go upstairs and take a nap? Then I'll fix us lunch a little later."

"I should go to the embassy and see what they can do in case your friend doesn't have any luck."

"That's a good idea. But why don't you call them first instead of going all the way across town? It might take a few days, even if you go through the proper channels at the embassy."

"I'll do that," she said standing.

"You can use the phone in my study," he said. "Follow me."

Phillip walked her to his study. She sat at the desk while he found the phone number for her. Then he left the room. She looked at the phone for several moments before picking it up. She didn't want to call the embassy, but it appeared she was out of options.

Brett had the rest of the day to kill. He was restless and anxious to get moving. He'd been in Guatemala a week, and he'd only managed to collect samples from one dead man. If this was a serious disease, and he no longer had any doubt that it was, it could rapidly spread beyond control.

He was more than a little worried about Kari. The registration clerk told him there were no messages for him. Without proper papers, she couldn't have flown to Chicago, but where had she gone? Did she have friends here in Guatemala City? Had she found some kind of transportation back into the jungle? Did she know Zolog and the Secret Police were looking for her? Or worse yet—had Zolog already found her?

Something Sanchez had said bothered him, and he was going to try to find some answers. It might also provide answers regarding Zolog's interest in finding Kari. Brett asked directions to the government offices of Tourism and Archeology, then with Tequila in the back of the Jeep, drove to the center of town. Soldiers there looked at him with a great deal of mistrust as he pulled up in the military Jeep and climbed out. Obviously he wasn't a soldier, but they didn't know what to make of him or his intentions.

Guards approached as Brett started to enter the large brick building. He showed them his passport. They carefully scrutinized his passport and CDC identification, they motioned him to continue. With all the guards and security, Brett thought the place seemed more like a fort than a government office.

Once inside, he looked at a list of all the offices, then found the one he wanted. On the second floor, he walked into a large atrium and approached the counter. A man in military uniform sporting a cluster of service ribbons greeted him at the Archaeology Licensing and Permits office. He was the opposite of Sergeant Pere with his pressed uniform a perfect fit, his hair greased into place, his dark mustache trimmed to perfection. In short, he was pure military.

"May I help you senor?" the man asked.

"I would like some information about Mayan tombs and archeological excavation."

"You can get information at a library. Do you wish to purchase a permit?"

"How would I go about doing that?" Brett asked.

"You have to fill out papers, and they have to be approved. That takes usually two to three weeks to complete. The cost is five thousand Quetzals." He pulled out a packet of papers and slid them across the desk to Brett. "What region are you specifically interested in exploring?"

"Does that matter? Are the permits issued only for a particular region, or will I be allowed to explore anywhere?"

The look on the man's face told him the answer. "If you are

approved, you must limit your exploration of tombs to a very specified area and under strict supervision. If you are caught digging in any area not specified in your permit, the penalty is quite severe."

"What is the penalty?"

"Digging in an unapproved region is twenty years in prison. The penalty is far more severe for possession of artifacts of antiquity from unapproved areas." He pushed a large geological map toward Brett. "What area are you interested in exploring?"

Brett pointed to the general area where he thought Wheeler had been exploring. "Somewhere in this area."

"That is in the heart of El Peten. That is strictly off limits for any kind of excavation," he said, staring sternly at Brett. "There are no permits issued within a hundred miles of that."

"What are those three areas marked in red?"

"It is thought those areas might be the sites of one or more ancient Mayan cities, and possibly the palace of one of the most important Mayan rulers. Excavating anywhere within the areas is completely forbidden."

That revelation stunned Brett. He thanked the officer, took the papers and left. Had he been mistaken about the region where Wheeler had been murdered? Or had Wheeler actually been exploring in a restricted area? Had Wheeler been involved in taking illegal artifacts? Maybe that was why he seemed so ill at ease when Brett met him.

Brett wondered if Kari knew what her father had been doing. If she was caught and implicated, she could spend the rest of her life rotting in a stinking prison. Was that why Zolog was looking for her? Even so, why would the loss of a few ancient artifacts bring out the head of the secret police? If the penalty for possession of artifacts was much more severe than twenty years in prison, what could that be? Brett couldn't believe Wheeler would have put his daughter at such risk. There had to be a mistake. Brett left the building with even more questions than he went in with.

He then drove to the library two blocks away. Row upon row of dusty books filled the huge spacious room. As far as he could tell, there were no more than two or three other people in the place. After searching for twenty minutes, he selected three books which were in English, took them to a desk, and began to read. He scribbled several pages of notes, then left.

Tequila greeted him with a wagging tail when he returned to the Jeep. "You're right, boy," Brett said, rubbing his dog's head. "Let's get the hell out of here."

With reluctance, Kari called the United States embassy and explained her predicament.

"What you've described shouldn't be a big problem," the man on the other end said. "This happens occasionally. We can call the University of Chicago and a relative to confirm what you've told us. They can fax us necessary identification information, then we can give you a temporary visa that will get you back into the United States."

"Thank you," Kari sighed.

"You'll have to come in to sign papers allowing us to get personal documents from your place of employment, bank, and so forth."

"I'll be right over."

"We close in twenty minutes. Come in first thing tomorrow, and I'll see what we can do to get things started for you. You realize we will have to contact the local authorities to tell them about your special circumstances in order to get them to forgo the usual restrictions and rules about your leaving. Strictly a formality," he assured her.

"Thank you, again" she said softly. "I'll see you first thing tomorrow morning."

Keiser was standing in the doorway and heard her final comments. "Looks like you're staying the night. Go have a nice warm bath and catch a nap while I figure out what to cook for dinner. There's a clean bedroom that is yours."

Kari smiled and nodded, trying to hide her disappointment. "Thank you, Phillip. I'll take you up on your offer for tonight." Then she left to take a much-welcomed bath and a nap. She would have dinner with Phillip, get a good night's sleep, then worry about the embassy in the morning.

Back at the hotel, Brett pulled out the notes he'd made while he was in the library. The evidence did in fact suggest that the restricted areas deep in El Peten were possibly the site of one or more ancient cities and probably also hid some of the richest long-forgotten tombs containing rare artifacts.

The problem was, the restricted areas were also where most of the deaths from the disease were reported. Was there a connection? If so, what was it? As usual, more questions than answers.

His mind turned to Wheeler, and he began to worry about Kari in earnest. Something had been bothering him the past two days, and it was becoming more bothersome the more he thought about it. What if Wheeler's murder wasn't a random act by thugs but rather a well-planned hit? A cold-blooded murder? And if so, why?

Then, a horrible thought occurred to him: had they also intended to kill Kari?

After feeding Tequila, Brett washed, had dinner and fell into bed. He was exhausted, worried, and knew he faced big problems ahead. Tomorrow was going to be a long, hard day.

But what day in Guatemala hadn't been?

Chapter 26

CDC Headquarters
Atlanta

M itch Quinn headed across the CDC campus to the Biological
Safety Level-Four Maximum Containment Laboratory, the
maximum security building known simply as "Bio-Four." A stiff
wind blew, thunder echoed in the distance, and dark, angry clouds
threatened, but Quinn didn't notice. His mind was on other things
during the short walk from his office in C-Building.

Bio-Four was unique among the buildings on the CDC
campus. There were no windows above the first floor. Large air
filters on the roof hummed constantly as heat from flame burners
poured out of vents.

The maximum containment lab held the world's most
dangerous infectious agents. It was the best equipped and most
sophisticated laboratory of the CDC. Bio-Four was a place of
deadly warfare, with locked doors and sophisticated security at
every entry. To enter Bio-Four was to pass into another world,
requiring phenol chemical showers, then squeezing into full-body

airtight PPPS hazmat suits—'positive pressure personnel suits.' The suits were then hooked to air hoses so that workers breathed reverse air that had been passed through flame burners and then triple filtered. The purest air on the planet. Nothing contagious went in that wasn't intended, and nothing came out.

The samples of blood, tissue, and body fluids that Brett had shipped from Guatemala were being tested and cultured in Bio-Four. After showing his ID and passing through security, which included a series of three metal doors requiring codes to enter, Quinn went to the third floor, took a phenol shower, changed into one of the blue total containment suits, attached a purified air hose to his suit, then entered through another locked door. After going through an airtight passage, he arrived at the main laboratory in maximum containment.

Locked freezers along one wall held the deadliest known organisms, including Ebola, Marburg, Hanta, smallpox, anthrax, SARS, multiple influenza viruses and dozens of others, including the recently identified A9-CN from Alaska.

Armed guards outside Maximum Containment, security checks, and locked entries on the main floor were in place to prevent the threat of terrorists stealing any of the live viruses. If that happened, the risk to a city or country could be more devastating than a hydrogen bomb. The locked freezers were also fireproof vaults that could withstand the intense heat of a fire or the force of a massive explosion.

"What have you got, Jan?" Quinn asked.

Dr. Janet Boggs looked indistinguishable from the twelve other scientists working in the max-contain lab of Bio-Four—blue space suit, air hose, Plexiglas face window, and special surgical gloves to allow movement with fine instruments. Janet Boggs, who had both a doctorate in microbiology and a medical degree and was board-certified in infectious diseases, was the most experienced and knowledgeable scientist in max-contain of Bio-Four.

She spent every working day in a containment suit, with only a thin layer separating her from certain death if the barrier was accidentally broken. Boggs was the go-to person for answers.

"Morning, Mitch. Well, since we've only had the samples for four hours, we obviously haven't learned much," she said with a hint of *how-stupid-a-question-is-that* in her voice.

"However, I think we can probably exclude bacteria as the causative agent. I did gram stains on some of the samples, all of which were negative, except this." She held up a test tube of darkish fluid. "This fluid from the chest cavity is growing Klebsiella, but my guess is that was a terminal event and not the cause. We have cultures cooking, so we'll probably be able to rule out bacteria for certain by tomorrow. We're making tissue cultures from the samples, and I'm just about to inject a solution containing portions of the samples into mice. If it's a virus, we'll know soon enough."

Quinn looked at her through his sealed Plexiglas face guard. He could only see her eyes, but the telltale squint of her eyes told him she was smiling. Boggs was steady, dependable, and never seemed bothered by the strange world of max-containment in which she lived. "Brett mentioned something about an odor of mildew," Quinn said. "Let's culture for fungus."

"We'll do that next," she said. "But tell me, when have you ever seen a fungus do what Brett described in the autopsy?" she asked.

"Never."

"I didn't think so. Cultures, sero-typing, protein substrates,

ELISA and DNAs are all being set up. Call me tomorrow. Who knows? Maybe we'll get lucky."

The Enzyme-Linked Immunosorbent Assay—known as ELISA—would test for traces of antigens or antibodies. Both of them knew it could take weeks to grow, isolate, and then identify a virus. A lot of luck was what they needed.

"Be careful, Jan."

"Of what, the boogeyman?"

When he finally completed the standard exit procedures, which included another phenol shower with the sealed suit on, followed by a standard shower, he dressed and left Bio-Four. He was glad to be out of there. To Quinn, max-containment was a world of another dimension, a world he was not comfortable in. He had the greatest trust and respect for Janet Boggs, but he would never understand how she and the other researchers could spend every working day in Bio-Four.

Zolog was a man running out of time. His future depended on finding the girl. She had to know something. And he would find out what it was. He wouldn't allow himself to think what would happen if she knew nothing. He couldn't afford to lose favor with the President at this critical stage. He had an idea that just might work. He crushed out his cigarette, stormed out and slammed the door of his office.

In addition to posting guards at both the train station and the airport, he had the entire block around the United States embassy under constant surveillance. Zolog's men were out of sight but stationed strategically so they could monitor everyone near the American embassy.

By international law, they were not authorized to detain or stop anyone from going into the compound, but Zolog didn't give a damn about international law. These were different times, requiring different rules. This was *his* country. They were at war. He could not allow the American woman to escape his grasp again.

His men were looking for a dark-haired, attractive young American woman, but since she might be wearing a disguise, every person within a block of the American Embassy would be stopped and questioned.

They would be ready.

The following day, a four-engine LC-111 from Mexico City touched down at the airport in Guatemala City just before noon. Tires met the blistering cement runway with the tortured screech of burnt rubber and blue smoke, and the plane taxied to the terminal. Brett greeted the team at the gate and broke into a broad smile when he spotted a ruddy-faced, gray-haired man with a beard, piercing green eyes, and an unlit pipe jammed into his mouth.

Ross Solt was the last of the team off the plane. Life moved at his pace, not the other way around. Solt believed most people were salmon—they always swam upstream against the current. He preferred to go with the flow, "drifting downstream'" with least resistance his motto. He believed you never had to chase problems. They always had a way of finding you. No reason to rush it.

"Ross, what a great surprise. What the hell are you doing here?" Brett slapped him on the back. "What about that equine encephalitis?"

Ross grinned at Brett. "Quinn finally decided the epidemic down here is more important than a little encephalitis. I missed the last party in Alaska, and I didn't want to miss another." Then he lit his pipe and blew fragrant cherry-blend clouds into the air. "Besides, you need me down here to take care of you."

The other four team members gathered around and chatted with Brett. Most of them had been together on other assignments at one time or another. The other members were Julie Thaxton, epidemologist; Peter Jacek, virologist; 'Doogie' Doyle, a red-haired Irish entomologist; and Robyn Shermis, bacteriologist. Solt and Brett were the two medical doctors and EIS agents on the team. The six made up an epidemiological SWAT team. They would explore every possibility in their relentless search for answers.

After unloading crates of equipment, the group went to the El Dorado where Sanchez had reserved rooms for them. They had lunch then headed to the Ministry of Health building, where Brett had arranged for a conference room to function as a "war room" for them to be able to plan their strategy. Five doctors from the Guatemalan health ministry joined them, and introductions were made all around.

"So, Brett, fill us in. What do we have so far?" Solt asked as he poured cups of dark coffee for everyone.

"Practically nothing yet," Brett admitted. He went on to tell them about his trip to see Dr. Crenshaw, the person with the World Health Organization who first reported the epidemic. "I examined one of the victims just before he died. I did a quick very limited autopsy on him and sent blood and tissue samples back to Bio-Four. There have been over ninety-five cases in the country reported in total. Only eight of the cases were in women."

"Well, 'Quincy', what did you learn from the autopsy?" Solt asked. The group laughed.

"The abdominal organs were becoming gelatinous. There was considerable hemorrhage and dark fluid in the abdominal and chest cavities. There was a distinct smell of mildew. My guess is that it's one of the hemorrhagic viruses. Extremely unlikely to be Ebola, more likely to be Marburg, but of course we haven't ruled out bacteria yet."

When he stopped, all laughter had long faded, and the room was silent for a moment. Then he added, "Nobody has survived more than twenty-four hours after the onset of symptoms."

Solt let out a whistle of concern. "Jesus, Brett, anything else you can think of that can make it worse?"

"Yeah, actually there *is* something else. The tropical storm you read about has devastated the southern half of the country," Brett continued. "None of the trains are running because large sections of tracks are gone. Bridges and roads have been washed away. We don't have access to a helicopter, so we'll have to do most of our traveling in Jeeps or trucks. That's going to make our job almost impossible."

Peter Jacek, known as "PJ" to his friends, was the oldest member of the team. He had been appointed by Quinn to oversee the operation of the team. Jacek would handle all the details and support of the assignment such as meals, travel, communications, and supplies. As EIS agents, Brett and Ross had more important things to do than to make sure food and water were available to the team, or to see that samples got shipped out.

"Brett, you've been here a week. Any suggestions on how we proceed from here?" Jacek asked.

Brett stood up and went to the front of the room. "In fact, I do. We don't have concrete proof of anything yet, but I do have some ideas. I don't think this disease is spread person-to-person. Otherwise, we'd have entire villages dead by this time, but that hasn't happened. It's probably a virus, it's obviously extremely virulent, but with low contagiosity. It's probably not the Hanta virus, it but acts like it, except much more deadly. In other words, we're not likely to come into contact with the organism, but if we do, it's fatal. We still have to prove that, but I'm almost certain that's the case."

"Those are big assumptions, Brett," Solt said. "Anything to support that?"

Brett tacked a large map of Guatemala on the wall. "There have been no big population outbreaks, just sporadic cases that seem to be occurring with greater frequency, and all the cases seem to have no connection with each other. There have been two clusters in these villages in the jungle—Lepudro and Del Norte. More of the cases came from scattered clinics up here in the northern mountainous region. As far as I know, nobody who has come into contact with infected victims ever got the disease. Crenshaw and his nurse at the clinic saw more than thirteen cases, but neither of them has contacted the disease."

"You're saying we're dealing with a vector?" Solt asked.

"That's exactly what I'm saying. I think the virus is carried by a vector. People get infected when they come into contact with the vector. If I'm right, finding the vector is going to be the key to identifying it and ultimately stopping it. Now, the million-dollar question is—what is the vector?"

"That's a big jump to make," Jacek said. "We don't even know what *it* is. You must have something more to go on other than just conjecture."

"As I mentioned earlier, so far there have been no cases reported in children. Mostly in men, only a few women." Brett pointed to the map. "All reported cases are roughly in these three areas."

Everyone leaned forward with interest. "Why those areas? What do they have in common?" Solt asked. He lit his pipe and began blowing puffs of smoke.

"That's what I'd like to know," Brett said. "Nothing, as far as I can figure out yet. Could be it's just a random grouping because of population areas. But I think there *is* a connection, and that's what we have to find out."

"Anything else?" Jacek asked.

"That's it. Gram stains are negative, so it's probably not a bacteria, but cultures are pending. As you know, some of these may take a few weeks."

Someone came in and handed a fax to Solt. "Just in from Bio-Four," Ross said, reading the fax. "Gram stains negative, as Brett already mentioned. Serology survey negative. It's almost certainly not Marburg. They did ELISA tests on the protein, but got zilch. No match. Electron microscopy also negative. They say it's possible none of the organisms survived the shipping of the samples."

Everyone knew that the lack of answers at such an early

stage didn't mean much. It had taken them more than six weeks to confirm the Hanta virus during the 'Four-Corners' outbreak near Mesa Verde that killed eighteen people. And it had taken more than five months to isolate the new A9-CN virus in Alaska. Legionnaires disease took over a year. And HIV had taken years to figure out. Occasionally they got lucky during the early initial screening, but usually not.

"So, what do we do now?" Jacek asked.

"Hopefully, examine victims before they die and get blood and throat cultures on them," Brett replied. "Then we try and find the vector. We ask them about every minute detail of their last few days before they got sick. We culture everything in sight—water, food, pets, livestock, sewage. And we start trapping rodents, birds, insects... everything that crawls, walks, or flies. It could be something as simple as mouse turds like the Hanta outbreak, or as tiny as mosquito spit. In the meantime, we can hope Bio-Four comes up with something."

"What about quarantines and roadblocks?" Jacek asked. "Shouldn't we at least try and contain the damned thing until we figure out what it is?"

"Like I said, I think there's more than a reasonable chance it's not spread from human to human. Roadblocks and quarantine would have done nothing to stop the Hanta outbreak. I'm almost certain we're looking for a vector. Mouse turds, mosquitoes, birds—could be anything."

"Almost certain? And what if you're wrong?" Jacek persisted. The room was silent.

"First, what I've found so far says that I'm right. Second, the Guatemalan government is strained to the max. They are in the middle of a civil war with rebels and still digging out from a very destructive tropical storm. Roadblocks would be currently out of the question. Our biggest problem at the moment is transportation. Quinn has contacted the Red Cross, the World Health Organization, and our own State Department for helicopters. The Guatemalans have refused to provide us with one."

"That's not entirely true," a voice from the back of the room corrected him. "It's not that we refused your request. The fact is, we don't have one available for you."

"Let me introduce Dr. Manuel Sanchez, the Minister of Health," Brett said. Everyone turned to look at the tall, stoop-shouldered man.

"First, I would like to welcome you to our country," Sanchez said as he lumbered to the front of the room. "Let me extend our gratitude to the United States for its quick response. My government will do everything it can to assist you. We are putting together the necessary supplies and providing trucks to get you where you need to go."

"I think we should split up into three teams, and each cover one of the three circled areas thoroughly," Brett said. "We'll cover more area and have a much better chance of turning up something."

"I disagree. I don't think we should split up," Jacek said. "We should stay together until we figure out what the hell we're working with. With this civil war going on, it could be too dangerous to split up."

"I don't agree," Brett argued. "We'll just be stumbling over each other. And we need to visit as many villages in these regions as possible to find out the extent of the disease."

"Ordinarily, I would agree with you, Brett, but Peter's right,"

Solt said. "It's probably too dangerous to split up at first. We don't want to get caught in a cross fire or become hostages of the rebels. And you yourself said that transportation is a big issue. Why add to our problems by spreading ourselves out miles away from each other?"

"I'm afraid I too have to agree with them, Brett," Julie Thaxton said. "You're single, but most of us have families. Staying together seems the only rational thing to do for now."

Sanchez pushed a black cigarette into his mouth and lit it. "We will provide military escort for you to ensure your safety while you are here. You will have nothing to worry about."

Bullshit, thought Brett. *Nothing to worry about?*

Chapter 27

After saying goodbye to Phillip the next morning, Kari started her long walk to the embassy. After two hours, she finally spotted the Stars and Stripes flying in front it two blocks ahead of her. The late morning heat was stifling, and she welcomed the shade of the few trees along the street. Her feet were sore and her blouse was damp with sweat.

As she paused in the shadow of the trees, two men jumped out of a hidden doorway and grabbed a woman walking ahead of her. The woman immediately began struggling and yelling. Before Kari could act, a car screeched to a halt beside them, a door flew open, and the woman was shoved in. Then the car sped off.

Kari froze. She started to tremble as memories came flooding back. She hadn't spotted the two men before they leaped out of the shadows and grabbed their victim. Where had they gone? She froze in fear as she looked around. A kidnapping in broad daylight seemed beyond belief.

Frantically, she looked around at her surroundings, spotted the front door to a large apartment building near her, and ran inside. Her heart was racing. She had to do something to help the woman. She saw a pay phone down the hall, ran to it, and with trembling fingers, dialed an operator and asked to speak to the police.

A gruff male voice answered. "*Sí.* What is it?"

"I just saw a woman being kidnapped."

There was a long, unsettling silence. Too long a pause, Kari thought.

"Where are you?" the voice on the other end asked.

"I'm a block from the United States embassy. Please help me. I'm not sure it's safe here."

"Near the embassy? You're an American, right?"

"Yes. Please hurry."

"What is your name?"

"Kari Wheeler."

"Stay where you are," the man said. "You could be in danger. We will send somebody to pick you up."

Kari hung up, filled with fear. Why did the police think she could be in danger on a busy street in broad daylight? She went to the front door and looked out the window. There were now more than a dozen men standing in a group, looking around at all the buildings. She started to open the door when she suddenly stopped.

They were wearing uniforms. They *were* the police. Had someone already called them? Or, Kari wondered, had she seen a kidnapping she wasn't supposed to see? Then an even worse thought occurred to her. *What if they were looking for her?* Her heart raced and her knees buckled. She might be wrong, but she couldn't take that chance. She stayed at the window watching, frantic about what to do next.

After a few minutes of talking on a portable phone, the men

looked around then broke off in groups of two and began walking rapidly toward various buildings in the vicinity. They were looking for someone, but Kari didn't know if they were there to help her or to apprehend her. The embassy loomed on the next block, but even if she sprinted, she doubted she'd make it. She tried to convince herself that she was being paranoid. But she couldn't take that chance.

She glanced out the window again. Two men were coming down the walk toward her building. She spun around, looking for an escape route. A wide stairwell led up to the upper floor apartments. She only hesitated a moment, then ran down the hall and opened a wooden door, but it led down to the basement. She didn't want to be trapped in a basement with no way out. She sprinted to the end of the hall and burst through a back door that opened into a narrow alley filled with garbage cans and dusty cars. She ran for a full ten seconds, then stopped. She flattened herself against an old garage door, out of view.

Her heart was thumping wildly, she was trembling, and drenched in sweat. She froze when she heard a door open, then close again. Had somebody stepped into the alley? Should she run for it, or hope they wouldn't spot her? She listened, but all she could hear was her own rapid breathing.

She finally leaned forward and glanced down the alley. She didn't see anyone. She knew she couldn't stand there all day. She decided her best bet was to stick to alleys and back streets, and work her way back toward the hotel and away from the embassy.

Her hopes of getting home soon were dashed. Tears stung her eyes and streamed down her face, and her lips quivered as she began the long walk back. Everything that had happened to her over the past week finally overwhelmed her. She collapsed against a tree in despair and sobbed.

The CDC specialized team spent the rest of the afternoon organizing supplies, transportation, and deciding on their route and plan of attack. It had been a long day for everyone, and the exhausted group returned to the hotel. After dinner at the El Dorado, Brett and the other members of the team went down to the bar for a nightcap. The atmosphere was as noisy and charged as it appeared to be every night. Guitar music, singing, and laughter filled the place. Two rounds of margaritas put the six of them in a better mood.

Brett was still stewing about Kari. Where was she? Had she managed a way to leave the country? Or had Zolog found her? Was she safe or now in police custody?

Solt struck a match and drew the flame into the bowl of his pipe, blew a small gratifying cloud, then turned and stared at Brett. "Something's on your mind, Brett. What's bothering you? Not worried about a stupid little epidemic are you?"

"We're getting older, Ross. Why do we still do this?"

"Do what?" he asked, downing a third of his tequila in a single swallow. "And, by the way, I'm not *that* old."

"You know, the usual stuff you and I do. Hanging out in shitty Third World countries, playing Russian roulette with epidemics, getting shot at, and—worst of all—being alone most of the time. Why haven't you asked for a permanent assignment in Atlanta?"

Solt drew a long breath through the pipe and blew it out slowly before answering. "And do what? A nine-to-five job doing cultures in the lab with an occasional trip to Bio-Four for my kicks? It'd be like asking Patton to work in a recruiting station during the invasion." Solt flashed his trademark grin and slapped him on the back. "Is that what has your guts in an uproar? You're not going soft on me, are you, Brett?"

Brett shook his head and laughed at him. "You're crazy, Ross."

"Hell, Brett, we're all crazy. That's why we're down here." He downed his tequila and grinned.

Suddenly heads turned toward the entrance to the bar. Brett followed their gaze, then broke into a wide grin when he saw Kari standing there.

"I should have figured it'd be a woman," Solt said as he relit his pipe. Brett slapped him on the shoulder and jumped up to go to meet her.

"Kari! Where have you been?" Brett asked in a low voice. He was relieved and ecstatic to see her. The emotions he felt surprised even him.

"I had some things to take care of," she said. "I've had a busy day."

"I've been worried about you."

"Why you were worried about me?"

"I mean, I didn't know where you were. I wasn't sure if... I'm glad you're here."

The strain of the past few days showed on her face. She gave him a quizzical look. "Why were you so worried about me?"

"Colonel Zolog was here looking for you," Brett said.

"Zolog? Who's he?"

"Head of the secret police," Brett said.

"The secret police? What did they want with me?" she demanded.

"He said he wants to ask you some questions. He seemed to think it was important. He didn't look too friendly. Do you know why he would be looking for you?"

"Maybe he wants to find out who murdered my father," Kari answered tentatively.

Brett nodded, but he didn't agree. Zolog wasn't out to help anyone. He was hunting, and Kari was the prey. What Brett didn't know was why. "Where were you today?" he asked.

"I went to see an old friend of my father's, hoping he could help get me out of the country without papers. Then I called the American embassy and was headed there when—" she paused...

"Well, Brett, you've been holding out on us," Solt interrupted her, as he stepped forward and held out his hand to Kari. "Ross Solt. And you are..?"

"This is Kari Wheeler," Brett said. "Kari's at the University of Chicago, and she's going to be heading back home soon." He didn't want to go into the details of her recent ordeal. "Kari, Ross here is an old friend of mine. What he lacks in manners, he makes up for with genius. He's down here with the rest of the team from the CDC."

Kari shook his hand and tried to smile. "Nice to meet you, Ross."

Brett could tell Ross was completely smitten with her the moment he laid eyes on her. Solt took her by the arm and made introductions to the rest of the team. The men had big smiles on their faces as they were introduced. Brett went to the bar and brought back a glass of wine for her. Everyone started talking at once.

Finally, Brett was able to pull her aside. "You started to tell me something. What happened today? Is the embassy going to help you?"

"I didn't make it." Then she told him what happened. "Brett, do you think they could have been looking for *me*?"

"I would have said 'no,' but after Zolog's unexpected visit, I'm not so sure. One thing I know for certain. You need to get out of the country—*now*."

"I can't leave," she said. "I don't think it's safe to go to the embassy. I have to go back the village where we were staying to get my passport, and I'll be able to get some of my father's things without having to make another trip back to Guatemala. He has valuable notebooks and papers there, and I can't just leave all of it behind."

Brett frowned as he mulled things over and sipped his scotch. After a few minutes of silence, he spoke.

"Maybe I can help."

"How?"

"You want to go back to your village. I'll take you if you'll help me while we're there. We'll be gone for about a week before we come back."

"I didn't plan to stay a full week. And I have absolutely no medical experience. How can I possibly be of help to you?"

"I'm going to need at least an entire week. And there's plenty you can do. Do you still want to go with me?"

"Of course. How soon can we leave?"

"First thing tomorrow morning." He wanted her out of Guatemala City before Zolog came around again.

She nodded. "I've had a rough day and I'm exhausted. I've got things to do to get ready. Good night everyone. It was nice meeting you." She turned to Brett. "Thank you. I'll see you tomorrow." She put down the wineglass and left.

"Now I know what's bothering you," Solt said. "Care to fill me in?"

"Nothing to tell, really."

"I don't know how you do it, Brett," Solt said as he watched Kari walk away. "You seem to attract beautiful women like most men collect parking tickets."

Brett said nothing. He hadn't "collected" anyone yet, but he was glad she was back. Finally, he turned to Solt. "I'm going back to El Petan jungle tomorrow. I want to get blood samples and throat swabs from a couple of the villages there, then I'll join the rest of the team in the northern mountains. I'll be back in a week. Do you want to come with us?"

"Us?" Solt asked.

"I'm taking Kari back with me. I could use your help."

"You don't want me to piss off Quinn, do you? Besides, Jacek's right, you know. We'll be safer staying together, especially with the military escorting us." Solt took a few deep draws from his pipe. "You sure you want to do this, Brett?"

"Do what?" Jacek asked as he moved to the bar beside them.

"I'm going back to El Petan," Brett said, annoyed with the intrusion from Jacek. "I want to get some samples and talk to some of the villagers. I think we just might get some answers there. I'll join up with everyone in a week."

Jacek shook his head. "We've already decided we're not splitting up. It's going to be dangerous enough as it is. Quinn won't allow it, and neither will I. What exactly do you expect to find there?"

"Tell me, Brett," Solt asked, "why *do* you want to go back? It's definitely not safe. This doesn't have anything to do with that girl, does it?"

"No. I have a hunch I need to follow up on."

"Care to share it with us?" Jacek asked.

"Maybe I'll have something more definite by next week. Have the rest of the team go into the northern mountain region as planned. You'll have military protection. I'll join you as soon as I get back."

"You're an EIS agent, and I can't physically stop you from going," Jacek said, "but it's my opinion as team leader that we should stay together as agreed to. It's obvious you're going to go off on your own no matter what I say. Just make sure you're back here in one week. We'll all meet back here and regroup. Maybe Bio-Four will have something for us by then.

If you think you really have to go, then for god's sake be careful, will you Brett? Quinn will have my head on a platter if you get yourself killed." Jacek looked at his watch. "Let's call it a night and get some sleep."

Brett had three important reasons for going back. He believed the answer to the epidemic lay somewhere deep in the jungle. And he wanted to take Kari back for her father's belongings. But more importantly, he knew he had to get Kari out of Guatemala City before Zolog found her.

Chapter 28

With extra fuel, food, and supplies, Brett, Kari, and Tequila once again loaded into the Jeep, and drove out of Guatemala City at the crack of dawn. He hoped to kill two birds with one stone by taking her along. Kari could get her passport and her father's things, while he could talk to the villagers and get some cultures. He just hoped like hell that he wasn't going to risk her life by exposing her to some lethal disease.

They had a long distance to cover, and Brett knew they were facing a rough trip. The flooding caused by the storm had finally receded, but the water had carved deep ruts into the road making travel difficult and slow.

Brett pushed the Jeep hard, and they made good time. They had several hours of traveling in the highlands before they reached the El Peten rain forest. Kari had been studying a map for some time as they jostled and bumped along.

"What are you looking for?" Brett asked.

"San Angelica is here," she said, pointing to a spot on the map. "We'll have to take a right sometime ahead. Fairly soon."

He glanced over at the map she held and said, "That's sixty miles from Lepudro and the clinic. I thought it would be closer." He wondered why Wheeler and Kari had made the grueling trip all the way to Guatemala City only to return two days later to the jungle.

"Why were you and your father in Guatemala City?" Brett asked.

"Business," she said without explaining further. "And mostly for supplies."

"What kind of business? Seems like a hell of a trip to make in the middle of the storm."

"Yeah, it was pretty rough," she said and continued looking at the map.

It was obvious that Kari had no intention of discussing it further. They drove on in silence.

They finally reached the tiny village of San Angelica late in the night. "That one over there," Kari said and pointed to one of the dark houses. When she knocked at the door, a light came on, and an elderly woman opened the door.

"Kari!" the old woman said, her bony hands pulling Kari into a hug. "*Nino pobre. Usted es seguro.* Poor child," she repeated as they hugged.

Kari introduced Brett to Juanita Toricilla, who continued to stroke Kari's hair.

"*Estas cansado, duerma*," Juanita said. "*Usted necesita el sueño, niño.*"

"She's telling me to go to bed," Kari whispered to Brett. "My room is in the back. My second mother," Kari said, smiling at the petite woman.

"Ask her if I can pitch my tent outside."

"Of course, you can," Kari answered for her, "but don't bother tonight. You can sleep on the couch."

"*El puede quedarse mientras el desea*," Juanita said, smiling broadly.

"You can stay as long as you wish," Kari said. "My father and I spent the past two summers here with Juanita. Seems like home."

After they moved their packs inside, everyone went to bed. Brett quietly opened the door and let in Tequila, who curled up on the floor beside him. The trip had been grueling, and both Brett and the dog were asleep in seconds.

The next morning, Brett took a cold sponge bath from an outside well, put on clean clothes, then pitched one of the large canvas tents that Sanchez had provided under a tree near the house. Then he set up a cot inside it. After Juanita gave them breakfast, he and Kari walked to the chapel at the center of town. Kari wanted to arrange a funeral mass for her father. The sun's heat was stifling, and they were drenched in sweat by the time they reached the church.

The village of San Angelica was like all the others scattered throughout the rain forest and highlands: rough dirt roads; dogs, chickens and donkeys roaming freely; crumbling houses with no windows, often without doors; plucked chickens, skinned jack rabbits, and red peppers all hanging from various doorways as flies buzzed around.

Life in most Guatemalan villages centered around the church, which was usually built on the center square of town. The adobe church in San Angelica had a tiled roof and primitive stained glass windows. A stone well shared the center square with the church. Religion and water were the pivotal pillars of life here, the padre both their social and spiritual leader.

A priest came out of the church as they approached. He stopped, and his face blanched as if he'd seen a ghost when he spotted Kari. "Kari—." The name seemed to catch in his throat, then he recovered. He quickly went to her and engulfed her in a hug. "Kari, my dear child. We are so sorry for you. We heard about your father. We didn't know what happened to you."

Tall and distinguished-looking, the priest had an aura of authority and self-assurance. He wore a beige cotton robe and sandals—practical garb in this a sweltering climate.

"Thank you, Father Hernandez." Kari introduced Brett and told the priest she was there to collect her father's things. She described the attack and how her father was murdered in cold blood.

"Guatemalan soldiers, right?" Hernandez asked.

"I don't think so. The man who shot my father was a giant of a man with only one eye and an ugly scar where his left eye should have been."

Brett noticed that Hernandez only nodded when he heard Kari's account of what happened.

"Do you know him?" Brett asked.

"No. I've heard of him, though," Hernandez said, then turned back to Kari. "Tomorrow night we will have a Mass for your father."

"Thank you, Father. That would be very nice."

It seemed to Brett that Father Hernandez was only too anxious to steer the conversation away from the man with the scar. Brett said, "I'm here with a team from the United States to investigate a new disease that appears to be spreading quickly. We would like to culture everyone in the village, including taking blood samples and mouth swabs. Can we have your support in this? The people in the village might be reluctant to have blood drawn, so I could use your support."

"Of course. Anything I can do to help, just let me know."

"Have you heard anything about the disease?" Brett asked. He had reviewed the list Maria had given him at the clinic, and three men who died of the disease were from San Angelica. But all three were at Crenshaw's WHO clinic in Lepudra when they died, more than sixty miles from San Angelica. That fact in itself seemed strange to Brett.

"There have been six deaths in this village over the past few months, but that is not unusual in the jungle," Hernandez said. He turned to Kari. "It's good to have you back."

"Thank you, Father."

Once again, Brett felt he had been cut short.

Near the town square, Brett put up a second tent, which would provide shade and shelter while serving as the testing center. Then he spent the rest of the day preparing for the next day's work. He and Kari would take blood samples and throat cultures from everyone in the village, and the tent would serve as their laboratory and clinic. They would collect samples from the food, water, soil, and animals, then store them in the tent along with the blood samples.

At dusk outside his tent, Brett spotted Kari down the road a short distance talking alone with Father Hernandez. He assumed they were discussing the funeral Mass for her father, but something about their actions seemed almost secretive, and their discussion looked intense. Did Kari know her father had been excavating in an unauthorized area? Brett wondered if he should tell her what he had learned. Then it occurred to him. She might have been involved all along and knew full well that what they had been doing was illegal.

He and Tequila spent the night in the tent. With the flaps tied back, there was enough breeze blowing to make it fairly comfortable. The next morning after a quick wash and breakfast, Brett showed Kari how to label the vials and take throat cultures, then he started taking blood samples from the villagers. Juanita helped by keeping a list of everyone who had been cultured, and made sure the word got out that everyone had to be tested.

While Juanita and Kari worked in the tent, Brett collected samples from the wells in the village, a nearby stream, and from a cistern that collected rainwater. Then he took milk samples from goats and two cows. He even took samples from the soil and sewage area.

A brief, hard downpour in the middle of the afternoon brought welcome relief from the heat and gave them a chance for a work break. Brett went to find Father Hernandez after the rain had stopped. He had something he wanted to discuss with him regarding Kari's father's funeral.

After dinner, Brett followed her to her father's room so she could go through his trunk. She knelt down, opened the lid and sat a moment and stared into the trunk. The she reached in and pulled out an exquisite silver and jade necklace, and held it up to show him.

"It's beautiful," he said

"My father gave this to me for my sixteenth birthday." Then

she put it on and fastened the clasp.

"Don't forget to get your passport," he told her.

"Thanks. I've already got it packed, along with his notebooks. He recorded extensive information about every discovery."

Then she then selected a few items she wanted buried in memory of him, including a picture of him with her mother. Brett could see that Kari got her beauty from her mother.

"She died of cancer when I was twelve," Kari said before he could ask. Her eyes were moist with tears.

Brett put his hand on her shoulder. "Are you going to be okay?"

She nodded without answering, picked up the items she had selected, and gently closed the trunk.

Later they made their way to the church. Once there, they saw that the things she'd selected—the photograph of her parents, a watch Kari had given her father, his well-worn hat, and one of his favorite books, *Self Reliance* by Emerson—had all been carefully placed on a table in front of the altar.

"He never wore the watch," Kari explained to Brett. "He was afraid of losing it." She smiled at the memory, but tears ran down her face. She draped a black nylon scarf over her head. Candles were lit, and people from the village began filing into the church.

The children went to the front of the church and sang a song in Spanish. When they finished, as he had discussed earlier with Father Hernandez, Brett picked up a guitar they'd provided for him and went to stand among the children. He began playing *Amazing Grace,* and the children sang the words in Spanish. There was not a dry eye in the church.

Following Mass, Father Hernandez led a procession to the cemetery, swinging the incense holder in front of him as he walked.

All the items Kari had brought were placed in a small token grave, which was then filled in. Each person placed a rock on top, then it was covered with flowers. It was believed that the rocks would hold a person's soul there forever, and would remain with them.

Wheeler would not be forgotten; his soul would remain. He would be remembered by the simple, good people of the village. Finally, a headstone with a carved cross was placed on top. Father Hernandez said a brief prayer, then everyone quietly turned toward their homes.

Brett and Kari remained at the rock and flower-covered mound for several minutes for a private goodbye to her father.

"Thank you for everything," Kari finally said, and took his hand as they walked back to the village.

Back at Juanita's house, Kari went immediately to bed and fell asleep, emotionally exhausted. Brett went to the tent and sat outside looking at the sky late into the night with Tequila lying beside him.

He thought about the events of the evening. He thought about the brevity of life and the finality of death. Most people seemed to be searching for the meaning of life, but he had decided long ago that it was a futile search. To him, there was no meaning to life, and as far as he was concerned, they were wasting their time looking for it.

Tequila rolled onto his side and put his head against Brett's leg. Brett scratched his head behind his ears.

A shooting star fired across the sky for a brief second, then it was gone. Vaporized.

Like everything else eventually....

Over the next three days, Brett and Kari worked long hours collecting dozens of samples, which they put in coolers filled with the dry ice. They were due back in Guatemala City in three days, but Brett planned to visit another village before they returned. He decided this would be their last day in San Angelica. They would leave for the next village the first thing in the morning.

Chapter 29

The third morning began with tearful goodbyes between Juanita and Kari. Brett wanted to speak to Father Hernandez, but was told the padre had left earlier that morning. Brett packed the Jeep and they drove off.

"I know I'll never be back," Kari said as she turned and looked back at the shabby village. "I hate the jungle, but part of me is going to miss this place. Hard to believe, isn't it, that anyone could miss this? But I know I will. My father's memorial grave will always be here."

Their next stop would be Del Norte, twenty miles away. Seven men from Del Norte had died at Crenshaw's clinic in Lepudro. As far as Brett could tell, none of the men who had died were anywhere near their own villages when they got sick. Why? What was the connection? The obvious answer was to find out what the men were doing when they were away.

"Did your father know any of the men from Del Norte or San Angelica who died of the disease?" Brett asked Kari.

"Yes, we knew all of them," Kari answered.

Playing a hunch, he asked, "Did any of the men work for your father?"

"Many of the men in surrounding villages helped my father at one time or another. My father paid them to go on short trips with us when we went exploring for tombs."

"Did any of them get sick when they were with you?"

"Yes."

He slowed the Jeep. "How come you didn't tell me this before?"

"Because it didn't seem important. Why, what's the connection?"

"I don't know that there *is* a connection. The seven men from Del Norte all worked for your father?"

"As I said, many of the men worked for him at one time or another. It was a way for them to make a little money."

"I mean, were they with your father on one of his trips when they got sick?"

"No," she said. "Why? Do you think there's some connection?"

"Possibly. I don't know yet." Wheels were starting to spin in his head. He was scrambling to put it all together. Maybe—just maybe—he'd stumbled onto something important.

Once they were set up in Del Norte, Kari began taking throat cultures and labeling the vials while Brett drew blood samples. She was proving to be an invaluable asset. That evening after dinner, they went to interview the three women whose husbands had died of the disease. Just as Brett suspected, each man had been on an excavating trip to earn money. Brett believed he may have found the link he'd been looking for.

His began to wonder if the answer to the mysterious disease lay buried somewhere inside Mayan tombs. Had a deadly vector been uncovered by tomb raiders?

That would explain why the men were miles from their homes when they died and why nobody in the villages had gotten the disease. He guessed that the three large areas where outbreaks had occurred would prove to be sites of ancient Mayan civilizations and would be dotted with crumbling tombs.

There was still much work to be done. He had to find out exactly what it was inside the ancient tombs that might have carried the virus. In order to do that, he needed to find an unexplored tomb to begin his search. He was also anxious to tell the team what he had learned. He would finish collecting the blood, soil, and water samples, then pack up and get back to Guatemala City as soon as he could.

It was absolutely vital to let Solt and the rest of the team know what he'd learned so far.

That night, Brett stretched out on the cot in his tent. Finally, he thought he might be getting close to finding some answers. He was too tired to even consider dinner. An hour later, he had just dozed off when Kari appeared at his tent. She said, "Guess what I just learned? A five-year-old girl here in the village may have died of the disease two weeks ago."

"What?" Brett asked, jumping off the cot, now fully alert. "A young girl? Are you sure it was the same disease?"

"Well, there's no way we can know for sure what the girl died from," Kari said. "But her mother described symptoms that sounded exactly like what you described. The girl had a headache, fever, then became violently ill. The next morning, she was dead. A local medicine man told her it was because of some kind of a curse."

"Well, we know for sure it wasn't a curse. We have to talk to the mother and find out everything we can about the little girl."

He suddenly had a nagging thought in the back of his mind that he might have been premature in his suspicions about the tombs. There were the deaths of three women he had yet to fit into his theory. And, it seemed almost certain that the little girl couldn't have been inside a Mayan tomb. "Ask the mother if we can talk to her."

"Okay, but not tonight. They're probably already asleep. I'll ask her in the tomorrow morning. Good night." She petted Tequila, then left.

Brett lay down again but sleep didn't come. The news of the little girl's death had created serious doubt in his theory, just when he thought he'd discovered the likely source of the disease. His mind went over various scenarios that might explain it, but none of them seemed plausible. After fitful tossing and turning, he finally fell asleep in the early morning hours. Daylight arrived far too soon.

Kari and Brett spent the morning drawing blood and taking throat cultures. After lunch, they went to visit the mother. Like the rest of buildings in the village, the house was little more than a shack with no door. The windows had no glass in them. Brightly painted religious artifacts were displayed throughout the small house.

The mother seemed frightened. Kari smiled and tried to reassure her. "Thank you for talking to us. I know this is a difficult time for you." The woman nodded, wiped her eyes, then told them basically the same story Kari had related about the little girl's illness. The mother vehemently denied that the girl, who was only five years old, had been out of the village recently.

Kari put her arm around the woman. "I'm so sorry for your loss."

The woman nodded. "I've lost Carlita. Now I have no one."

"Where is your husband?" Brett asked.

She shot him a stern look, then said, "He is gone."

"When will he be back?" Brett continued. The woman only continued to stare at him.

Then Brett understood. The husband wouldn't be coming back. Had he died, or had he just abandoned them? He wanted to know more about it, how long the husband been gone, where he had gone, or if he'd had contact with the little girl recently.

"May I look around?" Brett asked.

"*Sí, vaya a continuación. Está detrás allí,*" the woman said quietly.

Kari nodded to Brett to go ahead, but the look Kari gave him wasn't exactly friendly. Brett excused himself.

Five minutes later, he returned and sat down. The woman was softly crying into a scarf that she held to her face. Brett knew the interview was over. They stood, thanked her, expressed their condolences, and left.

"She seemed frightened," Brett said. "She wasn't telling us everything."

"Afraid? The poor woman just lost her child," Kari shot back. "What you saw was a distraught woman who had just buried her little girl. Then we barged into her home with a bunch of questions. And what were you doing, going through their home?"

Brett could tell that he had not only upset the mother, but Kari also. He was too close to stop now, though, and he was sure the answer was within his grasp. He thought a second, then said, "I need to get samples from her."

Kari stopped in her tracks. "Samples from whom?" When he didn't answer, her eyes widened. "The mother?" He didn't reply. A look of incredulity crossed her face. "You don't mean the little girl, do you?" Kari stared at him in disbelief. "They're going to let you dig up her body. Forget it. Christ!"

"Kari, that girl's death may be the key to this disease. She wasn't exposed to anyone in the village who had the disease. How, then did she come in contact with the virus? Why didn't anybody else get sick?"

"I don't know, maybe she was bitten by a mosquito, or fleas, or ticks—who knows?"

"Yeah, maybe," he said. His theory suddenly had a large crack in it, and he felt he was back at square one. Everything had fit into place until the death of the little girl.

Kari went back to the tent to continue taking throat cultures. Brett spent an hour collecting blood samples from dogs, goats, and chickens in the village that the boys in the village helped him catch.

When he was finished, he walked over to Kari where she was drawing blood from a young boy. Her clothes were damp with sweat, and covered in a layer of dust. When she finished, the boy looked at his Band-Aid, then sat on the floor of the tent and started playing with Tequila, who had wandered in with Brett.

"I think you've found a new profession," he said, admiringly.

"Nope. That's it for me," she said, pulling off her latex gloves. "I'm finished here. How are you doing?"

"Done. Time to pack it up again. Put your hands out." He poured alcohol over her hands as she cleaned them. He was dreading the trip back. She'd be leaving for Chicago once they got to Guatemala City. "Thanks for your help," he said. "I couldn't have done it without you."

"Sure, you could, but I'm glad I could help, regardless."

The usual afternoon thunderstorm hadn't materialized, and

the heat was suffocating. She wiped her hand across her forehead and pushed damp strands of hair away from her face. "Get the Jeep," she said as she came out of the tent.

"Are we going somewhere?" he asked. "We still have to pack."

"That can wait till we get back. Let's go. I've got a surprise."

With Tequila in the back, they headed out of the dusty village as the afternoon heat seemed to intensify. Thick, humid air shimmered from the jungle floor. A few minutes later, Kari pointed for him to pull over into a clearing. "I think this is it," she said as they stopped. She climbed out and started down a steep hill.

Brett got out, Tequila jumped down, and they followed her. The temperature dropped a refreshing twenty degrees in a distance of only a few dozen yards. They heard the sound of falling water and felt a fine, cool mist just before arriving at a clearing. A steep rock wall sloped down to a wide, shallow pool, which was fed by a small cascading waterfall that dropped twenty feet over a cliff and splashed off rocks before finally plunging into the pool. The collision of water onto rocks sent a constant mist into the air creating a permanent rainbow in the afternoon sun.

"Unbelievable. This is fantastic," he said. "How did you know about this place?"

"A couple of people mentioned it to me. They thought we might enjoy it. It's too shallow to swim in, but they said it'll cool us off." Kari turned her back to him, hesitated a moment, then unbuttoned her blouse and took it off. She unsnapped her shorts and let it drop. Wearing only her underwear, she stepped into the shallow stream and moved toward the waterfall. She was partly hidden by a faint misty prism of a rainbow.

Brett stripped to his boxers and followed her. Tequila barked and jumped into the stream with enthusiasm, sending up showers of water. The cooling water cascading over them washed away the dust and grime of the last few days. It was the most refreshing shower Brett ever experienced.

After they'd been under the waterfall long enough to get clean and cool off, they waded down the stream a short distance and found a large inviting rock in the middle of the stream. They sat down, and dangled their bare feet in the flowing water. Tequila splashed up and down the stream, then shook a wide spray of water and found a place under a tree to stretch out and doze.

"Can you believe this place?" Kari asked, running her hands through her wet hair.

"Yeah, air-conditioner and shower built into one," he said, but his mind wasn't on the waterfall. It was on the lovely woman sitting on the rock beside him. He glanced at her legs glistening with water. He said nothing, but his heart raced a mile a minute.

He leaned over, picked a stone from the stream and skipped it across the water. He counted five skips before it finally disappeared. They sat there in silence for some time; the only sound the sound of the cascading waterfall.

"What are you thinking?" she finally asked.

"A lot of things. I'm thinking about the trip tomorrow. And the fact that you'll be leaving and heading back to Chicago." He turned and looked into her eyes.

After a few moments, she said, "I'm going home, but I know nothing will ever be the same again. The last two weeks have changed everything."

He quietly looked at her but said nothing.

She continued in a soft, but serious voice. "My father is dead, and now I'm alone. I have so much to take care of when I get back, so many decisions to make." She sighed and stared at the water. Then she looked up at him. "I want you to know I'll never forget these past ten days."

"You're right, not many people get to experience floods in the jungle, a deadly epidemic, all the while sleeping in tents and churches and traveling around in an old Jeep shot full of holes."

"Or have your father murdered in front of you," she added. "It's been a nightmare. Worse than losing my mother." She looked up at him. "But at the same time, in a strange way, this past week has been..." She didn't finish the sentence, but looked down. "I'll never forget you Brett Carson."

"Don't make it sound so final," he smiled. "Once we're back in the States, we can keep in touch... maybe catch up from time to time."

Her next words brought him up short.

"I can't deal with the future right now."

He said nothing and skipped another stone across the water. The afternoon shadows grew longer. They finally stood up, waded to the shore, dressed, and drove back to Del Norte.

They were quiet during the short drive back. Tomorrow would be the long drive to Guatemala City and, Brett thought, the end of their time together.

Chapter 30

Zolog stomped up the steps and down the hallway toward his office. He was a troubled man. Things had not been going well, and he was under the gun to get results. His only lead to uncovering the source of smuggled artifacts had been murdered, and his daughter was nowhere to be found. He wasn't even sure if she knew anything, but right now she was his only hope, and time was running out. He had promised the president he could end the war quickly; that promise was based on his ability to stop the smuggling of ancient artifacts, thereby cutting off funding to the rebels.

He opened the door to his office and immediately saw the shadow of a man sitting near the window. The man had his feet on Zolog's desk. Zolog's senses went on full alert when he realized who it was.

He snapped to attention and said, "*El Presidente,* what a pleasant surprise." He had been caught completely off-guard and tried to maintain his composure. President Jorge del Manguinos didn't to stand to greet him or remove his boots from Zolog's desk, a fact that did not escape Zolog.

"I thought it was time you and I had a talk," del Manguinos said as he blew smoke from his dark cigarette. "You told me you were going to wrap things up quickly. You also said you were going to keep me informed. I am concerned because I've not heard anything from you. I thought you would have something for me by now."

The tone of his voice left no doubt about his anger. He dropped his feet to the floor and sat forward, grinding out his cigarette in an ash tray. Before Zolog could respond, the President continued. "You're not keeping anything from me, are you?"

Zolog had only a split second to consider his answer. Any delay would suggest to del Manguinos that he was either lying or he had something to hide. Yet, he didn't know how much if anything the President knew about Wheeler's death and the disappearance of his daughter. Zolog was on treacherous ground.

He put his hat on a shelf and walked deliberately over to another chair and sat down. "We encountered a snag in our plan, but we've already put another plan in action. There will only be a temporary delay in achieving our goal of cutting off the rebels' money source."

"How much of a delay?" del Manguinos asked as he pulled another dark cigarette out of his case and lit it. After a long, slow draw, he continued, smoke popping out of his mouth with each word. "I hope you know what is at stake," he said. "Time is not our friend. To put it bluntly, we need the fighting to end *now*. If we don't win soon, the rebels will take over, and the country will be in chaos. We need a total, decisive victory, and we need it now!" He pounded the desk to make his point.

"I expect to have answers within a few days," Zolog said.

"Then I can expect to hear from you within a few days." The President stood up, smashed out his cigarette and walked out.

After the door closed, Zolog paced back and forth across his office. The president was in a foul mood, and time was running out for both of them. For Zolog, there was only one way the war could end, and that was with total victory.

If somehow the inconceivable happened and the rebels won, both he and the president would face a firing squad. If there was a settled peace, the president would be allowed to step down and Zolog would be forced out of the army. Not making the rank of general would be the least of his problems.

He had to move quickly. Every effort had to be put into finding the girl and hope she could provide answers regarding the smuggling of Mayan artifacts out of the country. Zolog knew he had made a mistake when he decided to follow Wheeler instead of bringing him in for questioning. He wouldn't make the same mistake with the daughter.

Something still troubled him—who had killed Wheeler? And why? Zolog picked up a small ancient carved statue of a Mayan chieftain from his desk and flipped it back and forth in his hands as he contemplated what had happened. What was he missing?

Suddenly he stopped fiddling with the statue and stared at it. Sometimes answers were within arm's reach. He realized he was holding it in his hand. Wheeler was killed because he knew too much or because he'd discovered something he wasn't supposed to know. Did it have something to do with the smuggling of Mayan artifacts and the influx of money? That almost certainly meant that whoever killed Wheeler would also be looking for his daughter.

If he was right, it was now a race to see who could find her first. If they found her – whoever they were – they would no doubt kill her also. They had probably intended to kill her at the same time they killed her father, but they had been interrupted, and she'd escaped. If they got to her first, he would be left with nothing.

He stood up, grabbed his hat, stormed out of his office, and slammed the door. He had an idea.

Brett and Kari enjoyed a late dinner with Juanita, then they said good night. He went out to his tent, undressed in the dark, stepped out of the tent and poured a bucket of water over himself to rinse off sweat. Feeling refreshed, he toweled off and had climbed onto his cot when he saw a shadow approaching. The flap of the tent opened and Kari leaned in.

"Hello," he said.

"May I come in?" she asked.

"Sure," he said and sat up.

She wore one of his shirts he'd given her, and her legs were bare. "I want to thank you for driving me back here to get my father's things. You should have been with the rest of your team. I caused more work for you when you already have enough to worry about."

"You're welcome, but you don't have to thank me." The truth was he would have driven her to the moon if she'd asked. Standing there, she was the most beautiful, sensuous woman he had ever seen.

She leaned over and kissed him tenderly on the lips. His heart was racing again. He said nothing, not sure what he should do next. Was that just a "thank you" kiss, or was it something else?

His uncertainty was soon answered. She unbuttoned her shirt and when it fell open, he could see the pale fullness of her breasts in the dim moonlight. His breath caught in his throat as he looked at her. He had dreamed about this, but she was more exquisite than he had even dared to envision. He stood, pulled her to him, and kissed her with a passionate kiss. He kissed her neck, softly pushed her hair from her face, then kissed her neck. He pulled her shirt off her shoulders and gently held her arms behind her, causing her breasts to thrust toward him. He traced his tongue lightly over her nipples and kissed them. Her breath on his neck was hot, and her hair had the faint fragrance of flowers. He drew her to him.

He hesitated. "Are you sure...?" he whispered in her ear.

She pressed her lips against his in a passionate kiss that left no doubt about her intentions. "I've never wanted anything more in my life," she said in a throaty voice.

He ran his fingers through her hair as he kissed her lips, her neck, and her breasts. He pulled her shirt completely off, lifted her onto the cot, and stretched out beside her. His fingers traced the contours of her body as his hands slid the length of her thighs. He kissed her stomach, then lower.

She tensed when his tongue sent a pleasing jolt through her. "Oh... wait," she whispered, but her body said otherwise.

She made no move to stop him and pushed her pelvis toward him. Her body shuddered and she moaned. Her breathing was deep and rapid as she reached down to guide him into her. He felt her softness open to him, and he slowly entered her.

Brett didn't want to rush. He pulled out slowly while looking into her eyes.

She looked at him. "What? Did I do something wrong?"

"You're beautiful. I want to savor this." He kissed her and gently slid in deeper. She moaned softly. He slid out again, and once more pushed slowly into her. Then she wrapped her legs around him, pulling him deep into her and moved her pelvis against him, faster and faster.

Her body trembled and her breath came in short gasps. He could no longer hold himself back when he felt her muscles spasm tightly around him, and he felt a sudden intense release of his own. They lay in the dark entangled in each other's embrace, breathing hard.

"You're incredible," Brett whispered in her ear as he pushed damp hair from her forehead. He held her in his arms, and his fingers gently closed around one breast, which felt hot to his touch. After a few minutes of lying quietly together in the dark, she rolled over and straddled him. Her pelvis gently pushed against him in a very seductive way as she leaned over and kissed his chest.

"I don't think I can right now," he whispered in her ear. But he was wrong.

She reached down and gently wrapped her fingers around him, her touch as light and soft as feathers. She then gently held him against her, and he could feel the heat and softness of her body. Slowly she pushed him deeper into her, and he felt himself grow hard inside her.

Oh god... oh...." she whispered between breaths. The second time was even more intense than the first, and left them both exhausted.

"I guess you were wrong," she smiled teasingly.

She moved beside him and slipped her arms around him. He pushed her hair aside and kissed her neck, then held her in his arms. He felt more contented, happy, and fulfilled than he had ever felt before. He didn't want the night to end. Tomorrow was full of too many uncertainties; lying beside her warm body in the cool, dim moonlight was—at this moment—perfect. Then he drifted into a deep, much needed sleep.

Sometime during the night, she slipped out of the tent.

Chapter 31

CDC
Atlanta

Mitchell Quinn was staring at a disturbing new report he'd just received when his phone rang.

"Mitch, this is Jan. How about coming over to Bio-Four and taking a look at something."

"Sure. Be right there." Quinn hoped to hell that meant they'd finally found something. His concern was that the disease was exploding right in front of them while they struggled to find out what it was. He had just received a very disturbing report, and the thought of another trip to max-containment didn't cheer him up.

After going through the phenol shower and putting on his full-body suit, then attaching his reverse air breathing hose, Quinn entered max-containment and found Janet Boggs working at the dissection table. "What've you got, Jan?"

Dr. Boggs was dissecting the mice they had injected with tissue samples Brett had collected from his autopsy. "Take a look," she said. All ten dead mice had been laid out in a row. A few had been dissected so their organs could be individually examined. "The mice died within twelve hours after we injected them. We examined their blood. There was almost no immune response. Their immune system was overwhelmed, and death was probably too sudden to get any kind of serology change."

Quinn stared through his Plexiglas mask at the table. "That means sero-typing is out. Not enough time for antibodies to respond. What's the next step? DNA typing?"

"Exactly. Brett was right about one thing—this is a hot one. We're pretty sure it's not bacteria. Of course, we never thought it would be."

"Anything on fungus cultures yet?" Quinn asked.

"Yes and no. Come see and I'll show you what I mean."

He followed her into the dimly lit control room containing both the TEM and SEM—the transmission and the scanning electron microscopes. A green light from the control panels reflected off their Plexiglas masks.

"What have you got?" he asked as he adjusted the focus on the screen. They both stared at the monitor.

"This is liver tissue," Jan said. "We're looking at hepatocytes at fifty thousand times magnification." Tens of thousands of hexagonal-shaped structures were attacking the liver cells. The viruses were devouring cell structures and reproducing at an unbelievable rate.

"A hemorrhagic virus?" he asked.

"Don't know. It's not Ebola. Could be Marburg. But I've never seen anything like it before on EM. You asked about fungus. Now take a look at this." She switched to another screen. Fungus mycelia strands and spores were filled with the same hexagonal structures.

"What do you make of that?" Quinn asked.

"We didn't culture any fungus from the samples Brett sent. So on a hunch, I inoculated a culture of *Stachybotrys chartarum* fungus with some of the material. The virus is growing and thriving on the fungus mycelia, but it isn't killing the fungus. It's kind of a symbiotic relationship. I tried it with other fungi, but didn't get the same result. That might explain the mildew smell Brett described."

"Maybe that means the victims were infected with both the virus *and* the fungus," Quinn said. "Brett thinks the epidemic might somehow be related to ancient Mayan tombs. That would fit into his theory."

"My guess is that the virus weakened the immune system, and the fungus grew uninhibited until the virus completely devoured the entire body. I don't think the fungus acts as a pathogen, rather more like an opportunist. But that's all just speculation at this point. It also explains something else."

"What's that?"

"How the virus could survive in dark tombs for centuries. What if the virus lived inside the mycelia of the thick mold inside the tombs."

"We need to know what the hell this virus is," Quinn said. "We need the DNA identification as soon as possible. We'll be getting several cases of blood and throat cultures from the team in a day or so. If we're lucky, maybe we can get a sero-typing from that. Entomology section is going to have a million insects to screen to see if one species might be a vector."

"For now, that's all we have," Jan said.

"Actually, there may be something else," Quinn said dejectedly. "I just received a disturbing report, if it turns out to be true."

"What's that?" Boggs asked.

"It appears there's been an outbreak in New Mexico."

"New Mexico? Oh, god. How many?"

"At least four dead. Of course, we can't confirm it without sero-typing or any other way to identify it. But it sounds like the same disease."

"Guatemala and New Mexico—what's the connection?"

"I don't know that there is one," Quinn said.

"What do we do now?"

"Pray that they're wrong."

The trip back to Guatemala City was hot and dusty. The past week, which had been emotionally and physically draining, left both Brett and Kari exhausted. Now they faced the inevitable; they would be going their separate ways. They had traveled through the jungle together and shared many emotional ups and downs the past ten days, including a funeral mass for her father, and making passionate love in a tent by moonlight. Ten incredible days; in reality a very short time, but in some ways, it seemed like a lifetime to Brett.

During that time, they had been inseparable, but tomorrow Kari would fly back to Chicago and her real life. Fate had caused their paths to cross, but only briefly. Now it was coming to an end.

Brett knew he had to put thoughts of Kari behind him and concentrate on the real reason he was down here. He had to get back to the team to tell them what he'd learned. Even though Brett couldn't explain the little girl's death in Del Norte, he was still convinced the answer to the disease lay buried deep inside dark Mayan tombs. He just had to figure out a way to prove it.

Finally, he said, "Kari, the secret police are looking for you. I'm worried that they may stop you at the airport."

"I have my passport now, and I haven't done anything wrong."

"I know, but they could still find some reason to detain you." He reached in his pocket and pulled out something and handed it to her. "I think you should use this."

"What's this?" she asked as she took it and looked at it. Then she looked back at him, her mouth open in disbelief. "You stole that mother's identity card?"

"I just borrowed it. I got the idea when we were visiting her. You both have dark hair and on quick inspection of that ID photo, you could pass for her. You can send it back to her once you're in Chicago. Zolog is looking for an American girl named Kari Wheeler. They're not looking for this woman. This way you can buy a ticket using her name, and the secret police have no way of identifying you. You won't need any other ID until you arrive back in the United States. Then you can use your own passport."

She stared at the plastic ID card, frowning.

"It may be your only way out of the country," Brett said. "Otherwise, you might be a guest of Zolog for a very long time."

"I don't look exactly like her. What if they spot the difference?"

"They won't."

She finally nodded agreement and put the ID in her pocket. He turned his attention back to the road.

He dropped her off at the El Dorado, then drove to the Ministry of Health building.

Everyone from the CDC epidemiological investigative team was sitting around in the meeting room drinking coffee. Over the past week, they'd visited and cultured more than seven villages. The mood inside seemed anything but cheerful. Sanchez and the five other doctors from the health ministry who were assigned to help them were also there. Sanchez nodded at him and continued smoking his dark cheroot. The room was too quiet, and everyone looked grimly serious. Brett could tell something was wrong.

"Welcome back, Brett," Solt said, jumping up when Brett walked in. "You finally made it back. I was beginning to worry about you."

"Told you not to worry," Brett said to the group as he accepted a cup of coffee from Solt. "What's going on, Ross? Did you turn up anything?"

"Maybe, maybe not," Peter Jacek said. "First tell us what you've found."

Brett pulled out his folded notes and glanced at them. "The Mayan Empire flourished for over 2,000 years. Archeologists have discovered that the region we are in contained the densest populations per square mile in human history."

Jacek spoke up. "Besides a history report, have you found anything pertinent to the epidemic we were sent down here for?"

Brett continued. "Do you know that in the year 950 A.D., more than ninety-five percent of the Maya population mysteriously died off? Historians and archeologists speculate that this massive collapse could be attributed to bitter wars, or due to a severe drought and fire storms. Most think it was a combination of these factors."

"Get to the point Brett."

"What if the Mayan population suddenly disappeared not because of war and famine, but because of a deadly virus—the same virus we are now facing."

He was met with stony faces and silence.

He continued. "I brought back a Jeep full of blood samples and dozens of other types of samples from two villages that I visited. I interviewed ten of the wives from San Angelica whose husbands died of the disease. All ten of the men were away when they got sick and died. Do you know what they were doing? They were excavating Mayan tombs. The same with the men from Del Norte who died. And six of them had been with Professor Wheeler, an archeologist from Chicago. I'm fairly convinced that the disease might somehow be related to the ancient tombs. What we have to figure out is exactly what that connection is."

"Mayan tombs? Are you serious, Brett?" Jacek asked.

"I told you last week that I thought the disease is carried by a vector, and I still believe that. The pattern of reported deaths is not that of person-to-person spread within a village. Rather, the cases occur in clusters, and not everyone—or even most—within the region of the clusters get the disease. This is the pattern of vector spread disease. The question is, what is the vector?

"The organism could be in the soil of the tombs," Brett continued, "or in the lichen or the mold inside the tomb, insects or rodents that inhabit the tombs, bats, snakes—whatever, or even inside the bones and rotted tissue of the dead that are buried there. Ancient tombs, buried for centuries, and are suddenly exposed to fresh air and the light of day."

"Do you seriously believe old tombs could be the source of the disease?" Jacek asked. "Another 'Curse of the Pharaohs'?"

"I'm convinced of it."

"Well, Brett, that's an interesting theory, but it appears your tomb idea is way off base. Seems that we may have been on a wild goose chase and lost valuable time because of your 'vector' theory. And now it may be too late to contain this thing. I think we've gotten ourselves into one hell of a fix."

"What are you talking about?" Brett demanded.

"We just learned that there's been an outbreak of a disease in New Mexico," Solt replied. "Our best guess from what we know about it so far is that it's going to be the same disease as the one down here."

"New Mexico?" Brett was stunned. It didn't make any sense.

"At a monastery, to be exact. And as far I know, there sure as hell aren't any Mayan tombs in New Mexico," Jacek said. His voice was both accusatory and angry. "At your recommendation, we didn't put up road blocks or establish regional quarantines. And who knows where the hell the disease has spread to by now. We followed your suggestions, but it only succeeded in setting us back weeks. Five more people that we know of in Guatemala died this week. We were able to examine and culture two of them in one of the villages just after they died. Now it may have spread too far to ever be contained."

Brett could feel the heat rising in his cheeks. What the hell had happened? How could he have been so wrong? Everything about his theory had fit perfectly. Except for an outbreak in New Mexico, and the little five-year-old girl's death—a fact that he had chosen not to tell them. Jacek was right. It seemed he had screwed up royally.

"Actually," Solt said, trying to ease the tension in the room, "they haven't proven that the outbreak in New Mexico is the same disease."

"Not actually proven, but we know it's the same," Jacek said.

Brett stood there a moment trying to make sense of it, then put the coffee down and left.

That evening, Kari walked into the El Dorado lounge and found Ross. "Good evening, Kari," Solt said with a big smile as she joined the team at a table. "Welcome back. Come have a drink with us." He held out a chair for her and then held up his hand to summon the waiter

"Have you seen Brett?" she asked.

"Not since this afternoon," Solt replied. "But I expect he'll be dropping in sometime."

"I wanted to thank him and say good-bye. Where is he? Why

isn't he here?" she asked.

"Don't know where he is right now. I know he's not in his room. He made a bit of a mistake, and it's my guess he's out somewhere trying to work things out in his own mind."

"What kind of mistake?"

"Well, it seems that he made a wrong assumption about the epidemic, and now we've got big problems. Have you ever heard of 'The Curse of the Pharaohs'?"

"No."

"Well, in 1967, twelve archeologists—six Americans, and six Brits—were exploring a newly discovered network inside one of the lesser Egyptian pyramids. They had worked themselves into a deep, narrow passage in the pyramid and stumbled on an ancient black Egyptian sarcophagus, which they pried open and examined the contents. When they returned to their camp that night, they all became violently ill, and within a day, ten of them were dead. The two surviving men were immediately put on a plane back to London. One died en route, but the last man survived just long enough to tell his story at the hospital. Then, a pathologist became ill and died a day after doing autopsies on the two men who'd been flown back."

Kari stared at him, her mouth open in disbelief. "What killed them?"

"There was a lethal fungus growing on old cheese left in the tombs to provide food to souls as they made their way to heaven or wherever they were supposed to go. When the fungi were exposed to oxygen, the spores began to grow immediately and produced an extremely poisonous toxin. The archeologists breathed in the spores and within hours were overwhelmed with the toxin. The story was big, and news media called it 'The Curse of the

Pharaohs.' The name stuck. Brett thought maybe now it could be the same kind of thing was going on inside Mayan tombs. But it looks like he was wrong on this one. And we lost valuable time because of it."

"How do you know he's wrong?"

"Because there is an outbreak of the disease in New Mexico. In a monastery of all places. And there are no Mayan tombs in New Mexico."

"They're not going to fire him, are they?"

"Fire Brett?" Solt said, and let out a bellowing laugh. "He's the best EIS agent we have."

"What's going to happen now?"

"Brett is a driven person," Solt explained to her. "He won't allow himself to be defeated. He won't dwell on possible mistakes. His focus will be to find the cause of the disease and stop it."

"You like him, don't you?" she smiled.

Solt sat there a minute staring at his beer before answering. "Brett's the most unique man I've ever met. You can trust him with your life. I consider him my best friend." He looked at her. "How about you? You like him?"

Kari felt herself blushing but remained silent.

"Yeah, I thought so," Solt answered for her. "How well do you know him?"

"We just met ten days ago. But it seems like I've known him a life time."

"That's the way Brett affects people. He's a complicated guy, and there's a lot about Brett you probably don't know. Did you know he gave up a career in music to go into medicine?"

"Yes, I heard him play."

Solt lit his pipe and puffed cherry blend while he spoke. "Did he tell you he almost became a surgeon?"

"A surgeon? No, he never mentioned that." Her eyes widened.

"I didn't think he would. He was chief resident, finishing his last year of surgical residency at Duke when he dropped out and decided to join the CDC."

"He was going to be a surgeon? I'd never have guessed that. I don't see Brett standing in a surgical suite all day."

"Well, you're right. Standing in an operating room ten to twelve hours a day wasn't his style. But that's not why he quit. He was a very skilled surgeon and four months away from completing his residency when something happened, something he couldn't deal with." Solt paused to finish the remains of his beer.

"Late one afternoon, a twelve-year-old girl was brought to the hospital. She'd been hit by a car while she was riding her bike. She was alert and talking with the ER staff and Brett before surgery, but she was in considerable pain. An emergency CT scan showed a ruptured spleen and torn kidney, so Brett took her to surgery.

What they didn't know was that her aorta had also been damaged, and before they could repair it, she bled to death on the operating table. He was devastated and blamed himself, even though there was nothing anyone could have done. It was the second young patient he'd lost that week, and that was it for him. He quit the next day. That's his one fatal weakness."

"What's that?"

"He can't handle losing—in anything. It's the demon in his life. He is driven to succeed. Or die trying."

Kari looked at him for a moment, then put her wineglass down and stood. "Ross, when you see him, please tell him goodbye for me. I have to leave first thing in the morning." She headed toward the door, then stopped and turned to look back at Solt. Her eyes were moist. "And tell him..." She paused a moment. "Never mind. Take care of yourself, Ross."

Kari smiled at the group and shook their hands. "It was nice meeting all of you," she said. "Sorry to rush off, but I have an early morning flight." Everyone at the table started to stand, but Kari left before they could finish their goodbyes.

Solt wanted to say something, but no words came to mind as he watched her disappear into the crowd.

Solt was climbing into bed when there was a knock on his door. After pulling on a robe, he hesitantly opened it and looked out to see Brett standing there.

"Come on in," he said.

Brett stepped into the room.

"Where've you been all day, Brett? And what are you doing wandering around this time of night?"

"I've been trying to get more information on the outbreak in New Mexico, but there's no way I can learn anything important while I'm down here. I'm flying back home first thing in the morning."

Solt stood there, looking at him. "Brett, you know more about what's going on down here than anyone else. You can't leave. Besides both Jacek and Quinn will be pissed as hell."

"My job isn't to keep them happy. I might learn something in New Mexico that could yield an important clue. I'll only be gone a couple days. You're headed into the mountain region tomorrow where more than sixty people have died. I'll catch up with you as soon as I can. Will you take care of Tequila for me?"

He led the dog into the room. He closed the door and left.

Chapter 32

Brett caught the early morning flight and arrived in Atlanta late in the afternoon. Most of the leaves had fallen, and the sunlight, unimpeded by bare trees, bathed his apartment in late afternoon orange glow. It was a good afternoon for a run, but he had too many things to do. Time was of the essence.

Inside his apartment, he poured a stiff scotch, then checked the mail and phone messages. He knew Ross would take good care of Tequila, but he missed the damned dog. And he realized he really missed Kari. At least both of them were safe.

His biggest concern now was what had happened in New Mexico. He needed to talk to Quinn. He showered, changed into fresh jeans and a sweater, then left for the Emergency Operations Center at the CDC.

He showed his ID badge to a guard and entered the newest building. When he punched in his code, the frosted glass doors slid open to reveal the large rectangular room the size of a gymnasium. It teemed with electronic communications equipment. The CDC Emergency Operations Center, known by everyone as the 'EOC', was a highly sophisticated medical intelligence war room filled with rows of computers, fax machines, and dozens of phones, all focused on the most current dangerous diseases around the world. Huge flat-panel monitors filled the wall along the front of the massive room, some displaying various detailed maps, some displaying hot spots of diseases around the globe with updates as they arrived, and others displaying weather conditions, maps, and current political conditions in various areas.

More than one hundred personnel staffed the center. The intelligence nerve center was tied directly to the Department of Defense and its bioterrorism division. It also tapped into every state health department and the World Health Organization.

The busy team of people in command center had been tracking mad cow disease, SARS, West Nile, bubonic plague, avian flu virus, swine flu, and a particularly virulent strain of tuberculosis. But the newly discovered outbreak in New Mexico moved the outbreak in Guatemala to the top of the priority list. Records from every county in every state would be reviewed and cross-referenced to try and turn up any new cases. Deaths from unexplained infections would be put under the microscope.

Brett found Quinn staring at one of the monitors and slid into the chair beside him.

Quinn sputtered and nearly dropped his coffee. "Christ, Brett, what are you doing here? Why aren't you down in Guatemala with the rest of the team?"

"We heard about the outbreak in New Mexico. I need to know more about it. Is it the same disease?"

"There's nothing definite yet, but it looks like it could be the same disease. Four deaths at a monastery in the mountains north of Santa Fe." Quinn eyed him. "So, what are you doing back here, Brett?" The tone in his voice was less than friendly.

"I want to check it out."

"Check what out?"

"I need to go to New Mexico."

"What the hell for? The New Mexico state health department is going to look into it, and we're running all the records in the state for the past six months. Besides, since we don't yet even know what we're dealing with, it's going to be hard to prove or disprove if the cases in New Mexico are the same disease," Quinn said. "It may turn out to be nothing."

"But you don't believe that, do you?" Brett asked. "That's why you're here at command center."

"Yeah, it's probably the same virus," Quinn said. "I'm going to send Laura Bauer there to work on it as soon as she gets back from Turkey."

"When does she get back?"

"She's leaving Turkey day after tomorrow. She can probably be in New Mexico first thing next week."

"Not soon enough. We have to check it out now."

"*We*? Forget about New Mexico," Quinn said sternly. "You've got enough to do in Guatemala. I already talked to Peter Jacek. He told me what happened. So, you goofed up. Everyone's entitled to one. You're not going to prove anything by running around New Mexico by yourself. I want you back down there with the team. They need your help."

"Mitch, the answer to this whole damn mess might be in New Mexico and I'm going to find it. I need a few days to check it out. Then I'll fly back down to Guatemala."

Quinn sat there a moment, staring at the screen. Finally he

said, "You've got three days. By then Laura should be there and you can get your ass back to Guatemala."

"I need a week."

"Don't push it, Brett. Three days, and I shouldn't even be doing that." Quinn looked at him awhile then said, "I thought you wanted some vacation time."

Brett went over to the coffee console, poured himself a cup and returned. "Yeah, but not right now."

"I didn't think so," Quinn said, smiling. "Go check it out, then get your butt back down there with the team. They need you there. I'm getting a lot of pressure on this one, especially since the press found out about the outbreak in New Mexico."

Brett sipped his coffee and glanced at the monitors.

Quinn looked up at the giant screens with global maps, updated text and graphs. "We're tracking a lot of bad stuff right now, but your disease takes top billing. The command center is going twenty-four seven on this, and I'm moving it to the number one priority. Dictate a quick report before you leave to bring us up to date on what you know." Quinn let out a slow sigh and ran his hand through his hair. Then he leaned forward. "Brett, if this virus finally breaks out, we're in for one hell of a mess. If the bird influenza and this thing in Guatemala both start spreading at the same time, it'll be total chaos. The pandemic of all pandemics."

Brett nodded in agreement. "That's why I have to go to New Mexico."

As he stood to leave, Quinn grabbed his arm. "Dictate that report before you leave. You're not going to shoot anyone or steal anything again, are you?"

"You never know, Mitch."

Brett left the Emergency Operation Center and walked over to his office. He took his Federal EIS badge out of his desk and dropped it into his briefcase, along with other items he might need. He rarely carried his badge because he usually didn't need it. But the badge gave him the authority to gain access to property or information if that ever became an issue. He didn't want to take any chances. He only had a few days, a week at most, to check it out and return to Guatemala.

He wasn't ready to give up on his theory. He was troubled by the outbreak in New Mexico, and he intended to investigate it. He logged onto his computer and did an internet search on Mayan tombs and artifacts. He printed out more than three dozen pages of material, which he'd take with him for later reading. On a hunch, he next typed in Forrest Wheeler and Mayan. More than two dozen sites came up, and he printed all of them. Reading all this would have to wait.

He wrote a quick summary on his computer and had just emailed it to Quinn when his phone rang. He decided to let the voicemail take it. It was Ashley Berkley. "Hi, Brett. It's me. I heard you were back in town. I really want to see you. I called your apartment but you weren't there." After a long pause she said, "Give me a call sometime." Click.

He stared at the phone. He didn't know why she had called.

She'd already broken it off. They had nothing to talk about. He and Ashley were too different. And things had happened in the El Peten jungle that made their differences even greater.

He knew two things for certain. He wasn't going to call Ashley, at least right now, and he missed Kari much more than he wanted to admit.

**Hortuedo village
In the Varapaz Valley,
Northern Guatemala mountains**

Solt needed a break. It had been a long, hot, grueling day. He sat on a packing crate in the shade of one of the army trucks, trying to find relief from the oppressive heat. It was late afternoon, but the temperature was still well above 100, and thick, humid air hung deathly still without a hint of a breeze. Solt slapped his neck to kill a biting insect, then pulled out his pipe and pushed cherry blend into the bowl. Tequila lay in the shadows beside him. The dog had been listless since Brett left. Solt looked around as he drew a flame into the pipe.

Seven military trucks and several large tents were spread out at the edge of the town of Hortuedo. A large antenna had been erected in a clearing for communication. More than a dozen Guatemalan soldiers had set up camp, presumably to provide protection. Solt sensed that their presence actually made the situation more unstable and dangerous.

Over the past three days, the CDC team had cultured nearly everyone in town. They had cultured the animals, the water supply, the soil, inspected the sewage, and collected thousands of insects. They closely monitored the patients who visited the World Health Organization clinic in the town where fourteen patients with the disease had died.

This was the second village they had visited. So far, there had been no new cases reported since their arrival in the region. Peter Jacek was growing impatient. "We've turned up nothing since we came here," Jacek said as he wiped sweat from his forehead. He pulled up an empty crate and sat down beside Solt. "There's no escape from this damned heat and miserable bugs. Where are all the cases? From all the panic about this, I thought there was supposed to be an epidemic."

Solt shook his head at Jacek's shortsightedness. Ross sucked on his pipe then said, "It's no different than any other disease we chase. You know that. Long periods of waiting, then boom—an outbreak somewhere."

"Well, I'm thinking we should go back to Guatemala City."

"And do what?" Solt asked as he blew out a blue cloud.

"We've collected enough samples," Jacek argued. "Now we wait to hear from the lab or wait until there's another case. Since it seems to be sporadic, we're just chasing our tails out here."

Solt couldn't think of a logical argument to counter Jacek's reasoning. He had to admit, the sweltering conditions in the Varapaz Valley were grim. A shower and a cold margarita seemed like a very good idea right now. Since there were no patients with the disease to examine and culture, there was no reason for them to stay.

Julie Thaxton was walking rapidly toward them. Covered with a layer of dust and sweat, she had been collecting soil, water, and animal samples. "I think we just got a break," she said, breathlessly wiping damp hair away from face. "They think another case just arrived at the clinic here."

"Let's go," Solt said, and the three of them headed for the clinic with Tequila trotting closely behind.

One of the government health department doctors who worked in the village met them at the door of the small adobe clinic. "I think we have a new patient with the disease. He arrived less than an hour ago. There's something different from all the others about this one, though."

"What's that?" Solt asked.

"He's an American."

Chapter 33

CDC Headquarters
Atlanta

Brett gathered up everything he would need for the trip, then left his office and walked over to Bio-Four. He hoped they might have some answers for him. After showing his ID and passing through security, he went to the men's locker room, showered, dressed in a full body suit, went through a phenol shower, attached his air hose, and finally entered the steel door into the maximum-containment laboratory.

Is that Brett Carson under that smart-looking space suit?" Janet Boggs asked.

"Don't they let you out every hour or so to play with the other kids?" he shot back.

"I guess you're here for an update. We haven't got much, but

I'll show you what we have so far," she said.

"Jan, what do you know about the outbreak in New Mexico?"

"New Mexico? Is that why you're here? Actually nothing," she said. "The computer spit out a list of deaths that were clustered and seemed to fit the similarities to your disease in Guatemala. We'll need viral DNA to prove if it's the same, and so far we've gotten zilch."

"So, it's possible the small outbreak in New Mexico is totally unrelated, right?" Brett asked.

"Of course it's possible. But my gut feeling is that it's the same disease. But if you want me to prove it, I'll need material to test. Otherwise, we're just guessing."

"Then I'll have to get it for you," Brett said.

"How are you going to do that?"

"I'll figure it out as I go."

She shook her head and smiled through her Plexiglas mask. "You're one of a kind, Brett. By the way, we do have a DNA profile of your virus. It doesn't match any others that we have. Just like the A9-CN in Alaska, you seem to keep turning up new ones for us. What I want to know is, where were these viruses before the outbreaks?"

"That's the question that may never be answered. But if my theory is correct, we might get lucky with this one."

"You have a theory about this virus?" Jan asked.

"Yeah, but now I've got to prove it."

"And how do you plan on doing that?"

"Like I said, I'll figure it out as I go. Were there any other recent deaths on the computer search that sounded similar besides those at the monastery?"

"Operations center turned up only one other death that

might fit the disease, but of course that's very difficult if not impossible to prove," Boggs said. "There was a death in Chicago last Christmas. An elderly priest, I believe—a monsignor. There was a lot of similarity with his death that suggest it could be the same disease. Because of the similarities to your cases, we decided to do more testing."

"And...?"

"His ELISA serology tests match the samples you recently sent."

"I need a copy of that case," Brett said. He couldn't make sense of it. How could a virus from Mayan tombs kill a priest in Chicago and a little girl in a Guatemalan village? Or for that matter, monks at a monastery in New Mexico? The obvious answer was that he'd been wrong about the connection to Mayan tombs.

Brett knew for certain he was going to New Mexico and decided he was going to stop in Chicago on his way. He had a lot of questions that were bothering him, and answers to some of those might be found in Chicago.

And he wanted to see Kari.

Hortuedo village
the Varapaz Valley,
Northern Guatemala mountains

The nurse at the Hortuedo clinic provided Solt and Jacek with masks and gloves. The World Health Organization doctor who ran the clinic motioned them over to a bed in the corner.

"From what you've told me about the other cases, this man has all the symptoms."

Solt nodded. "What do we know about him so far?" he asked as he reached for a stethoscope.

"He's an American, an archeologist from the University of Arizona. He's with a small group of graduate students and assistants. He first came down with symptoms last night. They brought him to the clinic about an hour ago."

"Are they still here? We'd like talk to them."

"They're over in the cantina getting something to eat. I didn't want to expose anybody. As far as we can tell at this point, it's one-hundred-percent lethal," the doctor said.

Solt nodded. He glanced at the IVs hanging.

"We're giving him broad spectrum antibiotics. And he's extremely dehydrated. He had episodes of severe vomiting last night and a high fever.

His years of practicing and teaching internal medicine at Columbia had given Solt an uncanny skill at quickly assessing a patient. He leaned down close to the man. "Can you hear me?" he asked into the man's ear.

The man nodded almost imperceptibly.

"Can you talk?"

The man just stared with dulled eyes half closed. It was obvious that breathing had become his all-consuming task.

Solt opened the man's shirt. He was startled by the dark purple splotches of hemorrhage discoloring his chest and abdomen. He put his stethoscope to the man's chest and listened to the gurgling sounds of air-sacs filled with secretions from an apparent overwhelming pneumonia. He checked the abdomen for enlarged liver or spleen, but the abdomen was soft, devoid of tone. Certainly, there was no organomegaly. He palpated for enlarged lymph nodes but found none. The disease had ravaged the body far too quickly for lymph nodes to respond.

The man was unable to communicate with them, and there was nothing to gain at his bedside other than exposing themselves to the disease, so Solt motioned for them to leave. They took off their gloves, gowns, and masks and put them in a plastic bag. "Burn everything in the bag, then scrub thoroughly," Solt instructed the nurse as they washed their hands.

Outside, Solt said, "We need to talk to the people who brought him in."

"They're still across the road at the cantina," the clinic doctor told them.

"Since none of us has actually seen a case, we don't know if this is the same disease," Jacek said.

Solt stuck an empty pipe in his mouth and looked at Jacek with disdain. "Don't be ridiculous. Do you really think that archeologist in there just has indigestion?"

"No, of course not," Jacek conceded. "You're right. Which brings me to something that's been bothering me. Why the hell is Brett back in Atlanta? He's the one person among us who has actually seen a case, and he did an autopsy. He knows what the disease looks like. We need him here now. Why the hell did he leave? Damnit, we finally get a possible break, and he's off chasing phantoms."

Solt couldn't think of a good argument. In fact, he agreed with Jacek. But he wasn't about to tell Jacek that he'd be willing to bet that Brett would be on a plane for New Mexico at his first opportunity.

They approached four people sitting outside on a small patio having dinner, and introductions were made all around.

"Can you fill us in on specifics?" Solt asked. "How long has he been sick?"

"His name is Steven Koop... Professor Koop," one of the young female graduate assistants said. "He complained that he was coming down with something last night after dinner. We didn't think much of it, and assumed that he was probably getting a cold or the flu. He spiked a fever, then began throwing up. It seemed to let up, and we all went off to bed.

When we got up this morning, it was obvious that he was deathly ill. We immediately packed up and brought him here to the clinic. Will he be alright?" she asked with concern in her voice.

"We can't say for certain," Solt said as he filled and lit his pipe. "But I must warn you, he is a very, very sick man. In all honesty, there's a chance he won't make it."

They all looked shocked, and one young woman started to cry.

"Has anyone else gotten sick?" Solt asked them.

"No, nobody so far," a young man answered. "I'm Nick Jindal, an assistant professor and an associate of Steven's. I usually accompany him on these trips."

"How long have you been down here?"

"We left Phoenix three weeks ago, and we've been at our digging site for two weeks. Two days ago, we stumbled onto a new undiscovered tomb, something we've never done before. When we explored it, we found more than a dozen artifacts that are probably more than fifteen hundred years old. It was an incredible find. Steven was very excited, as we all were."

Solt drew smoke through his pipe and blew out a cloud as he took in what he'd just heard. "So, within approximately twenty-four hours of discovering the tomb and the artifacts, Professor Koop became ill?"

"Yes, that's correct."

"Is anybody else in your group sick?"

"No. Should we be worried?" Nick asked.

"I can't really say for certain, but I don't think so," Solt answered. He put his elbows on the table and leaned toward them. "These artifacts you discovered—exactly who handled them?"

"I'm pretty agile, so I crawled into the tomb and handed everything out to Steven. I had latex gloves on because I'm allergic to all the mold on everything." He paused a moment then said, "I guess Steven was the only other person to actually handle them after that. They're over a thousand years old, and very fragile, so we were very careful with them."

"What did Professor Koop do with them after you handed them to him?"

"He dusted them with brushes to remove the worst of the grime and mold that coated them, then he packed each piece in plastic bubble wrap."

Solt assumed Koop might had inhaled some infectious agent when he dusted the artifacts before packing them. Everything fit with Brett's theory. Since no one else was sick, the disease appeared to be carried by a vector rather than being spread person-to-person. Mayan art. It now seemed entirely possible that the dust and fungus that enveloped the artifacts could be the source of the disease. Clearly, Brett had been right about that too—except for the little matter of an outbreak in New Mexico.

At that moment three new military Jeeps came roaring into the village with a cloud of dust billowing behind them. They pulled up beside the group and slid to a sudden stop. Solt knew something was wrong.

Chapter 34

During the flight to Chicago, Brett began to read the material he had downloaded from the internet on Forrest Wheeler and his contributions on Mayan history. Brett was surprised by the voluminous amount of material written about Wheeler and the work he had done. He had been highly respected in the field of archeology.

However, that made Brett even more puzzled about Wheeler's activity in Guatemala. Why was a man of his reputation digging in an unauthorized area? More important, why was he murdered? Was it simply a case of robbery and greed? Or—as Brett suspected— did it involve something far more mysterious?

After landing at O'Hare, Brett checked into the Drake, then took a cab to the University of Chicago. The first thing he wanted to do was see Kari. He missed her more than he wanted to admit.

He went to the administration building, found her office phone number in the directory and called her.

She answered on the first ring.

"Hi, Kari. It's Brett."

"Brett! I've been thinking about you. How are things going in Guatemala?"

"Progressing slowly. We hit a few snags. I'm in Chicago for a day. Do you have time to see me?"

"Chicago? You're here? Where?"

"I'm at the administration building."

"You're here on campus? My office is in the Social Science Research Building directly across the quad. Second floor. It should be easy to find." She paused a moment. "Wait—I have a better idea. There's a coffee shop in Swift Hall right behind the admin building. I'll meet you there."

When she walked into the coffee shop, he jumped to his feet. His reaction was just like the first time he had seen her in the El Dorado lobby; her stunning looks overwhelmed him. She crossed the room and gave him a quick kiss on the cheek. He'd hoped for more. But reality set in and he realized she was back home, had a boyfriend, and what they'd shared in Guatemala was in the distant past.

"It's great to see you, Brett," she said. "What a nice surprise. What are you doing in Chicago?"

"Just a stopover. I'm actually on my way to New Mexico." They found a corner tables, and he handed her a latte. "I have a few things to do here, and I wanted to see you. Can you have dinner with me tonight?"

"Oh, I'd love to, but I'm sorry I can't. I'm already have a commitment for this evening."

His heart sank. How could he have been so foolish? Why hadn't he called her earlier? He should have known she wouldn't be available on short notice, especially on a Friday night.

"No, it's nothing like that," she said, reading his face. "I'm having dinner with my aunt and uncle, my father's brother. He's helping me sort out the estate. How about tomorrow?" she asked.

He forlornly shook his head. "Tomorrow's out. I have an early morning flight to Albuquerque." He sipped his coffee and looked at her. He found himself scrambling to find a way to be with her again. "I have an idea—why don't you fly to New Mexico with me?"

"Are you serious?" She squinted at the ceiling while she thought about it a moment, then said, "I'd love to, but I have so much to do here, and there are so many things that need my attention."

"We'd only be gone a couple days. Just a long weekend. It might do you good to take a short break and get away from things."

"I can't. The semester has started, and I'm teaching three classes. Where are you staying?"

"The Drake."

"I can't believe our bad luck," she said, glancing at the clock on the wall. "I've got a committee meeting, and I can't be late. Walk with me back to my office."

They walked across the quad to her office. He wanted to put his arm around her, but her kiss on his cheek told him they were friends, nothing more. She stopped at the door to her building. Then she did something that made him think maybe he'd misread things. She leaned forward and kissed him, this time on the lips. "Dinner with my family isn't until seven tonight. We could meet at Jimmy's for a drink after my meeting. That'll give us a little time to visit."

"Great. Where's Jimmy's?"

It's two blocks up on East Fifty-fifth Street. You can't miss it. I really have to go. I'll see you there later." Then she left.

That gave him a little time to take care of something else. He had already located the Anthropology Department on the campus map. He headed back across the quad and crossed Ellis Street to Ingerside Hall.

Several things about Professor Wheeler had been bothering Brett. Was it standard procedure for a reputable academic anthropologist to dig in unauthorized areas? Somehow, he doubted that. He knew there were also restrictions on exploring certain ruins in the U.S. The country involved had the right to grant or refuse permits to whomever they chose. Why would any anthropologist go off on their own against regulations to find artifacts? Was it possible Wheeler had gotten special permission from someone? If so, who had granted it? Why had he gone into an extremely dangerous situation and taken Kari with him?

And why was he killed? He had been traveling with the men for at least three days before he was murdered. Had it been just a random violent act by one of numerous marauding bands—or was it a planned murder? Brett realized his suspicions were weak. Ross would say he was chasing shadows—and he probably was. But something didn't feel right. And what was the connection between Wheeler and the disease? Again, just a coincidence?

He entered Ingerside Hall, a large stone building with ivy covering the front, found the door to the anthropology office, and went in. The receptionist smiled at him.

"I'd like to speak to the director if possible," Brett said.

"That would be Dr. Horn. Do you have an appointment?" she asked as she glanced at the daily appointment book.

"No. I just need a few minutes of his time."

"*Her* time," a voice behind him said.

Brett turned and saw a tall, attractive woman standing behind him. "What can I help you with?" she asked.

"May I ask you a few questions regarding Dr. Wheeler?"

Dr. Horn froze for a second, her face showing a moment of pain. "Are you a reporter?" she asked.

"No." He extended his hand. "I'm Brett Carson with the CDC."

She shook his hand. "I'm Sarah Horn. The CDC? What is your interest in Forrest?"

"Could we talk somewhere in private?" Brett asked.

"Forgive me—of course. Jonna, hold my phone calls for a few minutes." She went into her office and Brett followed. She sat at her desk and he took a seat in a chair next to a window. Late afternoon sunlight lightened the ambiance of an otherwise elegant but somewhat somber, dark cherrywood office lined with bookshelves.

"I can give you ten minutes," she said, glancing at her watch. "What do you want to know?"

"I have a few questions regarding Dr. Wheeler."

"Forrest was one our most outstanding faculty members," she said. "His loss has devastated us."

Brett sensed immediately that his death had meant much more to her than the mere loss of a colleague. Before he sat down, he had noted that several photographs hanging on the wall were of Forrest Wheeler and Dr. Horn. A possible relationship between the two of them caught Brett off guard. He was uneasy as to how to proceed.

"Was Dr. Wheeler working under the supervision of the university while he was in Guatemala?" he asked.

"I'm not sure exactly what you're asking, but professors do

their own work and research during their time off. The university doesn't tell them what to do. They're not on assignment."

"When anthropologists are in foreign countries, do those governments limit their digging and explorations to specified areas?"

"Of course. We just can't go to one of the pyramids in Egypt and start moving blocks around. If there's something in particular we want to explore, we go to the proper government agency, tell them our plans, and get their approval."

"What about within our own country? What if you were looking for American Indian artifacts?"

"Native American," she corrected him. "Well, that depends. If it was on private land, we would talk to the owner of the property. If it's on federal land, we would need to get a permit. If it's on a reservation, we would contact leaders of the tribal council." She leaned forward on her desk. "What does this have to do with Forrest?"

She obviously was not pleased with Brett's questions, but he needed answers. "I have reason to believe that Dr. Wheeler might have been excavating in unauthorized areas in Guatemala."

"Preposterous!" Dr. Horn shot back. "Forrest would never do any such thing. Where did you come up with that ridiculous idea? He's one of the most respected men in modern archeology. His discoveries are on display in museums all over the world." She glanced at a picture on her desk; Brett assumed it was of Wheeler. "Forrest was a very special man. We all miss him very much."

Brett realized he had touched a raw nerve. 'We all miss him' meant she missed him. Wheeler had been someone very special to her. "Well, I could be wrong about that," he said. "It's possible he got permission from someone in the government."

"Would you explain to me why the CDC is interested in

Forrest's activity?" Horn asked, her tone angry.

"There's an epidemic in Guatemala, and some of the men who worked with Dr. Wheeler died from the disease."

"And—?"

"And I think Dr. Wheeler was killed while he was digging in an unauthorized area. I'm wondering why he was there."

"Since neither of us knows whether or not he had permission to dig there, we have to assume he did. I knew Forrest well, and he would never dream of doing such a thing."

"Are there any records that document where artifacts were found?"

"Of course. Every archeologist keeps a journal with explicit details about where each piece was found. Our work would be meaningless without documentation."

"Would it be possible for me to see Dr. Wheeler's journal?"

"No, that's his personal property. You would have no right to do that. Forrest has a daughter who is on the faculty here. She might be able to help you."

"Yes, I know. I met both Kari and her father when I was down there."

"You met Forrest?" Horn's defenses softened visibly when she spoke. She looked down a moment, then she glanced at her watch. "I've got an appointment. I'm sorry I couldn't be of more help to you. Do you have any other questions?"

"Are there other archeologists digging in Guatemala?"

"I'm not sure, but it's possible," she said. "Central America is a place of great history and ancient civilizations. I think there might be a team from the University of Arizona down there now."

"Do you know where they might be digging? Is there any kind of registry that would list where they are?"

"No. As I said, most archeologists are away on their own time, doing their own work. But the Guatemalan government should have applications and registrations on file."

"Isn't it true that most—if not all—of them are digging in well-known tombs that have already been extensively explored? And that none of them are actually digging in newly discovered tombs?"

Dr. Horn stared for a moment, not answering, either because she didn't know the answer, or because she knew the truth about Wheeler but didn't want to acknowledge it. Finally she said, "I suppose that is true. Do you have any more questions?" she asked.

"No," he said, standing and extending his hand. "Thank you for your time."

She stood and shook his hand. She stared at him for a moment. "What was it you really wanted, Dr. Carson? This isn't about a disease. Forrest was murdered. He didn't die of some infection."

"Just information. I'm not trying to imply Wheeler was doing anything illegal. I'm just trying to find out why he was murdered. There might be a clue about the disease and how to stop it. Thank you for your time." He shook her hand and said, "I know this has been hard on you, and I'm sorry. In the very brief time I knew Professor Wheeler, and from what Kari has told me about him, I know he was a special person."

She smiled at him and nodded. He had definitely been right about Wheeler and her. She cleared her throat, and her eyes started to moisten.

"Thank you for your time," he said softly, then left.

Outside, he headed down the steps toward the grassy quad and glanced at his watch. If he rushed, he had just enough time to check something else.

Chapter 35

Hortuedo
the Varapaz Valley,
Northern Guatemala mountains

A tall military officer with knee-high black boots stepped from one of the Jeeps and walked toward them. From the ribbons and the uniform, Ross Solt could tell he was a highly decorated colonel. And from the escort he had, Solt could also tell he was someone with status and rank. Then he saw the patch on his sleeve that identified him as Secret Police.

The man walked up to the table. "I am Colonel Zolog, head of the Secret Police Section of the Guatemalan government," he announced in a voice that was anything but friendly. "You are the Americans here investigating a new disease, correct?"

Jacek stood up and extended his hand. "I'm Doctor Peter Jacek with the Centers for Disease Control. I am in charge of this task force, and these are two of my colleagues."

Zolog nodded but did not acknowledge Jacek's extended hand. "I need to speak to Doctor Carson at once. Please get him."

"I'm afraid that's not possible," Jacek said.

"Why not?" Zolog shot back.

"Because he's not here," Jacek replied, clearly annoyed with the unfriendly and intimidating attitude of Zolog. "We don't know where Brett is. We haven't seen—"

"What do you mean, you don't know where he is?" Zolog shouted and slammed his fist down on the table, his face contorted in anger. "He is supposed to be here. He can't roam through the country at will."

Solt pulled his pipe from his mouth and decided to step into the fray. "Are you telling us that we are under some kind of travel restrictions while we're down here trying to help you?" He stared Zolog directly in the eye.

"You are in this country as our guests. We want you to stay in designated areas where our troops can provide protection for you."

"Let me set you straight on something, Colonel. We are here because your government asked us to come. We are trying to track down the source of a virus, and that means we are under no travel restrictions of any type. If your troops get infected and your forces are decimated, I can guarantee your president isn't going to be pleased. And we will make sure he knows who was responsible."

Zolog's face was deep red and the muscles in his neck bulged. "An American woman may be involved in matters of the government that are extremely important. We need to question her."

"What does that have to do with Brett?" Solt asked.

"We believe Doctor Carson knows where the woman is. That would make him guilty of harboring a fugitive, which is a very serious crime."

"Kari Wheeler is a fugitive?" Solt asked. He realized he had made a mistake as soon as the words left his mouth.

"You also know this woman? Do you know where she might be?"

"What has she done?"

"That's what we want to ask her!" Zolog stared at him for a full minute, anger carved in his face. Finally, he said, "If you see Dr. Carson, tell him it would be advisable for him to contact my office immediately."

With that, Zolog spun around and went back to his Jeep. His guards followed. He turned back and stared at them for a moment before he climbed into the Jeep. They roared out of the village just as quickly as they had arrived, leaving a dust cloud behind them.

Jesus, Brett. What have you done now? Solt wondered, as he put his pipe back in his mouth.

University of Chicago

Brett walked back across the campus quad. Maybe he had been wrong about Forrest Wheeler. But something was still bothering him, something in the back of his mind that he couldn't quite grasp. He was missing something. He decided to go the museum on campus and look at some of the Mayan pieces. He found the Walker Museum on the northeast corner of the quad. The hours on the door indicated he had thirty minutes before closing time.

He found what he was looking for on the second floor. Five rooms were filled with cases of ancient artifacts from the archeology department. The majority of the pieces were Aztec or Mayan, and he noted that the majority of them had been discovered and donated by Wheeler. There were cards telling something about each artifact and its estimated age. A few of the Mayan artifacts were estimated to be more than three thousand years old. He spent several minutes at various pieces, reading the notes that accompanied them.

He was in the second room when a voice startled him. "Sir, I'm sorry but we're closing now," a woman said.

As he left the museum, he knew he had to get a look at Wheeler's journal. Something was still nagging at him, but he couldn't put a finger on it. He knew he was missing something. The early evening sun was low, and the breeze blowing across the quad was chilly. Brett walked north on Fifty-Fifth Street until he came to Jimmy's Woodlawn Tap, just "Jimmy's" to the locals— famous for its jazz, cold beer and fantastic greasy hamburgers. University students and staff had already jammed into the three large rooms for Friday night drinks. He found a small table against the wall and ordered an Amstel Light.

He kept thinking about the dozens of artifacts in the museum he had seen.

Then it came to him.

He suddenly realized what had been bothering him. How had Wheeler gotten the artifacts that he discovered out of Guatemala? The government had established strict controls to prevent smuggling of valuable artifacts, and the penalties were severe. How had Wheeler managed to smuggle so many pieces out of the country? Out of areas that were strictly off limits?

He was sipping his Amstel Light when Kari found his table.

"Isn't this great?" she said as she sat down. "I love Jimmy's on the weekends. I've been coming here since I started college."

"We have a hangout like this in Atlanta," Brett said, "but it's not quite this rowdy."

She ordered a beer. "They've got great burgers here. I can't stay, but you may as well eat while you're here."

"Maybe later," he said. "Have you reconsidered going to New Mexico with me?"

"I'm sorry, Brett, but it's just not going to be possible right now. I have so much to do."

He nodded. He'd guessed as much, but he was still disappointed.

"Sarah said you talked to her,"

"Who?"

"Sarah Horn, director of the anthropology department. She said you were asking questions about my father. What was it specifically you want to know?"

"I was trying to find out all the sites where your father had been digging. I wanted to see if there was any connection to the disease. It was a long shot."

Kari's beer came, and she took a drink, then put her glass down and looked at him. "Why didn't you just ask me?"

"Okay, I will. Do you know the locations of the past few sites where your father was digging?" "No, not exactly. I didn't pay much close attention to where we were. It was all dense jungle and looked pretty much the same. I knew the general regions we were in, but not specifics. Occasionally, we might get lucky and find coordinates for a tomb we'd found, but not always." She leaned back in her chair and took another drink of her beer.

"Do you know who gave your father permission to dig in unauthorized areas?"

"Who said they were unauthorized? Where did you get that notion?" she asked with an edge in her voice.

Brett didn't want to tell her he had already talked to officials in Guatemala and he knew the areas were off limits. Instead of answering, he asked, "Who were the men you were traveling with on your last trip?"

"I don't know. We had never worked with them before, and they weren't from any of the local villages." She looked at him, trying to figure out what he was really asking. "Why do you want to know so much about my father? What does any of that have to do with the disease?"

"Could I look at his journal?"

With that she leaned forward and put her elbows on the table. "If I had it, I might let you look at it. But it's missing."

"Missing? You mean it was stolen?"

She looked warily around at the crowd. "Maybe... I don't know. I'm not sure. I'm not even sure I brought it home with me from Guatemala. I was sure I did, but now I can't find it. Maybe it just got misplaced when I was packing some of his things." She glanced at her watch. "I've got to run. Can't be late or my family will start to worry about me. It's been great seeing you again, Brett. Please call me when you get back. And get yourself a burger. They're fantastic."

She leaned over the table and kissed him. It was more than a peck on the cheek, and he could taste her lipstick. "Take care of yourself," she said and disappeared into the crowd.

Chapter 36

Hortuedo village
Northern Guatemala mountains

"He's dead," Solt announced as he walked up to the rest of his group who were sitting around drinking their morning coffee at their camp. Professor Steven Koop had died twelve hours after arriving at the WHO clinic in Hortuedo.

"None of his group has come down with any symptoms," Julie Thaxton said, sounding perplexed.

"No, they all seem fine," Solt said in agreement. "They're scared to death and obviously very upset, but nobody's sick." The CDC task force had cultured the members of Koop's group when they first arrived, and they were now watching them closely, but none of them had exhibited any symptoms. He jammed his pipe in his mouth. "Let's go talk to them."

The CDC team and the members of Koop's group went across to the café and found an outside table. A discussion followed about what to do with Koop's body. The group wanted to ship the body back home for burial, but Solt explained to them that that option was out of the question. Koop's body was now a giant culture medium for the deadly virus.

"Are you going to do an autopsy on him?" one of the group asked.

"No," Solt said. "We're not going to do that for two reasons. First, we aren't pathologists. We never do autopsies. Second, this disease is too dangerous to do an autopsy. One of my colleagues did a very limited autopsy last week on a victim, but that was risky as hell."

Solt wasn't about to attempt even a limited autopsy. But he was going to get samples. Wearing mask, gown, and gloves, Solt carefully and methodically took biopsy specimens from the liver and lungs. He was sweating under the gown, and his hands were trembling slightly when he finished. There was no room for the slightest error. Finally, he slid a long needle into the thorax and aspirated blood fluid from the chest cavity. After filling ten vials with blood and fluids he had drawn from the body, he was finished.

Outside, he had Jacek pour phenol over his gloves, then he removed his mask, gown, and gloves and put them into a bag to be burned.

The clinic was temporarily evacuated while the staff completely sterilized the floor and walls with diluted Clorox. Solt gathered everyone together to explain what they had to do. Jacek seemed to be completely undone by the recent turn of events, and he was more than willing for Solt to step forward and take charge.

"You need to contact his relatives and explain what happened,"

Solt said as he addressed the group from Arizona. "Then we will burn the body, and the ashes will be sterilized in phenol. After that, the ashes can be safely shipped back home for proper burial. It's far too risky to do it any other way."

People nodded and started to leave, when Koop's assistant asked, "Is it safe for us to go back to the site to retrieve our belongings? And what should we do with the artifacts we found?"

Solt tapped cherry blend into the bowl, put the pipe in his mouth, and lit it before answering. It was his way of giving himself time to think through things before coming to a decision. "I think only one person should go back."

"I'll go," Jindal volunteered."

"Okay. Collect only what you absolutely have to have. While you're in the camp, you'll need to wear a body suit, mask, gloves, and we'll give you a phenol bath when you come back."

"What about the artifacts? Can we collect them? Otherwise our trip down here would have been for nothing."

Solt realized this might be an opportunity to get cultures and study relics that might be the vector for the disease. "It's possible that the dust and mold covering the artifacts are the source of the disease. You definitely can't bring all of them, or even go near them. However, I would like you to collect two of the smaller relics and carefully place them in sterile sealing bags, then lock those in a metal container we will give you. Remember, you'll have to wear gloves, mask and body suit while there and handle the items exactly as instructed. Don't drive into camp," Solt continued, "since the tires might kick up infected dust. Park a short distance away and walk to the camp. Try not to disturb anything. Get only the essential items and get out of there as fast as you can. Our next main objective is to get everyone in your group home alive."

Then turning to his own team, he said, "We have work to do."

Jimmy's Woodlawn Tap
Chicago

Brett ordered a cheeseburger, fries, and another Amstel Light. Everybody jammed into Jimmy's seemed to be talking at the same time; the noise was deafening. It seemed to him that he was the only one who was alone. Friday night and he was alone again. He'd never really experienced loneliness until he'd met Kari. But tonight after she left, he felt it wash over him. His second beer came, he took a drink and pushed his personal life aside for the moment.

Had her father's journal been stolen or just misplaced? Who would want to steal it? What value could it be to anyone, unless it contained information that someone didn't want to get out? There was always the chance it hadn't even been stolen. Maybe she had just misplaced it. But that journal just might have a clue to the disease if it noted exactly where Wheeler had been digging.

He realized he was still trying to prove that he had been right about the disease being somehow connected to Mayan tombs. He had to let go and accept that he had been wrong. The outbreak in New Mexico seemed to prove beyond any doubt that he had been wrong. Why couldn't he just accept it? His food came, and while he ate, a jazz group started playing, adding to the clamor.

He left Jimmy's and headed back toward campus. It was dark. He crossed the quad again and went back to Ingerside Hall. Like most buildings on campus, the main doors into the building and the laboratories inside remained open, but most of the private offices were closed and locked.

Inside, the large halls were dim and empty. Very few faculty members would be working late on a Friday night. At least that was what Brett was banking on. He looked at the registry at the entrance. Dr. Forrest Wheeler's office was on the second floor. On his walk from Jimmy's, Brett twice had the feeling that he was being followed. But he hadn't spotted anyone. Even so, he looked around the hallway and glanced outside the door, then he took the wide marble stairs and found Wheeler's office.

As he'd expected, it was locked. Light spilled under the door from one of the offices farther down the hall. Someone was working late. Brett pulled out a pocket knife, inserted one of the small blades into the lock and twisted back and forth a few times while jiggling the handle. The lock didn't give. It wasn't a dead-bolt. He tried sliding the blade between the door and the frame, down past the lock. On the third try, the lock snapped back, and he opened the door.

Just then, the door down the hall opened. Brett quickly slipped inside and closed the door as quietly as he could. Footsteps approached, then continued on down the hall and faded down the stairs. Brett let out a slow, deep breath. He waited a few more minutes but heard no other sounds in the hall.

Street lamps provided faint light through the window, and

as his eyes adjusted to the otherwise dark office, he was able to make out things; desk and chair, bookshelves, file cabinets, and a computer. Several boxes filled with papers were stacked along the floor. Where to start looking?

Brett pulled out his penlight and passed its tiny beam over the desk, looking for some kind of notebook. Stacks of journals, tablets and spiral notebooks covered the desk. He flipped through a few of them, but nothing detailed the location of any artifacts. He wasn't sure what kind of notebook he was looking for. What he hoped to find were maps or geo-survey coordinates to locations of the tombs. Next, he looked through the bookshelves. He found several ring binders filled with lecture notes. He spotted a file cabinet and went over to open it.

Then he heard footsteps again.

He leaped to the door and quietly turned the lock. He hoped they would continue down the hall. They didn't. He heard the sound of keys being sorted. He looked around—there was obviously no place to hide inside the office. Who was it? Kari? Sarah Horn? Campus police? Or someone else? Had he been followed?

A key finally slipped into the lock. Brett reached the window at the same moment, shoved it up several inches, and slipped through it as the door opened. He hung by his hands on the stone window sill. Lights came on inside, then he heard the person moving toward the window. He looked at the bushes two stories below him and knew it was too far to jump. He grabbed onto the ivy vines that clung to the old stone building and started climbing down. The vine suddenly snapped, and he fell into the bushes below.

The impact of the fall knocked the wind out of him, and he strained to catch his breath. Brett looked up and saw the lights in the office go off. He was hidden from view by the bushes, but he could see the shadow of a figure standing at the window.

When the figure disappeared from the window, Brett crawled out from the bushes, brushed himself off, and headed up Ellis Street to find a cab.

Back in his room at the Drake, he climbed out of his clothes, showered, and crawled into bed.

He didn't notice the message light blinking on the phone.

Scar stood in the shadows of the dark room and stared out the second floor window of Forrest Wheeler's office. He wasn't sure what had happened, but he had lost the American doctor. He had followed Carson from the restaurant, hoping he would lead him to the woman. But he'd lost him. He cursed under this breath.

Scar's long flight from Guatemala had arrived more than seven hours earlier. He hadn't slept for over thirty hours. But he was close to finishing the job he had been sent to do, and the excitement of having the woman again gave him a new surge of energy.

Fortune had not been on his side, and he'd been on a losing chase since he arrived in Chicago. First, he went to her office at the University of Chicago campus, but she had already left. He found the address to her apartment and walked the twelve blocks there to wait. When she didn't show, he headed back to the campus.

He couldn't believe his luck when he spotted her walking

into a busy restaurant. He followed her in, aware that because of his size and the worn leather patch over his eye, more than a few turned to stare at him. He had ignored them and shoved his way through the crowd.

The woman met the American doctor and joined him at a table. Scar thought they were there for a meal, so he found a spot at the bar and ordered beer and a burger. He was famished. After he ordered, he turned to watch them, but the woman had vanished. He waited for a while to see if she would return. Once he realized she wasn't coming back, he decided to follow Carson to see if he would lead him to her.

Carson had led him to this office, but Scar had lost him too. The big man quietly left the office and headed back out into the night. Fatigue numbed his mind, and he fought to concentrate.

It didn't matter where she had gone for the evening. She would eventually be going back to her house. That was where he would wait for her. He assured himself he would find her within the next twenty-four hours. Maybe yet tonight. She would be his—until he decided to kill her. Their only concern was that she was dead; they didn't really care how he did it, or what he did to her before killing her. He would not kill her immediately.

He remembered what she looked like naked in the jungle before the shooting started—and a new surge of adrenaline made his heart hammer in anticipation.

Brett sat at his gate in the United terminal at O'Hare International Airport, sipping hot coffee and waiting to board flight 259 to Albuquerque. He had called Kari's apartment, but there'd been no answer. When he spotted her walking down the long concourse toward him, he broke into a wide grin.

She stopped in front of him and put her small carry-on case down. "Do you still want some company?"

"You're serious? Of course I want you to come," he said and leaped up to hug her. Then he quickly glanced at his watch. "We board in fifteen minutes. I'll have to get you a ticket."

"I guess you didn't get my message. I already have a ticket." She sat down beside him and took a drink of his coffee. "You look beat. And you've got an ugly scratch across your cheek. What were you doing last night?"

"Just my usual Friday night on the town," he said and smiled. "I can't believe you changed your mind."

"Well, it's the weekend, so I'll only miss a day or two at the most. You haven't told me what you're going to be doing in New Mexico."

"We're going to a monastery," he said, breaking his bagel in half and handing half to her.

"A monastery? I wonder why you forgot to mention that when you asked me to go." Then she laughed. "A monastery?"

"What made you change your mind?" he asked.

"I was disappointed that we weren't going to get to spend more time together. So, I moved a few appointments around and freed up some time. Actually, I don't like being alone right now. I spent the night at my aunt and uncle's house." After a moment, she added, "And if I can learn anything more about what happened to my father, I'm not going to miss the opportunity to help clear his name."

The overhead speakers announced that their flight to Albuquerque was ready for boarding. As they waited for their row to be called, a vague question crept in his mind. Was that the real reason she'd changed her mind about going with him? Or, did she know that he'd been to her father's office? Had she been the one following him? He decided not to over analyze it. Whatever the reason, he was glad she was here.

Scar spent most of the night on the street, watching and waiting for the Wheeler woman to return to her apartment, but she hadn't shown up. Fatigue was now like a strong sedative that had taken over his mind and body. Chilled, stiff, hungry, and tired to the point of collapse, he decided to find a room. He didn't want to collapse on the street and have to deal with the police.

Four blocks later he found what he was looking for. The young blond girl at the front desk of the University Ramada Inn stared at him as he paid for the room in cash. She didn't bother to ask for identification. She slid a key across the counter to him, and he left.

He unlocked the door to room 215, stumbled in, fell across the bed and immediately slipped into a deep sleep.

Chapter 37

New Mexico

Three hours later Brett and Kari landed in Albuquerque, rented a Ford Taurus, and headed north toward Santa Fe.

"Ever been to Santa Fe?" Brett asked, while adjusting the air conditioner.

"Once, as a child," Kari said, "but I don't remember much about it. My mom was an artist, and she had a few paintings in a gallery there."

"It's always been one of my great get-a-way places," he said. "It has a gentle peacefulness to it. Not the most beautiful place by a long shot, but it's comfortable. More like a well-worn sweatshirt on a fall day."

Just before noon, Brett pulled in front of the New Mexico State Health Department located on the west side of Santa Fe.

They went inside and walked to the front desk.

"Hello, I'm Dr. Carson with the Centers for Disease Control in Atlanta. Could I speak to the director please."

An attractive middle-aged woman with long streaked hair pulled back into a ponytail glanced at his identification. She was dressed "Santa Fe" with full-length skirt, sandals, and brightly colored blouse. Silver bracelets hung on her wrists. "He's not in on Saturday," she said. "He'll be here Monday morning."

"Then I need to speak to him on the phone."

"I'm sorry, but he's not available on weekends."

"Maybe you can help me then," Brett said. "I need copies of the records you have on the recent deaths at the San Sebastian Monastery."

"Oh, isn't that a dreadful situation?" she asked.

"Yes, it is. I'm on my way there to investigate it. That's why I need copies of the records today."

"I'm sorry, Dr. Carson, but I don't have the authority to release them."

Brett pulled out his EIS federal badge and shoved it toward her. "I need those records today. So, either get the director on the phone now, or else figure out another way to get authorization for release of the documents. I can get federal agents in here to confiscate them if necessary. I'm sorry, but this can't wait until Monday."

She seemed taken aback by his demand and stood there a moment, then went into an office behind the desk and closed the door. She returned fifteen minutes later with a folder containing copies of the records. She was much friendlier now and smiled when she handed him the folder.

"Here are the papers you wanted. I also put a card with our director's name and phone number in case you need to contact him. I included a map with directions to the monastery."

"Thank you for your help," Brett said, and they left.

"Were you really going to call in federal agents?" Kari asked as they climbed into the Taurus.

"Nah, just wanted to muscle her a little. A pretty good act, huh?"

She punched his arm. "Federal agents....," and shook her head.

It was nearly one o'clock and they hadn't eaten since sharing a bagel back in Chicago. "You hungry?" he asked. "I know a great place for lunch."

"Great. I'm famished," Kari said.

The Coyote Café was one of his favorite haunts in Santa Fe, a second-story open patio restaurant that overlooked the narrow streets, two blocks from the Plaza and Governor's Palace.

"You're right," Kari said, as they walked out onto the patio and found a table under the shade of a tree. "This is a lovely place. I need to make a couple of calls. Order for me. I'll be right back."

He noticed men glancing at her as she walked away. He ordered lunch and cold beers for them. He was sipping his beer and wondering what lay ahead for them when Kari returned and slid into the chair across from him.

"You look deep in thought," she said. "Are you okay?"

"I'm fine. Let's have some lunch," he answered, as their food arrived. They laughed and chatted as they ate their tortilla soup with sliced avocados, followed by chicken enchiladas with mole poblano sauce and Mexican rice. Kari made it easy for him to forget his problems. She was the easiest woman to be with he'd ever met. He was mesmerized by her eyes, the way her eyebrows arched when she was puzzled, the way her lips looked when she smiled.

She caught him staring at her. "What?" she asked, blushing.

"Nothing. I'm glad you're here."

"The heat's getting to you," she said, standing up. "Let's go."

Borga,
Guatemala

A late afternoon thunderstorm turned the sky black. The sky opened, and rain fell in sheets, blown sideways by a stiff wind. A solitary figure hunched under a poncho made his way along one of the alleys of the slums of Borga. The streets were nearly dark except for the frequent ear-splitting thunder and blinding lightning bolts that streaked to the ground.

Wearing old, worn clothes under the poncho, he looked like any of the peasants who roamed the streets. He stopped beside a rundown warehouse and looked up and down the deserted alley. No one would recognize him, but the situation demanded extra caution. After satisfying himself that he hadn't been followed, he climbed the steps to the loading dock and banged on the door.

Torrents of water poured from the tin roof onto him as he banged again. With the combined noise of the rain hammering on the tin and the booming thunder, he wasn't sure he could be heard. He banged on the door again. After knocking a third time, he heard the lock turn, and one of the large doors slid open.

Armando Galvez stood there, staring. It took him a moment for the face under the hood to register. "Padre—what are you doing here?" he burst out when he recognized the face.

"Keep your voice down," the figure said as he pushed past him and stepped inside.

"Come in, come in." Armando looked up and down the alley before sliding the door closed behind them. Armando's damp shirt was open, and perspiration beaded his face.

"What happened to you?" Father Hernandez asked. The hot, stuffy dark warehouse made Hernandez feel as if he were suffocating. The stale, dust-filled air smelled of woodchips and cleaning solutions.

"Working," Armando said, "just working."

"Two things have come up. We've got problems," Hernandez said.

"What do you mean, Padre? What kind of problems?" he asked, rubbing the back of his hand across his sweaty forehead, smearing dirt as he did so.

"Colonel Zolog is on a rampage. The government has stepped up their security. You know what the implications are if they find out about us. Everyone has to be instructed to be extremely cautious. What happens in the next few weeks could decide the war. Zolog is both smart and dangerous. Talk to no one—and watch your back. Or you might find yourself lying on it—permanently!"

Armando nodded. He suspected the priest hadn't risked coming to the warehouse just to warn him. He sensed there had to be more, but for the moment, he couldn't figure out what it was. He hated surprises, especially bad ones. He began to sweat more profusely. At least Father Hernandez was unaccompanied. Armando pulled out a soiled hanky and blotted his face and neck.

"No, of course not, Father." He tried to hide his panic. Had he been discovered? "We will make sure that doesn't continue."

"Make sure it doesn't."

"By the way," Armando asked, "what about the murder of the American archeologist, Wheeler? That's going to be a very big loss for us." Almost all of the valuable artifacts they'd shipped over the past few months had been discovered by Wheeler. "What are we going to do now?"

"Never mind," Hernandez said sternly. "It's not your problem. You'd do better to look out for yourself and the warehouse instead of worrying about things that don't concern you."

"Is there anything else, Padre?" Armando asked, wanting this to be over and done with.

"There is another reason I came to see you. A team of doctors from the United States who came down to study a disease. They could prove to be a very big problem for us."

"Disease? What disease? How could that be a problem for us?"

Hernandez stared at Armando Galvez with a look that sent a chill through him. "You don't worry about the disease. Pay attention!"

Armando grew rigid. "Yes, Padre. What do you want me to do, have them killed?"

The priest shook his head. "No, we don't want the Americans killed. The last thing we need is for some United States airborne division descending on us. We only want to delay them."

"Delay? I... I don't—" Armando stammered.

"Figure out a way. They've headed north to the Varapaz Valley region. If they do find something regarding any disease, then make sure no one else learns about it. But get it done quickly. There've been some complications over the past two weeks."

"Complications? What kind of complications?" Armando asked.

The priest waved the question away. "Find out what you can,

and stall them. Keep them in the mountains and out of contact with the outside world. If things get out of hand, we may have to kill them. But that will be a last resort."

Father Hernandez pulled the hood over his head. "I'm sending some men tomorrow to help you. Use them to increase security here, and to keep a tight rein on the American doctors."

He paused and looked directly at Galvez. Also, there are rumors that someone has been skimming off select artifacts for themselves and dealing with foreign art dealers on their own. I hope for his sake that the rumors are false. Don't screw this up, because if you do, when we're through with you, there'll be nothing important left for the firing squad to shoot."

Hernandez slid the door open and checked the alley carefully. Once he decided it was safe, he hurried back out into the storm and disappeared.

"Bastards," Armando spat out after Hernandez left. After three shots of Tequila and stewing about the situation, Armando decided that stalling the American doctors wasn't an impossible task. All he had to do was come with a plan and get others to carry it out.

Chapter 38

Brett and Kari left Santa Fe and drove north toward the monastery. He rolled down the window and took in the view of the open plains dotted with pinion pine and sage. The only sound was the wind blowing through the pines. The quiet vastness of the southwestern plains was quite a contrast to the jungle. The jungle was a constant presence, intruding into every sense, a place always in motion and never at peace: the incessant noise of birds and howler monkeys, water dripping from everything, and the smell of wet earth and rotting vegetation.

A gust of wind blew a tumbleweed across the road in front of them. He noticed Kari glancing occasionally in the car mirror.

"What are you looking for?" he finally asked.

"Making sure we're not being followed," she said.

"Why would anyone be following us?"

"Just being cautious."

Her answer didn't entirely satisfy Brett, especially since he had been followed when he went to Forrest's office the night before. He found himself glancing in the mirror occasionally, then decided that was a useless exercise. Except for an infrequent car, they were alone on the long stretch of road.

"Have you noticed that whenever I'm with you we're always traveling somewhere?" she asked. "At least this car is better than that damned Jeep."

"Actually, I was kind of growing fond of that thing. It had spirit."

"Spirit? If it's anything, it's possessed, some kind of rusted torture device."

She laughingly continued, "And I'd also like to remind you how you've always put me up in the best accommodations. A church balcony, a tent in the middle of the jungle, and now a monastery."

"Yeah, first class all the way." He turned and looked at her, a big grin spreading across his face. "You're definitely going to be the object of great attention at the monastery. The only woman for miles around."

"What if they won't let me in?"

"They have to. You're Dr. Wheeler, my assistant, and we're here on official business."

"What exactly are we going to be doing at the monastery?" she asked.

"We're going to get samples. I have to know for certain if it's the same virus. And I need to know if there's a connection between the monastery and the jungle in Guatemala. We may be missing a big piece of the puzzle."

"So, are we going to culture everyone at the monastery like we did in the villages?"

"You are," he said. "That's your job. My job is to figure out how to get samples from the four monks who died."

"How are you going to do that?" she asked with great interest.

"I'm going to dig them up," he said. She looked at him as if he were crazy, but said nothing.

Late in the afternoon, he turned off highway 191 onto a narrow gravel road consisting of dangerous curves and steep climbs that wound its way up a deep canyon of the Carlos mountains. The low afternoon sun bathed the canyon in a muted orange light.

The road came to an abrupt end in front of a large iron gate. Brett pulled up to the gate and stopped. Behind the fence stood the three-hundred-year-old adobe buildings of the San Sebastian Monastery. He hoped he would find the answers he was seeking inside that fence.

The damned job didn't used to be this tough or complicated. He got out of the car and went to the gate and rang a bell.

A monk in a brown robe and sandals came to the gate. "This is private property. May I help you?"

Brett stepped up to the gate. "I'm Dr. Brett Carson with the Centers for Disease Control, and this is my assistant, Dr. Wheeler." He showed the monk his federal badge.

"Yes?" the monk said. "What can I do for you?"

"I would like to speak to the person in charge. May we come in?"

"Wait here," he ordered, and he walked away.

"Well, I'd say that went pretty well," Kari remarked sarcastically.

Five minutes later the monk returned, unlocked the gate and opened it. "Park your car over there," he said, pointing to a spot inside the gate. "I'll take you to Father Menendez."

After Brett parked the rental car, the three of them walked along a stone path that led them to an adobe brick building where an old heavy oak door hung massive iron hinges. The sun had dropped behind the mountains, the evening shadows grew longer, and the temperature in the mountains had already started to fall.

The monk knocked at the door. The thick, weathered oak door finally swung open, and the monk accompanying them turned and left. A silver-haired man with a trim beard greeted them. "I'm Father Menendez, the director here at San Sebastian. Please come in."

Brett shook his hand and made introductions again. "I'm Doctor Carson from the Centers for Disease Control, and this is my assistant, Doctor Wheeler. We are here to investigate the recent deaths at the monastery."

"The CDC? What is it exactly you want to know?" Menendez asked. His face registered alarm.

"Well, to begin with, how many deaths have you had at San Sebastian?"

"Well, that depends. Over what period of time?"

The last three centuries, dick head! The muscles in Brett's jaw flexed as his anger rose to the surface. "Let's start with only recent deaths," he said, trying to keep his emotions in check. " F o u r ," Menendez said without hesitating.

Brett already knew that. So why did he feel he had to drag the information out of him? "When was the most recent death?"

"Brother Jonathan, seven days ago."

Brett also knew that. It was obvious Father Menendez was answering his questions truthfully, but he certainly wasn't elaborating and wasn't going to provide any information that wasn't specifically asked for. "When was the first death?" Brett asked.

"Three months ago," Menendez replied.

"Three months ago?" Brett repeated. That was a surprise and a disturbing bit of information. The three-month spread between the first and the most recent death concerned Brett. That didn't fit the pattern of a contagious epidemic, especially since the men were confined in a relatively small area and exposed to one another on a regular basis. There was also the possibility that the earliest death was unrelated to the more recent deaths. Maybe they were chasing a dead-end here.

"What did the doctors say about the four deaths?" Brett asked. "Do you have copies of their medical records?"

"As you are well aware, we are more than seventy miles from the nearest town. So, we don't always have a doctor available to us."

"Are you saying that the monks who died never saw a doctor or went to a hospital?"

"When Brother Jonathan became ill, we sent for a doctor from Shiprock. Unfortunately, by the time the doctor came the next morning, Brother Jonathan was already dead."

"So, his death is the one that really started the investigation?" Brett asked.

"I wasn't aware that there was an investigation." Menendez shot back.

Yeah right, there's no investigation. I came all the damn way out here just to watch men run around in brown robes! Brett knew he was about to lose control, and he couldn't afford to let that happen because he needed answers. Answers that the priest seemed reluctant to provide. Brett stared at the priest a moment before continuing. "We are investigating the deaths here at San Sebastian. We think the four monks may have died of the same disease."

"Certainly, we want to help you in any way we can," Menendez said with a disingenuous smile.

Ever heard of the sin of lying, Father? Brett's quick-fire temper had gotten him into trouble more than once, and he knew he was going to have to keep it under control if he was going to get any cooperation from the monks. "Do you have copies of their death certificates?"

"They're not kept here," Menendez said. "They are on file at the archdiocese offices in Santa Fe."

Brett was getting nowhere fast. "We're going to need to get blood cultures on everyone at the monastery, and I want to talk to the monks."

"Of course, but it's too late for you to do anything tonight," Menendez said. "There's no reason for you to drive all the way down the canyon tonight. I'll make arrangements for you to spend the night here. You may join us for the evening meal and talk to the brothers tomorrow. By the way, we live by strict rules here and we expect you to respect them while you're our guests."

Brett had assumed they would be staying at the monastery. They thanked Menendez for his offer. Kari was unhappy about being given a room in a separate building from Brett, and after everything she had been through, Brett couldn't blame her. She insisted on knowing where his room was. After putting their things in their rooms, they went to the dining hall where the monks were already seated at long rough wooden tables. Oil lamps on the wall provided the only light.

Menendez stood and spoke. "Before I give the blessing for the meal," he said, "I would like you all to welcome Dr. Carson and Dr. Wheeler. They are from the CDC in Atlanta. They will be spending the evening with us." After he gave the blessing in Latin, monks served the dinner, delivering plates already filled with each person's portion.

The meal consisted of freshly baked sourdough bread, sweet potatoes, baked chicken with pine nuts, and red wine poured from a clay pitcher. Brett was surprised at how delicious the food tasted. After the meal, Brett cornered two of the brothers and questioned them before they left for their evening mass at the chapel. He learned that the monks had been sick only a short time before they died; all had died within a day after getting sick.

Just as Brett started to ask more specific questions, a deep, brass bell echoing off the canyon walls sounded the call to evening prayers. He would have to wait until the next day to get more information.

"You are welcome to join us for evening prayers," one of them said as they left.

While that was not on his list of things to do, Brett decided it might be prudent to do so under the circumstances. They followed the monks up the path to the adobe brick Chapel of Saint Francis del Marco. Candles provided the only light, revealing rough-hewn beams, primitive stained-glass windows, and Spanish-tiled floor. Brett and Kari sat in the back on a bench by themselves. The monks sang Gregorian chants, then Father Menendez led the prayers. After the service, everyone filed out quietly and went to their rooms. A monk escorted Kari to the building where she was staying.

Brett's was a small cell-like room, long and narrow, with only a cot and a little wooden stand. A single open window with no glass allowed moonlight into the otherwise dark room. None of the windows in the adobe dormitories had glass in them. Brett was exhausted. He washed his face from a jug of water sitting on the stand, stripped down to his shorts, and climbed under a sheet and a heavy wool blanket. Cold night mountain air poured into the room, but the blanket was warm, and he fell asleep almost immediately.

Sometime during the night, Brett woke out of a deep sleep and became aware of a presence in his room. The moonlight was temporarily blocked by a dark form moving between him and the open window. Suddenly, a monk was climbing onto his cot on top of him. Brett looked over, but the face was hidden in the dark shadow of the hood that covered it.

"Hey!" he grunted. Muscles tensed, and Brett braced himself to throw the person off, when the figure moved closer, inches from his face.

"Shh... it's me."

"Kari—what are you doing?"

"I didn't want to be alone tonight," she said. "It's lonely on the mountain at night."

"How did you get in here? And what's with the robe?" Brett whispered, starting to laugh.

"It was in my room. I needed something to wear," she said, "and I figured the robe would be a good cover if someone spotted me sneaking in here."

She crawled under the blanket. He pushed the hood back, brushed the hair away from her face, and kissed her gently. Even through the robe he could feel the contours of her body. They lay there for several minutes.

Kari seemed restless. She fidgeted with the blanket and pillow, then kicked a bare leg out from the robe. "I can't sleep," she finally whispered.

"Yeah, me neither." Brett was bone tired, but sleep was suddenly the farthest thing from his mind now. She looked at him with a serious look on her face, then she kissed him. It was a long, sensuous kiss.

"I have an idea," she said, as she rolled over and straddled him. She leaned forward and kissed him again. The hood fell over her head and covered both their faces.

He pushed the hood off her head for the second time. Slowly he reached down and pulled the bottom of the thick robe up to her waist. She was wearing nothing beneath the robe. His hands slid up her thighs, and he arched up to meet her as she pressed herself against him.

Her fingers urgently guided him into her. His hands went behind her and pulled her tightly against him, forcing himself deeper into her. She flipped the hood back, but it kept falling over her head as she leaned over him. Her legs were clamped against his sides, and her hands were on the bed, leaning over him as she moved against him.

His hands slipped under the robe and found her breasts, and her skin was hot to his touch. "I guess we don't need this," she said and suddenly sat upright, clawed at the monk's robe and pulled it off over her head. He held her hips as she pressed against him with slow, purposeful motion, her head down and her hair spilling over his chest. After a long moan, her breath caught in her throat, the muscles in her legs tensed, and he felt her tighten around him, causing him to release deep inside her. With a final shudder, she fell beside him and tried to catch her breath.

"Now you can go to sleep," she whispered.

"Oh, god..." he said, breathing hard.

"Exactly, Brother Brett," she said with a giggle. "By the way, they never did tell us the rules. I wonder if this violates one of them?"

"You are totally crazy," he whispered in her ear with a breathless, raspy voice. He took her hair in his hands, pulled her face to his and kissed her with a long passionate kiss. "By the way, where'd you get that robe? Isn't someone going to be missing it?"

"Would you like me to leave now so I can return it to the owner?"

"No," he said and held the blanket so she could slide under it beside him. She put her head on his pillow. Moisture on the side of her face glistened in the fading moonlight. He stroked her hair and kissed her again.

They curled up again.

"I should go before the monks find us together," she said.

"Not yet," Brett said, hugging her. They held each other and kissed, then with slow, tender, deliberate moves, they made love again. Brett finally fell asleep with Kari beside him on the narrow cot.

Chicago

When he finally woke, Scar stood up, stretched, and looked out the window of the University Ramada Inn. It was Sunday morning. He'd slept an entire day. His mouth was dry, his muscles were sore, and he was starving.

After a hot shower, he put his clothes on and went out for breakfast. Over a pile of eggs and pancakes at Denny's, he planned his day. Kari Wheeler hadn't returned to her apartment. She must have shacked up somewhere for the night. Possibly even for the weekend. But she was certain to be at work on Monday, and that meant she'd be back at her apartment today. He smiled as he gulped down a cup of coffee.

The damned weekend had screwed up his plan. If they had sent him a day earlier, she'd be dead and he'd be back home in Guatemala.

It didn't matter; he'd get her today. She would have to come back to her apartment.

Chapter 39

San Sebastian Monastery
New Mexico

When he woke to the sound of the morning chapel brass bell, Kari was gone. He washed, dressed and went to breakfast. She was already sitting at a table eating. She barely acknowledged him as he sat down. He wondered which monk was missing his robe this morning.

A plate of cornbread and sausage was placed in front of him and as he started to eat, a voice sounded behind him.

"How was your night, Dr. Carson?" Father Menendez asked.

Brett wondered for a second if the priest had learned of Kari's trip to his room. "Fine, thank you, Father," Brett said, turning around to look at him. Swallowing a piece of cornbread, he said,

"We're sorry to inconvenience you, but as I mentioned yesterday, we'll have to culture everyone at San Sebastian, and I'll need to talk to the monks."

"I will assemble the brothers and you may talk to them."

"I would rather talk to them individually," Brett insisted.

"I will arrange for that," Menendez said and left.

After breakfast, Kari was given a room where she could take blood samples from each monk, which she labeled and put on ice. While she was busy doing that, Brett took quick samples of the soil and from the spring that provided their water source.

Then he interviewed several of the monks after Kari had drawn their blood for sampling. They seemed much more reluctant to talk to him than they had been yesterday. It was obvious to Brett that someone—namely Father Menendez—had clamped down on the monks since last night. Brett realized he wasn't going to learn anything meaningful from them, and he was starting to get pissed off.

They finished just before lunch. Kari walked up to him and ripped off her sterile gloves with a snap. "I want to point out that every time I'm with you, Brett, I'm either bouncing around in some vehicle or drawing blood for you. You're going to have to plan something different for our next date."

"Come on, I'll buy you lunch at the Brother's Café," he said.

After lunch, Menendez and two other monks approached Brett. "I assume you've gotten what you needed," Menendez said.

"Almost," Brett replied. "I have a few more questions. And I need to get samples from the four monks who died."

Menendez looked shocked at his last statement. "I don't understand. What do you mean, the four monks who died?"

"We need to exhume the bodies so I can get samples from

them," Brett said.

Menendez reacted immediately. "We've cooperated fully with you. But I think you've used up your welcome here."

"I didn't realize I had been welcomed," Brett shot back.

"I think you'd better leave." The two monks beside Menendez seemed prepared to see to it that it happened.

Brett looked Menendez straight in the eye and said, "Tomorrow we need to dig up the bodies so I can get samples. Then we'll leave."

"Desecrating bodies of our dearly beloved in Christ is not something we approve of, and I don't believe you have the authority to exhume bodies on the monastery's private property," Menendez said through clenched teeth, as his face turned red with anger. "We've done everything we could to assist you. You've invaded our privacy, and we tolerated it in order to help you. Now I must insist that you leave. I will not allow you to dig up the bodies of our dead."

"I know it's not pleasant, but it's something we have to do."

"Do you have a warrant? If you don't, then leave," Menendez insisted.

Brett flipped out his badge and held it in front of him. "I'm a federal officer. I can call in federal marshals if necessary. If you think I've invaded your privacy, just wait until the marshals and the press who are sure to follow get here and start swarming all over the place. Somehow, I don't think you want that to happen, do you? We're going to exhume the bodies for testing, either by just me or with a dozen marshals and the press in attendance. Your choice."

Menendez glared at Brett, his lips pressed into a thin line, and the veins on his forehead bulging. He turned and started to walk away, then stopped and turned. "Do it, then get out and leave us alone." He walked away.

"Well, I'd say that went pretty well again, wouldn't you?" Kari said when they left the dining room.

Brett smiled at her. "Gotta get rough sometimes. The problem is to know when."

"And you think you've mastered that?" she asked.

"I might need a little work on it."

"Federal marshals? Geez... "

He walked her back to her room.

"Keep your door locked," he said, then kissed her.

"The 'window' is an open hole in the wall with no glass. So why bother to lock the door? Are you worried about something?"

"Well I'm just—"

"I have a gun," she interrupted.

Brett stool there a second. "What do you mean, you have a gun?"

"I brought my father's revolver. I decided at the last minute to throw it in with my luggage. After what happened in Guatemala, I've become much more cautious. Actually... I've become more afraid. I'm afraid at night; I'm afraid to be alone."

"You brought a gun? How did you get it through airport security?"

"Obviously you can't go through security with a gun in your carry-on, but it's not a problem if you just disassemble it and pack the separate pieces in luggage that you check through."

"I don't think you can—"

"Yeah, you can. Detach the cylinder and put in your hair rollers. The barrel detaches and goes in with your hair dryer."

Brett shook his head in disbelief, then said, "Well, I don't think there is much to be afraid of. The monks seem pretty harmless."

"Then why did you tell me to lock my door?"

"Just being cautious. See you in the morning."

Back in his room, as he was getting undressed, there was a knock at his door. He opened it. A monk stood there, one of the burly monks who accompanied Menendez around the monastery. "Father Menendez would like a word with you, Dr. Carson."

Brett didn't have a good feeling about the situation, but he slipped back into his clothes and followed the monk across the courtyard to the building where the director lived. He couldn't imagine why he was being summoned so late at night.

Menendez opened the door before they knocked. He stood in the doorway. "Tomorrow we will dig up the bodies as you requested. The brothers will help you so we can insure the dignity of the dead. We expect the bodies to be handled with respect. We will have a mass for them tomorrow. Then your business here will be finished." He closed the door without waiting for Brett's response.

The monk who had accompanied Brett turned and left, leaving him alone in the dark.

It was obvious that they were not going to make it easy for him. They had to be hiding something. It just didn't make any sense. He was only there to find out why the monks had died. As he crossed the courtyard and walked along the long colonnade toward the building where his room was located, a hooded figure stepped out of the shadows. Brett stopped. For a second, he thought it might be Kari. But the deep whispered voice proved him wrong.

"They didn't tell you everything," the voice whispered, the face hidden beneath the darkness of the hood. "There have been five recent deaths here, not four." The man's breath sent faint puffs of vapor from the hood into the chilled night air.

"Five? When was the fifth death?"

"A week ago. Brother Steven."

"A week ago? How did he die? Why aren't there any records of it?"

Silence.

"Where is he buried?"

"On the side of the mountain with the others," the voice whispered.

"I only saw four new graves."

Silence. Brett waited. No answers came.

"Why are you telling me this? What's going on? What are they trying to hide here? Why all the secrecy?"

He waited for answers, but the figure had already melted back into the shadows and disappeared. Who was he? Why had he decided to feed him information? Brett had an uneasy feeling. Was he being set up, maybe being led into a situation that could have serious consequences?

He felt he was getting close to uncovering something, and the closer he got, the more threatened others became. What he intended to do tomorrow was illegal and could cost him his job. He had no authority to demand that bodies be exhumed. That would require a court order signed by a judge. He had gambled that the monks' need to keep secret whatever it was they were hiding was far more important to them than the sanctity of the recently dead bodies of the four—or five—monks. His gamble had paid off for now. But he was working on borrowed time.

Back in his room, he stared at the sky for over an hour through the open window as his mind searched for answers before he finally fell into a troubled sleep.

Chapter 40

The next morning after breakfast, Brett and four monks carrying shovels and picks walked up the mountain path to the cemetery behind the chapel. Nothing identified the area as a cemetery except for the recently turned earth and the small stone markers that had been used to mark the graves of the monks of San Sebastian for the past three hundred years. The stone markers looked as if they were part of the rock that made up the mountain.

Wearing body suits, surgical masks and latex gloves, that Brett had insisted on, the monks started digging up one of the graves. If he was right, they were about to uncover the deadly virus, and he didn't want to help the disease spread. He looked around, trying to spot a fifth grave. Why would they want to keep him from knowing about it? Was there in fact a fifth grave, or had the secretive figure in the shadows been trying to send him on a wild goose chase?

The whole damned situation at the monastery made Brett furious. His job was to figure out how to stop a terrible disease and try to save lives, but the monks of San Sebastian seemed determined to prevent him from doing that.

Why?

Brett pulled off his mask and walked up to Brother Daniel, who was overseeing the project. "What are you hiding here that you're so worried about?" Brett asked. "Why have you refused to cooperate with me and help me get to the bottom of this?" His questions brought only icy stares.

"We are cooperating. We aren't hiding anything from you, Dr. Carson."

"Don't you care about the other monks' safety?" Brett continued. "You haven't been honest with me."

"We haven't been dishonest with you," Brother Daniel said in his deep voice.

Brett couldn't contain his anger any longer. "First of all," he snapped back, "there have been five recent deaths, not four. And the first death was only six weeks ago, not several months ago. And finally, Brother Jonathan's death ten days ago was not the most recent. There was the fifth death a week ago that you forgot to tell me about."

"We didn't want people coming around and asking questions," Brother Daniel said.

"You mean people like me?" Brett asked.

After a moment of icy stares, he finally said, "Yes. People like you."

"Why not?"

Just when Brett thought Daniel might be forthcoming with some answers, Menendez walked up to inspect the site. The monks had dug up the first coffin and were moving it onto a flat area. They pried off the lid, revealing a body wrapped in white linen. Brett put his mask back on, put on gloves, and carefully unwrapped the body. He pushed a long needle into the chest cavity, then into the abdomen and drew back fluid. He squirted the fluid into a vacuum tube, sealed it, and put it in the ice chest he had brought.

Next, he pushed the syringe into the right upper quadrant of the abdomen and sucked back liver tissue and again put that into a tube and packed it in ice. Finally, he pulled out a scalpel, made a small incision on the abdominal wall exposing the liver and cut out a small piece. The smell of mildew poured from the incision, overpowering even the smell of death and decay.

Brett nodded to them that he was finished with the first body.

The monks wrapped the body in a new piece of linen and nailed the lid shut again. Menendez sprinkled holy water on the coffin and scattered a handful of dirt over the coffin in the shape of the cross. *"In nomine Patris, et Filii, et Spiritus sancti,"* he said.

Then they lowered the coffin back into the ground with ropes and covered it up, finally replacing the stone.

They repeated the process for three more graves. It was exhausting work, and the heat of the day and the dry warm breeze that kicked up dust added to their discomfort. Chipmunks scurried around the ground, and an occasional silent shadow moved over the men as buzzards, smelling death in the air, soared overhead, silent sentinels to the morbid scene below.

It was late afternoon by the time all four bodies had been dug up, tested, then buried again. They put the masks, gloves and needles into a burlap bag, which was then taken into the woods and burned, then the ashes were buried.

Brett walked up to Brother Daniel. "Thank you," he said.

Daniel nodded and put his hand on Brett's shoulder. The touch was one of reconciliation, a touch that said he understood. Brett wondered if the voice in the shadows had been Daniel.

After dinner, instead of going to the evening service, Brett went back to his room and put on dark clothes. He was exhausted, but there was one thing he still needed to know, and he hoped to get answers tonight. Keeping his distance from Menendez was probably a good idea until he was finished.

He waited in his room for two hours. Except for a full moon that cast long shadows, the night was dark and quiet. He slipped quietly through the open-air window and kept to the shadows as he made his way to the dormitory where Kari was staying. He crouched down and waited to make sure no one had followed him. Rather than risk running into one of the monks in the hallway of the dormitory, he jumped up and slipped through her open window and dropped to the floor.

"I thought you'd be too tired tonight," she whispered as she sat up, rubbing her eyes.

"I've got something to check out. Give me the revolver," he whispered to her.

"Why. What are you doing? What's going on?" she whispered as she took it out of her duffel bag, handed it to him and put a handful of cartridges in his pocket.

"Did you notice anything unusual about this place?" he asked.

"You mean something besides a bunch of men in robes living alone on a mountain?"

"Yeah, besides that. Did you notice the large building in the center of the compound?"

"What about it?" she asked, suddenly interested.

"Well, for starters," he whispered, "it's always locked. There's always someone outside the door during the day, guarding it. And there are several lines going to the building. Coaxial cables, phone lines, power lines, and satellite discs. I asked myself, why would a remote monastery that uses oil lamps to light their buildings need coaxial cables and satellite dishes?"

"Good question. What does it mean?"

"I'm going to find out. Stay here and wait for me."

"You're not leaving me behind. I'm coming too." She slipped on her jeans and a shirt and was out the window right behind him. He didn't argue with her.

They moved through the shadows toward the large building, now bathed in silver by the moon that hung low in the sky. They crouched down in the shadow of a bush to watch and listen. He saw nothing that would suggest they had been spotted or were being followed.

Suddenly he thought he heard something, too faint to locate the source. "What was that?" he whispered. He pulled the Colt out of his belt. "Is it loaded?" he whispered into her ear. His question was met with silence. In the dark shadows, he couldn't tell if she nodded or shook her head. She had put a fist of cartridges in his pocket earlier. He didn't know if that meant it wasn't loaded, but he didn't have time to load the revolver in the dark.

Brett didn't intend to shoot anyone, but the mere presence of the gun might prove to be the difference between life and death for them. He pulled the hammer back and cocked it. The cylinder rotated slowly. He could only pray that it delivered a round to the firing chamber, that the firing pin would find a cartridge rather than just air. The cold steel felt heavy, and he found it both unfamiliar and comforting at the same time.

Somewhere from the dark shadows, Brett heard a footstep, a dull thud, then Kari grunted and fell. He caught the shadow of something slamming into him. At the moment of impact, light flashed in his eyes as the gun discharged with a deafening sound. He felt the kick of the recoil, and at the same moment something struck him on the side of his head with a tremendous blow, blinding him for a brief second. Brett staggered and collapsed.

Brett slowly opened his eyes to an annoying bright light. Father Menendez stood over him with a flashlight, surveying the scene. Several other monks who had been awakened by the shot had gathered around. Kari sat on the ground, holding her stomach.

"Are you hurt?" Menendez asked as he leaned over to look at her.

She moaned, then asked, "What happened?"

Menendez swung the beam of light into Brett's face. "What about you?"

Brett put his hand to his bleeding head. "Just a scrape, I think."

"What the devil do you think you're doing?" Menendez snapped. "You could have killed someone! You sneak around at night on private property where you weren't invited, try to break into a building, then you shoot at us."

From Brett's point of view, he was the one who could have been killed. He hadn't shot at anyone. The gun had discharged when someone struck him. But he knew that was a technicality they had little interest in. He gingerly touched the side of his head and felt warm blood on his face.

"Your welcome here has expired. I insist that you leave first thing in the morning. You're now trespassing," Menendez said.

"There have been five deaths here," Brett shot back, "not four."

"Who told you that?" Menendez asked, obviously caught off guard.

"If the truth about the number of deaths got out," Brett shot back, "the authorities would be coming to investigate, and you don't want that to happen. You've been lying to me, and I want to know why. What are you hiding that you're so worried about?"

"Be gone in the morning," Menendez hissed, "or those marshals you talked about will be here to arrest you." Then he turned around and stormed off. The rest of the monks wandered back to their rooms.

Brett looked at Kari, who had staggered to her feet again. Brett hadn't finished what he had set out to do, and he sure as hell wasn't going to let Menendez stop him. But sunrise was less than three hours away. He was quickly running out of time and options.

"Are you okay?" he asked Kari as she clutched her stomach.

"Just got the wind knocked out of me," she said through clenched teeth. "My stomach's going to be sore. What about you?" She reached for his head. He flinched at her touch. "You're bleeding. You need to get that sutured."

"We don't have time for that. Go back to your room," he urged as he worried about her safety. "They'll be watching us. Keep your door locked."

"What good is that going to do with an empty window?"

He handed her the gun. "They won't think about coming through the window. Besides, I don't think they'll bother you. You're no threat to them. But don't be afraid to use it if you have to."

"Where are you going?"

"There's something I have to do," he said, and slipped away into the shadows.

Chapter 41

Brett knew he was running out of time, and he had to get a look inside that building. If for some reason the monks discovered that he hadn't returned to his room, they would come looking for him. And the night was fading fast.

Slipping among shadows to avoid the brilliant moonlight, he crossed the large, open courtyard until he came to a clump of bushes near the mystery building in the center of the compound. The sparse foliage provided no cover between him and the building. He would be exposed. Crouched over, he ran to the building and dove flat against it in its shadow, the side opposite the moon. He listened for any sound or movement. He wanted to be certain he hadn't been spotted. But he couldn't wait any longer.

He got to his feet and moved along the wall, looking for a way in. The thick wooden door was locked, and picking locks was definitely not his forte. He had never really picked a lock; opening the worn lock to Wheeler's office on campus didn't count. Two large windows along the wall were also locked. He looked around the corner.

The next side was bathed in full moonlight, which had the same effect as being lit by a spotlight. He'd be spotted easily, but he noticed a small open window high on the wall, at least twelve feet from the ground. He wasn't sure he would able to get to it. He wasn't even sure he could fit through it. But it seemed to be his only chance for getting in.

He wished he'd brought gloves and a mask. If his hunch was right, the building could be crawling with the virus. He might be climbing into a death trap; he would make a concerted effort to be cautious.

He slid along the wall quickly until he was directly under the small window, then started to pull himself up by clawing at the adobe bricks. The brittle, sun-baked brick cut into his fingers, and occasionally small pieces crumbled under his weight. Almost within reach of the bottom of the window, his fingers cramped, and he didn't think he could make it.

Sticky blood and shards of crumbling adobe covered his fingers. If he slipped and fell, he knew he wouldn't be able to pull himself up a second time. Gripping the brick with every bit of effort he had in his right hand, he stretched his left hand up and felt his fingers touch the bottom of the window sill. Using his feet to help push, he finally got a grip on the sill with both hands.

He hung there for a moment, exposed in the moonlight, while he caught his breath. He pushed the window open as far as he could reach, then he pulled himself up and wedged himself through the narrow opening. He fell onto a table several feet below him, then rolled off and onto the floor. He lay there for a few moments recovering from the fall and listening for any response to the sound of his falling.

Slowly, he got to his feet and tried to flex life back into his bloody, cramped fingers. He pulled out a small medical penlight from his pocket and moved the tiny beam of light around the building. He was on the second floor, which housed numerous computers, servers, fax machines, and phones—just as he had suspected from the lines and cables going into the building. No oil lamps here; strictly twenty-first century high-tech stuff. He wanted to turn on one of the computers and see what information it held. But he was out of time.

He hurried down the wooden stairs to the ground floor. It was a large, open room filled with crates and packing material. He pointed his light at one of the crates. It had been shipped from Borga, Guatemala. He continued looking around and saw a long shelf that ran the entire length of one of the walls.

Mayan artifacts! The monks were collecting or distributing Mayan artifacts. A wave of euphoria swept over him. He had been right all along. The ancient artifacts must indeed be the vector for the disease! Everything made perfect sense now.

Dozens of the artifacts were sitting on the long shelf. The pieces were apparently being cleaned, polished, and made ready for shipping. Gold, silver, pottery, jade. His light moved over the long row of priceless artifacts; he doubted any museum in the world held a finer collection. He glanced at the addresses on some the crates that had been sealed; apparently, they were ready to be shipped.

There was something else that bothered him, and it took him a moment or two for it to register. Every artifact had two or three identical pieces beside it. Every piece seemed to be in triplicate.

"What are you doing here?" a voice asked, barely above a whisper.

Brett jumped and spun around. He tried to penetrate the darkness and thought he could make out the dim outline of a figure in the corner. Was it the same whispered voice he had heard before? He couldn't tell.

"What are you doing here?" the hushed voice asked more urgently.

"I'm looking for some answers."

"How did you get in?"

"I scaled the wall and slipped through the window at the top."

"Clever. But stupid."

"What's going on here?" Brett demanded.

A long moment of awkward silence followed. Brett stood still. He couldn't see the door in this darkness and had no obvious escape route. He hadn't even considered the problem of getting out.

"You've made a serious mistake," the voice finally answered, more sternly. "You and the woman are in grave danger. You have to leave the monastery immediately."

"Is that a threat?"

"No. I'm warning you. Leave now. It's your only chance."

Brett's mind raced to make sense of it all. The answer to the disease was on display in front of him, but he was being warned that his life was in danger if he didn't leave.

The first faint hint of pink in the sky was visible through the window. "You have to go," the voice demanded. "It may already be too late."

"Too late for what? Why would we be in any kind of danger?"

"When they find out you were in here, the chances are slim that either of you will ever leave San Sebastian."

Suddenly, Brett understood. *They're making fake duplicates from original artifacts!* He couldn't figure out why they would want to do that, but he didn't have time to dwell on it. One thing he did know—it seemed they would do anything to keep that secret from getting out. And now he understood the warning. If word got out that dozens of fake Mayan artifacts were being distributed throughout the world, the price of Mayan art would plummet.

The shadowy figure had already moved back into the dark shadows and disappeared.

Brett's heart was racing. Now he knew why they couldn't let them leave the monastery after what he'd discovered. Who had warned him, and why? He used the penlight to find the door, quietly unlocked it, cracked it open to look outside, then quickly slipped through and disappeared among the shadows.

Squatting low, Brett sprinted across the courtyard and scrambled under a shrub while his mind raced over his situation. He had to come up with a plan, and he had to do it quickly. The tissue and blood samples he and Kari had collected were stored in a container in an underground root cellar. He had to grab Kari, collect the samples, and get to the car without being spotted. Faint pink along the horizon told him he had only a few minutes of darkness left for cover. When the sun was up, so were the monks.

If he succeeded in getting Kari and the samples to the car,

there was still one final problem he would have to deal with—the locked steel gate at the entrance. He tried to remember whether it unlocked from the inside with a latch or if it required a key.

There was no way the car could ram through it; the steel gate was capable of stopping a large truck. As a last resort, he could try to shoot the lock off. If he couldn't open the gate, they would have to scale the wall and try to escape into the hills by foot, an option he hoped they wouldn't have to use.

Their best chance of escaping would be for him to forget about the samples, get Kari, and leave immediately. But he'd come too far. He had no intention of leaving without those samples. He ran to his room, scrambled through the window, grabbed his pack and keys, then left, all in less than a minute.

The stars faded as the sky grew lighter. Keeping to the shadows as much as possible, he sprinted to Kari's room. She had the Colt, and he had told her to use it. Now he hoped she didn't shoot him. He ran the final distance, leaped up, and silently dove headfirst through the small window opening. He fell to the stone floor with a jarring thump to his chest. He heard the click of the Colt's hammer.

"Kari," he whispered, "it's me. Don't shoot."

Suddenly she was clinging to him. "Brett, I was so worried."

"Shh. Get dressed," he said and started tossing her clothes to her. "We have to get out of here now. Not a second to lose."

"What's the rush?" she asked.

"I'll explain later. Right now—just move!"

"God, look at your head," she said with concern. "There's blood everywhere. Oh no, your hands are bleeding too. Where have you been?" She reached for the water pitcher.

He grabbed her arms. "No time for that now. We have to leave!"

Kari pulled on her jeans, jerked a T-shirt over her head, pulled on her sandals and grabbed her backpack. "Ready," she said.

"We're going out through the window. I'm going to get the samples. You get the car. Here are the keys." He pulled them out of his pocket and handed them to her.

"Can't we go together?"

"No. Move as fast as you can to the car, get in, and don't make a sound. I'll be at the gate. Wait for my signal with this penlight. If you see one flash, start the car and drive to the gate as fast as you can. If you see two flashes, get out and run to the gate. That means I couldn't unlock it, and we'll have to go over the wall and try to escape on foot."

"Escape from what?" She had a firm grip on his arm.

"The monks. Apparently, they don't intend for us to leave. Take the Colt. Shoot anyone who tries to stop you."

"You can't be serious."

"One flash, you start the car and come get me. Two flashes, you get out and run. Got it? Let's go." And with that he was gone.

Kari crawled out the window and dropped to the ground. She gripped the keys and ran to the car. She squatted down against the side of the car, listened for any sound, then reached up and quietly opened the door. She slid into the car, put the key in the ignition, and waited. Her eyes searched the darkness for a spot of light. The Colt lay on the seat beside her. Her hands were shaking so badly she wasn't sure she could even start the car.

What was happening? Why would the monks want to hurt them? Had Brett completely flipped out? She remembered his bloodied face and hands, and his warning seemed real enough.

There—she thought she saw a brief, faint light. But she wasn't sure. Had she imagined it? She fumbled with the key. Just as the engine turned over, she saw it again. There was no question about it this time. She jammed the car into gear, turned on the headlights, and stomped on the accelerator. As the tires spun in the dirt, she caught a glimpse of Brett in the beam, waiting at the gate.

She hit the brakes and slid to a stop. One side of the gate was open. The car door flew open. "Move over!" he yelled at her. Then he popped open the trunk, loaded the container filled with the samples, slammed the trunk and jumped in behind the wheel.

Kari turned and to see a half dozen monks in the early morning light racing toward the gate and waving their arms furiously. Brett floored the accelerator. Two of the monks caught up to them and ran beside the car, yelling at them and banging on the windows as they tried to open the doors. The spinning tires threw dust and stone into the air as the car swerved and raced toward the gate. A second later, the Taurus was through the gate and heading down the road.

"I'm shaking all over," Kari said, looking back at the commotion at the gate. "I think I'm going to throw up."

"Don't," he said as he watched the monks in the rearview mirror.

"What happened?" She choked with fear.

Ignoring her question, he concentrated on driving as he recklessly pushed the Taurus through the curves. He raced down the canyon, leaving San Sebastian behind in the early dawn.

Chapter 42

Hortuedo
Northern Guatemala mountains

Ross Solt tossed and turned on his cot, unable to find relief from the intolerable thick, humid air inside the tent. Sweating and miserable, he sprawled across damp, rumpled sheets. It would have been far more comfortable sleeping outside under the open night sky, but the frequent unexpected thunderstorms and hoards of mosquitoes made that an impossibility.

Tequila looked up and barked just as the tent flap slapped open.

"We've got problems," Jacek announced. "Seems we had visitors last night." The tone in his voice spelled trouble.

"And...?"

"You'd better come take a look for yourself."

Solt jumped up, slipped into his khaki cargo shorts, jammed

his feet into a pair of sandals, and went outside.

"What's the problem?" he asked.

"Look," Jacek said, as his arm made a sweep over the field where all the trucks were parked.

The result of the raid on the camp was startling. The tires of the trucks had been slashed, and their supplies were scattered across the field. The rest of the CDC team was picking through the crates and boxes, assessing the damage. A hollow feeling grew in the pit of Solt's stomach.

"Where are the tissue samples?" he asked, already afraid of what the answer might be.

"Gone," Jacek said.

"You're certain? You've looked everywhere?"

"They're gone. No question about it."

Solt let out a long sigh of defeat. The day wasn't starting out well. He walked over to a crate they'd used as a table, poured himself a cup of coffee from a metal pot, and took a sip.

"So, they stole our samples, slashed all the tires, and left us stranded here. And the shortwave antenna is gone. Clever. We can't chase them, we can't even report it. It'll be at least another two days before Sanchez can get more trucks out here." Solt looked out over the field. "Who would do this? And why?"

"Well, thankfully everyone is safe," Julie Thaxton said quietly.

"That's where you're wrong," Solt said. "There's somebody out there carrying around tubes of contaminated blood and tissue that are swarming with one of the deadliest viruses we've ever encountered. A weapon potentially as devastating as a nuclear warhead."

"You think they could possibly know what's in the vials?"

"Either way, it's bad," Solt said. "If they know what they have, they can use it to blackmail the government. If they don't know what it is, they might dump it somewhere that could kill hundreds of people. If we're lucky, they'll get careless, infect themselves and die quickly. What we don't want is for them to use it for ransom or as a weapon."

"How do you know it was the rebels who did this?" Jacek asked.

"What do you mean?" Solt asked as he sipped more of his coffee.

"You said they could 'blackmail the government,' implying that it was the rebels who did it. In fact, maybe it was government troops who did this. After all, weren't they the ones who were supposed to be guarding us?"

Solt thought about that while he pushed cherry blend into his pipe, then lit it. "Why the hell would they do that?"

"Okay, then what did the rebels have to gain by doing this?" Jacek asked.

"None of it makes any sense," Solt said. "Either way we still have two big problems. We're stuck out here in this god-forsaken miserable mountain jungle, and someone has glass tubes of blood that'll kill whoever comes in contact with it. I don't even want to think about what else could go wrong."

He puffed on his pipe, staring out at the field. "I want to know what the soldiers guarding us were doing when this happened. We need to find a way to get the hell out of here. I don't think we're welcome down here by either side."

"Damnit!" Jacek said disgustedly. "We're stuck here with no way to get out or to get help. Guess that means we're going to have to start hiking out."

"Not necessarily," Solt said and nodded at a small cloud of dust coming toward them.

New Mexico

When they finally headed south again onto highway 191, Kari turned to Brett. "Okay," she said with a tremor in her voice, "what the hell was that all about?"

"Five more minutes and we might never have been heard from again."

"You're joking, right? They're monks, for god's sake! What reason would they have to want to hurt us?"

Brett struggled to regain his composure. "I stumbled onto something that we weren't supposed to see. It's possible we might never have left San Sebastian alive because of it."

"What? They'd have kept us prisoners? They're monks! You don't really believe that, do you?"

The voice from the shadows kept coming back to him. *You and the woman are in grave danger.* Brett said, "Yes, I think they would have."

"Tell me, what did you find that was so important and dangerous?"

Brett rolled his window down to let in the fresh morning air and glanced in the rearview mirror again for the umpteenth time. "I broke into that large building in the center, the one with all the cables and wires."

"You broke in? How?"

"I scaled the old adobe wall and slipped through a window—"

"You scaled a wall?" she interrupted. She was struggling to grasp what Brett had done and what he'd seen. "That explains the cuts on your hands. What did you find inside that's so important that they'd want to kill us?"

"Just as I suspected, one room was filled with modern electronic equipment—computers, faxes, printers, servers, phones. There was even a satellite hook-up."

"Why would a monastery need that kind of equipment?"

"I'm not sure."

"And the other room?" Kari asked.

"Mayan artifacts."

"Mayan artifacts?" She sat upright. "What do you mean Mayan artifacts?"

"Dozens of them. It looks like the monks clean them, package them, and ship them out to museums and collectors around the world."

Kari sat stunned. "I don't understand. Where would they get them?" He turned and looked at her but didn't answer. "Do you think the monastery is involved in smuggling?" she asked.

He wasn't surprised when she'd used the word smuggling. "That's exactly what I think. And I don't think they'd take kindly to being discovered."

"That's crazy. Why would a monastery be involved in smuggling?"

"That's what I'd like to know," he said glancing in the mirror again. "There's more."

"More? What else?"

"There were multiple duplicates of each piece."

"Duplicates? What do you mean *duplicates?*" she asked, trying to comprehend what he was saying.

"The monks of San Sebastian are doing more than just dealing in smuggled Mayan artifacts. From what I saw, they are duplicating them, then probably selling them pieces to dealers and collectors for a fortune."

"Making duplicates? That's absurd. I don't believe it. Why would they do that? And why would they want to kill us for finding out about it?"

"If word of that got out, the value of any Mayan artifact would become nearly worthless overnight, if you couldn't prove which is the copy and which is the real one."

"I—I can't believe it."

"There's one thing I am pretty sure about," he said.

"What's that?"

"They'll do *anything* to keep anybody from finding that out."

"Are we in any kind of danger?"

He shrugged. He wanted to put her mind at ease, but the truth was, he didn't have a clue what lengths the monks might go to, to keep their secret safe.

Once in Santa Fe, he drove straight to the state health department. He pulled on surgical gloves, unloaded the samples from the trunk, and gave them instructions to ship them express to the CDC in locked, chilled containers marked 'Bio-Hazard'. Then they headed out of town. On the outskirts of Santa Fe, he stopped at a drive-through for coffee and bagels. He had trouble getting his wallet out of his pocket because of his swollen, cut fingers.

"For god's sake, your hands are a mess," Kari said. "You shouldn't even be driving." She pulled money out of her purse and paid for the food. "Pull over and I'll drive."

"I'll be fine. Just hand me a coffee." He didn't want to admit it to her, but fatigue was overpowering him. His mind was foggy from lack of sleep. His hand trembled as his fingers bent slowly around the Styrofoam cup.

"We need a doctor to take a look at those fingers."

"I am a doctor, remember?"

"I mean a doctor who isn't as stubborn. Do you want cream cheese on your bagel?"

"No." He took the bagel from her and bit into it. Then something occurred to him. "Did you or your father know a Monsignor Cardone in Chicago?"

"Yes, we knew him. Why?"

"According to the state medical records, he died during Christmas of what was probably the same disease. His serum titers tested positive for the same virus. I was wondering if he had any kind of connection with the monastery. That might explain his death."

Brett also had seen something else at the monastery that troubled him. After they turned back onto the highway, he sipped his coffee and asked, "How involved were you in your father's work?"

"Very little. He was an archeologist. I teach social anthropology. I only went along on his last two summer trips to keep an eye on him. And I didn't do a very good job," she said, her voice fading off.

"You can't be responsible for what happened to him."

Kari sensed there was something else bothering Brett. "Why are you asking me about my dad's work?"

"A label on one of the packages at the monastery was addressed to him."

"What? Do you think he was involved somehow with that monastery?"

"I'm sorry, Kari. I think your father may have been involved in smuggling."

"How did you come up with that bit of fantasy?" she snapped. "That's ridiculous! How can you possibly accuse him of something like that? Maybe you think I'm a smuggler too."

"I know you don't want to believe me, but I have pretty strong evidence that he was."

"Evidence? What evidence?" She was almost shouting. "Is that what you were doing in Chicago? Checking up on him?"

"It's likely that many of the pieces he collected were obtained illegally from unauthorized areas, then somehow shipped out of Guatemala."

"Are you trying to ruin his reputation? My father was a great archeologist, highly respected by his peers. He spent a lifetime making important discoveries. Many of the pieces in museums are ones that he saved from either being destroyed or being sold on the black market to greedy art dealers. I don't know why his name was on one of the labels. But he was not a smuggler, and just in case you're wondering, neither am I!" she shouted. "And I know for damned certain he would never have been involved with some damn counterfeit artifacts."

They drove in silence for several miles, then she said, "Guatemalans are desperate, and are stealing their own heritage for pocket change. I don't know how he got the pieces out of the country, but my father was rescuing the artifacts from cheap plundering—pieces that otherwise would be lost forever. Instead, they are now in museums around the world. He gave them to museums. He didn't sell them!"

She had just admitted that her father had been taking artifacts from unapproved areas and that she had known about it. On the surface, it sounded innocent enough. But what Brett had discovered at the monastery wasn't innocent. From what he could tell, it was an operation center for international smuggling and distribution of both authentic and fake Mayan artifacts. Then there was the issue of producing counterfeit pieces.

They drove on in silence, a volatile tension in the air between them. He was relieved when she finally slept during the last forty minutes to the airport. There was a lot about the beautiful woman beside him he didn't know. Had she been involved in her father's smuggling? Was she an international thief or an innocent accomplice?

Brett realized that nobody could ever fully know another person. There was always a secret part to everyone, something private and inaccessible to others. What was Kari's secret part?

He rested his swollen, cut fingers on the steering wheel as he struggled to stay alert. He hadn't slept in two nights, and every muscle ached. He wondered what the first symptoms would be if he'd contracted the deadly virus.

He tried to calm his concern by telling himself he hadn't touched any of the artifacts. But the fact remained: he had put himself at great risk with close contact to the virus. And at the moment, he felt miserable.

Quinn was right, he did take too many risks, and it was eventually bound to catch up with him, if it hadn't already.

One thing was for damned certain. He'd been right about some of the tombs being connected to the disease. It also seemed obvious that the virus was being carried by certain artifacts. At least five monks at San Sebastian had come into contact with the artifacts and died because of it. He was still left with many questions that had no answers. Why did only some of the tombs seem to carry the deadly virus? Why weren't all the artifacts carriers? Why were the incidences of those dying so erratic and unpredictable?

Once arriving at the airport in Albuquerque, they would go their separate ways. Kari was flying back to Chicago, and he was headed for Atlanta.

When she had cleared security, Kari started to go down the concourse to her gate. He rushed over to her and grabbed her arm. "Kari—I'm sorry. About everything."

"Why don't I believe you?" she said. Her eyes were red.

"I sorry I implied your father was mixed up in any of this. More than likely, he had no idea what was going on," Brett said.

She started to walk away, then stopped. "You have no idea what you've done." Then she stormed down the concourse to her flight.

Or maybe her father wasn't involved at all, Brett thought, as pieces of the puzzle started to fit together. Thoughts formed in his mind; maybe now he understood. *Professor Wheeler was murdered because he had also discovered the secret—that the monastery was making counterfeit duplicates!*

He stood watching her walk away from him. He turned and started down his concourse. He was bone-tired, and his mind was a tangle of thoughts. He had hurt her deeply at a time when she had already suffered so much and also given so much to help him.

She was the best thing that had happened in his life. He stopped and turned around. He wanted to run after her and tell her he was sorry.

But she was gone.

Chapter 43

Hortuedo
the Varapaz Valley
Northern Guatemala mountains

Nick Jindal pulled up in Brett's battered Jeep wearing the scrubs that Solt had given him to wear. The CDC team had him take those off, gave him a quick phenol washing as a precaution, then he changed into his own clothes.

"Can we use the Jeep to take our group back to Guatemala City?" Jindal asked.

"Sorry," Solt said. "We had visitors while you were back to the excavation site, and all the truck tires have been slashed. That old Jeep is our only transportation out of here, and right now we need it more than you do. I'm in a bit of a rush, and I have things that need to be taken care of immediately. I'll send trucks back to pick up you and my team."

"Ross, you won't have enough gas to get you back," Julie Thaxton said.

Solt tamped tobacco into his pipe and lit it. After taking a couple of deep puffs, he said, "Hell, Julie, we've got plenty of gas." He nodded toward the trucks.

After Jindal unloaded the gear from the Jeep that he had brought back, they siphoned the gasoline out of one of the trucks, filled the Jeep's tank, and all the extra fuel cans. Solt threw his things in the back of the Jeep and climbed in. Tequila barked excitedly and jumped onto the back when Solt started the engine, and they sped from the village in a growing cloud of blue exhaust smoke.

Brett fell asleep before the plane left the ground, and only woke up in Atlanta as passengers crowded the aisle, pulling luggage from the overhead bins. The three hours of sleep had helped, but he still felt wrecked. He needed to crawl into bed and sleep for a day.

He grabbed a cup of Starbucks in the airport and took a cab to his apartment. He was conflicted, confused, and dissatisfied. The closer he got to the truth the more things became unraveled. Now he was almost certain Wheeler had never been involved in the smuggling or the fake Mayan artifacts. They'd probably murdered Wheeler because he had somehow discovered the very thing Brett now knew. Brett knew he was close to solving the mystery of the epidemic but feared he might have lost Kari in the process. After a quick shower and change of clothes, he headed to the CDC. It was late afternoon, but he needed to see Quinn before he left for the day.

Brett knocked on the door to Quinn's office, then went in without waiting. Quinn took one look at him and said, "For god's sake, Brett—what the hell happened? Your face is a mess, you're bleeding. And look at your hands! Care to tell me what happened to you? You're crazy, you know that?"

Without waiting for a response, Quinn burst into a tirade. "You've really done it this time. Culler, the Secretary of State—that Culler—called me. The bishop of the archdiocese of New Mexico called me, and the director of the New Mexico State Health Department called me. They said you threatened to send federal marshals into a monastery in New Mexico, attacked a monk in the middle of the night, and exhumed four bodies without a court order. Secretary Culler says you've pissed off the Guatemalan government. Not to mention that you came to the wrong conclusions in Guatemala about the epidemic and set us back weeks. And from your appearance, I assume you got into some kind of fight. Did I leave anything out?" he shouted.

"Got any cream?" Brett asked as he poured himself a cup of coffee, then sat down in a chair.

"Cream?" Quinn glared at him. Then he saw something in Brett's face, and his frown softened. "You've got something, don't you? You found out something in New Mexico. Let's have it."

"Looks like I was right after all," Brett said as he stirred his coffee and took a sip. "The disease is related to the Mayan tombs—actually Mayan artifacts, to be more exact. It seems the saintly brothers of

San Sebastian have been involved in smuggling Mayan art into the country. When artifacts were delivered to the monastery, so was the virus, and five monks are dead because of it."

"You mean four of them are dead."

"I mean five," Brett said. "My guess is they've been trying to cover up the deaths to protect their smuggling operation."

"Smuggling what? Why in hell would a monastery be involved in smuggling?" Quinn asked. "You're not leading us down another dead end with this, are you? You're certain about this?"

"I scaled a wall, broke into a building, and saw the artifacts with my own eyes. From what I could tell, it looked like they were making multiple duplicates of the original pieces, then shipping the fake pieces all over the world. They must be making a fortune from it."

"We received news from Solt and the team two days ago," Quinn said. "An American archeologist down there exploring tombs died two days ago. Solt is convinced it's the same disease. He's sending us the samples. If this turns out to be the same disease—and I'm sure it is—it looks like you were right all along. Mayan tombs, or more specifically Mayan artifacts, will probably prove to be the vector," Quinn said. "But it's still just conjectures until we can prove it. There's a small problem that's got me concerned, though."

"What's that?" Brett asked.

"We lost contact with the team two days ago and haven't heard from them since."

"Probably something to do with a storm," Brett said.

"Yeah, probably." But Quinn didn't sound convinced.

"There is a more immediate problem. We've got to get into the monastery. Now!"

"What are you talking about?" Quinn asked.

"We have to stop the monks from shipping out infected artifacts. They could be responsible for spreading the virus worldwide."

"And how do you propose we do that? We don't even have any proof yet that the pieces are carrying the virus."

"Get a search warrant," Brett shot back. "Go to San Sebastian, grab the artifacts, and we will have our proof. Bio-four will find the viruses on the artifacts and we're done."

"A search warrant for the monastery? On what basis? What crime have they committed?" Quinn asked.

"International smuggling, for a start," Brett said.

"You tell that to a Federal judge. Who do you think he's going to side with?" Quinn asked. "A bunch of monks who live peacefully inside a monastery, or some crazy doctor from the CDC who has just pissed off the Secretary of State? As I said, you've already got half the government after your hide. I'm assuming you're right of course, but it's obvious we just can't do that. We'll test the samples from the dead archeologist first and see what that shows." Quinn went to the coffee pot and poured himself a fresh cup, dumped in a packet of NutraSweet and stirred it with his pen.

"We have to get into the monastery," Brett persisted.

"What do you want us to do, invade it?" Quinn asked.

Brett shot back, his voice filled with anger. "Yes! First of all, they're committing federal and international crimes involving smuggling, as well as making fake pieces and selling them. More importantly, they're shipping pieces around the world that could cause a pandemic involving one of the deadliest viruses we've ever seen! Are we going to sit on our asses and let that happen?"

"We're not the police," Quinn said. "It's our job to track down diseases, not criminals. I don't give a damn if the monks make a million fake copies. We'll need to have definite proof before we do anything regarding the infection. As soon as we get the samples from the archeologist who died, we'll test them and compare them with your samples from the monastery. That will probably take Bio-Four at least forty-eight hours, if we're lucky."

Brett's fuse finally blew. He leaped out of his chair and slammed his fist down on Quinn's desk. "Mitch, this virus makes Ebola look like a mild cold. It may already be too late. But you'd damn well better do something and figure out a way to stop them!"

Quinn took a deep breath and blew it out with a huff. "Okay, Brett, let's say I agree with you. Any ideas on how I'd do that?"

"We can tackle it from two different angles. We can use their illegal international trade violations to get a search warrant. That'll get us into the monastery. Then you can invoke a court-ordered quarantine. Federal marshals could stop and inspect all shipments going into and out of the place. That at least will stop any infected pieces from being shipped out."

Quinn looked out the window as he mulled over Brett's suggestions. Finally, Quinn turned and said, "There's nothing we can do until Bio-Four confirms that your samples from the monastery are the same virus. Then we'll see what we can do."

Quinn looked at Brett's hands holding the coffee cup. "Jesus, Brett, look at you. You're a mess. How come none of my other agents come in looking like this? Looks like you haven't slept in days, and your hands couldn't even hold a pen. Go to the ER and have your hands looked at, then go home and get some sleep. You're always playing it too close to the edge, and it's going to catch up with you."

"I could use some sleep." Brett put the coffee cup down, stood up and left.

Chicago

Scar made his way down a dark street to the address he'd been given, the large old mission church of Saint Teresa of Mercy, in one of the poorer sections of Chicago. In this forgotten neighborhood, most of the streetlights didn't work. The church serviced mostly a population of derelicts, drunks, homeless, and burned-out drug addicts. While the church made every effort to provide spiritual guidance, the truth was that for these people, soup and blankets were more important to them than their souls or eternal life. Their problems were more immediate rather than eternal. A large dark crumbling cement grotto on the street near the front entrance contained a statue of Saint Teresa and smelled of urine.

No one took notice when the huge man with a worn eye-patch stepped through the thick oak door, moved down the aisle, and silently slipped into a confessional. Scar hated the confining space, the stagnant air, and most of all—he hated the darkness. Sweat ran freely down his face and soaked his shirt as he felt his stomach tightening.

"You let the woman get away," an unfamiliar voice on the other side of the lattice scolded him.

He didn't like taking orders from a stranger. He knew the man was with the organization because they had sent him here, but he didn't like it. "I'm watching her apartment," he countered. "I'll have her soon. She won't be a bother anymore."

"It's not that simple. She went to New Mexico. She was in the monastery," the voice continued. "She was in the monastery!" the voice repeated.

The huge man sat, trying to decide if he should speak. But he said nothing. Silence. The person on the other side said nothing, and the silence stretched painfully into a full minute, then two. He hated the silence, almost as much as the darkness. Sweat ran down his back. He feared nobody. But the cramped space of the dark, stagnant confessional combined with the silence was beyond his tolerance.

Scar wondered if the priest on the other side knew how much danger he was in. Scar didn't intend to sit there and be scolded by a damned stranger, even if he was part of the organization.

The voice finally broke the silence. "Everything's changed now. She was there. She knows everything. We have to do damage control."

"I will have her before the day is over. She won't get away again," Scar argued. He'd been standing outside in the cold for days without food or rest watching her apartment, thinking about what he was going to do to her before killing her.

"No," the priest demanded. "As I said, everything's different now. We need to know how much she knows, and who she's talked to." After another pause, the voice continued. "There's more."

He slid a note under the lattice. Then the voice was gone and Scar was alone again in the confessional. He grabbed the note, stuffed it in his pocket, and left Saint Theresa to attend to the poor without his help.

Chapter 44

CDC Headquarters
Atlanta, Georgia

Mitch Quinn let out a deep sigh. This was unquestionably the most bizarre and potentially deadly situation he had been involved with since he had been appointed head of the EIS Division. He believed what Brett told him regarding the monastery, but he couldn't do anything about it right now. He didn't want to take on everything that would be involved with breaking into a monastery. Not yet, anyway. The CDC had enough problems to deal with already without tackling something that wasn't their concern.

Once they got the blood and tissue samples Solt had taken from the dead archeologist in Guatemala, they could compare it with the samples from the dead monks. If they were the same organism, then and only then would he worry about how to deal with the monastery.

He closed his eyes for a second and rubbed his forehead. It was a damned complicated mess. But they appeared to be close to getting answers.

Then the phone reserved for "Emergency Situations Only" rang. Quinn felt his pulse quicken as he grabbed it.

Brett didn't bother to go to the ER, but instead went back to his apartment and ordered a pizza. He took a cold Amstel from the fridge, then went into his living room to check his voice mail. There were two messages. He hoped one would be Kari. He was disappointed when he heard the first message was from Ashley. The second caller left no message. It could have been anyone so he dismissed it.

He decided to call Ross Solt and dialed the number, but there was no sound on the other end. No dial tone, no busy signal, nothing. He hung up, redialed, and got the same result. Dead silence. He would try again later.

He called Kari's apartment in Chicago but got her voice mail. He left a message for her to call him back.

The pizza arrived, and he opened another beer. As he ate, he wondered what his next move should be. Suddenly he sat up straight, nearly knocking over his beer. Where was Kari? She should have been back at her apartment by now. *You and the woman are in grave danger* kept screaming in his head.

How stupid of him. Why had he let Kari go back to Chicago alone? He had been tired and not thinking clearly. He went to his desk to look for a paper with a number on it. It wasn't there. He started to open a drawer, then froze. The hair on the back of his neck tingled and his breathing stopped. He distinctly remembered dropping his overnight bag on the chair when he first came home, and it was now sitting on the floor. It had been moved since this afternoon.

Someone had been in his apartment!

He thought maybe he'd been followed when he was in Chicago. Had somebody had been here in his apartment as well? Were they still here?

With his senses on full alert, he listened but heard nothing. He took a quick walk through his apartment, checking windows and the back door. The backdoor wasn't locked. He didn't remember if he had locked it. He turned the deadbolt and checked it to make sure it was secure, then walked back into the living room. Maybe he had been mistaken. Maybe he had put the bag on the floor—but he was certain he hadn't. He checked the front door to make sure it was locked, then shrugged it off. Maybe he was wrong about the overnight bag.

By the time Brett finished his pizza, the past several days finally caught up with him. He fell asleep on the couch with an empty pizza box beside him. He woke up an hour later from the pain in his hands. He took two Percocet, showered and finally climbed into his own bed.

He stared at the darkness, worrying about Kari, and still wondering about the overnight bag and the unlocked back door. He wondered if he should call her department in the morning or call Sarah Horn. Brett was frustrated because he didn't know her uncle's last name. He needed to know she was okay.

Chicago

O nce back in Chicago, Kari didn't go home, but rather to her uncle's house, where she had stayed the night before flying to Albuquerque with Brett. She had left some clothes at her uncle's, and she wasn't ready to go back to her empty apartment. After dinner with her aunt and uncle, she told them she had to go to her office, and that she'd be back later.

Instead of going to her office, she took a cab to St. Peter's Cathedral on Washington Street. She had been surprised and shocked when Brett mentioned Monsignor Cardone's name. Known to her as "Father Joe," she and her father had been friends with him for years. Father Joe Cardone had approached her father three years ago with an idea for getting more artifacts. She and her father weren't Catholic, but they had shared many dinners with Cardone and always enjoyed his company. He had become a close friend of the family. They were in church on Christmas Eve when he had gotten sick, and they had attended his funeral the day before New Year's Eve.

Now she wanted to know what his relationship had been with her father regarding those Mayan artifacts. What exactly was the connection between the monastery, Father Joe, and her own father—if any?

She went to the large stone rectory beside the church and knocked at the door. The door opened and the assistant priest Father O'Higgins grinned when he saw who it was.

"Kari Wheeler. It's been a long time. What brings you out here at night?"

"Hello, Father. I'm sorry to bother you this time of night, but Monsignor Cardone had some of my dad's things, and I was wondering if I could get them."

"Everything in Monsignor's apartment was cleaned out after he died. Another priest is living upstairs there now. I'm sorry you had to make the trip all the way out here. What kind of things were you looking for?"

She tried to hide the crushing disappointment she felt. "Nothing important. Just a couple of sentimental things I wanted to get." She wasn't about to tell him the real reason for her visit.

"Do you want to come in for a while?" O'Higgins asked politely.

"Thank you, no. I don't want to bother you. Besides, I have to get back." She put her hand out to shake his. "It was nice seeing you again."

"Kari, please come back again sometime so we can visit."

Kari walked away and the door closed, but she had no intention of leaving yet. She needed to look around. She went to the front of the church, climbed the steps to St. Peter's Cathedral, opened one of the thick oak doors, and slipped inside the dark church. Tiny flickering light from votive candles reflected off the stone walls. Kari had been in the church a few times and knew her way around. She also knew about a loft that Cardone used as his private office. Few people knew of it, but she and her father had visited Father Joe there more than once. Cardone had an interest in Mayan history and art and enjoyed discussing it with her father.

The large, dark empty church was silent and felt more than a little eerie. She climbed the stairs to the choir loft at the back of the church. Then she walked to the back of the loft and climbed another flight of narrow stairs to a small door. She paused briefly to catch her breath and to listen. There was no sound from the dark void below her.

The door to Monsignor Cardone's tiny alcove opened with a loud squeak on its unused hinges which unnerved her. She left the door open to prevent further noise, and stepped inside. The alcove office looked exactly the same as she had remembered it. It apparently hadn't been touched since his death. Maybe no one else knew about it, or had just not bothered with it.

She pulled out a small flashlight she'd brought with her and moved the beam around the room. She didn't know what she was looking for. She went to a desk, leafed through papers, letters, and envelopes that were on the top of the desk. She quietly opened the drawers and looked through them. Nothing in the papers there seemed to be of any significance. In the bottom drawer she saw a ledger.

She pulled it out and leafed through the pages. There were records of sales, with huge dollar amounts beside them. Hundreds of thousands of dollars on each page. There were addresses of banks, an address in Borga, Guatemala, the monastery at San Sebastian—and her father's address! What did this mean? She slipped the ledger into her shoulder bag and looked around the room. She spotted a wooden trunk against the wall. There wasn't a lock on it.

She tried to open it, but the lid was too heavy to lift with one hand. She put the flashlight down and used both hands to open the lid. Just then she thought she heard something below in the church. She turned off the flashlight and waited. She hoped it was someone coming to light a votive candle or to pray. She took a deep breath and told herself there was no reason to worry. She had to remain focused.

She turned the flashlight back on and made sure the light was blocked from the view below and began to search the trunk. A strong odor of mildew poured from the trunk. Remembering Brett's warnings, she worried about exposing herself to the deadly virus. Had the disease in fact killed Cardone? She wrapped her scarf around her face so she wouldn't breathe in dust; she would be careful, try to protect herself, and promised herself to wash her hands as soon as possible.

Gingerly, she reached into the trunk, moved a folded cloth aside and stared down at Mayan relics. No—it couldn't be! Her head began to swim. Her own father, Monsignor Cardone, the monastery, and the disease all seemed to meld into one. Carefully she pulled out a clay statue, a necklace, a cup and what appeared to be two coins, each of which she put on the floor. Then she pulled out a knife, possibly a ceremonial knife used for sacrifice. She looked at the all the pieces lying on the floor in front of her.

She beamed the light into the trunk and continued to look around. On the bottom were several pieces of paper. They appeared to be inventory for the items that had been shipped. On one of them was an address for Borga, Guatemala, the same address she recognized from the ledger. She didn't know if the address had any significance, but it might be important. Her father's name and address in the ledger was more a little disconcerting. She folded the papers and put them in her bag along with the ledger.

Then she heard footsteps. She froze and listened. They seemed to be down in the main sanctuary of the church. She knew people occasionally came into the church at all hours to pray or light candles. She waited, but there was only silence. It was time to leave.

She quickly put the pieces back in the trunk and closed the lid. The heavy lid slipped from her fingers and slammed with a loud thud. The sudden noise filled the darkness and echoed off the walls, then the church was silent again. She held her breath, afraid to move.

Now there were definite footsteps on the stairs coming up to the choir loft. She raced out of the alcove and down the steps to the choir loft. She was headed toward the person who was coming up the other stairs since they were both headed toward the choir loft, but it was her only way out. She remembered a back stairwell out of the loft that didn't lead into the main sanctuary, and she ran to the door and raced down the back stairs. Once at the bottom, she burst through the side door out onto the street and ran to the corner.

She waved down a taxi and slid inside just as she saw a huge dark figure coming out the front door. She was trembling and shaking all over. Had somebody actually been after her? She remembered the papers and ledger in her bag and reminded herself to wash thoroughly. Her whole world seemed upside down. Nothing made sense anymore. Monks in a monastery were after them, her father had been murdered, and Father Joe may have died of a disease connected to Mayan artifacts.

And someone had been following her.

Chapter 45

After ten hours of uninterrupted sleep, Brett woke the next morning feeling like a new man. He yawned, rubbed his eyes, and dumped some Costa Rica roasted blend into a filter and started a pot of coffee. While the coffee was brewing, he shaved, took a quick shower, dressed, then poured himself a cup. He began sipping the hot brew when he saw there was a new voice mail.

"Brett, this is Kari. I need your help. Please call me the minute you get this. It's important."

He had been so exhausted he hadn't heard the phone ring last night. He grabbed the phone and punched in her number, but there was no answer. Now he started to panic. Why did she need his help? Where was she? Was she in some kind of trouble? He was growing more alarmed. You and the woman are in grave danger. How serious was the threat? Had something happened to her? Why had he let her go back to Chicago alone? He dialed the

Anthropology office.

When the department secretary answered, Brett asked to speak to Kari Wheeler.

"I'm sorry, Dr. Wheeler is not here."

That was not the answer he wanted to hear. He felt his heart skip a beat. "Do you know where I could reach her? It is extremely important that I talk to her."

"Just a moment—." Then the phone was silent for more than a minute. Finally the voice came back on line. "Dr. Wheeler is on emergency leave for at least a week."

Brett was stunned. "She's on leave? How long is she going to be gone? Where did she go? Is there any way I can reach her? It's very urgent that I do so."

"I'm sorry. We aren't allowed to give out personal information." Click.

Brett hung up and sat staring at the phone. Where would she have gone? He had to warn her of the danger she was in. Had she gone back to Guatemala? That seemed out of the question. What was he going to do now? Suddenly he stood up, went over to his desk, pulled a card out of his wallet, and dialed Sarah Horn. She was his last hope of finding Kari.

She answered on the second ring.

"Dr. Horn, this is Dr. Brett Carson. I'm sorry to bother you at home, but it's extremely important that I find Kari Wheeler. I thought maybe you might be able to help me. She left me a message last night. I've tried her apartment and can't reach her. Her department office said she left this morning on an emergency leave, but they won't tell me where she went, or why she left. It's extremely important I find her and warn her."

"Warn her about what?" she asked.

"I think her life could be in danger. I have to find her, and I don't know where to look for her. Do you know any friends or relatives I could contact?"

"Why would her life be in danger? Why don't you call the police?"

"It's not something the police would be able to do anything about. I think the same people who killed her father might kill Kari if they find her."

"Oh, my god." After a brief pause Horn said, "I'll make some phone calls, see what I can learn. I'll call you the moment I find out anything."

"Thank you."

Ten minutes later his phone rang.

"Hello."

"Dr. Carson, this is Sarah Horn. I contacted a friend of Kari's in the Anthropology department. She said Kari told her she was going back to Guatemala."

"Guatemala? Are you sure? Why would she go back?"

"She apparently had found some kind of information that might prove Forrest wasn't involved in anything illegal. She said she's trying to protect his reputation."

"Where did she get the information?"

"I don't know. Let me know the minute you find out anything," she said. "I'm worried about her."

"Yes, of course."

"He wasn't, was he? Involved in anything illegal?" she asked.

"No, he wasn't," he replied, wanting to believe it himself.

Kari was gutsy; she had been unable to save her father's life, so now she would do anything to protect his reputation. But she was walking into a trap. Both Colonel Zolog and the rebels wanted her, but for different reasons. Either way, her chances didn't look good.

His phone rang again.

"Get back over here," Quinn said. "Something's come up. We've got a situation here. I'm in the EOC."

He hung up before Brett could respond. Now what? The day seemed destined to be headed for total disaster. Brett made sure the door was locked when he left.

Quinn was in the large Emergency Operations Center, sitting at one of the computer consoles. The activity in the large situation room seemed higher than usual. Dozens of people were at computer terminals or milling about. All the huge display panels on the front wall were focused on Guatemala and the situation there. Quinn turned to Brett and said, "The team's camp in Guatemala was attacked."

"What do you mean they were attacked? Who attacked them? Is everyone okay?"

"Everybody's okay, but all the blood and tissue samples they took from the American archeologist who died were stolen. Now we've got nothing except the samples you brought back from the monastery. They don't have any idea who it was. The tires on the trucks were slashed, the communications tower destroyed, and all their gear broken into and scattered across the camp."

"When did this happen?" Brett asked as a sense of fear began to grow. The situation had finally exploded. The team was still in danger—and Kari was missing.

"Two days ago," Quinn said. "Ross wasn't able to contact me until just now. Why would anyone do that? And why would they want to steal the samples?"

"The same reason the monks didn't want anyone to know about the deaths in the monastery. If word gets out that an extremely lethal virus is carried by Mayan artifacts and that some of the pieces are duplicated fakes, the market for those will collapse," Brett said. "Someone is desperately trying to make sure that that information doesn't get out."

"According to Jacek, they're in a hell of mess down there now." Quinn turned in his chair toward him, then paused a second. "I've decided to bring the team back home. The situation is just too unstable and too dangerous. If you're right about the monastery and Mayan artifacts, there's little else for us to learn in Guatemala. Certainly not enough to warrant any further risk to the team."

"Then it's mandatory we get back inside that monastery," Brett said. "At this moment, that's our only source to prove this."

"Yeah, it seems that way. But it's going to be difficult and it'll be one hell of a mess, politically, legally and any other way you can think of."

"If we're going to do anything," Brett said, "we have to do it now before the monks get rid of everything and cover their tracks."

Quinn nodded as he read a fax that had just been handed to him. "Based on what you told me earlier about what's going on inside the monastery, a federal judge is issuing a warrant even as we speak. You'd better damned well be right about this. Our asses are on the line when we send marshals into that monastery," Quinn said. "We'll both be gone faster than a snowman in July if you're wrong." Quinn picked up his phone. "Kate, have Kaufman from the FBI call me as soon as possible on an urgent matter. And I need to speak to both the Federal Marshal's Office and the State Health Department of New Mexico."

Quinn looked at him and said, "I'm going to move on this as if everything you say is accurate. I hope to god you are."

"We also have to get word out to the public about the dangers of handling any artifacts from Guatemala," Brett said. "Infected pieces probably have already been shipped to god knows where. We need to send out a warning."

"One thing at a time, Brett," Quinn said. "Let's do our job and get the proof we need, then we can sound an alarm. We're sticking our necks out enough already by invading the monastery. We simply can't risk spreading fear and panic throughout the entire art community and every museum in the world without definite proof."

Brett went to Google Earth and downloaded an aerial photo of the monastery to show Quinn where the main building was located. "There's a large steel gate at the front of the monastery that is locked. The door to the building you are interested is located here, and it's also locked. My guess is the best approach would be to land several officers by helicopter and take them by surprise. Let me know what happens." Then he turned to leave.

"What do you mean, let you know what happens? Where do you think you're going?" Quinn asked. "We're going to need your help. You're the only one who's been inside the place."

"You've got the aerial map. That's all you'll need."

"You're going with us when we go into that monastery, understood?" Quinn barked out. "We'll fly there tomorrow, as soon as the judge signs the warrant and everything else is in place. Be ready to go. And make sure I can reach you."

Brett nodded at him, then walked away. The hell with the monastery. He'd done his job; they could handle it from here.

His task now was to try to find and save the life of the woman he loved.

Chapter 46

Brett needed to get back to Guatemala as soon as possible, but he had to know where to start looking for Kari. Guatemala was a big country, filled with remote villages and thousands of square miles of jungle. If he was to have any chance of finding her, he had to find a way to narrow his search. Kari hated the jungle, and she wouldn't have gone back without a very compelling reason. But it was a trap—a deadly trap. And he was quickly running out of time to save her. Maybe he could find a clue at her apartment or her office, which meant a trip back to Chicago. He only hoped he wasn't wasting valuable time.

He raced back to his apartment, packed everything he would need, then stopped at the door. He had another idea. There was something else he had to take care of first. He picked up the phone and dialed.

"Ashley, can you meet me for coffee? It's important."

"What is it, Brett? What did you want to talk about?"

"It's not about us," Brett said hurriedly. "I've got an exclusive for you. A big story. You're going to want to hear it."

After a moment of silence, she answered him. "All right," she said. "Meet me at Murray's."

When Ashley walked in, Brett stood and extended his hand. She moved past his hand, kissed him on the cheek, then slipped into the booth opposite him. She leaned across the table and laid her hand on his.

"Brett, I've done a lot of thinking. I was angry and upset when you had to leave so soon the last time. I'm sorry about some of the things I said. I was wrong."

"There's no reason to apologize, Ashley. You were right. We are too different."

She carefully withdrew her hand. "So... you don't think we should even try—."

"No," he finished her thought.

She glanced at the menu, then pushed it aside. "You've found someone else, haven't you?"

Brett let out a sigh. "I thought maybe I had, but no, it didn't work out."

"Just for the record," Ashley said with a confident smile,

touching his hand again, "I'm not giving up on you. I've got more patience than most of the other women out there." She grabbed her pocketbook, sorted through it, and finally pulled out a pad and flipped it open. "Okay, tell me about your big story."

They ordered from the menu and over lunch at Murray's Pub, Brett told her in detail about the deaths in Guatemala and at the monastery in New Mexico. Ashley wrote rapidly while he talked.

When he finally stopped, Ashley put her pen down and looked up at him. "You're sure about all this? You realize I have nothing to back this story up. Just your word."

Brett held up his hands, showing her his swollen fingers with cuts and punctures on them. "I was there. None of this is conjecture. Your story could help save lives and stop any further spread of the disease."

"You're absolutely certain about everything, including the monastery?" She continued to write furiously as he described exhuming the bodies of the dead monks, about his break-in at the monastery, and about the duplicated pieces of Mayan art he found there. He told her about his narrow escape.

She put her pen down and stared at him. "Aren't you going to tell the authorities? Something has to be done to stop them. Let's call someone."

"I'm going to tell you something, but you have to give me your word that this cannot in any way leak any of this to the general public for twenty-four hours. Promise?"

"Yes," Ashley said. "Tell me."

"Sometime tomorrow, a combined force of the CDC and federal marshals will be going into the monastery to seize all the artifacts and stop all shipping out of there."

Ashley resumed scribbling more notes. "Unbelievable."

"You promised," Brett reminded her. "Nothing in the news about the monastery for twenty-four hours. We don't want to warn them."

"What's the name of the virus?" she asked.

"What?" he asked. "Officially, it's catalogued as the 'MEH-130 virus,'" he said. "We call it the 'Mayan virus.'"

She looked up at him and nodded. "The MEH-130 virus," she repeated as she wrote. "What do the letters mean?"

"Mayan-epidemic hemorrhagic virus. The letters and numbers are just for our cataloging or describing viruses, just like the swine flu is labeled H1N1. Your article is going to help stop the spread of the disease." Brett said. "When word gets out about this deadly infection associated with Mayan artifacts, and that many of the pieces are fake, the market for Mayan art will vanish overnight. You're going to help save lives."

She frowned as she looked over her notes. "If the virus is spread by the artifacts, how come only a few people who come in contact with it get infected? Why didn't all the monks die?"

"We'll probably never know for certain the answer to that. But my guess is that the limited pattern of infection is due to several factors. First, some of the artifacts have more fungus on them, and therefore more virus. Second, during the cleaning or handling of the artifacts, the virus is probably spread by the dust that covers them. It depends on how it is cleaned, brushed, handled, and so forth. We saw the same thing with the Hanta virus outbreak. That particular hemorrhagic virus is carried on mouse feces, and is spread in the dust. Only a few dozen people got infected and died, even though the mice that carried the virus were widespread. But it was one-hundred percent fatal."

When she finally finished writing and put her pen down, she looked up at him with a look of both shock at what she had heard, and admiration for the man across from her. "Thank you. This is... incredible." She paused a moment as if weighing her words carefully. "Brett, about us..."

He interrupted her. "You were right, Ashley. It wouldn't work. We want different things from life. You're a smart, beautiful woman, and you'll find someone who wants the same things you do."

She stared at him a moment, then nodded and looked down. She recovered quickly. "Thanks for the exclusive. You're right, this is really big. My editor's going to have a stroke over this one."

"You're a good reporter. You deserve the story. Who knows? You might win the Pulitzer. Take care of yourself, Ashley. I really have to run. I've got a plane to catch." He started to get up.

"Brett" she said, "nobody knows what the future holds. Who knows, maybe someday—"

He stood up. "Yeah, who knows." He leaned over and kissed her quickly on the cheek. Then he left.

He took a cab to the airport and caught the next flight to Chicago. He knew the odds were stacked against his finding anything that would help him locate Kari. He hoped he wasn't wasting valuable time; time that might cost Kari her life.

Once in Chicago, he took a cab to her house and had the driver let him out a block away. He wanted to make sure there were no surprises waiting for him. Since his discovery at the monastery, he knew his life was also in danger. He didn't intend to walk into a trap. He strolled down the street in front of her house, but didn't spot anything unusual. Nobody sitting in cars, no one on the sidewalk. He walked around to the alley behind the house. He didn't spot any nosy neighbors peeking out windows, no dogs around to sound the alarm. Everything seemed quiet. He opened the gate to the back yard and went up the walk to the back door. He opened the screen door and tried the back door. It was locked.

He unscrewed the handle from the screen door and used it to smash the corner of the window on the back door. Then he reached in and unlocked it. He waited inside, peeking out the window to see if anyone had seen him. Satisfied that he hadn't been noticed, he went down the hall into the living room.

He looked around the room. It was sparse, clean, and neat. There was a pile of mail that had accumulated over the summer while she had been in Guatemala and a basket of laundry in the hall. He groaned when he looked at the mail. He couldn't possibly search through all of it, but whatever he was looking for probably wouldn't be in that pile anyway.

He went to her phone, then played back her voice messages. The last message was silent, nobody there. He remembered having a similar call with only silence on his own phone.

At her desk by a window, he riffled through papers, and through the drawers of the desk, but there was nothing there that would help him find her. He'd been with her two days ago, but it seemed like a lifetime since he'd seen her.

He moved quickly through the other rooms, which were clean and orderly. He found nothing there. He went back to her desk. There had to be something he could use. He spotted an old ledger lying on the shelf above her desk that he had missed the first time. He pulled it down and opened it. It apparently had belonged to Monsignor Joseph Cardone. Why did Kari have it? He leafed through pages and pages of accounts, which recorded sales in the hundreds of thousands of dollars. What did the figures mean? Things only grew more tangled and confusing the more he searched.

He quickly flipped through several pages. On one page, someone had circled an address in Borga, Guatemala. Was there any significance to it? He tore the page out, folded it and put it in his shirt, then continued flipping through the pages.

It suddenly occurred to him. These represented sales of Mayan artifacts! In the back were the addresses of museums and art dealers around the world. Whose ledger was it? Was it Kari's? Or her father's? He opened one of her drawers and pulled out checks, notes, and letters. Her signature was distinctive, crisp and decisive. It was obvious the writing in the journal wasn't her handwriting. As he flipped through more pages, he came across something else that quickened his pulse. He tore out three more pages from the ledger and folded them.

As he glanced out the window, he spotted a police cruiser going slowly down the street. It was definitely time for him to leave. There was the possibility somebody had seen him breaking into the house.

He went to the kitchen and looked out the window. He didn't see any activity, and there were no police cars in the alley. Time to get out. He ran out the back of the house, jumped over the fence, and disappeared down the alley.

Three blocks later, he stopped for a moment to catch his breath and to figure out his next move. It was early evening, and he was hungry. But he had no time for food. He still had no idea where to look for Kari. He had to think of something else. Everybody in her department would have left for the day, so he couldn't question them. He started walking toward the university. A plan formed in his mind. It was a wild idea. A long shot at best, but it was all he could come up with.

"Where the hell is Brett Carson?" Quinn yelled out as he slammed the phone down. People working in the EOC shrugged and stared at him. Quinn had tried calling his office, his apartment, and his cell phone with no luck. Brett had simply disappeared. He was a rebel, stubborn and independent, but he had never before disobeyed a direct order. Something must have happened to him.

Quinn was furious. Brett had convinced him to put his ass—in fact his entire future career—on the line, and now he was nowhere to be found. Dammit! Quinn knew that Brett understood the importance of tomorrow's incursion into the monastery. They needed him to help carry this off. Where the hell was he?

"Find Brett Carson and get his ass over here now!" Quinn yelled out to everyone in the room. He dropped into his chair at the console and let out a sigh. It had been a very long day, he was tired, he was hungry, the thick coffee in the bottom of his cup was cold, and right now he was in a damned rotten mood.

Chapter 47

Chicago

D arkness came quickly this time of year, and the glow of
the streetlights reminded Brett that he was running out of
time. His plane left for Guatemala in less than twelve hours. Brett
walked to the university campus and went across the quad to the
Walker Museum. He went up the front steps and tried the main
front doors. He wasn't surprised to find them locked.

At the back of the building, he saw a loading dock with a
receiving ramp leading down to a large metal overhead door. Over
the door was a single security light. He looked around but didn't
spot any security cameras. He tried all the doors hoping that one
might have been left unlocked. They were locked tight.

There was a wooden door beside the large metal overhead

door. That would be his best bet. Looking around, he found a board and used it to smash the security light bulb. Then he found a large rock beside the building. He glanced around to make sure nobody was walking close by, then smashed the door with the rock next to the lock. Holding the heavy rock with his cut and abraded fingers was difficult. He hit the wooden door several more times, wincing with pain each time he did. The wood was starting to splinter, but the noise was loud, and he paused to listen and see if anyone had heard him.

It occurred to him he'd never broken into any place before this assignment. Now, it seemed that was all he did. He tried again, this time pressing his body against the door as he smashed at the lock to put extra pressure on the wooden structure. With a loud crack, the door suddenly burst open as the entire deadbolt mechanism tore away from the frame. He waited for an ear-piercing alarm to shatter the night—but nothing happened.

Relieved, he dropped the rock outside, slipped through the door, and closed it again. He turned into the darkness of a warehouse and immediately stumbled into a crate, smashing his shins.

"Shit," he said and snapped on his small medical penlight. He was probably just wasting his time and risked getting caught in the process; but he'd had run out of options and had no other place to look. The problem was he didn't even know what he was looking for. The warehouse was filled with dozens of boxes stacked and lying about, varying in size from small boxes to large shipping crates.

He made his way through the maze of boxes and crates, glancing at the labels. Then he spotted two boxes sitting on a long wooden bench. There was a wooden frame around them, and they smelled of mesquite and wood shavings. He'd seen similar boxes at the monastery. He looked at the labels. They were both addressed to Forrest Wheeler. The return address on the first one was missing; the return address on the second box was from Borga, Guatemala. Brett recognized the town from the ledger; he peeled off the label and put it in his pocket. He didn't have time to chase down false leads, but at the moment he had nothing else.

The thing that had been puzzling him was how were artifacts smuggled out of the country, and was Wheeler working with the monks or the Church? Some of the questions seemed to have obvious answers; others had no answers.

Wheeler had used his expertise to find undiscovered tombs and recover priceless artifacts. They were then shipped out of the country under the protection of the Church to the monastery in New Mexico. Brett suspected that Wheeler probably hadn't known what was going on inside the monastery or about the duplicated fake artifacts.

When they realized Wheeler had discovered their operation, they murdered him to protect their secret. But who were 'they'— who murdered him? It didn't seem logical that only the monks were involved in the scheme. Brett couldn't believe that the monks had anything to do with his death; smuggling was one thing, murder something else entirely. He presumed that somehow the rebel forces and the monks were working together. The rebels must have killed Wheeler, because he presented a huge risk to their money flow.

Was Kari also a threat to them? She'd had been to the monastery and now she too knew the secret inside those walls. The same people who killed her father would also need to silence Kari.

He wanted to know what was inside the crates. He assumed

they were Mayan pieces, which meant they could be harboring the virus. He couldn't leave them. Somebody would eventually open them, possibly exposing them and others. He had to make sure that didn't happen. He pushed the beam of his penlight around the room until he found what he was looking for.

A white Chevy Caprice police cruiser slowed to a stop, then slowly backed up. The campus police officer rolled the window down and looked toward the museum receiving ramp. Something didn't look right, but he couldn't spot anything out of the ordinary. He continued staring, trying to decide what caught his attention.

The security light was out.

Probably just a burned-out bulb. It happened frequently enough around campus. He'd report it and maintenance would replace it in the morning. He decided to take a look around while he was here. He grabbed his flashlight and climbed out of the car.

As he approached the loading ramp, he saw that a portion of the wooden door was missing. And there was broken glass on the cement dock. He looked up. The light bulb hadn't burned out; it had been smashed.

He turned off his flashlight and walked back to his car. He started the engine, quietly pulled into the driveway up to the edge of the ramp and turned the engine off. Whoever was inside would be in for a surprise when they came out. He drew his revolver and put it on the seat beside him, then reached for the mike to his radio.

"Unit 902 requesting back-up at the loading ramp behind the Walker Museum. There has been a break-in, possible robbery in progress."

"Copy, 902. Two units will be there shortly. Keep your channel open."

"Copy." He heard the dispatcher announce a 'ten fifty-three' for possible robbery in progress, followed by a 'code-two,' instructing the backup units to proceed immediately with lights flashing but without siren.

He waited for a minute, then took his revolver and flashlight and climbed out of the car. Backup would be there any second, but he decided to have a look inside. He had the element of surprise on his side. With pistol in one hand and flashlight in the other, he slowly pushed open the splintered door and slipped inside.

Brett was running out of time, but he had to sterilize the pieces in the crates so nobody would be exposed. He pushed his penlight around, looking for a closet with cleaning supplies but not finding one. He tore open the cabinet doors below the work bench and found a bottle of Clorox among other cleaning items. Perfect—just what he needed.

He opened the bottle of Clorox and dumped half of it into a

bucket. Then he took a screwdriver from the tools lying on the bench and pried open the first small crate. He pulled out wood shavings, then pulled out the first artifact and put it in the bucket, bathed it thoroughly, then set it on a bench to dry. Then he did the same with the contents inside the second crate. Then he scrubbed his hands at the sink and poured alcohol over them. He searched the boxes but found only wooden shavings. He poured the remaining Clorox into the boxes to soak into the mesquite shavings. Everything had been sterilized and he knew no one would get infected by the virus from these crates.

He looked around with the tiny penlight, but found nothing else of interest. All he had to show for his efforts was an address that might or might not mean anything. He'd already used too much time. Time to leave.

As he turned, he noticed a beam of light flicker briefly over the far wall. Someone else was inside! He'd been spotted. Probably the campus police or security. Every nerve in his body kicked into action. He couldn't afford to get caught. He had to get to Guatemala without any delay. He had to find another way out of the building—if there was another way.

He snaked his way through the boxes and crates, away from the door he had broken in. There had to be another way into the museum the next floor up. Occasionally, he caught sight of light flashing behind him. Whoever had the flashlight was following him. The first door he tried was locked.

What if all the doors leading up into the museum were locked? He quietly ran to the next door. It opened with a loud metallic click. He slipped through it, ran up the stairs two at a time, and found himself on the first floor. Lights from the campus quad coming through the large, front windows lining the hall provided ample light, but also left him exposed in the open hallway.

He went to the large double doors at the front of the museum, but at the last second, he changed his mind and stopped. The police would probably be watching the front door as well. His footsteps echoed off the marble floor of the empty building as he ran down the hall toward a red exit light over a door. The door on the side of the building was intended for emergency exit only. There was a warning not to use the door, and a large metal bar for the alarm.

Without slowing his pace, he hit the bar, threw open the door and burst out into the night with an ear-piercing alarm blaring behind him. He slipped between two buildings, headed toward the main library and melted into a sea of students going into and out of the library.

While he waited for his plane at O'Hare, Brett finally reached Solt by phone. "Ross, I've been trying to reach you for a couple of days, but I understand you've had some trouble down there."

"Brett, good to hear from you. Yeah, we've got a mess down here. It looks like neither the government nor the rebels want us here, but for the life of me, I can't figure out why. Quinn wants the team to fly back to Atlanta. I heard you had a scare at the monastery. What the hell happened?"

"I'll tell you the full story over beers when I see you. This is one story you're not going to believe," Brett said.

"Damnit, Brett. How come you're always doing the fun stuff when I'm not around? We'll be back tomorrow, so you can buy me that cold beer and tell me all about it."

"You're going to see me sooner than that, Ross. I'm on my way down. I'll be in Guatemala City in approximately six hours."

"You're coming back down? Why? Quinn is sending us all home. He thinks it's too dangerous and unstable for us to stay here."

"I've got to find Kari."

"Kari?" Solt blurted out. "I thought she was in Chicago. What's she doing back here?"

"We're about to board, and I don't have time to explain it now. Meet me at the airport with the Jeep and all the gas you can get. I'll need some supplies also. When you get to the airport, keep an eye out for Kari. I don't know when she left, and we might get lucky and spot her when she's still at the airport. Gotta go."

As Brett turned to leave, something on the large TV screen caught his eye. The words "deadly Mayan virus" lit up the screen on CNN. An anchor was detailing the dangerous new virus, and telling everyone to stay out of contact with any Mayan artifact or any art piece from Guatemala.

Ashley had come through for him; that news piece would put a halt to the trafficking of Mayan art for a long time. Follow-up articles could add more details, and decrease the risk that anyone else would come in contact with the virus.

The assault on the monastery at San Sebastian would create a media frenzy, and the world would finally learn about the ancient Mayan killer virus!

Chapter 48

Six hours later, the Mexicana Airlines 757 landed in Guatemala City and rolled to a stop. Brett woke at the sound of the tires hitting the concrete, and yawned. He'd forced himself to sleep on the way down, because he wasn't sure when he'd find time to sleep again. He got off the plane, made his way through the crush of people and went through customs. When he stepped outside, he saw Ross Solt and the dog waiting for him by the Jeep. The rest of the team was standing nearby with their gear, waiting to catch a flight back to Atlanta.

Tequila barked and leaped from the back of the Jeep and ran to Brett, nearly knocking him over. The dog whined and rubbed against him while his tail wagged frantically.

"Looks like he missed you," Solt said as he shook Brett's hand and slapped him on the back. "Actually, we all did."

There were greetings all around, which included a mixture of handshakes, laughing, and loud barking. Jacek walked up to Brett and put his hand on his shoulder. "Brett, we're all sorry about doubting you earlier. It's just that with the outbreak in New Mexico—"

"Forget it, PJ," Brett said with a slap on the back. "Let's concentrate on what we have to do now. I want to thank all of you for the work you did while I was gone," he said. "Sorry I abandoned you. When I get back to Atlanta, I'm buying you all dinner at Murray's."

Solt noticed Brett's hands. "Brett—look at your hands. What happened to you? Were you in a fight?"

"Just a few cuts and scrapes. You didn't happen to spot Kari here at the airport, did you?"

"No, but with the chaotic crowd in this place, you wouldn't be able to spot your own mother," Solt said. "What's going on? Is she in trouble?"

"I've got to find her. Her life is in danger, and she doesn't know it." A fear that kept gnawing at him was the possibility that she was already dead.

"Listen," Solt said as he leaned close and spoke so no one else could hear, "Quinn's been looking for you, and he's mad as hell."

"You didn't tell him I was coming down here, did you?"

"No. He didn't ask, so I didn't have to lie. He thinks something happened to you. Now he wants me to fly to Albuquerque and meet up with him and the federal marshals. Looks like I'll be going to the monastery after all."

Brett threw his gear into the back of the Jeep. "Ross, thanks for taking care of Tequila and getting the Jeep filled with all the supplies. I'll try to keep in touch with you. Be careful in the monastery."

"Where are you headed?" Solt asked. "What are you going to do?"

Brett started the engine. "I don't have the slightest idea, Ross. She could be anywhere in the whole damned country. But I have to try to find her." Then he jammed the Jeep into gear and sped away, waving as he disappeared into traffic.

Solt shook his head as he watched his friend disappear. "Shit," he said, then picked up his bags and headed toward the boarding area with the others. I should have gone with him.

Borga, Guatemala

After four grueling hours of travel on a rough road, Brett arrived in Borga in the late afternoon. He had decided that he would start his search at the address in Borga. It was another frustrating hour of driving around the crowded, dirty city before he finally found the address that was circled in the ledger. It turned out to be a rundown warehouse deep in the slums of the crowded city. The large tin-roofed building stretched along a narrow, dusty, litter-filled alley.

He wasn't sure what he had expected to find at the address from the label he'd found, but it wasn't this. He sat in the Jeep several buildings away and watched the warehouse. There didn't seem to be any activity. No one went into or out of the warehouse. For all he could tell, it was an empty building. He had a growing fear that he followed a dead end, that Kari wouldn't be here, and he'd wasted valuable time.

Now that he was here, he had to at least check it out. Maybe he could find someone or something that would lead him to Kari. He wanted to make sure he wasn't walking into a trap, but time was scarce. If Kari was here, she might be in danger. He had no means of rescuing her. Either way he was in a losing situation.

He put Tequila in the shade under the Jeep and gave him a bowl of water. He considered taking the dog with him for an extra set of eyes and ears but decided against it. He walked down the alley, watching the building for any activity and looking over his shoulder to see if he was being followed. The whole set-up bothered him.

He climbed up on the loading dock and slid the large shipping door open a crack as slowly as he could and tried to peek in. He saw nothing. After being in bright sunlight, the building inside was dark to his eyes that hadn't yet adjusted. He slowly pushed the door another few inches and slipped inside.

He moved away from the door and ducked down to wait as his eyes adjusted to the muted afternoon sunlight diffused its way through windows covered with thick grime. Finally, he could make out shadowy forms. The large building was eerily silent.

Even through the sharp scent of fresh sawdust, he could detect something familiar and jarring. The smell of blood and the stench of death. He moved toward it. He almost tripped over the body in the darkness.

A short, heavy man lay sprawled on the floor on his back, blank eyes staring up at nothing. A dark pool of congealed blood marked where his genitals had been shot away. Another bullet through his gut spread a crimson blotch on his shirt. Whoever shot the man had not intended a sudden death. His death had been slow and agonizing as he slowly bled to death with both a gut wound and his genitals shot off. A revolver lay on the floor near him.

Brett looked around and spotted something that sent a chill through him; the necklace Kari's father had given her was clenched in the man's fist. Kari had definitely been here. Brett picked up the revolver. Only one bullet was spent. Five live rounds were still in the cylinder. But the dead man had been shot twice.

Who had fired the second shot? Where was that gun? Brett stuck the gun under his belt. Why did the dead man have her necklace? Maybe there had been a struggle and she had fired in self-defense. He wanted to believe that. But who fired the other shot?

What happened to Kari? Was she still somewhere in the building? Brett pulled the necklace from the dead man's grasp and stood to leave. He jumped when a huge man walked through another doorway. The man seemed equally shocked to see Brett. After hesitating a moment, the man moved toward him. Brett grabbed the revolver and aimed it squarely at the man's chest.

"Don't move!" Brett ordered. The man stopped.

Brett was in awe at the size of the man—arms thick as tree trunks and his chest as wide as the doorway he had just walked through. Brett guessed him to be six-eight, as tall as the door. Even in the dark building Brett could make out a dark patch over his left eye. He realized he was standing face-to-face with the man who had murdered Forrest Wheeler. A violent, ruthless man capable of anything. The man who intended to kill Kari—or maybe already had. Brett knew that any mistake, any slip-up would probably be his last. He realized his back was vulnerable and glanced around to make sure they were alone. He didn't want to join the dead man on the floor.

"Donde esta la muchacha?" Brett asked. Scar didn't move.

"Where is the girl?" Brett repeated through clenched teeth, his patience gone and a huge dose of fear flooding his body with adrenaline. "I know she was here. Where is she?" Brett snapped at him.

Dead silence. The huge man remained silent.

Had he already killed her? Had she somehow managed to escape? Or had she been taken someplace else? Brett looked around. What should his next move be? Brett realized the fear of losing Kari was the worst fear he had ever experienced.

"Kari!" he yelled out. He waited and listened. He thought he heard something, but couldn't be sure. Time was running out; every minute he stayed put his own life in danger. He pulled back the hammer, and the barrel rotated a new cartridge into firing position. "Where is she?" Brett demanded.

The man didn't answer him; he just stood in the doorway, filling the space. Then Brett heard a faint groan that was Kari's voice. Kari!

At that same moment, there was a loud screeching noise as the warehouse doors were shoved open and several policemen stood outside with their guns drawn. "Suelte el arma ahora!" *Drop the gun now* one of them yelled at him. At the same instant that Brett dropped the revolver and raised his hands, the huge man slipped back into the shadows and silently disappeared through the doorway into the other room.

The police rushed in and surrounded Brett. Then they spotted the body on the floor. One of the policemen looked down at the body. It was obvious he was dead, but the policeman kicked his boot against the body to be certain. He aimed a flashlight at the dead man's face. "It's Senor Armando Galvez," he said. Then he threw Brett a stern look. "You are under arrest, *gringo*. Don't move!"

New Mexico

The CDC team took a flight back to Atlanta, but Solt took a different flight to Albuquerque, where he met up with Quinn and the federal marshals. As soon as Solt walked across the tarmac in Albuquerque to meet Quinn, he could tell something was wrong. Solt had never seen Quinn that mad.

"Where the hell is Brett?" Quinn bellowed out.

"Guatemala."

"Guatemala? Shit! This operation into the monastery with marshals was his idea. He's supposed to be here. Now he's down there on his own, dealing with rebels, a hot virus—and who knows what else."

"Zolog. Zolog is also after him."

"Who's Zolog?"

"Colonel Zolog is head of secret police, and a real mean son-of-a-bitch from what I understand."

"Secret police? What the hell did Brett do down there?" Quinn let out a sigh. "And who leaked the story to the press of a "Mayan virus" that it was on every cable news show this morning? Do you have any idea what kind of mess we are going to be in if we bust into a monastery and then find nothing? And it's already all over the news?" I don't even want to think of the consequences if we are

417

wrong. Hell with it. Nothing we can do about it now. Let's go."

Two helicopters containing eight marshals, Quinn and Solt were racing over the New Mexico terrain toward the monastery of San Sebastian. After an hour, they were over the Carlos mountain range, then they followed the Chaco River basin into the deep, dark Canyon de Chelly. The red tiled roofs of the buildings of the monastery came into view at the top of the mesa. The helicopters slowed and began a descent into the monastery.

As the helicopters hovered over San Sebastian, something unusual happened below them. At least two dozen monks ran from various buildings toward the large building in the center and gathered at the door.

"Damnit!" Quinn yelled into his headpiece to the pilot. "We have to stop them. We don't want them to get inside. Get us down now!" He had hoped that they would surprise them and avoid this from happening. The last thing he wanted was to cause mass confusion and possibly infect more people in the resulting chaos.

The door to the building opened, and all the monks rushed inside. They were probably trying to destroy everything before they could be stopped. Just exactly the thing Quinn didn't want to happen. Both helicopters dropped quickly. The powerful backlash from the props sent dust and fine stones swirling into the air in a thick cloud. Marshals leaped from the other helicopter. Quinn and Solt jumped out after the marshals in their plane were out. Guns drawn, the marshals ran to the door, with Quinn and Solt right behind them.

"Stop!" Quinn yelled to the marshals over the sounds of the helicopters. "Don't go in there." Then he stepped through the doorway and yelled to the monks, "Everyone out! Now!"

The monks inside froze at the sight of the marshals with guns drawn. No one moved. Most of them had artifacts and molds in their hands. Strewn across the floor were dozens of pieces they had already smashed.

"Drop what you are holding. Leave everything inside the building," Quinn told them. "Then move outside."

The marshals stepped aside as the monks filed out. The monks stood together in a group, and the marshals formed a circle around them.

Quinn stepped up and addressed everyone. "There is a possibility that some of the art pieces in there are carrying a very deadly virus. No one is to go back in there until our contamination team has arrived. Understood?"

Marshals closed and guarded the door. Large containers of phenol and alcohol were carried from the helicopters, and everyone had to wash thoroughly. The monks who had been inside were ordered to take off their robes and put on chem suits provided for them.

Solt unloaded a container from the helicopter, slipped into a max containment suit, which had a portable sterile air supply tank, opened the door and went inside. He found several broken pieces of pottery and statues on the floor. But the monks hadn't had time to destroy everything; there were dozens more still on shelves or in boxes. There were still pairs of duplicates that hadn't been destroyed. He used large forceps to drop pieces into a container that would be taken back to Bio-Four for analysis and culturing. He looked around and shook his head in amazement when he realized Brett had scaled the wall with his bare hands and climbed inside.

Then he spotted something that made his heart leap. The building wasn't empty. Standing in the shadow of one the corners was a monk, holding a knife. It appeared to be a Mayan ceremonial knife. The sudden sight of him in the shadows was startling. Solt's heart thumped against his chest. He didn't know what the monk intended to do with that knife.

"What are you doing?" Solt asked, his voice muffled by the isolation suit and head cover. No answer.

"Let's go outside, okay?" Solt continued. "It's not safe in here for either of us." He stepped aside and waited.

Finally, the monk moved past him and out into the sunlight to the shock and surprise of everyone out there. Solt let out a relieved sigh, looked around, then stepped outside and closed the door.

After the last monk was sanitized and had changed, the marshals moved everyone into the dining hall. The chief federal marshal stepped up to Quinn.

"Well, Doctor Quinn, looks like we're just about finished here. There are vans on their way here to take the monks down to Santa Fe to the federal building and arraign them. We'll need copies of all the information you can find, including photos, documents, reports, etcetera."

Quinn extended his hand. "Thanks for all your help."

The marshal smiled. "I must say, this has been an interesting assignment. We've never invaded a monastery before."

"You realize we don't really have an ax to grind with the monks here," Quinn said, "and we won't be bringing formal charges against them. We just wanted to make sure they didn't infect half the world by shipping out artifacts that carried the virus. This is the only way we knew to stop them."

"Well, that will be up to the courts to decide, won't it? There is still the problem of both mail fraud and international trade conspiracy they are going to have to answer for. One of the helicopters will stay here and take you back when you're finished." Then he left to read the monks their rights and place them under arrest.

Chapter 49

Borga, Guatemala

"*Tenemos un asesinato,*" the officer spoke into his radio. The radio squawked back a response. "We're taking you into custody for the murder of one of Borga's outstanding citizens," the officer snarled at Brett.

Outstanding citizen? Who was the dead man? Who had tipped off the police? Brett wondered. Was this whole thing a setup to get him? As if to answer, the sergeant said, "Well, we didn't expect to find a murder." He jerked his head toward the offices and stairs of the warehouse. "*Compruebe fuera del lugar. Rápidamente!*" he told his men. They quickly spread out through the rest of the building, checking the other rooms. Brett noticed their uniforms and realized they weren't ordinary policemen. They were the dreaded Secret Police.

After a minute, the men returned. *"Es vacío. nadie aquí,"* one of the men said, indicating the place was empty.

"Tómelo," the sergeant said and motioned with his head toward the door.

"No, you've got it wrong. I didn't shoot anyone," Brett protested.

Police grabbed each of Brett's arms and pulled him toward the door and a waiting police van.

Brett panicked. He had only seconds before it would be too late to do anything. If they didn't hang him for murdering one of their own, he would most certainly rot away in a Guatemalan prison the rest of his life. One thing he knew for certain, he couldn't help Kari if he was sitting in a stinking cell. Acting more on impulse than reason, and using every bit of energy he could muster, he suddenly jerked free of the two men holding him, snatched the revolver from the floor in one swift movement, and fired once in the air. The deafening sound of the gun echoed through the warehouse and caught them by surprise.

"Caigas sus armas!" Brett yelled. "Drop them!"

Only the split second of surprise saved him. Momentarily caught off guard, the men dropped their guns. Another second and they would have realized they outnumbered him and could have easily overpowered him. He collected their guns and radios, then dropped them in an empty crate. His heart was racing and his hands trembled at what he'd just done, but there was no turning back now. He had to act quickly. He looked around and spotted a door. He pointed to it with his gun. "Get in. *Vaya!*"

Just then Zolog came in. He walked up to Brett, showing no fear, though Brett kept the gun aimed squarely at his chest.

"Well, Doctor Carson," Zolog said, "it seems we're both looking for the same thing. But apparently someone else got to her before we did."

That's why the Secret Police were here. They'd come expecting to find Kari, but she was gone. "Who?" Brett asked. "Where'd they take her?"

"That's what we'd like to know. Don't worry, we will find her. I just hope we don't find her dead—murdered, like her father and this man," he said, looking down. His eyes narrowed as he stared at Brett, his face seething with anger.

"Doctor Carson, you've made a real mess of things for yourself. Not just shooting Senor Gomez, but you've resisted arrest and assaulted police officers. I hope you realize that you are in very serious trouble."

Brett had just fallen into one hell of a mess. He motioned to the closet. "Get in there," he ordered. He kept glancing at the door, concerned that others might come in. If they saw that he had a weapon, they would gun him down.

"I promise you, you won't get far," Zolog said.

Brett feared he might be right.

Zolog glared at him, but he moved into the closet. The door had an old iron latch, but no lock. Brett jammed a piece of wood into the latch, then moved two heavy crates against the door for added security. The crates would act to block the sound of yelling and banging and would keep them from knocking the door down. He would call the police station after he was well on his way. He didn't want a roomful of Secret Police suffocating in a tiny closet with no air or water.

Things had suddenly taken a severe turn for the worst. Brett was a fugitive wanted for murder. He had both the rebel forces and the Secret Police after him. He had to find Kari before time ran out for both of them.

He went to a desk in the office and riffled through papers and maps hoping to find a clue, but wasn't even sure what he was looking for. The desk was littered with letters, invoices, billing sheets, inventory, but no reference to Kari or her father.

He kept glancing over his shoulder, afraid that Scar might appear again. After a minute of frantic searching the office, he figured he was pushing his luck. It was time to get out while he still could. The police had called in a report when they tried to arrest him, and others would soon start looking for them. Brett hoped he'd remembered to take all their radios. He didn't want to walk outside and find the warehouse surrounded by military police.

He slid open the large door, looked around to make sure he wasn't walking into a trap, and ran down the alley. As he started the Jeep, Tequila jumped in, and Brett tore down the alley. He had to get distance between himself and the military police, but he also had to figure out where the hell he was going. Where would Kari have gone? Had she killed this Gomez to revenge her father's death or to protect herself? Or had someone else shot him?

Twenty minutes outside of Borga, he pulled under the shade of a tree and stopped. He turned on one of the police radios that he had kept, contacted a police station, and told them where to find the men he had locked up in the warehouse. He didn't want them to suffocate from the heat and lack of water.

He pulled out maps and opened them. Swatting at insects, he wiped sweat from his eyes and downed some water. After pouring water for Tequila, Brett stared at the maps but didn't have a clue where to start looking. He closed his eyes for a minute and tried to think. What would Kari do? Where would she have gone on her own? He ran through a dozen scenarios in his mind. Would she have gone to Guatemala City? Or back to San Angelica village? Why had she even come back to Guatemala in the first place?

The most likely scenario was that someone had her. The question was, where would they take her? Since it wasn't Zolog and the Secret Police, it had to be the rebels. He made a decision. He looked at the map, saw what he was looking for, then drove off. There was one person who just might have some idea what happened to Kari. Brett hoped he'd made the right choice.

Brett knew the military police would launch an all-out effort to find him. But he figured he had several hours lead on them because they wouldn't know where he was headed. After that, the odds were in favor of the police.

After two hours of hard driving, he sped into San Angelica village, drove up to the adobe church and slid to a stop in a cloud of dust. He jumped out of the Jeep just as Father Hernandez opened the door and stepped out.

The priest's face registered shock as he recognized Brett.

Borga

Within ten minutes of Brett's call, a squad of military police arrived at the warehouse, rushed inside with guns drawn, and after making sure the building was secure, kicked opened the closet. Nine soldiers and Zolog poured out of the tiny room.

Zolog's face was distorted with rage, and he stomped out into the middle of the room in a fit of anger. The men knew that an angry Zolog was a dangerous beast, and everyone moved back to give him room. Zolog was running out of time and was furious at the American doctor who had gotten in his way. Carson had moved from being an annoyance to a dangerous hindrance that Zolog intended to remove permanently.

If he found Carson, then he had a chance of finding the woman. If the doctor knew the whereabouts of the woman, Zolog knew he would talk before he died. Find Carson and find the girl. Zolog had to move quickly. He thought he knew where to begin his search.

Four Jeeps and a personnel truck filled with heavily armed soldiers roared out of town.

The grotesque body of Armando Galvez, on the floor of the crumbling warehouse, was forgotten and left alone to bake in the heat.

San Angelica village

"Doctor Carson. What brings you back here?" Father Hernandez stumbled over his words. The expression on his face showed confusion. "I didn't expect to see you here."

"I need to find Kari. Her life is in danger."

"Why do you think I'd know where Kari is?"

Brett reached in his pocket and pulled out the ledger sheets and shoved them in Hernandez's face. "There's your name," Brett snapped, pointing to the paper. "You've been involved in smuggling Mayan artifacts. You welcomed the Wheelers to the village so you could keep an eye on Kari and her father."

"I'm not sure what you're talking about."

"Cut the crap, Padre. We know what's been going on inside the monastery in New Mexico. Right now, federal marshals are in the process of arresting the monks and shutting down their operation. Every news show in the world has already broadcast a warning about the Mayan virus. You couldn't give away an artifact right now. Besides, who would want them since two-thirds of them are fake?"

Hernandez's face went white. Finally, he spoke. "You don't know what you've done. You've just sealed the fate of the rebels."

"What do you mean?"

"Those Mayan artifacts are our war bonds," Hernandez said. "The money we make from selling artifacts pays for guns and ammunition to continue our fight against the terrorist government that is choking the Church and our people. Without money for supplies we cannot fight."

"Thousands of people have either been killed outright by government death squads or have disappeared," Hernandez continued. "Priests have been murdered, nuns raped, and the peasants are subjected to unbelievable terror. The rebels are strong and determined. Given time, they will eventually defeat the government forces, but that takes money. Lots of money, and no country has come forth with money or supplies to help us."

Hernandez continued: "Monsignor Cardone, a priest in Chicago, lost his entire family here in Guatemala to government death squads.

He knew somebody had to do something to help the poor peasant rebels in their cause, so he came up an idea of how we could help them. We—the clergy of the Church—formed an underground organization. We became the source of money to support their war. The monks in San Sebastian receive Mayan pieces that we smuggle out, find buyers for them, then ship them to art dealers around the world. The money is then sent back into Guatemala."

"Why are the monks duplicating them?" Brett asked. "Once word gets out that half the pieces are fake—and possibly infected with a deadly virus—they will all become worthless."

"Ancient artifacts are quite valuable and the market for them is very hot at the moment. But as you may guess, they are also quite rare. We would never be able to find enough of them to pay for our supplies."

"So you made duplicates of them in order to raise more money," Brett said. "And you used Wheeler to help you find more."

"It was an arrangement that helped both of us. He didn't know exactly what the artifacts were being used for, but I'm sure he had guessed. We let him select a few of the more valuable pieces to give to museums."

"But when he somehow found out you were duplicating the artifacts, you had him killed," Brett said.

"We had nothing to do with the murder of Forrest Wheeler. The rebel forces did that. He posed a huge risk to their flow of much needed money. I knew nothing about it until it was too late," Hernandez said, looking away.

"The clergy has taken on the responsibility for financing the rebels' cause because it is a war that is just. Without our efforts, there would be no funds to continue the struggle. But committing murder was not part of it. Forrest was my friend. Once he discovered what we were doing, the rebel leaders felt his death was necessary to keep the knowledge of fake artifacts a secret."

"You cold-hearted bastards!" Brett shot back.

"We knew nothing of the plan to kill him. The clergy would never kill someone. But let me ask you, if you were leading an army of men into a battle in which hundreds would probably be killed, but you could save all of them by sacrificing the life of one person, would you do it? Would you kill one to save hundreds?"

Brett just glared at him while the muscles in his jaw tensed. "There's a dead man in a warehouse in Borga—"

"A dead man?" the priest interrupted. "In the warehouse? Who?"

"Some short, grungy, heavy guy. "I don't know his name," Brett said, his face turning red. "Kari had been there. Why was she there?"

"That warehouse is where we collect all the artifacts," Hernandez said, "then ship them out of the country to the San Sebastian monastery. Armando Galvez—the dead man—was in charge of the shipping. But I have no idea why Kari was there."

Hernandez looked at the revolver stuck in Brett's belt. "Did you kill Galvez?"

Brett ignored the question. "If you didn't have anything to do with Wheeler's death, then tell me where I can find Kari and maybe save her life," Brett finally said.

"I don't know where she is. But if the rebels took her, she's probably already dead."

Brett could feel the blood drain from his face.

Hernandez paused, then said, "There is a slight chance they may have taken her to one of their camps, which are in a very rugged area at the southern end of El Petan," Hernandez said.

Brett unfolded a map and spread it on the hood of the Jeep. "Show me, Padre."

The visibly shaken priest pointed to an area on the map. "The largest camp is well hidden in steep, rocky canyons, and difficult to get to. I'm sorry I can't narrow it down any more than this," and he circled an area of at least twenty square miles. "Government forces have not been able to find their camp, so believe me, it is well hidden. Doctor Carson, you have to know that we had nothing to do with—"

"All I want to do is find Kari. That's a large area you pointed on the map. Can you narrow it down any? I'm running out of time."

Father Hernandez looked closely at the map and finally nodded. He pointed with his finger. "This area is very steep and treacherous. There is no way of getting in without being spotted. If you find the canyon, you will probably find Kari—if she's still alive."

Brett jumped back in the Jeep, jammed it into gear, and with tires spinning, sped away.

A few minutes later, five military Jeeps raced into the village of San Angelica and slid to a stop in front of the adobe church. A faint cloud of dust and oil from Brett's Jeep still hung in the air, but it appeared to a shocked Father Hernandez that the military secret police were in too much of a hurry to notice. Blood drained from the priest's face when he saw Colonel Zolog jump out of the Jeep and storm toward him.

"Padre, we're looking for an American girl. I believe you know her," Zolog said.

"I presume you mean Kari Wheeler," Hernandez answered.

Zolog cut him off. "You know exactly who we're looking for. The Wheelers spent their past three summers living here in the village. We also know she visited you here two weeks ago. Have you seen her or heard from her since then?" Zolog stared at him as if he were trying to see through him.

"No, I haven't seen her in at least three weeks. Not since—"

"Have you seen an American doctor by the name of Doctor Carson?"

Hernandez frowned and made a pretext of struggling to remember. Zolog stepped up and slapped him across the face with a gloved hand. Hernandez reeled from the stinging blow, jerked back, and caught himself from falling.

"Padre, I don't have time for games," Zolog snapped. "We are all out of time, and so are you. Let's go inside the church so we can help refresh your memory. We are in a hurry, and I'm sure we can help you remember." Zolog nodded to two soldiers, who took Hernandez roughly by the arms.

Except for a deepening crimson area on his cheek, Hernandez's face was pale. He feared that once he went inside the dark church, he might never see the light of day again. Hernandez was a devoted servant of God, but he definitely wasn't prepared to meet his Maker. Not today.

Chapter 50

Brett turned the Jeep onto the road leading back into the El Petan rain forest and raced into the deepening night. He drove until midnight, then he stopped by a clearing at the top of a rise. He and Tequila ate food and drank water. He curled up under a thin blanket with the dog beside him, the Colt in his lap, and fell asleep.

He woke at dawn and headed to the Xultun ruins, the lowlands of the rain forest. It was a gamble and if he was wrong, he would never find her. It was his only shot. If the rebels had her, her life was in extreme danger. They were certain to kill her, but they would torture her first to find out how much she knew. He was also concerned that she might have been exposed to the virus and could be dying somewhere out there alone.

He had only a vague idea of where he was headed since the details on the map looked nothing like the jungle, but he pushed both the Jeep and himself to the limit. Brett was driven with blind rage, and his body was numbed by fatigue. The muscles in his jaw were tense and his knuckles white from holding the wheel in a vise grip.

For the first time in his life, he knew he could kill someone, something that was unthinkable to him before now. In fact, if anything happened to Kari, he intended to do just that.

He flew recklessly over the rutted path, nearly flipping the Jeep once or twice. The shocks and springs were so bad that the Jeep refused to roll over; it was dead weight on its steel frame. The engine ran smoothly, but blue smoke began pouring from the exhaust, a warning that the engine was being pushed beyond its limits.

Still, Brett didn't let up. He then noted a more serious problem: he was running low on fuel. He had two ten-gallon cans left. It was a toss-up whether he'd run out of gas before the engine blew up.

The fuel gauge pegged on empty. He stopped and poured one of the cans of fuel into the tank. Using his Geo survey map, he thought he had just enough fuel to get him to where he was headed but nothing to spare. He didn't even know if Kari had been taken to one of the camps, or to which one. If he had guessed the wrong location, he would at a dead end.

There were four or five hours of daylight left. He ate a tortilla roll and gave two to Tequila, who gulped them down and sniffed the ground for more. They were both going to be hungry when this was over. He couldn't even dare think about how it would turn out. There was nothing in his favor.

The sky grew darker and a deep rumble of thunder shook the ground. He flipped on the headlights just as the clouds opened up with a driving downpour. Loud cracks of lightning echoed through the jungle. He stopped and pulled a piece of canvas over himself and Tequila. He was soaked, cold, and completely exhausted. He huddled under the canvas while the rain pelted them for more than an hour. He was losing time and would be short on daylight.

As soon as the rain stopped, he started the Jeep and spun away in a swirling cloud of blue smoke. The rain had turned the rutted road into a muddy mess, and his speed was cut in half as the Jeep bounced and splashed its way through the ruts.

He was concerned at his slow progress; the jungle had become thicker with tangled with vines and roots. He tried to stay outside the ruts and pushed the Jeep harder as daylight faded. Branches slapped at the windshield and stung his face. More than once, he and Tequila were jarred from their seats as the Jeep slammed into potholes. With all the deep ravines, swamps, downed trees and rivers, it was easy to lose direction and get completely disoriented

He had to slow down and settle for steady progress rather than have the Jeep break down. He drove twelve hours through the night fighting washouts, bogs, ruts, swarms of mosquitoes, and stinking humidity. He had pushed himself to the limit.

His arms were heavy as lead, his mind numb, and he was on the verge of collapse. When sunlight finally broke through the jungle in long thin shafts of orange, both he and the Jeep had nearly reached their limits. At times he had double vision from fatigue.

The Jeep was burning oil at an alarming rate. He'd pushed the four-cylinder engine beyond its limits, and it was finally succumbing to age and wear. He'd used his last can of fuel sometime during the night, and it was now running on fumes.

He was in four-wheel drive and grinding up a steep bank when the engine finally died. Out of fuel or a ruined engine—he couldn't tell. The silence was sudden and descended around them. Brett wanted to close his eyes a few minutes to rest. He couldn't afford any lost time, but he had to close his eyes for just a few minutes. He fell asleep sitting in the seat.

When he woke, the sun was almost overhead, and he was drenched in sweat. He'd slept nearly three hours. Tequila rested his head on Brett's leg. Brett jumped out of the Jeep, stretched, then spread his map on the hood and turned on his GPS. It was hard to get a signal, and he prayed it was accurate. If Father Hernandez had been honest with him, he was less than three miles from the steep, rocky canyon of the Xultun ruins, the rebels' camp.

He tied a water bottle to Tequila, took one for himself, grabbed the Colt, the GPS, and started walking. He had four lousy bullets. He should have taken the police guns. He and Tequila set out on the most direct route to the canyon. He covered the distance as rapidly as he could, but travel through the jungle was never fast. In the back of his mind, the worry kept surfacing that he might be looking in the wrong place.

That meant he was stranded in the jungle with no fuel. The temperature climbed as the sun moved higher, and sweat poured from his head. He occasionally soaked his shirt in a stream and tried to cool off by wrapping it over his head.

Late in the afternoon, they stopped and he sat down. He was on the verge of collapsing. He needed to rest. Then—he heard something!

A voice, a cough, a noise—something that wasn't jungle. He and Tequila moved carefully in the direction of the noise. They came to a clearing and nearly walked directly into a village. He grabbed Tequila just in time, and they slid back into the jungle.

He worried that Tequila might bark and give away his position, but at the same time he felt safer with the dog by his side. He scanned the area; there were several dozen shacks, dirt roads, a few dozen military trucks and Jeeps, and at the edge of town, a large tanker truck. *LA GASOLINA* was painted in large red letters on the tank. He spotted three or four dogs roaming around the small village. They could spell big trouble if they sensed him or Tequila.

Brett squatted down and surveyed the area. He finally spotted armed guards situated on the top of hills, which gave them a good view of anyone coming toward the village. They looked bored, but they were heavily armed and therefore posed a huge threat. He kept watching and finally located three separate teams of two guards each.

A few people were milling around, bringing in water or food, but the village seemed to be settling down for the night. It would be dark soon, and at the moment, he didn't have a plan. And all he had was a revolver with just four rounds.

Because of the condition he was in, he couldn't physically have fought off a child. He was cut, scratched, bitten, sweating, hungry, and barely able to move. He certainly couldn't take on armed guards with just four bullets.

The task of rescuing Kari seemed to have no chance of succeeding. He wasn't even sure she was down there, and if she were, where they were keeping her.

As he waited and watched, it became almost impossible to see the guards in the fading light and deep shadows. He couldn't tell if they were still there, but he doubted the rebels would let the village go unguarded at night. The guard teams were still out there somewhere.

Just as darkness was settling in, Brett spotted a man walking to the edge of the village. A few hundred yards away at the base of a steep stone cliff, the man disappeared into the rocks. Brett tried to decide what had happened to him, then realized the man must have slipped into one of the numerous caves in the canyon. The rocks formed a natural camouflage to the entrance, and Brett knew he never would have spotted it on his own. He watched to see if anyone else followed, but no one did.

He worried again about Tequila giving away his position, but that was a chance he would have to take. It wasn't just Tequila he had to worry about.

If any of the dogs from the village caught their scent or spotted them, the ensuing barking would be certain to give them away. Hanging as far back in the shadows of the jungle as possible, he worked his way around and finally spotted the entrance to the cave. He stayed in the shadows, and listened.

He peered into the darkness of the cave. It didn't seem to make much sense to go in. He didn't know what was in the cave or how many people were there. He didn't even know if Kari was here in the village.

From somewhere inside the cave he heard a cry, then a loud slap. Then another cry, this time weaker. Tequila's hair bristled on his neck, and a low deep growl grew from his throat. "Quiet, boy," Brett whispered directly into his ear and rubbed his head to calm him. But the hair on the dog's neck stayed erect and he was on full alert.

"Down, boy. Down," he demanded. Tequila reluctantly went down. "Stay," he ordered and pointed to the ground. The dog would be safer outside and could warn him if anyone tried to follow him in. Brett crouched low and moved silently into the cave entrance.

Chapter 51

Oil lamps from deep inside the cave cast strange, flickering shadows on the rough walls and crevices. After moving along the wall for a hundred feet or so, Brett saw that the cave widened where the oil lamps were located. Kari stood in the middle of the cave, her hands tied over her head to a hook in the ceiling. Her blouse was ripped open and hanging in shreds. A huge man with a patch over one eye—the same man that was in the warehouse, the man they called Scar—stood in front of her, leering at her.

Brett peered into all the dark spaces around the cave, but no one else appeared to be there. The man who had murdered her father and tried to rape her was now beating her and threatening her with much worse.

Scar reached out and grabbed her, pulling her toward him. She strained against the rope, but couldn't escape his hands groping her. Filled with blind rage, Brett acted on raw instinct. In one swift move, he whipped the Colt from his belt, pulled back the hammer as the gun was coming up, and said, "Don't move, you fucking bastard!"

At the sound of Brett's voice, Kari screamed hysterically. Then she jerked at the ropes holding her and yelled, "Brett! Help me, help me!"

Kari screamed again, a wild, crazed scream as she struggled against the ropes. She was sobbing and incoherent. At the first sound of Brett's voice, the huge man disappeared into the darkness of the cave. Brett ran up to her and held her a few seconds, then started working at the knots in the rope holding her. "Kari, I'm going to get you out of here. But you have to be quiet. I don't want to wake up the whole damned village. Do you understand?"

She nodded.

"Does he have a gun?" he asked while trying to untie her.

Her body was shaking and she kept sobbing. She didn't answer him.

He grabbed her again, this time more firmly. "Kari, does he have a gun?"

"Yes," she managed through the sobs.

Brett struggled with the rope holding her and finally got her untied. Then he dragged her back into shadows and out of the light as Tequila ran up to them. "We have to get out of here," he said, and started half dragging her back toward the cave entrance.

Then they both heard the sound of the gun being cocked.

"Get behind that boulder and stay down. Keep Tequila with you."

She crouched behind the boulder with the dog. Brett knelt with the gun poised, waiting and listening. Brett couldn't tell if Scar had gone deeper into the cave, or if he was just outside the radius of light, waiting at the edge of the darkness for him.

It was certain death if he followed Scar into the dark shaft, since Brett would be backlit by the torches while Scar remained in total darkness, invisible to Brett. Brett fell to his stomach, but kept the Colt out in front of him. If Scar fired, he had a better chance of surviving if he was lying down. The problem was, they had to get out of the cave. Now!

He and Kari were trapped. If he stood up, Scar would have a straight shot at him. If he waited, they were bound to be discovered, and neither one of them would get out alive. He aimed the gun at the darkness and waited, trying to weigh his options. Any second, he expected Scar to fire at them, which would sound the alarm and bring help. Brett had walked into a trap of his own making.

Then he heard a cry from deep in the darkness, a hideous, dreadful sound that echoed through the cave. The sound grew closer. Brett held the gun ready and prepared to fire, not sure what was happening. A moment later Scar stumbled toward the light, holding the Spencer revolver down by his side. In his other huge fist he held a seven-foot bushmaster by the neck. Blood trickled down from two small holes in Scar's neck. Brett immediately realized what had happened.

The deadly snake had struck the huge man in the neck. In minutes there would be massive swelling and Scar would die an agonizing death. As his jugular veins closed off, blood would engorge his head to the point of bursting, and finally his airway would close and he would choke to death.

Scar's huge fist had crushed the neck of the bushmaster, but its dying body still coiled and flipped in reflexive, non-purposeful movements. Scar's face had already started to turn deep red and his breathing began to sound raspy and labored as the swelling from the deadly venom squeezed shut his airway. He shuffled past Brett and continued on out of the cave still holding the snake, the man and the snake both in their death throes.

Brett ran over and dropped down beside Kari and held a finger to his mouth to tell her to be quiet. If they were lucky the villagers just might be too focused on Scar to bother with them—for a few seconds at least. He figured they had only a slim chance to make it out, but if they stayed in the cave, they were trapped for certain.

They had to take the chance and get out now. Kari had already pulled on her jeans and boots. Grabbing her hand, he half dragged her to the mouth of the cave, up a steep embankment, and pulled her back into the cover of the dark jungle.

They scrambled and tripped several yards deeper into the jungle, then sat down to catch their breath.

"Why are we stopping?" Kari asked as she gasped for breath. "They're going to find us."

"Shh. I think I can find the Jeep, but we're out of gas." Brett was trying to calculate their chances of getting away. He figured they had no chance of escaping on foot. The guards would have been alerted to their presence by now and would be looking for them.

"Come on, let's go!" Kari whispered and pulled at his arm. "Let's get out of here."

"Wait a minute. Let me think." Brett squatted down in the brush. He knew they wouldn't make it on foot, not through the jungle, and they were certain to be caught when daylight came. If he and Kari managed to find the Jeep, which seemed a remote possibility at best, they were still out of gas. Kari tugged at him, trying to get him to leave. But Brett didn't budge. He was trying desperately to come up with a plan. Suddenly he had an idea, a crazy scheme, but it seemed their only chance, even though it was a slim one at best.

"You stay here with Tequila," he told her. "If I'm not back in fifteen minutes, then the two of you head out of here. Get as far away from here as you can."

"Where are you going? You're not going to leave us here, are you? Don't leave me!" She was on the verge of becoming hysterical.

"Shhh. You have to wait here," he said in a stern voice. "I'll be right back. Wait fifteen minutes, then if I'm not back, you have to leave without me. Understood?"

She nodded and knelt down with Tequila to wait. He handed her his watch, then was gone from sight.

He remembered the fuel truck parked at the edge of town. It gave him an idea that just might improve their chances for getting out alive. He needed fuel. A crowd had gathered around Scar, watching him die with a twisting bushmaster in his hand. It was the diversion Brett needed. Crouching low, he ran down the steep hill into the town, slid between houses, and dove under the fuel truck. The area reeked of gasoline.

He spotted several ten-gallon fuel cans sitting off to one side. Most of the cans were empty, but four were filled. He twisted the top off two of the filled cans and poured the contents of one of the cans on the ground under the truck. He pulled his shirt off, twisted the sleeve and jammed it into the spout of the second can.

He reached in his pocket for a match, then realized he didn't have one. He swore at himself for such a stupid oversight. He sat crouched under the truck trying to figure out what to do next. A dog suddenly snarled in front of his face, its teeth bared, saliva drooling, ready to attack. Without a moment's hesitation, Brett smashed the dog in the nose with his fist, using every bit of strength he could muster. The dog went down without a sound. His heart racing to a dangerous level, Brett jerked his head around in every direction, but it seemed he hadn't been spotted.

Time was running out. The fifteen minutes were just about up, and Kari and Tequila would be heading into the jungle without him. Then their chances of finding each other in the dark were slim at best.

He needed to find a way to ignite the gasoline. He opened the hood of the truck, pulled loose a battery cable and created a spark with a loud snapping sound against the other terminal while he held the gasoline-soaked shirt close to it. The shirt immediately burst into flames. He dropped the flaming shirt on top the open gas can sitting beneath the truck, grabbed the two full cans, and raced back out of town the way he had come. He didn't know if the truck would blow up or if the shirt would burn out without igniting the gasoline.

He stopped and knelt down at the side of a house where he could still see the fuel truck. Flames were flickering beneath the truck where he'd poured the gasoline on the ground, but it looked like it might burn itself out. Somebody yelled. Everybody turned, then started running toward the truck. He had been spotted. His plan had failed.

He turned and struggled up the hill with the two cans and into the jungle, then suddenly stopped, turned around and squatted. He grabbed the Colt, took careful aim and emptied all four rounds into the side of the tanker. Gasoline spewed from the holes, cascaded down the truck and onto the burning ground, feeding the fire which grew into an inferno. Everyone stopped for a second as they tried to figure out what the gunshots meant, then they started running toward the truck and the spreading flames.

Brett picked up the two heavy cans again and continued running. He tore into the jungle in the direction of where he had left Kari and Tequila. Suddenly a deafening blast and a brilliant yellow light lit the night. A gust of wind from the shock wave of the explosion knocked him down, but he scrambled back to his feet and kept running to where he thought they should be. He stopped and looked around but couldn't see anything in the darkness. He was late. They had already left. He continued on a few yards, listening. He didn't know which direction to take.

"Over here," Kari said.

Brett ran over to them. "Come on, let's get out of here," he said. They took off at a run in the direction of the abandoned Jeep.

Twenty minutes later, they stopped to rest and catch their breath. The ten-gallon cans were heavy, and Brett's arms were aching with fatigue.

"They won't have a chance of catching us in the dark," he reassured her. "But by morning, they'll be out looking for us. And they're going to be madder than hell. If we're lucky, we should be long gone by then."

"Look at us," she said. Her shirt hung in shreds, he wasn't wearing a shirt, and they were muddy and covered with cuts from the branches. "How far do you think we can get on foot?"

"Just far enough. We've got to keep moving. We have a lot of ground to cover. There's a blanket and water in the Jeep." He took her arm. "Are you okay? Did they hurt you back there?"

"Let me carry one of the cans," she said, ignoring his question.

"We have to work together if we're to get out of this."

"I have a better idea." He found a long stout branch, slipped it through the handles of the gas cans, pulled it across his shoulders, and stood up. A can dangled from each end. "Let's go."

The three of them moved through the jungle in the darkness of night, fighting their way mile after mile through tangled vines, bogs, and fallen trees. More than once Brett's foot caught on a root and threw him to the ground.

They stopped twice to rest then continued on. After two hours of steady progress, Brett grew concerned. They were near the clearing on the hill, and they should have stumbled across the Jeep by now. If they missed it in the dark, they would have no chance of finding the Jeep. The intense pain in his shoulders from carrying the ten-gallon cans made him nauseated. He didn't have much strength or endurance left. He knew he simply couldn't go much farther without collapsing.

Finally, he stopped and put the cans down. His cramped arms were useless. In the pitch-black night of the jungle, they could easily miss the Jeep and go miles beyond it without realizing it. He hoped they hadn't already done that.

"Are we lost?" Kari asked as she dropped to the ground. "Do you know where we're going?"

"I don't know yet. I think we're okay." But he was far from okay. He had reached the end. He wasn't sure he could stand up again, let alone pick up the heavy cans and continue on. If they waited here until morning they would eventually be found by the gang from the village.

Tequila came over to him and licked his face. Brett tried to gently push the dog aside, but Tequila kept licking him. Then

Brett had an idea. Tequila might be the one to save them.

"Tequila, go home," he ordered. The Jeep had long ago become home to the dog, and Brett gave the command "home" to the dog when he wanted the dog to stay in the Jeep. "Home," he repeated sternly.

Tequila's head came up, he sniffed the air, then took off on a trot into the jungle. Brett struggled to his feet, managed to shoulder the cans again, and turned to Kari. "Let's go," he said. Kari pulled herself and followed.

After ten minutes of going in the direction that Tequila had run, Brett stopped. He whistled. Tequila barked a response off to the right. They followed the sound. Within a minute he came to the Jeep sitting in the clearing where he had left it. Tequila was standing on the back seat, and started barking excitedly with his tail wagging.

Brett dropped the cans, put his arms around the dog and hugged him. Then he poured a bowl of fresh water for him from one of the canteens, and Tequila gulped it down immediately. Kari stumbled into the clearing and stopped. "We made it," she said with a weak voice.

"Yeah, we made it." Brett strapped one of the cans to the carrier on the side of the Jeep and poured the other into the gas tank. Kari climbed into the front seat, and Tequila lay down on the back seat where he always traveled. Brett pulled a blanket from the back and wrapped it around Kari, who was starting to shiver from fatigue and hypothermia. Then he climbed in and started the engine.

It sputtered and belched a cloud of smoke, but it started. "It's burning oil like crazy," he said. If we don't push it, maybe it'll get us most of the way out of here."

He turned the Jeep around and headed back the way he had

come. This time he was satisfied with slow steady progress. He was in no hurry as long as the Jeep didn't die. Within minutes, both Kari and Tequila were sound asleep, but he struggled through the night to stay awake and to keep the Jeep moving.

Just before dawn, he poured the second can of gas into the tank, and continued on.

His eyes were swollen with fatigue. His face and bare chest burned from dozens of cuts from branches and thorns, and his fingers were stiff and painful to move. As he drove, he tried to think of the safest place for them to go.

The military police would be looking for both of them. Villages were out of the question because there might be rebels there who would also be looking for Kari. He decided that in spite of the threat from Zolog and the Secret Police, he would head to Guatemala City and get Kari out of the country and back to Chicago.

Chapter 52

By midmorning, Brett's body finally gave out. Trembling with cramps and fatigue, he stopped in a small clearing and turned off the engine. He climbed up onto a large flat rock that was bathed in a small pool of sunlight pouring through the trees and stretched out with a sigh of relief. Every muscle in his body ached. Total exhaustion and lack of sleep had drained his body and left him trembling and weak. His hands were stiff, his split fingers were sore, and his arms were nearly useless.

Kari climbed up beside him and spread the blanket on the rock. She wanted to talk, but he immediately fell into a deep sleep. So she curled up beside him and also fell asleep. They slept for more than two hours. When they woke, the sun was directly overhead and burning down on them. Tequila was lying beside them on the rock, his head up and alert, guarding them.

Brett sat up, put his hand to his painful shoulder, and rubbed it. He felt more dead than alive. They hadn't eaten in a day, and his mouth felt like cotton. They both looked like vagabonds—his torn jeans was covered with dirt and grime, her blouse hung in shreds, and her jeans were covered with dirt and leaves. They were scratched from tearing through the underbrush when they escaped. There was a red blotch across Kari's face where she'd been hit. Crusted blood marked the cut on his face.

She woke up and rubbed her eyes. He brushed a leaf out of her hair and gently pushed her hair back out of her face.

"Well, Kari Wheeler, you've made this assignment one I won't ever forget. Why did you come back to Guatemala?"

"I had to try and clear my father's name. I had to prove that all the work he did was valid."

"How did you intend to do that?"

"I wasn't sure. But I thought I'd find a way."

She propped up on one elbow and looked over at him. "Thank you for saving my life. The past few weeks have been the worst of my entire life," she said. "But in a way that I can't explain, they've also been the most unbelievable... That is, if we survive this."

He saw a brief look of disappointment in her eyes. They both felt it. The past four weeks had changed their lives forever. The jungle was a steaming, miserable, dangerous place, but he doubted either of them could ever again experience life as intensely as they had in the jungle. And now—one way or another—it was nearly over.

"How did you find me?" she asked.

"I found an address in your house," he said.

"You broke into my house? Why?"

"I'd have broken into Fort Knox in order to find you, if I had to."

She stared at him for a moment, then leaned over and kissed

him. "Thank you for rescuing me, again. Every time I'm in need of something, you seem to show up."

"Well, we're not out of this yet."

"Where's Ross and the rest of your team?"

"They're gone. The CDC decided it's too dangerous here for them. The fighting has gotten intense. Their camp was raided, equipment stolen or broken, and they thought their lives were in danger. Ross flew to New Mexico, but the rest of the team flew back to Atlanta."

"Why did Ross fly to New Mexico?"

"Right about now, Ross, Quinn and a dozen or so federal marshals are storming into San Sebastian."

"I need to know, Brett. Was my father involved with what was going on inside the monastery?"

"No. Your father knew nothing about the art forgery and duplicated pieces being produced. You were correct when you said your father was only interested in saving some valuable pieces for museums. But he somehow discovered that the monks were making duplicates and selling them to art dealers and museums around the world for an insane amount of money. Monsignor Cardone—"

"Father Cardone—he was friends with my father. I've known him since I was a little girl. Was he involved with this?"

"It was Cardone who thought up the scheme to acquire large sums of money by first smuggling artifacts out of the country, then duplicating them and shipping them around the world. The monks sent the money to the rebel forces to continue their fight. They couldn't risk their secret getting out."

"So, they killed my father," she said.

"No, not the monks. The rebels killed him. They couldn't

risk anyone learning what the monks were doing. Then the rebels' money would dry up. They'll do anything to keep that from happening, and they will kill you if they can find you. You were supposed to die that day, too, but it didn't go as planned."

"I thought the Secret Police were after me."

"They are," Brett said. "Zolog thinks you probably also know what your father had learned. If Zolog can stop the smuggling, the rebels will quickly run out of money, and the civil war will be over."

"So, everybody's looking for me," Kari said, fear creeping into her voice.

They lay on the blanket, looking up at the sunlight filtering through the trees. They didn't speak for several minutes. They both realized the dangerous situation they were in was far from over.

"What would you like right now?" she asked.

He looked over at her with a devilish smile. She punched him on the arm and said, "I mean other that."

Finally, he said, "I guess a cold beer would be great right now."

"I'd like a Sautter's pepperoni pizza with olives," she said.

"Olives?"

"Yeah," she said. "Sautter's has the best. It's a small pizzeria just off campus. Spicy pepperoni and hot cheese."

He looked at her, surveying her face, her hair, her eyes. Dirty, disheveled, tired and weary, she was incredibly beautiful.

"What?" she asked. She returned his gaze for a moment, then stared out at the jungle for a few minutes before she finally asked, "Where do we go from here?"

"I'm going to get you to Guatemala City and on a plane back to Chicago."

Kari was quiet for a moment. "I mean you and me?" her voice

had softened.

That was a question he wasn't prepared to answer because he didn't know the answer. "I don't know," he said. He regretted it as soon as the words left his mouth. "What are you going to do when you get back?"

"Try to pick up the pieces of my life," she said. "Take care of my father's financial affairs. And my job at the university will keep me busy."

"And your boyfriend is waiting for you," Brett added.

She nodded and smiled. He wanted her to scream No! You and I have each other—but she didn't. He hadn't lost her; he realized she'd never been his.

"Will we see each other again?" she asked.

It wasn't 'call me the moment you get a chance'. She seemed to be making it clear how she felt about the situation.

"You've got your job at the university," Brett said. "You have a life back there. And I'll be off on another assignment at some other god-forsaken place."

"Brett, we have to stay in touch. I need to know you are okay. I want to hear from you."

"I promise to call you," he said. "I also want to know how you are doing."

She nodded, then leaned over and kissed him again. "Thanks for saving my life back there. Thank you for everything. I will never forget you."

"We'd better get going," Brett said standing up. "It's not over yet. We're low on fuel, we have no food, and everybody in the damned country wants our hides."

They got back into the Jeep and continued on. Kari sat looking straight ahead, her eyes moist and her lip trembling as she fought to maintain her composure.

F ive hours later, they stopped at the edge of a hill, looking down on Guatemala City sprawled out below of them. "You have to go to the airport, buy a ticket, and get the hell out of Guatemala as fast as possible," Brett said. "Take the first flight out. Don't wait around for the best flight to Chicago. Just get out of the country. Everybody is looking for you, and they're sure to be covering the airports."

He pulled out a clean shirt from his pack and handed it to her. "Get rid of that torn blouse and put this on. Buy a hat and sunglasses at the airport. You should be all right."

"Won't they be looking for me? As soon as I buy a ticket, they'll have me."

"They'll be looking for Kari Wheeler. So, use Juanita's I.D. again." Then he handed her most of his cash. "I can't drive you any closer. The Secret Police are looking for me, too, and the way this Jeep is belching oil, it's like a billboard pointing at me."

With tears rolling down her cheeks, Kari leaned over and kissed him. "What's going to happen to you?" she asked. "The Secret Police want you for murder. Everyone else on your team has left, and now you're down here by yourself. How are you going to get out of the country?"

"Don't know yet. I'm working on it. I have to disappear for

now," he said. Suddenly he jumped out of the Jeep, went to her and held her in his arms while she cried. He held her face in his hands and kissed her. They hugged each other like two lovers who knew they would never see each other again. Finally, he wiped her eyes and said, "Walk into town and grab the first taxi. Then go to the airport and get on the first plane out of here."

She nodded silently, looking down at the ground.

"Kari, in case one of us doesn't make it, and we never see each other again—"

She put her hand over his mouth. "Don't say that. Don't even think it."

Brett merely nodded, got back in the Jeep, looked back at her and said, "Take care of yourself, Kari Wheeler. I will never forget you." Then he drove away. Tequila's head came up and stared back at her, ears up and alert, as if he were wondering why she wasn't coming.

Kari waited until they were out of sight, the dust had settled, and silence returned. Then she started walking down the hill into Guatemala City. Tears were flowing freely, and she could do nothing to stop them.

When they had stopped to say goodbye, Brett caught sight of dust from the road on the other side of the mountain. Zolog and his men were gaining on him. He hadn't said anything to Kari because she had been through enough and he didn't want to alarm her. He needed her to focus on getting on a plane. He didn't want her frozen with fear and make a mistake.

Brett had heard the faint sound of engines from time to time and was aware they were being followed. Zolog was relentless and steadily gaining on him. The worn-out Jeep was hemorrhaging oil and its engine was gradually slowing; they were closing on him. Brett knew he wasn't going to be able to outrun them. He would do the next best thing; he would lead them away from Guatemala City and Kari. He would make sure she would escape to safety, but he couldn't say the same thing for himself.

He couldn't even remember exactly how he'd gotten himself into this mess, with the head of Guatemala's Secret Police after him. If they caught him, it was prison at the very least. Almost certainly it would be worse.

Brett had to concentrate on not allowing that to happen.

Chapter 53

Six weeks later...

University of Chicago

The last class of the day was over, and Kari was in her office gathering up papers she needed to work on that night. She had resumed her routine of research and teaching the past few weeks since returning to Chicago, but her life had been changed forever. In the jungle she had witnessed death, seen her father murdered, was nearly gang-raped, suffered intense loss, was held captive, and experienced love. She had seen and lived life on the raw edge.

Her time was filled with classes and lectures now, all predictable and orderly. But she was alone, for the first time. Her boyfriend was putting pressure on her to make a commitment and move in with him. But she kept putting him off, telling him she needed more time. She knew the reason why, but couldn't admit it, even to herself.

She kept waiting for Brett to appear, but he hadn't. She thought Brett would call her when he returned to the States, and couldn't understand why he hadn't. She was worried he might not have made it out of Guatemala, and she hadn't called Solt because she was afraid of hearing bad news. She went to Jimmy's on weekends with friends, who worried when she often turned quiet. They knew she had been traumatized, and they tried to help her out of her depression.

The past was gone. Done. Over. Time for her to move on with her life. She knew she could never recapture the past, but the present seemed so tediously routine.

She put her father's house on the market—the home where she had been raised. She had planned to move in, but at the last minute changed her mind. She decided there were too many memories there. She moved into a nice condominium a few blocks from campus and filled it with new furniture. She was beginning a new chapter in her life, and she brought nothing with her from the past except memories.

In case one of us doesn't make it... he had said. Tears started to well up again as she thought of Brett Carson. She brushed them away with the back of her hand, put her papers in her briefcase, and closed it.

She cried easily these days. She chalked it up to all that had happened to her over the past two months. Friends worried about her and suggested that she see someone to help deal with her grief and her depression, which seemed to be increasing. But she ignored their advice, because she knew the real reason. She often cried herself to sleep at night.

Her work finished for the day, she locked her office and left the Social Science Research Building and started across the campus quad. The leaves had fallen, and an unseasonably warm early December breeze swirled them across the ground in short gusts. The days were shorter now and once again, the late autumn sun was low in the sky. She headed home, feeling very much alone.

Some days were harder than others, and today was especially hard. She hadn't heard from Brett since she'd left Guatemala, more than six weeks ago. Not a letter, not even a phone call. She didn't know if he had been captured, if he was rotting in a prison somewhere, or if he had managed to get out of Guatemala. She had been putting it off for fear of hearing bad news, but decided she would call Ross Solt at the CDC tomorrow and ask if he'd heard from Brett.

Halfway across the campus quad, she heard a dog bark. Something about the sound of that bark stopped her in her tracks. When she turned, she spotted an old, battered Jeep parked on the lawn under a tree. She starting walking across the grass toward it, and a broad smile spread across her face when she saw the familiar worn seats, bullet holes in the door, and faded paint.

Tequila, who had been lying in the grass, spotted her and ran to her. Kari dropped her briefcase and pulled the big dog to her. She then spotted Brett leaning against a tree.

She ran over to him and hugged him. He took her in his arms and kissed her. "I've missed you, Kari Wheeler."

She was crying too hard to answer.

"Why are you crying?"

"Shut up," she said and gently punched him.

He held up a pizza box. "Have a slice of pizza. It's from Sautter's. I hear they're the best."

She smiled, wiped her eyes, and sat down on the grass beside him. She took a slice of pizza and bit into it.

"You didn't steal it, did you?" she asked, nodding toward the Jeep.

"What—that? Yeah, actually I did. I figured they owed me," Brett said. "Besides, I needed it more than they did. They were probably just going to scrap it."

"How did you get it here?"

"Well, it was Ross's idea. I couldn't fly out of the country since Zolog and the secret police were hot on my trail. And I couldn't get Tequila into this country if I went through customs. I wasn't about to leave him. Ross suggested that he fly down, and he and I drive the Jeep back and bring the dog. So, we did. We detoured around Mexico customs at the border in Texas by going cross-country off-road, and here we are."

She sat up. "Are you telling me you drove all the way from Guatemala in that?"

"Ross and I both had vacation time coming, so we thought what a great way to spend some time together, and a way to get Tequila here. I found a rebuilt engine and transmission. After a week's work, it was ready to go. The hardest part was driving through Mexico. We actually had to hide from the police twice and barely escaped the drug cartel. It was quite a trip. More than thirty-five hundred miles."

With her eyes still moist, she leaned over and kissed him again. "I've missed you," she said. "I was certain they caught you after I left. I saw the dust from the troops chasing us, and I knew they were getting close. How did you get away?"

"I abandoned the Jeep and took off on foot with Tequila. They had no idea which direction I was headed, so they had to search everywhere. A few of the men stayed to guard the Jeep in case I came back."

"Where did you go? Why didn't they find you?" Kari asked.

"Just like you, I walked down the hill into Guatemala City and hid out in the slums at the edge of town. Late that afternoon, I called the airport and made reservations for a Brett Carson and Kari Wheeler for a flight the next day back to Chicago."

"What? Why would you—"

"Because," he interrupted, "they immediately contacted Zolog, just as I wanted them to. He forgot about the Jeep and sent all his men to the airport to set a trap for us for the following day. Except you were already gone, and I had no intention of showing up. When the soldiers left, I doubled back, got in the Jeep, and drove off."

"With clever scheming like that, you could have been a career criminal."

"I am a criminal," Brett said. "I've broken into several buildings, including your house, assaulted police, blown up a truck, stolen a Jeep, and exhumed bodies illegally without a warrant."

"So, you're a wanted man."

He smiled at her. "I certainly hope so."

She punched him in the arm, and they kissed again. They sat huddled in the grass together and talked while the leaves blew around them and the afternoon sun dropped lower. Tequila had managed to plant himself squarely between them on the grass.

Finally, Kari stood up, brushed leaves from her jacket, and

said, "Why don't you come back to my place and I'll open a bottle of chianti."

"That thing you said about us being too different...," he said.

"Maybe I was right about that all along." She looked at the Jeep and shook her head. "For instance—you know, I'm just not sure I can be seen riding around in that."

"You'll learn to love it," he said and they climbed in. "It's what they call a 'classic'."

"Are those new?" she asked.

"What?"

"Those," she said, pointing to bullet holes.

"Only a couple. The rest are old."

"I don't want to know, do I?"

"No."

With the three of them once again loaded inside, the Jeep pulled away and headed down the narrow leaf-strewn street as the streetlights came on and the late autumn day faded into twilight.

The End

Acknowledgments

A special thanks goes out to all the readers of my earlier manuscripts. They provided invaluable ideas, corrections and continued encouragement with this book. These include Rob Solt, Beth Bruneau, Robin Strong, Bob Strong, Michael Palmer, and many others that are too numerous to list. A thank you to everyone for your time and suggestions.

I also want to thank all the editors for their expert guidance and corrections of my manuscript. These include Jack Adler, Cynthia Nesserman, Jonathan Sanger, Gary Provost, Barbara Norville, and Joyce Wedge.

Thank you to John Prince and Hallard Press for their tireless work and efforts to get this book into publication.

And a very special thank you to my wife Cathy, my best friend, my best editor, the person who continues to inspire and encourage me.

About the Author

Dr. Keith Wilson is a graduate of the Ohio State University College of Medicine, where he earned several academic honors, and was chosen outstanding senior student in medicine and graduated *cum laude*. He was elected to AOA Medical Honorary Society in both his Junior and Senior years. He completed his diagnostic radiology residency in Denver, Colorado, where he was also chief resident. He was the director the MRI Section at Toledo Hospital and was the medical director of the PET-CT / MRI outpatient office. He also worked exclusively the last fifteen years at the Promedica Breast Care Center, specializing in diagnosis of breast cancer.

In addition to four published books, Keith has also written several short stories and has won awards, among them the Hemingway Short Story Contest and The National Writer's Club contest.

Since retiring, he and his wife, Cathy, now divide their time between Ohio, Cape Cod, and Florida.